MW00810413

Voices in the Drum

Voices in the Drum

Narratives from the Native American Past

R. David Edmunds

University of Oklahoma Press : Norman

This book is published with the generous assistance of the McCasland Foundation, Duncan, Oklahoma.

Library of Congress Cataloging-in-Publication Data

Names: Edmunds, R. David (Russell David), 1939– author.

Title: Voices in the drum : narratives from the Native American past / R. David Edmunds.

Description: Norman : University of Oklahoma Press [2023] | Includes bibliographical references and index. | Summary: "Features nine stories, each focusing on a fictional character who is a composite of historical indigenous Americans. Spanning human history in North America from the 1400s to the late 1900s, the fictional characters interact with real historical figures and participate in actual events, giving readers a sense of how tribal peoples reacted to the disruptive changes forced on them by European colonizers and U.S. government policies"— Provided by publisher.

Identifiers: LCCN 2023005952 | ISBN 978-0-8061-9276-5 (hardback) | ISBN 978-0-8061-9277-2 (paperback)

Subjects: LCSH: Indians of North America—History—Fiction. | LCGFT: Historical fiction. | Short stories.

Classification: LCC PS3605.D59 V65 2023 | DDC 813/.6—dc23/eng/20230530

LC record available at https://lccn.loc.gov/2023005952

The paper in this book meets the guidelines for permanence and durability of the Committee on Production Guidelines for Book Longevity of the Council on Library Resources, Inc. ∞

For Sally: Memories of . . .

Whip-poor-wills and fireflies flashing at dusk in an Indiana forest . . .

* * * * * *

Rain falling softly over grey stone walls in the Yorkshire dales . . .

* * * * * * *

Dragonflies skimming across the still waters of the Okavango Delta . . .

* * * * * *

The aroma of piñon smoke wafting at sunset across the plaza at Santa Fe . . .

* * * * * *

Cilantro.

RDE

Contents

Preface

During the summer of 1983, I was invited to present a paper at a conference titled "Indian Self Rule: Fifty Years under the Indian Reorganization Act," which was sponsored by the Institute of the American West. Held at Sun Valley, Idaho, the conference program was organized around topics such as the Indian New Deal, termination, self-determination, and Native American poetry and featured twelve speakers, both Native American and non-Native American. Some were academics, others were writers or poets, while the remaining were tribal officials (some employed by the Bureau of Indian Affairs [BIA], others working for the tribes). I agreed to discuss the relocation of tribal people from reservation communities to major urban areas through the BIA's relocation program, which served as a focal point for federal Indian policy during the middle and late 1950s, and to evaluate the impact of the program on those people who had participated in it.

The sponsors anticipated that the conference would be well attended (who wouldn't enjoy three days in Sun Valley in mid-August?), and everyone expected the audience to be a town-and-gown assemblage composed of some academics but also many tourists, history buffs, and tribal people. Speakers had been asked to limit their formal presentations to about half an hour, followed by the usual questions and comments. Although I had some familiarity with the relocation program, I had not previously spoken on this subject, so I spent some time during the early summer months of 1983 gathering materials, including statistical data and other information on who had been moved where, how long they had remained in the urban areas, and how many people had returned to their old reservation communities. I wrote the paper, typed it up, proofread the completed manuscript, then attempted to read through it, as if I were presenting it to an audience.

It bored me to tears. The paper was chock-full of facts and figures about the numbers, ages, and gender of tribal people who had left their reservation homes. It also delineated how many had secured new jobs in the cities, the wages that they earned, and how the BIA had assisted them after their relocation. But it provided little information about the emotional impact of the relocation process on the people swept up in this federally marketed migration. In short, the paper really had little to say about the wear and tear of everyday struggles on the lives of flesh-and-blood individuals forced to scramble for an existence in an unfamiliar, urban, working-class America. My original paper was full of statistics, not people. I tore it up and threw it in the trash can.

In response, I decided to incorporate some of the facts and figures I had included in the original paper with the wealth of information I had received from personal friends and acquaintances who had previously navigated the relocation maze. After leaving the University of Oklahoma, I had taught for several years at the University of Wyoming, where I served as the faculty adviser for the Keepers of the Fire, the Native American student organization on campus, and several members of the organization had grown up in families who had originally been relocated to Denver. During my tenure at the McNickle Center at the Newberry Library, I became good friends with former "relocatees" in both Chicago and Minneapolis-St. Paul, and while teaching at the University of California at Berkely, I served on a faculty with several individuals who had been relocated to the Bay Area. All of the above (and many others) had willingly shared stories of their own or their families' experiences, and these personal stories were far more interesting than raw data generated by the myriad reports of the BIA. Moreover, during the previous decade, I had spoken to numerous town-and-gown audiences across the Great Lakes region and the American West, and I had learned that most individuals who attended such presentations preferred narratives that focused on people rather than statistical analyses.

I knew that it would be almost impossible to humanize any attempt to survey the broad scope of the many people swept up in the relocation program, so I decided to create a fictitious Native American family and to focus on their experiences as a microcosm of the trials and tribulations endured by tribal people resettled in the cities. Since I felt that I had a better grasp of conditions encountered by relocatees in Denver than in most other relocation centers, I decided to place the family in the Denver metropolitan region during the height of the relocation period and "turn them loose." Consequently, the Summer Hawk family emerged on the pages of my narrative as the standard-bearers for the many tribal people lured into the program. I hoped that their story and the stories of their family and friends would help to explain, to a greater or lesser degree, the broader saga of the thousands of Native American people who left rural reservations for new homes in the cities during the 1950s.

I'll admit that I initially had some doubts about delivering a paper based on the experiences of composite historical characters, but "Summer Hawks in Concrete Canyons" was a huge success. When my session on the program ended, I was approached by perhaps a dozen members of the audience, either asking for copies of the paper or inquiring if it was part of a larger study. I assured them that the paper, in addition to the other presentations on the program, would be included in conference proceedings that would be published later in the summer by the Institute of the American West.[1] They could purchase copies from the institute. But in the aftermath, I was encouraged by the audience's reception. Although I continued to harbor doubts about how such a format would be received from some of my more conservative professional colleagues, the saga of the Summer Hawks obviously had piqued the interest of many members of my audience, and it evidently encouraged them to read more on the plight of urban Indian communities.

Since that time, I have utilized similar composite-character formats when I have presented papers or addresses to other town-and-gown audiences, and I've been rewarded with similar responses. On several occasions, editors from state or regional historical journals who were part of the audience have approached me following the presentation and solicited the paper for publication in their journals. In addition, I also have used copies of these papers as reading assignments in both undergraduate and graduate classes and found that they spurred discussion and often encouraged students to pursue additional, more detailed or in-depth reading. Through the years, students have repeatedly suggested that I incorporate some of these vignettes into a single volume, so I have decided to do so.

But in planning this volume, I knew there were many important chapters in the Native American experience that I had never addressed in the town-and-gown presentations. Some were much too important to omit. Consequently, two of the chapters in this volume have been written specifically for inclusion in *Voices in the Drum* and were not previously presented to an audience. In addition, most of the other chapters have been edited and lengthened from the original papers that were presented to town-and-gown audiences. These changes have been made to enhance a similarity in the formats among the chapters and to keep the length of the separate chapters somewhat parallel.

All but one of the chapters follow a similar format. They begin with a lengthy section that introduces readers to the primary characters in the chapter and sets the stage for the events that will exemplify and offer insights into the characters' actions and lives, which in turn, I hope, illustrate specific or important facets of the Native American experience. Following the initial narrative, each chapter includes several pages that place that narrative within a more traditional academic discussion of the broader scope of Native American history during the period. This more traditional, second section is documented and provides readers with citations to additional, more detailed, or specialized academic studies that furnish supplementary information about these events. With one exception (chapter 3), the chapters then conclude by returning to the original format, featuring a brief epilog which focuses on characters previously discussed in the narrative, or individuals or events related to them.

As readers wend their way through the pages of these narratives, I am sure they will encounter certain recurring themes. There are a multitude of interlacing issues (both triumphs and tragedies) that constitute the saga of Native American history, and no single story or storyteller can encompass them all. Obviously, chapter 1 asserts that American history does not begin in 1492 and that the people who inhabited pre-Columbian North America followed many patterns of cultural development also found throughout Eurasia and Africa. Subsequent chapters focus on other elements of Native American history, but several facets of this story continually reemerge. One important (but often overlooked) part in this ongoing chronicle is the critical role played by tribal women. Thankfully, during the past three decades, that oversight is slowly being redressed, but much remains to be done. I hope that some of the chapters in this volume can contribute to that remedy.

Other themes also emerge from the narratives. There is no singular "Indian culture." Different tribal people have always lived in different ways, even within the defined parameters of single tribal groups. Moreover, tribal cultures have always been adaptive; they have never been fixed in stone. And finally, in the face of considerable adversity, tribal people have persevered. Since the early twentieth century, tribal populations in the United States have markedly increased. Contemporary tribal people are active members of a modern American nation.

A word or two about terminology. In all of the essays, I have used *Indians, Native Americans*, and *tribal people* interchangeably. I also have used both *tribes* and *nations* to designate indigenous groups who identify with a particular political or cultural entity (e.g., Apache, Potawatomi, Ojibwe, Lakota). In some instances, where it seemed appropriate, I have used tribal names applied to a group of people by another tribe (e.g., Apachu, rather than Dene in chapter 1). In some chapters, I also have attempted to utilize names or other terms taken from tribal languages. Since the translation of tribal languages into English is sometimes uncertain, I may have made some mistakes. If so, they are my own, and I apologize for them.

Occasionally, in creating dialog between characters within the chapters, I have used racial terminology and other language common to the time and place of the conversations. Some of this terminology may be offensive, but I have used it to illustrate the racial attitudes of particular characters at that time and to indicate that such attitudes impacted Indian people. Obviously, these are neither terms that I personally use nor attitudes or opinions to which I subscribe.

In October 1985, at the annual meeting of the Western History Association in Sacramento, California, I participated in a panel that focused on the teaching of Native American history. The other members of the panel were Terry Wilson (Prairie Band Potawatomi), Charles Roberts (Choctaw), and Jack Forbes (Powhatan-Lenape). After opening statements in which each of us briefly discussed our method of presenting information and engaging students, we fielded the customary questions from the audience, then mostly fended off the usual inquiries regarding instructional materials, testing techniques, and other pedagogical paraphernalia. Not satisfied by what seemed to be our rather simplistic approach, one member of the audience questioned why we still relied on a simple verbal interchange with members of our class. In reply, I answered that I taught the beginning survey of Native American history as a "hook," a class designed to interest students in the subject. I wanted them to enroll in other classes in Native American studies. I added that I believed I could do this most effectively through focusing on the experiences of Indian people. Charles Roberts and Jack Forbes then commented that they did the same thing. And Terry Wilson put it in a nutshell: "Hell, we're Indians. We tell stories," he said. We all laughed and nodded our heads.

Some of those stories echo, like voices in a drum.

Acknowledgments

Many individuals have contributed to this volume. The late Clay Reynolds, the director of the Creative Writing Program at the University of Texas at Dallas, graciously read two chapters and made helpful suggestions. So did Theda Perdue, the Atlanta Distinguished Professor Emerita at the University of North Carolina, Chapel Hill. Professor Don Hickey, of the History Department at Wayne State University in Nebraska, also read a chapter and provided useful comments. Parts of other chapters were read by the late Helen Tanner of the Newberry Library; Gerald Vizenor, professor emeritus of Native American studies at the University of California at Berkeley; Stephen Warren, professor of history and director of the American Studies Program at the University of Iowa; and Professor Kenneth McIntosh, chair of the Department of History at Clarendon College. My granddaughter Emmaline ("Emmie") Adams carefully proofread some of the chapters, looking for typos and so on. Two of my daughters, Brooke Adams and LeeAnne Edmunds, and my neighbor, Michael Saadeh, graciously provided emergency computer assistance. And finally, my wife, Sally, has listened patiently (well, sometimes) as I read parts of most chapters aloud to her as she sat with our two Airedales in the family room, or alone, amid the clutter in my study. To all of you: many thanks.

In addition, other people at the University of Texas at Dallas leant a helping hand. Professor Monica Rankin assisted me in better understanding the innuendos of Spanish slang and nomenclature. Carlos Palomino provided technological support in my ongoing war with my computer. Sally Mandiola arranged for publicity photos, and Travis Goode and the interlibrary loan librarians at Eugene McDermott Library procured materials from other libraries so quickly that I often was amazed at their efficiency. Again, many thanks.

Securing photographs to illustrate this volume proved to be much more difficult than I originally had envisioned, but fortunately, I benefitted from the assistance of a cadre of cooperative, professional curators and archivists. Among those who were especially helpful were William Bomar, executive director of Moundville Archaeological Park and director of museum studies at the University of Alabama; Lindsey Vogel-Teeter of the Pueblo Grande Museum in Phoenix; Regan Steimel of the Indiana Historical Society Library; Kelly Lippie of the Tippecanoe County Historical Society; Selena Capraro of the Amon Carter Museum of American Art; Blain McLain, archivist at the John Vaughan Library at Northeastern Oklahoma State University; Jenna Rulo, of the Woolaroc Museum and Wildlife Preserve; Alyce Tejral and Nancy Carlson at the Genoa US Indian School Foundation and Museum; Jim Gerencser at the Carlisle Indian School Digital Resource Center; Richard Truitt, at the Cumberland County Historical Society; and Sarah Bseirani, a member of the Still Picture Reference Team at National Archives and Records Administration.

I would also like to thank Alessandra Tamulevich, the senior acquisitions editor at the University of Oklahoma Press, who has shepherded me through this most recent publication gauntlet and who has supported the publication of this volume, which differs considerably from the usual standard academic monograph published by most scholarly or university presses. Her advice and expertise have been invaluable, and I more than appreciate her efforts expended in getting this volume into print.

Two more. I would like to thank the many members of the town-and-gown audiences (particularly Native American people) for their good words following my presentations and for their encouragement to combine these vignettes into a volume. I also want to thank the students in my classes who also suggested that I collect and publish these chapters. Their interest in this project has been encouraging.

And finally, I would like to acknowledge the influence and encouragement of a scholar, gone but not forgotten. In 1969, as a PhD student at the University of Oklahoma, I was privileged to enroll in a graduate writing seminar taught by Professor Savoie Lottinville, who, from 1938 to 1968, had served as the director of the University of Oklahoma Press. Unquestionably, I learned more about writing history in that one seminar than in any other class I have ever matriculated.

A Rhodes Scholar with a graduate degree from Oxford, Lottinville impressed on the class that almost all good historical writing focuses on people and that effective history invites or enables its readers to identify with the people swept up in the times or events it discusses. It is a lesson I hope I have learned. Although Lottinville was not present when I tore the initial draft of the relocation essay to pieces and replaced it with the Summer Hawks saga, I think he would have smiled. The chapters in this book owe much to his tutelage.

City-States and Sleeping Serpents

Pre-Columbian North America Reconsidered

In early October of the Gregorian calendar year 1392, a middle-aged Native American man sat beside his hearth as dusk fell across a community that modern archaeologists have called Moundville, a town of about three thousand people located on the Black Warrior River in western Alabama. His heart heavy with sorrow, the man, Serpent Who Sleeps, stared into the dying embers and grieved for his dead nephew. The dead man, Walks Quietly, had been his sister's eldest son, and since his people traced their families through the female line, the grieving uncle had been closer to his nephew than had the dead man's father. Walks Quietly had suffered a compound fracture of his leg in an accident in the neighboring forest, and when his friends had carried him back to the town, Serpent Who Sleeps, as the paramount leader of the community, had instructed his followers to bring the wounded man into his house, located atop one of the smaller mounds in the settlement.[1] Serpent Who Sleeps had sought the assistance of his leading healers and holy men, and in an attempt to purge him of the rapidly spreading infection, they had applied poultices, prescribed the Black Drink, and subjected the injured man to sweat baths.[2] But their medicine had failed. Walks Quietly had entered the spirit world and had been entombed beside one of the large mounds, overlooking the river.

At least Walks Quietly had journeyed into the darkness with all the accouterments that his status demanded. Since his clan traditionally had supplied the leadership for the town, his kinsmen were a royal family with considerable wealth and influence. Walks Quietly was buried with a vast array of ritual or ceremonial objects, including axes, fashioned of precious black stone, and copper maces, carried over the trade routes from the Great Lakes region. While the priests had performed their burial ceremonies, Walks Quietly had been wrapped in a blanket of shell beads and entombed with bundles of ceremonial arrows, their points manufactured from both flint and obsidian. Since the people in the town were followers of the Southeastern Ceremonial Complex (a loosely structured set of religious beliefs shared by many indigenous people residing from Georgia, across the Southeast, to eastern Texas and Oklahoma, and as far north as St. Louis), his kinsmen had adorned the dead man's body with shell gorgets embossed with symbols sacred to their faith: winged serpents, weeping eyes, and human hands portrayed with an eye in the palm.[3]

Although slaves were sometimes sacrificed to attend a royal personage in the afterlife, Walks Quietly was a relatively young man and had not yet achieved the status to merit such an honor.[4] Yet his uncle was aware that the young man's loss had considerable political ramifications. Like several other Mississippian communities, Moundville was ruled by a hereditary hierarchy comprising less than 10 percent of the population, and Walks Quietly had been the heir apparent to succeed Serpent Who Sleeps upon the older man's passing. Now his kinsmen must decide on a new successor, and although the clan was relatively small, Serpent Who Sleeps knew that the political infighting would be bitter.

The stakes were high. Located on a bluff overlooking the river, Moundville was partially surrounded by an earth and log palisade that enclosed almost 370 acres. Twenty separate mounds dotted its surface. The largest, laboriously constructed by his people's forebears, towered sixty feet above the surrounding ceremonial plazas and contained over 112,000 cubic meters of earth. Its summit held the great temple. Other mounds were topped by smaller temples, or the homes of Serpent Who Sleep and his kinsmen. The town contained playing fields where villagers engaged in stick-ball games, or *chunkee*, a game played with stone discs. It also included three fishponds where fish were bred and harvested for public consumption. Some plazas functioned as ceremonial arenas, while others served as small markets, facilitating the exchange of commodities from across the eastern half of the modern United States. In addition, other parts of the settlement were utilized by artisans whose mastery of pottery and woven goods had created a demand for these products throughout the region. Surrounded by fields of maize, squash, beans, pumpkins, and sunflowers, Moundville encompassed a population of approximately three thousand

Moundville during the Mississippian Era, painting by Caleb O'Connor. Courtesy of Moundville Archaeological Park, University of Alabama Museums. O'Connor's rendering features a priest in an animal-skin headdress and a clan chief with a stone axe in his hand, both atop an earthen mound looking down across a plaza where some residents of Moundville are playing at a ballgame.

individuals, but through an interlocking network of economic and military dominance, the community held sway over dozens of smaller settlements scattered up and down the Black Warrior valley. The population of this enlarged "city-state" approached ten thousand.[5]

Serpent Who Sleeps and his kinsmen enjoyed a life of relative luxury. As members of the ruling elite, they resided in houses constructed atop some of the smaller mounds. They wore copper or shell ornaments indicating their status. They were the owners of ceremonial objects which also enhanced their position, and at public ceremonies or festivals they were given the choicest foods and other goods. In some instances — occasions involving religion or military action — they held a life-or-death authority over their followers, and they often were attended by slaves, individuals purchased through regional trade or captured in warfare.[6]

Both warfare and trade had played pivotal roles in Moundville's expansion. Serpent Who Sleeps knew that his forebears had been forced to defend their homes at this fertile location in the Black Warrior River valley, and he had enhanced his family's status through his ability to gain control over many of the small villages which lay downstream from the settlement. A skilled warrior, Serpent Who Sleeps enjoyed several advantages over his more poorly organized opponents. Although intruders from regions beyond Moundville's permanent influence sometimes attacked traders from the town or occasionally skulked at night beneath the town's palisades, these assailants posed no more than a minor nuisance. On several occasions, Serpent Who Sleeps mustered his army and attacked the villages of his enemies, and his disciplined ranks of heavily armed warriors, fighting under his leadership, easily crushed his foes. Victory had been sweet. Although the less sophisticated village dwellers possessed little of material value, he took many prisoners, and his status among his people grew accordingly.

And yet in retrospect, when Serpent Who Sleeps thought back over his life, it was his experiences as a young man, when he had joined the far-traveling trading parties, that were the most significant. Many winters in the past, when the people were still led by his mother's brother, Strikes at Night, and when he, Serpent Who Sleeps, was a much younger man, he had joined with several other young warriors in a party led by Two Wolves. Born among the Hasinai, a people living far beyond the Great River, Two Wolves was an older man who had traveled in his youth and had arrived at Moundville with several followers of the Great Sun, a people who lived on the eastern bank of the Great River.[7] Two Wolves had married a woman from the Wind Clan and settled at Moundville with his wife's people, but he often talked of the lands to the west, and the young Serpent Who Sleeps and his friends had convinced the sojourner to guide them to these strange and wondrous places.

Their packs full of the beautifully inscribed shell gorgets for which their community's artisans and craftspeople were famous, Two Wolves, Serpent Who Sleeps, and four other young men from Moundville set out in the spring, traveling west through the pine forests toward the Great River. After passing through several small villages of tribal peoples, they arrived in the land of the Natchez, the people of the Great Sun, whose primary settlement lay less than a day's march east of the Great River.

Serpent Who Sleeps was surprised. Two Wolves and a few other residents of Moundville, or its surrounding villages, who had previously visited the Natchez, had spoken of their mounds and great temple, but when Serpent Who Sleeps arrived at their central village, he was taken aback that the residents of the settlement numbered less than those in his own village at Moundville. They, too, had erected a series of earthen mounds, but again, fewer than in the core area of the plaza and ceremonial center at Moundville. Some things were less surprising, however. Serpent Who Sleeps remembered that like the Temple Mound in his village, one of the three large mounds in the Natchez settlement also had a temple erected on it.

In some ways, the Natchez people were similar to his own; they grew the same crops, ate the same foods, worshiped the same gods, and feared the same demons. But in other ways, they were different. The Natchez spoke in strange and unfamiliar words, a tongue that differed even from the harsh language that Two Wolves learned as a boy in his Hasinai village. Two Wolves understood enough of the Natchez speech to serve as a translator for Serpent Who Sleeps and his companions, and the traders were welcomed in the Natchez village, but Serpent Who Sleeps felt uncomfortable in their midst and often wondered if their hospitality was genuine.

He was also wary of their political leadership. Like his kinsmen and other residents of Moundville, the Natchez also followed the guidance of a hereditary, paramount chief whose political position descended matrilineally, through the female side. Consequently, when a paramount chief died, the chieftainship was transferred down to the oldest son (his nephew) of the dead man's eldest sister; when the nephew died, the position of leadership again descended to his oldest sister's son, and so on. Of course, the demise of a potential heir (such as the recent death of Walks Quietly, Serpent Who Sleeps's nephew) upset the normal transfer of power and sometimes engendered bitter quarrels or even bloodshed among surviving siblings. Like other prominent or royal families, these rules of succession had the blessing of the shamans or priests of the Southeastern Ceremonial Complex, and Serpent Who Sleeps was quite familiar with this pattern of leadership. Indeed, his life was markedly determined by it. He had succeeded his uncle as the leading chief at Moundville; it had been expected of him. When he died, he too would be succeeded by a nephew

But what particularly troubled him when he first visited the Grand Village of the Natchez and continued to perplex him during the years that followed was the assertion among the Natchez that their "royal" family, who followed a pattern of matrilineal descent similar to his own, were direct descendants of the very Sun itself and were of a holy lineage far superior to that of other men. Since members of Serpent Who Sleeps's family continued to serve as the paramount chief at Moundville, he had always believed that his clan had been favored by the gods, and he had relished the special privileges that were associated with his rank, but the Natchez were led by a man whom they worshiped as a direct descendant of the Sun and who was referred to as the Great Sun by the Natchez people. Unlike Serpent Who Sleeps, who led his warriors in defending the village from its enemies and expanded Moundville's influence up and down the Black Warrior River valley, the Great Sun's primary purpose seemed to be ceremonial. He (or his personal servants) were responsible for ensuring that the sacred fire that the Great Sun's ancestors supposedly had brought down from the Sun burned perpetually in the temple atop one of the mounds, and he performed other ceremonial duties associated with keeping harmony in his village. The Great Sun was so venerated by his people that porters carried him about the village and to nearby regions on a special litter, while others attended him with thatched parasols, protecting him from the sunlight. When he appeared in public, he regularly wore a heavily ornamented helmet or crown adorned with white egret feathers.

A young man at that time, Serpent Who Sleeps asked Two Wolves if he could speak with the Natchez leader, but Two Wolves replied that such a thing was impossible. According to Two Wolves, the Great Sun could not be readily approached by common men and certainly not by strangers. He pointed out that Serpent Who Sleep was an outsider; he had no status among the class-conscious Natchez. Moreover, since he was unfamiliar with the highly stylized language needed to address the Great Sun, any attempt to speak to the man might be envisioned as an insult. Chagrinned, Serpent Who Sleeps pondered the elevated status of the Natchez leader and the veneration that his people seemed to shower on him. He was aware that his family also enjoyed a privileged status at Moundville, but it paled in comparison to the pomp and ceremony surrounding this supposed "son of the Sun," this Great Sun who seemed to dominate Natchez society.

During the remainder of his short sojourn in the Natchez village, Serpent Who Sleeps kept his opinions to himself, but after observing the Great Sun from a respectful distance, he became more suspicious of both the man and his position of prominence. The Great Sun was surrounded by priests or shamans, advisers, and other retainers who seemed to vie for his favor. According to many of the more numerous or common Natchez people, whom the Great Sun and his retainers called "stinkards," they (the stinkards) provided much of the labor that had built and maintained the earthen mounds that formed the center of the Natchez ceremonial centers. The stinkards also supplied the maize and other foodstuffs that went into the Great Sun's storage silos and cooking pots, although the stinkards admitted that during periods of food shortage, the Great Sun some-times redistributed some of these provisions back to the common people.[8]

Yet unlike Serpent Who Sleeps and his predecessors at Moundville, the Great Sun had never led his warriors into battle, or organized deer hunts in the forest, or ventured out on trading journeys to new or distant lands. Serpent Who Sleeps pondered this. "Obviously, the Great Sun was adept at Natchez politics, but he believed that the man was like a very tall stalk of maize, protected from the wind, and carefully grown and watered in a large pot of fertile soil. It would grow tall and heavy with ears of golden kernels as long as it was sheltered in a carefully tended growing pot. But if a great windstorm arose and threatened its height or if its cultivators failed to provide for it with the expected soil and water, it would collapse under its own weight and fall from the pot, crumpled, withered and dying. In contrast, productive and reliable stalks of maize, like successful leaders, needed to be buffeted by winds as they emerged and grew to maturity. They needed to endure the hot drought of summers and still produce a crop of kernels for those who relied on them. Astute and enduring leaders also needed to be exposed to the political and military winds that buffeted their worlds and to learn about new places and people. These trials and hardships strengthened them, offered insights into the ways of the wider world, and gave them the experience to meet many challenges."

In retrospect, Serpent Who Sleeps was glad that he had journeyed to the Natchez village. He had learned much during his brief encounter with the Natchez people. But he also remembered that he had been relieved when Two Wolves suggested that he and two other young warriors from Moundville continue on to other villages farther west. Serpent Who Sleeps had been fascinated by the variety of new and interesting items offered by Natchez traders on the plaza in their village, but Two Wolves had assured him that this assemblage of goods paled in comparison to the items bartered in more distant villages. The older man related stories of his youth, when he had visited another ceremonial center at the bend of a broad western river that rose amid legendary snow-capped mountains far to the west. This river (which pale-skinned men I would later call the "Arkansas") eventually joined the Great River, which flowed south near the Natchez village. Bartering several of their inscribed gorgets for a dugout canoe, Serpent Who Sleeps, Two Wolves, and two of the other travelers from Moundville, Hunts from Trees and Turkey Gobbler, had departed the Natchez village shortly before the summer solstice.

They had paddled north, hugging the western bank of the Great River, ignoring several small streams that entered the river from the west. They also passed two larger rivers that joined the Great River on the opposite shore, but when they reached the mouth of the Arkansas, Two Wolves immediately identified the stream, and they turned their canoe up the large western river, its banks still full with the aftermath of the spring runoff from melted snow in the legendary western mountains. They passed through a region of swampy lowlands, the banks often covered with huge stands of cane, then the river narrowed and deepened, and they followed the channel between low, tree covered mountains into what is now Oklahoma, where a community of Caddoan speaking Mississippian people flourished near the mouth of the Poteau River.

Serpent Who Sleeps found that this community, unlike his own, had established their village apart from their mounds and ceremonial center, and although they too were engaged in horticulture, they relied more on hunting, sending parties beyond the blackjack oak forests, seeking buffalo on the plains. In fact, it was their focus on the south and west, the Wide Land without Trees, that most fascinated Serpent Who Sleeps, for in addition to the rich variety of trade goods exchanged among Mississippian people throughout the Southeast, the people of the Spiro Mound complex traded for exotic western products, some of which Serpent Who Sleeps had never seen. While in the Wide Land without Trees, hunter-traders from Spiro had encountered wandering, nomadic people who told them strange tales of boiling springs, evil-smelling waters, and great serpents who lived beneath the earth and periodically spewed their hot breath in great columns of steam from the underground. But this region of frightful malevolence also produced obsidian, the dark, translucent stones whose fragments could be shaped into the razor-sharp knives and projectile points so valued by Serpent Who Sleeps and his comrades.

Indeed, the plazas at Spiro hosted a small, ever-changing cluster of traders, all bartering items that were then carried back and forth to villages throughout the Mississippian world. Serpent Who Sleeps and his comrades found that their gorgets and other inscribed items were in considerable demand, and they traded them for a broad spectrum of stone, ceramic, and additional goods offered by other traders. Some traders, who had arrived from the south, brought baskets full of finely crafted shell beads that they claimed came from the shores of the Great Salty Water, into which the Great River emptied. Serpent Who Sleeps had seen similar beads at Moundville, but not in such quantities. Others brought dugout canoes full of large stone celts, tools that could be utilized as digging stones, or hoe blades, although it seemed to Serpent Who Sleeps that such a use for these large stone tools would be wasteful. "Hoes and digging stones could easily be crafted from other sources. Celts of this size were in short supply. They should be utilized to fashion axe blades or other more specialized tools or weapons."[9]

Several traders offered ceramic or carved stone pipes, to which hollow wooden or cane stems could be attached. Some of the pipes were crafted or carved into effigies, usually of animals but sometimes of human figures. Many of the traders offered inscribed circular earspools, which were worn by many people at Moundville, Natchez, and other locations in the region. Varying in size, most of these earspools were carved from sandstone, or greenstone (argillite), although others were fashioned from clay, or copper.[10]

The quantity of copper items bartered at Spiro surprised the young Serpent Who Sleeps. Some of his relatives, or a few powerful shaman/priests at Moundville, had acquired copper implements or jewelry, but copper was not common at Moundville and was associated only with the ruling elite. At Spiro, copper also was utilized primarily by the chiefs and priests, but other villagers often adorned themselves with copper ear spools and other ornaments, and copper items were regularly bartered on the plaza. Serpent Who Sleeps was fascinated by the variety of copper trade goods. He previously had seen copper earspools, knives, and beads, but the numerous copper-wrapped wooden tools, staves, spear points, and even small copper celts were new to him. He was also amazed at the copper hair adornments, including copper plumes shaped like hawk feathers or small serpents, and at the effigies of humans or spirit animals also hammered out of copper and offered for trade. Other travelers who arrived from the north brought sheets of copper, hammered into breastplates and embossed with geometric designs or decorated with images of birds of prey, dancing gods, or human hands, with eyes peering from their palms. "Artisans at Moundville were skilled in their decoration of shell or ceramic items," he observed, "but who were the people who created these artfully crafted items of copper? Where were their villages? Where did they obtain the raw copper to create such objects?"[11]

Serpent Who Sleeps and his companions remained at the village near the Spiro Mounds for about two weeks, when three traders arrived from the west, bringing even more exotic goods. The travelers were from Two Wolves's boyhood village, a settlement of people speaking a language very similar to the villagers at Spiro but residing near a series of smaller mounds and communities

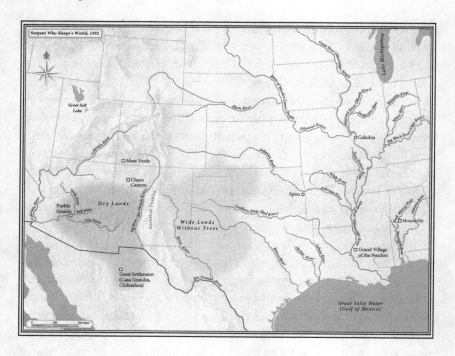

scattered along the Southern River, another large river, several days journey overland from Spiro, south, through rolling, forested mountains.[12] But these three traders, who like Two Wolves called themselves Hasinai, had boldly ventured out across the Wide Land without Trees earlier in the summer and had journeyed to the Dry Lands, where they had visited several villages of farming people who lived in houses constructed of bricks crafted of dried mud and who irrigated their fields through ditches that diverted water from nearby streams.

In conversations with Two Wolves, the Hasinai traders indicated that when they had first reached the Dry Lands, they found several small, deserted villages, sites where the western people once had lived and raised their crops but that were now abandoned and left behind as the former inhabitants had retreated back to the west, toward larger, more dependable sources of water. When the Hasinai traders finally arrived at the villages near the Big River, they initially were confronted by warriors who mistakenly identified them as "Saves" or "Apachus," ("strangers," or "enemies"), a name the people living near the river broadly applied to the increasing number of wandering hunters who recently had arrived on the high plains.[13] After some tense moments, the Hasinai travelers convinced the villagers that they were traders from the east, not Apachus, and the villagers extended a guarded welcome, but they also warned them to be vigilant; in addition to the drought, raids by of the new wandering people had forced them to abandon some of their eastern villages and consolidate their settlements closer to the Big River. They had grown more wary of strangers.[14]

The Hasinai traders had visited several villages scattered along the Big River that spilled out of the snow-capped mountains to the north then coursed southward for many days' journey until it turned toward the east and flowed somewhere, the villagers weren't sure where. (The Hasinai scoffed at the river's name; it wasn't "big" by Hasinai standards, but they kept their opinions to themselves.) But the villages were interesting places, similar yet very different from their own. Like the Hasinai villages that also shadowed rivers (that white men would later call the Red, the Sabine, or the Neches), these western villages also were built near plazas where trade was conducted. But instead of separate conical houses constructed of grass, or poles interlaced with limbs and dried mud, then thatched with grass, these western dwellings had been built of carefully molded dried-clay bricks and stones and arranged so closely together that many shared walls with their neighbors. They were covered with flat roofs, also formed of bricks and poles, which would have been become water-logged and washed away during the heavy rains of the Hasinai's homeland, but they performed adequately in the dry lands of the west. Indeed, some of the villages contained houses built on houses; people living in smaller brick houses constructed on their relative's roofs. All the Hasinai traders had seen houses erected atop earthen mounds, but they had never encountered groups of villagers living so close together, sharing homes with common walls and residing in lodges astride their neighbor's rooftop.

And, as the Hasinai had pointed out, the western villagers' temples or holy places were much different from their own. Mississippian temples resembled large, expanded houses and often were built atop mounds that abutted or towered over open plazas. In contrast, the kivas, the holy places of the western villagers, were subterranean chambers, usually sunk into the ground at different locations in their villages. The Hasinai traders were forbidden to enter these chambers, but from their locations and use, the Hasinai could tell that they varied in size and perhaps even in purpose. Some seemed to be used only by members of a single clan or kinship group, while others held much larger gatherings. All the kivas seemed to be entered by ladders extending down from the roof, which usually stood just above ground level. The traders did notice, however, that similar to the temples back in their home villages, women were given only limited access to these holy places. They could enter the kivas only with men's permission, and only for certain limited ceremonial functions.

In contrast to the limited attention they paid to the kivas, the Hasinai travelers had been fascinated by the new, exotic trade goods offered for barter in the clay brick villages. Like themselves, travelers from these villagers had also journeyed to distant lands and had obtained strange, enticing items from people who lived in sun-drenched valleys along the Gila River, many days journey to the southwest. They brought back small deerskin bags of blue and green stones, which the Gila River people had either dug from the earth or obtained from other strangers living to the north and west of their settlements. These stones, often interlaced with darker veins of black or brown pigments, were championed by local shamans and priests among the Gila River people who promised they would bring both good health and good fortune to those who carried and cared for them. The stones were readily traded among the Gila River people but were not common in Mississippian villages. A few of these stones had trickled through Spiro in the past, but they were relatively rare. Among the Mississippians, the stones were highly valued by those priests or political leaders fortunate enough to possess them.[15]

More dazzling, however, was the array of brightly colored feathers that had been obtained in the markets near the paved ball courts and wide canals constructed by the Gila River people. According to the traders in the Gila River settlements, they had bartered quantities of blue and green stones for the feathers which had been carried to their village by travelers from the south, from across the Great Desert, men who resided in the Great Settlement (Casa Grande) whose population numbered over two thousand and who had ties to the fabled cities of great stone mounds and temples further to the south.[16]

The Gila River people stated that the brightly colored feathers came from birds which lived in dense forests, far to the south of the Great Settlement, but men from that trading center had traveled to the distant region and had captured many of these brightly feathered birds, brought them back to the Great Settlement, and kept them in cages. There, the birds (scarlet macaws, military macaws, and other forest dwellers) were bred and raised for their plumage, the feathers then harvested and traded throughout the region. While in the Gila River villages, the traders from the Big River (the Rio Grande) had bartered for bundles of these feathers and carried them back to their villages, where they allowed the Hasinai visitors to examine them. The Hasinai admitted they had never seen such large feathers in such brilliant reds, multihued shades of blue, or iridescent greens. Although the price was high, the Hasinai traded for several bundles of this wondrous plumage. They returned to Spiro with a bundle of scarlet tail feathers, most as long as a man's forearm, and four patches of skin obviously taken from several birds' breasts, covered with much smaller bright blue-green feathers.[17]

Both Two Wolves and Serpent Who Sleeps attempted to trade for the feathers, but their Hasinai owners initially refused to barter. They planned to carry the plumage back to their home village and show the feathers to their relatives. Finally, after considerable cajolery, the travelers from Moundville pooled their resources and offered a large quantity of raw copper that they had acquired during their stay at Spiro; in response, the Hasinai traders agreed to relinquish two scarlet tail feathers, both as long as a man's forearm, and a patch of skin the size of a maize husk, covered with much smaller bright blue-green feathers, obviously taken from a bird's breast. The Hasinai more willingly bartered many of their blue and green stones, both to the travelers from Moundville and to other traders whom they encountered at Spiro.

Mound, by Michael Hampshire. Artist's rendition of a platform mound at Pueblo Grande, courtesy of Pueblo Grande Museum, City of Phoenix. Located near the Gila River, Pueblo Grande was a major settlement of the Hohokam people.

The Hasinai also answered questions, as best they could, about other places or people whom they had encountered in the Dry Lands. Serpent Who Sleeps was particularly curious about the people living in the Great Settlement, the people who bred the birds, and even more so about the legendary lands further south, the realm of "great cities where people swarmed like ants, and men lived amidst great stone temples and pyramids." The Hasinai claimed that the traders from the Big River (and they laughed when they used the term) villages who visited the Gila River people told them that although some traders from the Gila River traveled to the Great Settlement (Casa Grande), none had ever seen the fabled stone cities to the south. But in contrast, a few traders from the Great Settlement had ventured to those far-away lands and had returned with stories of great cites in valleys surrounded by mountains that sometimes spewed fire. They also spoke of powerful priests and nobles dressed in capes of brightly colored feathers, some taken from birds even more colorful than those bred in their settlement. They also mentioned large lakes, islands of flowers, and great markets where goods were traded on plazas that dwarfed those at Spiro or Moundville. But they had warned that the fabled land was steeped in warfare. Ranks of warriors armed with weapons edged in obsidian, fought for captives and slaves, some of whom were regularly sacrificed at altars atop the pyramid shaped mounds. There priests spilled blood to appease their gods and assure that the world would continue. Throughout his life, Serpent Who Sleeps had heard strange tales of such a place, but he had always assumed that it was a land of fables, of legends, not of men. Now he wasn't so sure.

"Strange lands!" thought Serpent Who Sleeps. "Strange people!" He had learned that the world was indeed a much larger place than Moundville and the Black Warrior River valley. But after their sojourn to Spiro and their encounter with the Hasinai who had visited the Dry Lands, Serpent Who Sleeps and his traveling companions longed for home. Two Wolves convinced them that the journey back to Moundville would be shorter if they first traveled overland to the Southern River, then followed that waterway downstream to its juncture with the Great River, just south of the Grand Village of the Natchez. From there they could retrace their earlier trail back to the Black Warrior valley. Moreover, as Two Wolves pointed out, the Southern River was dotted with villages of Hasinai and other Caddoan speaking peoples, many of whom were his relatives. They would provide a friendly reception and might have additional items to trade, other goods to be carried back to the Natchez villages or on to Moundville.

They left Spiro late in the summer. They carried packs full of items they had secured through the trade. Serpent Who Sleeps carried the macaw tail feathers in a lengthy piece of hollow cane to keep the feathers from being broken. They spent several days passing through low, heavily forested, but sometimes steep mountains (the Winding Stair and Kiamichi ranges), then followed a small river valley south until it emptied into the Southern River. Two Wolves recognized the terrain and led the party east, along the Southern River, then south as the river plunged toward the flatlands and pine forests. There the travelers encountered several villages of people who shared Two Wolves's language and who were eager to both trade and talk with the newcomers. The Hasinai traders whom Serpent Who Sleeps and his comrades had encountered at Spiro were from other villages, farther west, along the Neches River, so the western trade goods and reports of fabled lands in the west carried by the travelers from Moundville were new. They attracted considerable attention. The Caddo villagers were fascinated by their stories.[18]

The travelers bartered for a large canoe and continued on downstream, visiting other villages built along the riverbank. At first, Serpent Who Sleeps thought that the trade goods offered by Hasinai villagers along the Southern River were less attractive than those bartered at Spiro, but when they reached a large village located much further downstream, one of the villagers offered to trade a large pelt taken from an animal that Serpent Who Sleeps had never encountered. According to the villager, he had acquired the pelt from a party of scruffy traders who had arrived at their village earlier in the spring. They claimed they had come from the south, from a land covered by low trees and thorny brush and had followed the shoreline of the Great Salt Water for many days before reaching the village. The pelt had been taken from a great long-tailed cat, but not from a *kaccuv* (cougar), an animal that occasionally prowled the forests along the Black Warrior River. In contrast this skin, while also tawny, was a darker color, and was spotted with large, dark, irregular, roseate spots.[19] Moreover, this cat obviously was much larger, heavier, than a *kaccuv*. When Serpent Who Sleeps asked about the animal, he was told that the visitors from the south referred to it as an *ocelotl*, a name they said had been given to the cat by people who lived still further south, some of whom resided in white stone cities.[20] Once, Serpent Who Sleeps would have thought such tales pure non-sense. Now he believed they were true.

Serpent Who Sleeps was fascinated by the pelt, which obviously came from a very large cat, a powerful hunter. He had accumulated many blue and green stones at Spiro, and he traded part of them for the spotted skin. He believed that the pelt possessed powerful medicine, medicine that would enable its owner to also strike quickly like a cat and to surprise his enemies. He wrapped the pelt in deerskin and placed it carefully in the dugout canoe before he and his comrades departed from this last large village and paddled down the Southern River and back to the Natchez. When they arrived in the Great Sun's village, he kept the spotted skin concealed within the deerskin, then carried it overland back to Moundville. In the years since, it served him well; its medicine had remained strong. He wore it only when he went to war, and he regularly surprised and routed his enemies.

Thinking back on those days, he remembered how he and his fellow travelers had been greeted as heroes on their return from the west. He recalled how his uncle, Strikes at Night, and an assemblage of other senior kinsmen and priests, had listened with fascination to the information that he and the others had gathered in the west, tales of wide, treeless grasslands, snow-capped mountains, bone-dry lands irrigated by canals, and cities of countless people living in white stone houses. The large, spotted cat skin (his "war medicine skin") and the small sample of brightly colored bird feathers added credence to their accounts, but still, some of the older men remained skeptical.

They had heard another account of distant lands and great cities earlier in the summer. Prior to Serpent Who Sleeps's return, the two warriors who also had accompanied the trading party to the Natchez but who had not continued on to Spiro had returned to Moundville with a story of their own. After Serpent Who Sleeps's party had departed the Natchez village for Spiro, the two remaining visitors from Moundville, Snapping Turtle and Gander Man, had joined a small party of Natchez traders and had ascended the Great River to the north.

Snapping Turtle and Gander Man brought no brightly colored feathers or tales of broad plains or sunbaked canyons, but they had seen mighty rivers and the remains of a city so large that it dwarfed Moundville. Proceeding north up the Great River past the mouth of the Arkansas, they had traveled for several days, and although two smaller rivers (the White and the St. Francis) emptied their waters into the Great River's from its western bank, only smaller, non-descript streams flowed into the river from the east. The four Natchez traders, who had ascended the river once before, assured them, however, that they would soon see the Bokoshi Losa Ishtoa, the Big Black River (the Ohio), join the Great River from the east, and just before the Great River seemed to veer to the northwest the large, flooded tributary poured in from the east. Snapping Turtle and Gander Man privately concurred that the Big Black River's waters were green rather than black, but they wisely kept their opinion to themselves.

Passing the mouth of the Big Black River, they continued up the Great River, and three days later, they reached their destination. After paddling up a creek that entered the river on its eastern bank, they soon skirted a shallow backwater and approached a low bluff. Although they had been informed that the deserted city was larger than Moundville, both Snapping Turtle and Gander Man still were amazed. Stretching back from the bluff's edge was a series of earthen mounds, surrounded in the distance by the remains of a partially collapsed log palisade.

Wide eyed, they spent several days wandering through the abandoned city and its environs, marveling at the number of mounds, the remains of large open plazas (now overgrown with smaller trees and brush), and the deserted village sites scattered in the countryside surrounding the city for half a day's journey in three directions. Some of the mounds were circular, while others were long, narrow ridge-backed affairs, but others were four-sided, flat-topped pyramids, similar to some of the mounds in their home village. Yet the mounds at the abandoned city were so numerous and scattered over such a large area that neither Snapping Turtle nor Gander Man could count them; one, which dominated a large abandoned plaza near the location where they had landed their canoes, was huge. It seemed to have been built in tiers, and it towered at least one hundred feet (twice the height of the largest mound at Moundville), dominating the abandoned plaza that partially surrounded it. Both Snapping Turtle and Gander Man agreed that the flattened top of the structure, like similar shaped pyramids at their village, must have once held a temple or the residence of a great chief or priest, but the structure was no longer standing.

Although the city had been abandoned for many generations, a small village of people currently occupied a site on a plaza overlooking the creek, and their village served as a center of exchange for traders like Snapping Turtle, Gander Man, and their Natchez companions. The villagers, who followed a traditional way of life (hunting, fishing, and cultivating small gardens), lived in bark covered lodges and regularly hosted traders who periodically visited the abandoned city, since it sat at an important crossroads near the confluence of several rivers. Neither Snapping Turtle nor Gander Man ascended these streams, but they learned that just north of the abandoned city, the River of Wooden Canoe People (the Missouri) poured its waters into the Great River, while nearby, the River of the Alinouek (the Illinois), a smaller river that drained the tall-grass prairies to the north, joined the Great River from its eastern bank.

Neither Snapping Turtle nor Gander Man met any traders who had descended the Missouri, but they did meet with traders from the north. One party arrived via the River of the Alinouek, and another came down the Great River in strange but graceful canoes crafted of bark. Both groups carried ingots and hammered sheets of raw copper, which they eagerly bartered for the multicolored shells, engraved shell gorgets, and small bags full of beads from the Great Salt Water, which had been carried up the Great River by the two men from Moundville and their Natchez companions. The northerners spoke strange languages, but through translators in the village, Snapping Turtle and Gander Man learned of broad prairies along the Alinouek River but also of great freshwater seas to the north, seas often swept by heavy winter snows, seas whose shores were the source of the highly valued copper carried by the strangers.

Like Snapping Turtle and Gander Man. the traders from the north also questioned the village dwellers about the former resident of the abandoned city— Who were they? How did they build such monuments? Why had they left? Where had they gone? But the villagers had no answers. They referred to them only as the Old Ones, and they seemed to think that many had gone west, up the River of Wooden Canoes. Others had dispersed on the nearby prairies or had traveled eastward toward a river they called Wabasha, the River of Leaves. Yet their answers often seemed vague or contradictory. Some of the villagers suggested that they themselves were the descendants of the former residents, but they provided no answers on why or how the mounds had been erected or why the city had been abandoned. Although Gander Man, particularly, wanted to ask them additional questions about the past, both he and Snapping Turtle knew that such inquiries could not be made. They were guests in these people's village. It would violate all rules of manners and propriety to ask unwanted questions. Guests listened politely. They did not pry.

Snapping Turtle, Gander Man, and the Natchez traders lingered at the abandoned city for ten days, trading for copper and obsidian and exploring the neighboring region. They climbed the bluffs that contained the eastern margin of the bottom lands, and after venturing through a narrow band of timber, they found that the trees opened onto rolling prairies. They also traversed old trails that followed the flood plain both north and south of the city and found both regions dotted with the remains of additional mounds, and smaller, but also deserted villages. Where had all the people gone? What had happened to them? Their questions unanswered, after ten days they packed their newly acquired trade goods into the dugout canoes and returned to the Great River. They paddled south, carried downstream by the current, and eventually returned to the Natchez village. From there they carried both the stories of their experiences and their newly acquired trade good back to Moundville.

Snapping Turtle and Gander Man had arrived at Moundville in midsummer, well before Serpent Who Sleeps's return. Clan members, town elders, Strikes at Night, his advisers, and several priests had all listened to their account of the journey to the abandoned city, and although they were interested in their experiences, two or three of the older men assembled with Strikes at Night had previously visited the site. Indeed, these elders pointed out that in the time of their great-great uncles, a distant ancestor had journeyed to the city and found it still inhabited, although many of the houses were deserted and its walls in disrepair. The ancestor's account had been passed down through the years, but the few traders from Moundville who had made subsequent journeys north also reported either a much diminished population or finally, like Snapping Turtle and Gander Man, abandoned ruins inhabited only by a few villagers with little or no knowledge of what had happened. Strikes at Night, his advisers, and the priests had not been surprised at Snapping Turtle's and Gander Man's descriptions. Obviously, they had heard similar stories before, but like the recently returned travelers, they too had wondered at the city's demise. If the city had once been so large and powerful, and if it had collapsed, then what did the years ahead hold for Moundville?

Still sitting by the fire in his hearth, Serpent Who Sleeps arose, walked outside, and brought two small logs into his lodge, then placed one on the fire. The days were getting shorter, and the nights now brought a chill. When he had been a younger man, he had prided himself over his indifference to the seasons, but those days, like the travels of his youth, were things of the past.

Returning to his reveries, Serpent Who Sleeps pondered how in the years that had followed, he had learned that Spiro had declined as a trading center and its population had dispersed westward onto the Wide Land without Trees. The supply of exotic western trade goods had declined. He had grown older, and after Strikes Quietly had passed into the spirit world, he had inherited his position as leader of the people. The seasons had been good. He had understood politics. He had consolidated his family's power and enjoyed the support of his people. Although members of his clan still held dominant positions, he had established a series of minor posts which now were administered by commoners, and which he now continued to award upon merit. Moreover, Moundville's relationship with its outlying communities, while always tenuous, had been strengthened.

Indeed, in retrospect, Serpent Who Sleeps believed that his efforts had markedly increased his family's ability to maintain control over his incipient city-state, and although he doubted that the population of the community would grow much larger, he had looked forward to a golden age, a time of political and economic stability during which his people could live in peace, buttressed by economic prosperity and sustained by the community's rich ceremonialism. The now-deceased Walks Quietly had always been his favorite nephew, and Serpent Who Sleeps had carefully tutored the young man, preparing him as his heir apparent. Now Walks Quietly lay entombed near the Great Mound. The future of his family seemed less certain. Would Moundville, like Spiro, or the great abandoned city of the north also become deserted and forgotten? Would his kinsmen and neighbors, like the residents of those former places also be scattered to the wind? Would future travelers in the Black Warrior valley walk amidst neglected mounds and former plazas, overgrown with saplings and shrubbery?

And yet Serpent Who Sleeps remained optimistic. He believed that although some things changed, other things had permanence. Time, for Serpent Who Sleeps, was not a river. It was not the linear progression of the Europeans who eventually would occupy his river valley. In contrast, for the aging leader and his people, time was a great pond that always remained the same. Waves might sometimes ripple the surface, but things were unchanged. Regardless of who succeeded him, Serpent Who Sleeps believed that the community's endless cycles of existence would continue. The seasons passed, but the land and the people persisted. Some things changed, but most things were much as they always had been. They would remain that way in the future. The great cycle of life would continue.

On November 15, 2008, in his presidential address to the American Society for Ethnohistory, Colin G. Calloway, the John Kimball Professor of History and professor of Native American studies at Dartmouth College, initiated his remarks by stating:

> Growing up on the outskirts of a north England mill town, what drew me to American history was the presence of Indian peoples; what bemused me about American history books was the absence of Indian peoples. At the time I thought it was the limitations of Keighley Public Library's American history collection; I subsequently learned that was not the only problem.[21]

Calloway's initial perspective, while viewed from across the Atlantic, was quite correct. In 1967, Samuel Elliott Morrison's *The Oxford History of the American People*, a landmark volume by a distinguished, highly acclaimed senior scholar and a textbook used in many of the beginning American history college and university surveys during that decade and later, contained only a precursory chapter of fifteen pages (out of over eleven hundred total pages) on the pre-Columbian period. The chapter also included Morrison's admission that "when we try to tell the story of America. . . , the lack of data quickly brings us to a halt. . . . Thus, what we mean by the history of the American people is the history of immigrants from other continents."[22]

Obviously, during the following decades, some things have improved. Most modern American texts now contain at least a modicum of information on Native American people. Yet these discussions or data resemble the materials that also have been added in regard to African Americans, Hispanic Americans — even women, for that matter — separate subsections of chapters focusing on the role of these groups at different times or in relation to specific historical events, for example, urbanization in the late nineteenth century, the 1920s, or World War II. In other words, the general political-economic framework has remained the same; contributions of these previously marginalized groups have been added to the readily accepted framework, usually at the expense of diplomatic or military history, which currently are out of fashion among many historians in the United States.

But more so than other groups, materials on Native American history are often contained in special pictorial features, tucked into the middle of chapters, which elaborate on subjects mentioned in the text but often seem to be marginalized: they are added features apart from the primary focus of the chapter. Of course, this feature enables the author or publisher to introduce a quick discussion of cultural materials, complete with color photographs featuring copies of woodcuts, Tecumseh's tomahawk, paintings by George Catlin or Karl Bodmer, or even winter counts from tepee liners or buffalo robes. Special insets of Lewis and Clark among the Mandans and Hidatsas or Sequoyah and the Cherokee syllabary are particularly popular subjects, as are Navajo code-talkers during World War II or Mohawk steelworkers constructing high-rise skyscrapers. These added materials are welcome, but the body of the narrative still remains primarily a Euro-American story to which assorted Native American appendages have been attached.

Obviously, the primary problem for many historians in presenting a new understanding of Native people in the Americas is one of scope. Most start too late and focus too narrowly. Many historians who teach surveys of American history still stress that in 1492, when Columbus "discovered" America, the region encompassing the continental United States was a wilderness, sparsely inhabited by primitive peoples whose cultures had very little in common with the highly developed societies of Europe, Africa, or Asia. Indeed, after spending a few obligatory minutes discussing how Native American people arrived in the Americas via the land bridge, these introductory surveys dismiss Indian peoples as part of the primeval past. North America, therefore, especially those regions north of Mexico, existed in isolation, apart from the general mainstream of human development. The future United States essentially was an empty land, "a virgin wilderness" fervently awaiting the arrival of Europeans before becoming part of the "history of civilization."

Such an assessment, of course, reflects an ethnocentric European bias. Although Serpent Who Sleeps's world lacked some of the technological knowledge shared by Eurasians (notably, metallurgy and a written language), it exceeded the Europeans in other areas (agriculture and medicine). Obviously, many of the patterns and parameters that both scholars and laymen use to define "civilized societies" differ considerably among those rendering the definition, and all societies probably are "civilized" from their own perspective, but even if many of the cultural patterns commonly associated with the "civilizations" of Europe or the Middle East (non-American criteria) are used to examine American societies, the latter were "civilized" by any standard. The people of Moundville, Spiro, Mesa Verde, and Cahokia lived in complex societies that provided many of the opportunities and restraints found among similar cultures in Eurasia and Africa. And while Moundville or Cahokia hardly represented Rome "in all its glory," neither did their inhabitants resemble the barbarians. Serpent Who Sleeps was not Caesar, but he certainly was not Attila.

Far from being a cultural backwater, completely isolated from the broader mainstream of world history, North America shared many of the patterns manifested in Europe, Africa, and the Middle East. Just as in Africa or the Fertile Crescent, complex and sophisticated riverine cultures emerged, flourished, and then declined in the American heartland. Constructing large burial and effigy mounds, between 700 BCE and about 500 CE, the Adena people dominated the central and lower Ohio Valley. The Great Serpent Mound, an Adena earthworks in modern Adams County, Ohio, stretches almost one-quarter mile in length and appears to represent a snake with an egg in its mouth. The Adena people harvested surplus crops that were stored in ceramic vessels, and they traded in products from throughout the eastern United States. Adena craftsmen hammered raw copper into bracelets, beads, gorgets, and axes, and copper shell and intricately crafted stone objects adorn the graves of their leaders. A socially stratified people, the Adena villagers extended their influence up the Ohio Valley and over the Appalachians. Although they declined after 400 CE, they profoundly influenced those cultures that followed them.[23]

While the Adena people declined, another, perhaps more vibrant, way of life emerged in the same general region. Named the Hopewell culture or the Hopewell interaction sphere by modern archaeologists, this way of life flourished in the Ohio and Mississippi valleys from about 200 BCE through approximately 500 CE. A widespread cultural complex, the Hopewell phase encompassed a broad spectrum of people between the Appalachians and the Great Plains, and like the Mississippians, their trade networks stretched as far west as the Rockies. Also constructing large mounds, the Hopewell people were skilled artisans whose mastery of their craft reflected their specialization of labor. Conspicuous consumers, members of the Hopewellian elite adorned themselves and their dead relatives with copper jewelry, beaded shell blankets, and ornaments made of mica, embossed shell, and skillfully carved bone or wood. In some cases, gold and silver nuggets were hammered into foil that was combined with quartz crystals to adorn headdresses. Also steeped in religious ceremonialism, the Hopewellian heartland fostered a vigorous expansive lifestyle that was exported from New York to Oklahoma and from Minnesota to the Gulf of Mexico. Although their settlements remained smaller than the Mississippian people who followed them, they produced an urbane, attractive way of life.[24]

Far to the southwest and much less expansive, the Hohokam people of the Salt and Gila River valleys in Arizona flourished from shortly before the birth of Christ until about 1450. Desert farmers, the Hohokam people may have been colonists who migrated north from Mexico, or they may have evolved from local groups who combined their indigenous way of life with cultural influences from the Valley of Mexico. Their society probably was less stratified than the Mississippians, and their penchant for public works manifested itself in the construction of an extensive system of irrigation canals, rather than earthen edifices. Eventually, hundreds of miles of canals diverted the waters of the Salt and Gila Rivers, and population centers such as Snaketown and Casa Grande functioned as marketplaces for products from Mexico and across the Southwest. Moreover, as the years passed, the Hohokam people became more adaptive and continued to adopt a broad spectrum of ideas from surrounding people. Yet their ties to Mexico continued, for like their neighbors to the south, they also constructed the sunken courts on which the ceremonial ball games often were violently contested.[25]

A more expansive people, the Ancestral Pueblo villagers of modern New Mexico and northern Arizona were contemporaries of many of the Mississippians, and they too enjoyed a life bounded by their culture's rich ceremonialism. From population centers at Chaco Canyon, Mesa Verde, and other locations, they colonized much of New Mexico, establishing villages as far south as the Big Bend of the Rio Grande and as far east as the western fringes of the Great Plains. Incorporating over two hundred thousand logs, the eight major pueblos of Chaco Canyon towered as high as five stories, and the largest of the towns, Pueblo Bonito, contained over 650 rooms. More than one million carefully shaped stones were utilized in the construction. Irrigating their fields of maize with water collected in carefully constructed catch basins, the Ancestral Pueblos garnered their surplus harvests in storage areas within their pueblos. Led by a theocracy that combined religious and political influence, the Ancestral Pueblos followed a rich ceremonial life that reflected their systematic astronomical observations and the rhythm of the seasons. By 1400, the Ancestral Pueblos had spread down the Rio Grande valley, and colonizers had established outposts along the Pecos River, on the western fringes of the Great Plains. Trade networks exchanging turquoise, ceramics, and other valuable commodities stretched across the Southwest and as far south as Mexico, but a series of catastrophic droughts forced the culture to contract and consolidate along the upper Rio Grande valley and at other scattered population centers in western New Mexico and Arizona.[26]

And yet all these cultures pale before the majesty of the Mississippians. Although the site had essentially been abandoned before Serpent Who Sleeps was born, Cahokia, the Mississippian city that flourished just opposite modern St. Louis, Missouri, during the twelfth and thirteenth centuries was truly a pre-Columbian metropolis with a population numbering over ten thousand individuals within the city's core region and at least another thirty thousand other people, if the population of the neighboring Mississippian communities is included.[27]

Defended by a heavy log palisade supported by bastions, the central city comprised over two thousand acres, but the surrounding settlement encompassed an area over five times that size and was scattered over six and one-quarter square miles. Monk's Mound, which still dominates the site, overlooked the largest of the city's six plazas. Constructed by Mississippian laborers, each carrying a basket-load of from fifty to sixty pounds of soil, this massive earthen edifice was enlarged several times during the city's habitation. During Serpent Who Sleeps's lifetime, as today, it covered an area with a base measuring about eight hundred by one thousand feet. The mound itself contains approximately twenty-two million cubic feet of material. Flat topped, during the city's golden age, the monument was crowned with an enormous temple whose ground dimensions were 104 by 48 feet and which towered another 35 feet above the mound's summit.[28]

Cahokia contained an urbane population whose specialization of labor has been documented by extensive archaeological excavation. Some of the inhabitants cultivated the myriad fields of maize, beans, and squash that dotted the surrounding countryside. Others exploited the rich fauna, especially fish and other aquatic life available in the region's converging watercourses. Indeed, as at Moundville, fish were bred and raised in many of the barrow pits excavated during the mound construction. Some citizens were artisans, devoting most of their time to fashioning copper jewelry, carving stone, or crafting ceramics. Others engaged in trade, for several of the city's plazas functioned as open-air markets. But above all of these commoners ruled the city's elite, a privileged class who occupied the city's core area and whose homes, like those of Serpent Who Sleeps and his kinsmen, were located on the summits of several of the lower mounds.[29]

At Cahokia, this ruling class sometimes exercised a life-and-death control over part of its subjects. Mound 72, located about one-half mile south of Monk's Mound, served as the tomb for a Cahokian leader who had been buried with Mississippian splendor. Laid on a shroud embossed with twenty thousand marine beads, he was surrounded by grave goods including sheets of mica from the Great Smoky Mountains, rolls of hammered copper from the shores of Lake Superior, and conch shells from the Gulf of Mexico. Entombed near his feet were six other individuals (three male, three female), obviously sacrificed to accompany or attend him in the afterlife. Other investigations have revealed similar burials. Indeed, another excavation into this mound unearthed the skeletons of fifty-three young women, aged fifteen to twenty-five years, who also were the apparent participants (or victims) in a ceremonial sacrifice and a mass burial. Obviously, the residents of Cahokia lived in a very stratified society. We may not approve of their burial practices, but we must acknowledge that they lived in a rather well-defined, political system.[30]

And yet not all the Mississippians' efforts focused on the acquisition of luxury goods or political power or the construction of enormous earthworks. Archaeologists have pointed out that Cahokians, like many other people of pre-Columbian America, also spent considerable time and effort studying the heavens and calculating the passing of the seasons. One-half mile west of Monk's Mound stood a large circle of carefully placed log posts that functioned as an astronomical observatory. Standing atop the observation point in the circle's center, Cahokia's priests could calculate the passage of time by measuring the changing position of the sunrise on the horizon. The observatory could also be used to study the movement of the moon, or the other brighter heavenly bodies. Obviously, the residents of Cahokia pursued a myriad of interests and activities.[31]

So in retrospect, what is to be learned from an overview of these societies? Although the complex cultures of the pre-Columbian United States varied in their foci or sophistication, most shared many of the traits usually associated with the "civilized" nations or societies of Eurasia or Africa. Such comparisons can easily be overdrawn, for each culture is a unique entity, and all societies are civilized by their own standards, but since most modern Americans equate "civilization" with certain values or characteristics associated with the complex cultures of the "Western world," let's look at the Mississippians and Cahokia, in particular, within this "Western civilization" perspective.

Like the cultures that developed along the Nile, the Euphrates, the Tigris, and the Tiber, the Mississippians were a riverine people. They too emerged along a flood plain, utilizing the rich alluvial deposits of the river to plant and harvest an abundance of staple crops to support their population. For the Mississippians, as for the people of Egypt, the river also provided a major avenue of transportation. All these societies created monumental public works, many of which are closely associated with religion, death, or ceremonial centers. Most also featured culture-wide religious manifestations, with an established priesthood or clergy in control of carefully prescribed rituals for the management of their people's relationship with the powers in the universe. Indeed, many of the artifacts that have been recovered from these cultures (from Egypt and the Mississippians) are grave goods associated with the entombment of people of elevated status.

All of these societies were actively engaged in trade. They created and exported finished products whose intricate craftsmanship reflected a specialization of labor. In turn, they imported considerable quantities of luxury goods that were amassed and utilized for conspicuous consumption by a sociopolitical elite. In addition, most established public granaries where surplus harvests were stockpiled for future use during period of deprivation.

Although Serpent Who Sleeps exercised less political power than Pharaoh or Darius, and although the Mississippian communities were never combined in any centralized political unit, leaders of the individual communities did enjoy considerable power, and some—like the Great Sun of the historic Natchez people—were treated like veritable potentates. Certainly, the empires of Egypt, Rome, and Mesopotamia had first emanated from a single community or city-state, and attempts by Mississippian leaders to increase their hegemony may have constituted initial steps in such a direction. All of these societies were ruled by a social-political, and in some cases religious, elite who attempted to transfer their power through familial inheritance.

And finally, each of these societies eventually developed an urban focus. Great cities arose beside the Nile, Tigris, Euphrates, and Tiber. Of course, Cahokia, whose population probably never surpassed eleven thousand in its core area, (but which had another twenty to thirty thousand people living in smaller villages in the adjoining American Bottom region), could never rival these Old World cities in size, but by Western European standards it certainly qualified as a city. In 1200 CE, its population rivaled London's and was larger than any city in what is now Belgium, the Netherlands, or Germany.[32]

So why has the image of a sparsely populated and primitive pre-Columbian America persisted? Why have many historians and the general public continued to envision Serpent Who Sleeps's world as essentially a wilderness devoid of significant population or civilization?[33] The answers are obvious. First, the complex societies of the American interior did not extend to the Eastern Seaboard, and the first northern European travelers (mariners and traders visiting the Atlantic coast in the sixteenth century) did not meet the descendants of Serpent Who Sleeps and his people. Ironically, Hernando De Soto, whose expedition encountered several populous Mississippian chiefdoms or city-states in the 1540s, reported his findings back to Spain, but when compared to contemporary Spanish reports from Mesoamerica, the De Soto chronicles seemed rather inconsequential.[34]

A century and a half later, when French explorers and trappers penetrated the Illinois country and began to trade along the lower Mississippi valley, almost all the nascent or fully flowered Mississippian city-states or chiefdoms were gone. In a pattern similar to the rise and fall of similar but often larger states or societies in Europe and western Asia, Mississippian population centers had emerged, some had blossomed, then almost all had faded. In the eastern United States, these sophisticated societies typically had a lifespan of about five hundred years. Cahokia, for example, had emerged from a small village site in 700 CE, grew to a much larger settlement by about 900, and had reached its zenith approximately 250 years later. After 1200, the city had declined. Moundville, considerably smaller in size and population, existed as a small village in about 1000 CE then emerged as a major center of political influence about one hundred years later. It increased and maintained its position of preeminence in western Alabama until around 1450, but by 1500, it was basically abandoned.[35]

During the past century, historians and archaeologists have speculated about the causes of this decline, and they often have disagreed. Some scholars have suggested that Cahokia was swept by floods engendered by climate change.[36] Others have argued that the burgeoning population in the immediate area both polluted and deforested the region.[37] Some scholars believe that the introduction of new strains of maize encouraged many Cahokian farmers to move out of the American Bottom and scatter across adjoining prairies.[38] Others have posited that rivalries among the elite created political schisms that disrupted the relationship between the upper class and the commoners, which triggered an out-migration of the population.[39] The limited scope of this essay prevents any in-depth analysis of these differing hypotheses, but all these factors (to a greater or lesser degree) probably contributed to the city's downfall.[40]

Scholars also disagree over the destination of this out-migration. Many archaeologists and ethnohistorians believe that the bulk of Cahokia's population migrated westward, up the Missouri River valley, then scattered into smaller agricultural settlements on the eastern fringes of the Great Plains.[41] Others argue that many of Cahokia's residents gradually abandoned the American Bottom and moved up the Illinois River valley and onto the prairie regions of Illinois, and into Wisconsin.[42] Finally, some historians and linguists assert that at least part of Cahokia's population migrated east to occupy part of the Wabash valley.[43] But whatever their destination, by 1500 CE, for all practical purposes, the great city had been abandoned.

Moundville's decline shows some similarities. Christopher Peebles, a leading scholar of Moundville and the Mississippian peoples in Alabama, has traced the rise and fall of Moundville between 1000 and 1500 CE and has argued that like Cahokia, Moundville also developed a political elite that dominated both the city and surrounding settlements in the Black Warrior River valley. But after Moundville's zenith (during Serpent Who Sleeps's lifetime), Peebles suggests, the leadership failed, food production declined, and the city's participation in widespread trade networks declined. In response, much of the population of Moundville and the surrounding Black Warrior River valley, abandoned the region and relocated to smaller, more egalitarian villages along the Alabama River.[44]

Although much smaller than Moundville, Spiro's population had already declined during Serpent Who Sleeps's lifetime. Considerably less investigation has been devoted to Spiro's decline, but scholars assume that most of the villagers living near Spiro dispersed among Caddoan speaking people to the south and west, joining tribal people who would later be known as the Caddos, Hasinai, or the Wichitas. There is some evidence that others joined with the Tunicas.[45]

Regardless of their diasporas, another factor played an even more important role in the American public's assumption that pre-Columbian North America was devoid of any meaningful civilization or population: disease. Isolated from the Eastern Hemisphere and with no natural immunities to the Old World epidemics, Native American peoples fell before a pestilential scythe in unprecedented numbers. Although the exact figures will never be known, the effect was catastrophic. In Mexico, for example, the population dropped from about 12 million on the eve of the conquest to approximately 1.25 million a century later. Historians now estimate that in 1500 CE, the Native American population living north of the Rio Grande was somewhere between seven and ten million people.[46] Undoubtedly, the more diffuse population patterns of Indian people in the future United States and Canada may have prevented losses of a similar magnitude, but the population decline was still phenomenal. In the early 1540s, when De Soto marched across the South, Moundville had essentially been abandoned, but he encountered other populous settlements of Mississippian people throughout much of the region. But within a century, when Europeans began to settle in the region, many of these people were gone.[47]

In a similar scenario, tribal populations in the Northeast, which were flourishing at the time of initial European contact, were also much diminished by the second half of the seventeenth century. Of course, warfare and other disruptions also played a role, but here, as in the Southeast, disease was the biggest cause of depopulation. Historians estimate that in 1500, the Native American population of New England and the Middle Atlantic States reached two hundred thousand. The first recorded pandemic in the region swept through tribal villages between Cape Cod and southern Maine from 1616 to 1622 and may have killed as many as 90 percent of these villages' residents. Other epidemics also ravaged tribal villages from New England through Pennsylvania, also taking the lives of thousands. Regions once populated by numerous villages were laid waste, and tribal people who might have mustered a formidable resistance to European settlement were decimated.[48]

Pre-Columbian population figures for the Great Lakes area and the Midwest are more difficult to ascertain, but early French accounts of the impact of epidemics on specific tribes provide ample evidence of how native people in this region fared. For example, Jesuit records indicate that in 1615, the Huron settlements on Georgian Bay of Lake Huron contained between thirty and forty thousand people, but by 1640, after smallpox, measles, and influenza swept through their villages, their population was halved.[49] In the 1670s, the Illinois Confederacy numbered around ten thousand, but within one hundred years, their numbers had shrunk to 1,720; by 1800, they counted no more than five hundred souls.[50] Other tribal groups in the region also suffered major losses, and in the eighteen and nineteenth centuries, succeeding waves of epidemics (smallpox, measles, cholera, influenza, etc.) swept westward across the continent, decimating indigenous peoples, disrupting and dispersing their societies, and clearing the way for Euro-American expansion.[51]

There is an old familiar cliché utilized by many historians to describe the American experience. According to these traditional scholars, European pioneers landed on the eastern shores of North America, then advanced westward to conquer and transform an empty land, a place essentially untouched by human beings and devoid of any civilization—a "virgin wilderness." But such an interpretation conveniently ignores the accomplishments of the Mississippians and other pre-Columbian societies. The land was not empty. For centuries prior to 1492, North America had been traversed, settled, and transformed by Native American peoples. Like much of Eurasia and Africa, North America also had seen the rise and fall of sophisticated, complex societies. As Francis Jennings so persuasively has argued, Anglo-American settlers moved west into regions where the previous Native American inhabitants had been felled or dispersed by the epidemics. The settlers also moved west during what might be described as an emergent Dark Age for Native American people. Consequently, after 1700, Euro-Americans were not advancing into a "virgin wilderness." They were advancing into a "widow."[52]

August 2005

It was amazing! He really couldn't get over it!

Marvin "Rusty" Whiteside had just spent an hour in the Interpretive Center at Cahokia Mounds State Historic Park, and he had been dumbfounded by the dioramas and audiovisual presentation that focused on the size of the Mississippian city and the sophistication of its inhabitants. Who would have thought that a city of that size could have existed here on this floodplain in the thirteenth century? What's more, the video also pointed out that Cahokia was even larger than many cities in Europe at that time. Well, that was hard to believe, but the people who put the video together seemed to know what they were talking about, so he guessed it must be true. All this new information sure differed from what he had been taught when he attended Hickory Grove High School down in Randolph County, Illinois, back in the late 1950s. But that was over fifty years ago, and things had changed, he supposed.

Now it was August 2005—a new century. Rusty had just retired from his job at the post office at Sparta and had moved to St. Louis to be near his recently divorced daughter and his two grandkids, and he planned to see the sights in the "big city" while he still could drive his truck and get around. Through the years, several people whom he had known through his job as a rural mail carrier had told him he should visit Cahokia, but he had never bothered to take their advice. He had always figured that he already knew all he needed to know about Indians. Most of them lived out west, or in Oklahoma, or Wisconsin, or near Yellowstone Park, or in houses with totem parks, but all were gone from Illinois and Missouri. In elementary school, his third-grade teacher had talked about Indians at Thanksgiving, and Coach McConnell (who also had been his high school history teacher) had mentioned that Black Hawk, an old chief who once lived up by Rock Island, had a hockey team named after him. Coach McConnell had also shown their American history class and old black-and-white film (starring Errol Flynn and featuring Anthony Quinn as Crazy Horse) about Custer's Last Stand, but after that, Indians were never mentioned in class, and he had assumed that most of them had died out—except for the code-talkers, of course.

Boy had he been wrong! Following the recent video presentation at the interpretive center, a middle-aged, dark-haired woman had stepped to the podium in the auditorium and spent fifteen minutes talking about modern Indian people in the St. Louis region and in the United States. Rusty had been surprised to learn that over two thousand Indian people still lived in the greater St. Louis region and that their number was growing. Moreover, they worked at a lot of different jobs, like everybody else. The woman, Sally Pierre, was proud of her Peoria-Kaskaskia ancestry and seemed to know quite a bit about Indians and their business, in general. He wished he had had an opportunity to talk with her about lots of other things (both Indian lore and other stuff).

Rusty left the visitors' center and slowly climbed Monk's Mound, the huge flat-topped edifice that towered over both the center and the adjoining parking lots. The climb up the mound wore him out, and when he reached the top, he paused to catch his breath, but the view across the Mississippi River bottoms toward St. Louis and the gigantic stainless steel Gateway Arch that dominated the city's skyline caused him to stop and ponder. He always thought that Indian people had contributed little to the history of this region and that they had been swept away by the "floodtide of civilization." But now, standing atop a monument built centuries ago by human hands and then looking across the river at another more recently constructed landmark provided considerable food for thought. His understanding of both history and civilization certainly had been changed. Long before the French, or Spaniards, or Pilgrims, or whoever had settled and built a city in this place, other people — Indian people — had built their houses, raised their mounds, and established a trading center at this site near the juncture of these three large rivers. They, too, had planted their crops, raised their families, dreamed their dreams, and lived their lives to the fullest. Their footprints remained in the region, and they continued to leave those footprints into the present.

But damn, it was hot! Rusty was seventy-two years old, too old to be climbing up these mounds on a sultry afternoon in mid-August. He clambered down from the mound, got into his Ford pickup, started the engine, then turned on the air-conditioning. As he sat here, cooling off and catching his breath, he glanced through several brochures he had selected from a rack in the interpretive center. Most contained brief descriptions of Cahokia, or Mississippian, culture, but one listed a series of events scheduled to take place in the fall. Hmm ... A big get-together in October? Tribal people from Oklahoma and the Midwest coming together for a weekend celebration? The public was welcome? Well, it would be a lot cooler in October. He could drive over from St. Louis. Maybe bring his daughter and grandkids. The kids could climb up and down the mounds. And maybe that Indian woman would speak again. He hoped so. He'd like to ask her some questions. He wanted to learn more about Cahokia and the people who had built these mounds. He also wanted to learn more about modern Indian people who lived in St. Louis. What's more, he'd just like to talk with that woman. Hmm ... he wondered if she were married.

Suggested Readings

Crosby, Alfred W. *The Columbian Exchange: Biological and Cultural Consequences of 1492.* Westport, CT: Greenwood Press, 1972.

Echo-Hawk, Roger. "Ancient History in the New World: Integrating Oral Traditions and the Archaeological Record in Deep Time." *American Antiquity* 65, no. 2 (2000): 267–90.

La Vere, David. *Looting Spiro Mounds: An American King Tut's Tomb.* Norman: University of Oklahoma Press, 2007.

Pauketat, Timothy. *Cahokia, Ancient America's City on the Mississippi*. New York: Penguin, 2000.

Singleton, Eric D., and F. Kent Reilly III, eds. *Recovering Ancient Spiro: Native American Art, Ritual, and Cosmic Renewal*. Oklahoma City: National Cowboy & Western Heritage Museum, 2020.

Stuart, Gene. *America's Ancient Cities*. Washington, DC: National Geographic Society, 1988.

Townsend, Richard F., ed. *Hero, Hawk, and Open Hand: American Indian Art of the Ancient Midwest and Southeast*. New Haven, CT: Yale University Press, 2004.

TWO

Whispering Women and Shadowed Faces

Cultural Change and Commerce in the Western Great Lakes

Green Bay, 1679

Her back ached from lifting the heavy bales of furs she had helped haul over the gunwales of the immense canoe that had sailed away from the shelter of the island. Standing on the island's shore, she looked beyond the great canoe's former anchorage, gazing eastward through the narrow strait of water (Porte des Morts Passage), past the finger tip of the peninsula that separated the Bay of Stinking Water from Lake Michigame, the Big Lake, whose surface, though calm, looked gray and ominous.[1] The Potawatomi woman, Shadows on Her Face, recalled that four days before, when the great canoe arrived from Lake Michigame, the lake's blue water had rolled with gentle waves, and the great white wings that towered above the French vessel had billowed with the breath of the manitous. But now, the great canoe, which the Frenchmen called the *Griffon*, was filled with furs, and earlier in the day, French traders had loosed their moorings and had sailed through the passage, out toward open water.[2]

The woman was apprehensive. For the past two days, Shaota, the manitou who lived in the south, had caused the warm moist air to come blowing from his village. The Frenchmen boasted that these winds would carry their vessel rapidly to Michilimackinac. But Shadows on Her Face had her doubts. It was Mishiwa-kisis, the Moon of the Elk, and she knew that this was the season when climatic change came violently to Lake Michigame and her sisters. Often, when the wind blew so strongly from the south, Pondessa, the winter manitou, became angry and unleashed his icy breath, and great storms awakened Kegangizi, the water

monster, who lashed the lake with a wave torn frenzy. She had seen those tow-
ering masses of surf crash down on the northern shores of the island, and she
knew that even the gulls took refuge before such an onslaught of wind and water.

But since the *Griffon* had sailed, the southern wind had died. The Big Lake
lay smooth as a piece of stretched deerskin, but long lines of darkening clouds
shrouded the northwestern horizon. Shadows on Her Face was worried. She
knew that her husband, Onanguisse, the Light Which Shimmers, considered
the French men to be his friends. Their vessel, which now was somewhere out
on the open lake, was immense, and their Manitou on the Wooden Cross was
powerful. but Pondessa, the water manitou, was coming from the north, and
Shadows on Her Face feared for their safety.

She admitted that her people, the Neshnabe, the Potawatomis, needed these
pale-skinned Men with Hairy Faces. Their canoes were full of wondrous new
things that they traded to her people, and Shadows on Her Face was aware that
the Potawatomis and other tribes had now become dependent on these objects.
Indeed, Shadows on Her Face wondered at the many changes that had befallen
her people during the forty-five years of her lifetime, for she realized that many
of these innovations, both good and bad, had been brought by the Frenchmen.

Once, her peoples' lives had been simpler. But now they were more difficult.
Before the Frenchmen entered their villages, she lived on the opposite shore
of the Big Lake, and she remembered her early childhood, at the village on the
Muskegon River, where she had been born.[3] In those far distant days, she had
been raised by Sturgeon Woman, her grandmother, for her birth mother, Copper Bracelets, had died when she was a child of only four winters. Sturgeon
Woman had told her that when she was born, her aunts, who had assisted Copper Bracelets with the birth, were shocked when they first saw their sister's
child and discovered that the skin on her right cheek and part of her chin was
covered with a dark birthmark. Birthmarks were very rare among her people,
and none of the women had ever seen such a blemish. Some of her aunts had
whispered that the mark was a sign that the baby had been chosen by Kegangizi, the evil water manitou, and some said the child should be abandoned to
die in the forest.

Yet Copper Bracelets had protested, and the village elders had consulted
with Antler in His Hands, a powerful wabeno, a fire-handler much feared
and respected by the people. And according to Sturgeon Woman, the old shaman had examined her and had taken his medicine bundle into the forest

to consult with the manitous. When he returned, he informed her kinsmen that the darkened skin on her face was not the mark of Kegangizi but had been put there by the Wamigohuk, the thunderbirds, because while still in her mother's womb, this woman-child had already been struck by their lightning, and she would be blessed with many years and would render great service to her people. And because Antler in His Hands had provided them with these insights, the elders of her clan—the Sisko—the Muskrat People—had given the old wabeno tobacco and had asked him to assist in her naming ceremony. In response, he had chosen the name Shadows on Her Face, to commemorate her birthmark.

Her mother died when Shadows on Her Face was barely five years of age, but her grandparents shared her father's lodge, and she had been raised within their extended family. Both her grandmother and her father's sisters shared in her upbringing, teaching her the skills, duties, and obligations expected of a Potawatomi woman. But in some ways, life was hard. Before the Men with Hairy Faces arrived, her aunts and grandmother had cooked in pots they fashioned and fired from clay, but the vessels were fragile and easily broken, even when they were used with care. She had assisted her aunts and cousins in planting, cultivating, and caring for their small plots of maize and pumpkins, but their hoes, crafted of shell or stone blades attached to wooden hafts, easily shattered, and it seemed to Shadows on Her Face that her aunts were forced to spend more time repairing their garden utensils than utilizing them.

Her father and uncles supplied the family with elk, deer, bear, and other skins, which were sewn into clothing using sinew, with awls and needles made of bone or thorns, but the sinew often grew stiff and unwieldy, and the awls and needles quickly dulled and sometimes splintered. In retrospect, Shadows on Her Face marveled at Sturgeon Woman's patience, remembering her grandmother sewing by the fire, holding the clumsy bone needle in her gnarled and crippled fingers. Even the flint knives and scrapers, though initially sharp, soon lost their edges, and mussel-shell spoons, although easily fashioned, also shattered readily, sometimes flaking away into sharp edges that could cut the mouths or fingers of those who held them.

Of course, even in her early childhood, a few of the new and wondrous trade items had filtered into her village. Shortly after her mother's death, her father, Stands in the Water, had journeyed to the east and visited with the Wendats, farming people who lived on the eastern shores of another Great Lake to the north and east. These traders had welcomed the French into their lodges, and their black-robed shamans had established missions in the Wendat villages. In turn, these fortified towns became trading centers from which Wendat traders carried magical new objects to the Potawatomis and their eastern neighbors. Stands in the Water had returned to his village on the Muskegon with a shiny new knife made of a substance like copper, but much harder, and as silver as moonlight. And he had brought his grieving daughter six small circular objects, also made of metal, but colored golden orange, like oak leaves in the fall. Shadows on Her Face smiled when she remembered that she first thought they were a strange new kind of snail shell, and she had asked her father if he had caught the snails in the forest. Her father had simply smiled and handed her the brass hawks bells, which tinkled as she took them, and she had laughed with delight and had carried them into the wigwam to share her newfound treasure with her grandmother.[4]

In the months that followed, other strange and wonderful new items found their way to the Potawatomi village. Shadows on Her Face remembered Sturgeon Woman's happiness when her father gave her grandmother a shiny brass kettle. And during Tamin-kisis, the Moon of Strawberries, in the spring of Shadows on Her Face's sixth year, Sturgeon Woman had taken sinew and attached the brass hawk bells to a new doeskin dress. Shadows on Her Face beamed with pride when she wore the dress to the summer ceremonies, and the bells—she called them her "medicine shells"— jingled as she danced with her aunts and cousins. Through the years, she acquired additional hawks bells, which she had attached to other personal items. When her own children later asked her what they were, she laughed and told them they were special shells from the "medicine snails" in the forest.

But the happy days in Michigan soon ended. In the autumn following such feasting, the Wenros, or "neutrals," renewed their warfare against her people, and Shadows on Her Face and her remaining family fled north, through Michilimackinac to the northern shores of Lake Michigame. Meanwhile, the Nodaways—the dreaded Iroquois, the Serpents—attacked and destroyed the Wendat villages, and her people and their neighbors feared for their lives. Seeking shelter from the chaos, Shadows on Her Face and her family joined with other Potawatomis and traveled down the western shore of the Big Lake until they found new homes near the Menominees, the Wild Rice People, and the Ho-Chunks (Winnebagos), the People of the Big Fish, (sometimes called the People of the Bay). Here on the western shore of this great bay on Lake Mechigame, her people built a new village, and Shadows on Her Face grew to become a woman. Here also, at Mechingan, the new village on the western shore of the Bay, both her grandmother and father passed into the spirit world, and Shadows on Her Face became the wife of Onanguisse, the Light Which Shimmers, an influential young warrior from the Thunder Clan.[5]

Other tribes also fled the Iroquois onslaught, and they, too, built new villages in the region. Some of the Odawas, and the Tionnontatehronnons, or Tobacco People, close allies of the Wendats, settled near the Potawatomi village. The Ousakis, the People of the River's Mouth, established a new town on the lower Fox River. Meanwhile, the Mascoutens (Nation of Fire), the Miamis (People of the Crane), and the Kickapoos (People Who Make Journeys) formed new villages near the Fox-Wisconsin portage, close to the Outagamies, or Meskwakis (People of the Red Earth), who earlier had been driven westward from Michigan by the Ojibwes. This concentration of tribal peoples attracted the Men with Hairy Faces and their black-robed shamans. In the years that followed, both flocked to the Great Bay and to the lower Fox River.[6]

For Shadows on Her Face and her people, the pace of change quickened. She could remember when few warriors from her village possessed the Frenchmen's muskets, but now, many of them owned a firearm of some sort, although many of these weapons were in disrepair, and most of the warriors usually were short of lead and gunpowder. Still, all her adult male kinsmen now carried iron or steel knives or hatchets, and when they hunted smaller animals with their bows and arrows or speared fish in the shallows, they tipped their shafts with iron points, crafted from pieces of metal they salvaged from other broken tools or weapons. Both she and her daughter abandoned the old bone, shell, and flint utensils, and they now used steel or iron needles, knives, and awls to fashion their clothing.

Shadows on Her Face possessed a looking glass of such shiny surface that when she peered into it, she saw her own reflection, and she used the mirror to apply vermillion paint she had acquired from a trader. Recently, bolts of bright crimson and blue trade cloth arrived in their village, and Shadows on Her Face and her sisters had readily cut and sewn the pliable new fabric into long shirts and other garments that all members of their families now combined with more traditional skin or fur clothing. They continued to decorate their ceremonial clothing with shells, porcupine quills, and other age-old accouterments, but they now delighted in the bright glass beads, brass buttons, colored ribbons, and of course the "ringing shells" (the brass hawk's bells) and tinkling cones which they acquired from traders.[7]

As their reliance on French trade goods increased, the people's relationship with the Men with Hairy Faces intensified. When her own daughters grew to maturity, two of them took such traders as husbands, and her heart grew warm when she thought of her three grandchildren. Two years ago, one of these new kinsmen, the husband of her younger daughter, had left the Bay and journeyed back to the east; she doubted if he ever would return. But the husband of her other daughter, a man named Peltier, had settled down permanently and had been accepted by her husband's clan. Indeed, Peltier had readily learned the people's language, now dressed like a Potawatomi, and sometimes spoke in council. The Black Robes had first frowned on the union, but when Shadows on Her Face's grandson was born and her daughter agreed to stand before them and allow the Black Robes to make the sign of their manitou and sprinkle their medicine water over her and the child, the French shamans acquiesced and blessed the marriage.[8]

In retrospect, Shadows on Her Face admitted that that she, too, had been interested in the Black Robes' manitou. Unlike some of her kin, she had never participated in the Black Robes' medicine water ceremony, but the Black Robes seemed to be honest men, and they shared their food and other possessions with the people. Their chants and rituals fascinated her, and she believed that their Manitou on the Wooden Cross and his Mother of Sadness had powerful medicine. Surely these manitous held great power in the homeland of the Men with Hairy Faces. Yet here, at the Center of the World, others manitou held sway, and she believed that the Manitou on the Wooden Cross shared his power with Wiske, the trickster, and Tchaibos, Wiske's brother, and with Shaota, Pondessa, Kegangizi, and other powers in the universe.[9]

Yet the Black Robes were strange men. They refused to couple with women. Fish Crow, a quarrelsome old wabeno, claimed that the Black Robes rejected women because at night they preferred to pursue and mount moose in the forest. Shadows on Her Face had laughed out loud. Everyone knew the Black Robes were so inept, that in the midnight darkness of the forest they could never find their back to the village. Moose indeed! The Black Robes were frightened of even small animals—foxes and porcupines. And she was well aware that the crotchety old Fish Crow resented the Black Robes' growing influence and was jealous of the large numbers of tribespeople who listened to their stories about the Manitou on the Wooden Cross and his promises.

Moreover, on some things, the Black Robes gave good counsel. Like Shadows on Her Face, the Black Robes also became angry when her kinsmen and other Neshnabe drowned their hearts in Onontio's milk, then staggered, grew sick, and slept within their own retching. Through the seasons, the Men with Hairy Faces brought more and more kegs of the fiery liquid to the Bay of Stinking Water, and her people's appetite for this poison increased. Bitter memories! Sometimes, after several kegs had been emptied, joking words turned to quarrels. Then kinsman would fall upon kinsman, and the bright steel knives and hatchets would cause havoc, suffering, and sorrow. Women and children would weep, and Tchaibos would welcome new shadows into the spirit world, And sometimes, warriors or women whose thirst knew no quenching would barter away all their furs for such milk, and their families would go cold and hungry.[10]

Shadows on Her Face silently shook her head and sighed. Like Wiske, the trickster, the trade had many faces. A practical woman, she realized that her people relished the European technology, and what once had been luxuries had now become necessities. She still remembered how her grandmother had taught her to make fire-hardened pottery, but she doubted that her granddaughters could craft such items. Her daughters still wove reed mats and black-ash baskets, but they relied on the traders for thread, needles, knives, ladles, and other metal utensils. Moreover, few Potawatomi men now worked in stone, and they, too, relied on the Men with Hairy Faces for metal tools and weapons. Most of her adult male kinsmen remained skilled archers, but two moons ago, she listened with disgust to a nephew who had just completed his vision quest and who had boasted that now, since he was a man, he, too, planned to acquire a trade musket. *"Tukwap kitakwun"* — bows and arrows — he claimed, "were fit only for grandfathers, children, and the Outagamies."[11]

As Shadows on Her Face pondered these changes, she also wondered about her people's acceptance of the new trading system. Like a spider's web, it seemed to entangle all of them. Her kinsmen, of course, had always bartered among themselves and with neighboring tribes, but prior to the coming of the Men with Hairy Faces, such trade had been only a secondary economic activity; her father and uncles remained primarily hunters, fishermen, and warriors. But after her people moved to the Bay of Stinking Waters, they turned their face more and more toward the trade, scouring the lakes and rivers to the west, searching for

Meke, the beaver; for N'pshikwa, the mink, and for others of the animal broth-ers. And more recently, Onanguisse, her husband, and many of his closer kins-men had ceased their hunting and labored as middlemen in the trade, taking French merchandise to more western tribes and exchanging the goods for furs, which they then carried to Michilimackinac or traded to the Men with Hairy Faces, who brought additional wares to the Bay of Stinking Waters.

Shadows On Her Face worried about her people's new role as middlemen. The trade goods they carried and the changes that they wrought were like husbands: they brought pleasure and happiness to one's life, but they also took that life in new and different directions. Since the Potawatomis had become enmeshed in the trade, some age-old customs and traditions seemed to have changed. Recently, her husband, Onanguisse, and his kinsmen, met regularly with La Salle, Tonti, and other Men with Hairy Faces, and together they attempted to control the flow of beaver pelts that arrived at the Bay from more distant tribes. Yet their efforts to monopolize this trade seemed to violate traditional Potawatomi pre-cepts of sharing and generosity, and Neshnabe from other clans, and especially hunters or traders from different tribes, raised their voices in anger.

Leading this protest were the Outagamies. The Outagamies, whom the French called the Foxes, had arrived in the lands west of Lake Michigame many winters before many of the other tribes had been driven west by the Neutrals and the Nodaways (the Iroquois). The Outagamies had scattered in several small villages along the Fox River, but their largest settlement was at Ouestatimong, a fortified village of two thousand tribespeople on the Wolf River, a hard day's overland journey west of the Bay's western shore. Located on the far western periphery of the fur trade, the Outagamies were eager for French goods, and they initially welcomed Onanguisse and other Potawatomi traders into their villages. But the Outagamies were a proud people, sensitive to any slight, and they readily com-plained that Potawatomi middlemen charged higher prices at Ouestatimong for the goods carried to their villages than for similar goods traded at the Bay's shore.

More recently, however, these disagreements had taken a darker turn. For several generations, the Outagamies had warred with the Nadowaysiouek—the Sioux, the Prairie Serpents—who resided along the upper Mississippi. The Outagamies needed French firearms to repel the more populous Sioux, who threatened Outagamie hunting lands in the region between the Wisconsin and Chippewa rivers. And armed with French weapons, the Outagamies had more than held their own.

But some of the Men with Hairy Faces discounted the smaller Outagamie market and wished to carry their wares to the more populous Sioux villages. During the past winter, these French traders had tried to persuade her husband to accompany them through the Outagamie villages and on to the Sioux, but Onanguisse had refused. Early in the summer however, a few Ojibwes had accepted the French offer, but when the trading party passed westward through the Outagamie villages, the latter had attacked them, not wanting arms and ammunitions to be traded to their enemies. In the aftermath, Potawatomi traders feared to enter the Outagamie villages, so lead, powder, and other trade goods were in short supply.

In response, Outagamie warriors arbitrarily waylaid French traders on the Fox River and seized their merchandise. Blood was spilled, and both sides (the Outagamies and the French and their allies) now vowed vendettas. So far, none of Shadows on Her Face's kinsmen had become involved, but she feared that the conflict would continue and deepen. Moreover, her husband warned that unless the dispute was promptly settled, it would spread, engulfing the Mascoutens and Kickapoos as allies of the Outagamies and pitting them against the French, Potawatomis, Ojibwes, Ho-Chunks and other tribes.[12]

Shadows on Her Face relished the relative peace and security of her life at the Bay. She had no desire to see her people involved in a web of expanded warfare against the Outagamies and their allies. And she was even more wary about French attempts to enlist the support of the Potawatomis and other tribes in a proposal to attack the Nodaways—the Iroquois—in the latter's homeland. Recently, a spokesman for Onontio—the governor general of New France—had met with her husband and asked him to raise a large war party and to join with other tribal people and French soldiers to attack the Senecas in their homeland, near the Great Roaring Waters, below the Lake of the Eriehronons. She hated the Nodaways. They indeed were serpents, and she understood why her husband, her kinsmen, and warriors from other tribes fought to keep them from expanding into these lands west of Lake Michigame. But she saw no reason to attack them in their homeland. "Let them remain by the Great Roaring Water!" she insisted. Why kick a hornets' nest? She wanted no part of them. She had seen enough turmoil in her lifetime. The old ways seemed more difficult, but they were fraught with less uncertainty.

Still standing on the beach, Shadows on Her Face pulled her new trade blanket up around her shoulders. The wind had shifted, and Pondessa's cold breath was blowing from the north. La Salle, the Brown Robe (Franciscan-Recollet) Hennepin, and several of their comrades had earlier left the island in canoes, intending to follow the shoreline of the Big Lake south to the land of the Illinewek. Shadows on Her Face had no doubt that they would reach the peninsula, and if a storm arrived, they could safely put ashore. But the great canoe had gone northeast, toward the open water. There, Kegangizi would rage his wildest, and there, too, no shelter beckoned. Shadows on Her Face pulled the blanket more tightly around her shoulders, and the brass hawks bells, her "shells," jingled as she climbed the path that led from the beach to the village. Perhaps Wiske, the trickster, might intervene and fool Kegangizi; perhaps the north wind would fall away. But Shadows on Her Face was grateful that she was safe on the leeward side of the island. Mishawa-kisis, the Moon of Elk, was also the Moon of Storms.

Keewawnay Lake—Tippecanoe River Flowage, Indiana, 1838

She brought the quart earthenware jug of bourbon to the men at the makeshift table. The table wasn't much, just several rough pine planks supported by empty barrels and covered by a faded red trade blanket that overflowed the surface and draped down toward the rough puncheon floor. The five men sitting around it were seated on small wooden benches or empty kegs. At one end of the table, Massaw (Red Cedar Woman), her kinswoman, sat dealing poker from a worn deck of cards. In front of each player was a small pile of coins and a few multicolored banknotes issued by banks in Logansport, or Fort Wayne. Per usual, the largest pile of cash was loosely stacked in front of Massaw, at the end of the table.

Gashnezo (Whispering Woman) walked behind Massaw and quietly asked her if she needed any more of her "tonic" which she usually drank while playing euchre or poker with guests at her inn, located adjacent to Keewawnay's village, a short distance west of the Michigan Road (near Rochester, in modern Fulton County, Indiana). Massaw gave a slight nod of her head, and Whispering Woman poured three fingers of the amber liquid into the porcelain cup sitting near Massaw's pile of coins and banknotes. When she finished, Massaw looked up, politely thanked her, then exchanged knowing glances with her cousin as Whispering Woman walked away from the table to obtain another jug of bourbon for the American travelers who were trying their luck at Massaw's table.

"Go ahead, Chomokomon [Americans], drink your fill!" Whispering Woman mused, suppressing a smile. Big drinkers usually were big losers. "Make your bets and drink your whiskey!" Whispering Woman knew that the amber liquid in Massaw's cup was tea, brewed to look like bourbon. By the time the card games ended, the only sober person sitting at the table would be Massaw. What's more, Whispering Woman had no doubt that when the final hands were dealt, most of the remaining coins and banknotes currently scattered across the blanket would be stacked at Massaw's end of the table.

Whispering Woman exited the room, descended the stairs, and left the large, two-story log building through a rear door. She crossed an open covered porch and entered a slightly smaller log building where Massaw and Andrew Gosslieu, her Creole-French husband, kept stores of food, whiskey, and trade goods. One end of the smaller building also contained a large hearth and food preparation area, where Doga (Wakes Early), Whispering Woman's older sister, was slicing a slab of bacon into strips to be prepared for the next day's morning meal.

Looking up from her carving block, Doga asked, with a wry smile, "Is our relative winning?"

"Does the Tippecanoe River flood in the spring?" Whispering Woman replied. "I'm not sure about those three traders who work for the Ewing brothers, but both Pepper Grinder and that bumbling medicine-healer who rode in with him are well into their second jugs. When those two wake up tomorrow, their heads will throb like they were hit with a canoe paddle."[13]

"And I'm glad," she continued. "Pepper talks to all of us as if we were camp dogs. But that healer is worse. The more he drinks, the more he loses, and the more he loses, the angrier he gets. He passed through here last winter, just before the Black Robes' holidays, and he also drank too much then. He fought with another man, and Gossilieu made him leave. The only reason Massaw is letting him sleep in the house tonight is that he's with Pepper, since Pepper Grinder is a government man."

"What are they up to?" Doga asked.

"Massaw doesn't know," Whispering Woman replied. "But she hopes the whiskey loosens their tongues. She believes that Pepper Grinder plans to meet again with Menominee.[14] He wants to move more of our people across the Great River to the west."

"Where will the council take place"?

"That's what Massaw hopes to learn. While I was bringing in the whiskey, I heard Pepper ask her if Massaw could 'put up' four or five men at her house for several days in 'September,' which I think is the Chemokomon name for Zambogya-kisis (the Moon of Yellowing Leaves). Later, when two of the Ewing traders went out to urinate in the side yard, I overheard them talking that they believed the government wanted to bring people from several villages to one council, maybe here, near Keewawnay's lake."[15]

"If that is true," Doga commented, "then it will be a busy time. Many people will come and the government will pay us to feed them. Maybe we will have dances and more card games. The government men will also pay Massaw for food, and to sleep in her house. Massaw will need to buy extra food and drink to prepare for this. Maybe she will even cook the food for her guests."

Whispering Woman laughed out loud. Massaw's lack of ability as a cook was common knowledge among her relatives. Both Gossilieu, her husband, and Maurie, her daughter, good-naturedly teased her about it. Still laughing, Whispering Woman knew that any meals served in Massaw's house would be prepared by Doga and her, not Massaw.

Busy days ahead, but Whispering Woman was willing to do her part. She was well aware that Massaw served her family and her people in other ways. A skilled businesswoman, Massaw was a shrewd judge of human nature; she understood the ways of the Chemokomon. For many winters, she had managed her trading post/inn here at Keewawnay's village. Whispering Woman knew that Massaw was respected by those Potawatomi people whose villages still dotted the banks of the Tippecanoe and Yellow Rivers. Like Creole French and Chemokomon merchants, Massaw also turned a profit on her transactions, but like many other traders of Potawatomi descent, she too shared her wealth with her relatives. Hungry tribespeople were never turned away from Massaw's door. If government men such as Pepper Grinder and that drunken healer were planning to meet the village okimas (chiefs) to discuss the people's future, Whispering Woman wanted Massaw to be at the council, providing good advice.

But she also hoped the okimas would sell no more land to the government. Whispering Woman turned to Doga and asked, "Will Keewawnay sell his village site? What about Menominee and all his people up on the Mzaw-sibe [Yellow River]? Many of his people follow the Black Robes. Will the Black Robes also meet with the government men and speak in Menominee's behalf?"

"These are difficult times," Doga replied. "Keewawnay is much indebted to the Ewing brothers and to other American traders, and they have influence with the government men. Some say that Menominee will not sell his land, but that two winters ago [August 1836] other okimas, men who do not live on the Mzaw-sibe, already put their mark on the government paper. They believe that these other okimas have taken government money and that they have already sold Menominee's village, to which they have no claim."

"What will happen?" Whispering Woman asked.

"No one knows," Doga answered. "But Massaw thinks Pepper and the healer have come to meet with all the okimas who remain along the Tippecanoe and Msaw-sibe to convince them to accept the government's offer to move beyond the Great River."

Looking down at her butcher block and shaking her head, Doga continued, "Massaw also worries that if Menominee and other okimas refuse, Pepper will send the Blue Coat soldiers to force all of us from our homes and drive us west." She added, "Massaw and Gosslieu have already traded for a wagon to carry part of their possessions with them if we are forced to leave. Don't worry. She has promised me that we also can travel with them if the soldiers push us west."

Whispering Woman made no reply. She gave Doga a quiet smile, then walked away from her sister and out onto the covered porch that separated the storeroom from the main building. She carried another jug of whiskey back to the card game, received another quiet nod from Massaw, and set the jug down between Pepper and the healer. Whispering Woman then exited the room, returned to the covered porch between the house and the storeroom, and walked to a rough log bench near the porch's edge. The porch overlooked a small stream that flowed into Lake Keewawnay. Sitting down on the bench, Whispering Woman spat on the dirt beside the porch floor. She respected Massaw, and she was grateful to be living at the trading post. She gladly assisted her sister in Massaw's household, but she had no intention of ever removing to the west.

Five years earlier, in the spring of 1833, accompanied by her husband, Shigwnabek-Moewe (Flint Wolf), and her two adolescent sons, Gonkiwen-Giwesew (Snow Tracker) and Giwesew-Pikonya (Hunts at Night), Whispering Woman had journeyed to Logansport, Indiana, intending to remove across the Mississippi. Federal agents, including Abel Pepper, had promised them and other "Prairie Potawatomis" from the Kankakee River in Illinois that if they assembled on the Wabash, "government men" would conduct them west to new Potawatomi lands in Kansas.

They had assembled at Logansport, where other Indian agents, including Lewis Sands, had assured them that they would leave in May, but the removal had been delayed, and during the following two months, many tribespeople deserted the camp and returned to their villages. Whispering Woman's family had remained, and late in July, they had left Logansport and traveled across Illinois to Alton, where most of the diminished removal party boarded a steamboat and were carried to Fort Leavenworth.

But not Whispering Woman. While awaiting the arrival of the steamboat at Alton, her husband and two sons were among a small number of tribespeople who contracted cholera, which had been raging in St. Louis. When other Potawatomis were loaded onto the steamboat, Whispering Woman remained behind, caring for her critically ill family. To her dismay, neither the questionable remedies of the frontier physician employed by the government nor traditional healing methods passed down from her elders had any effect. Her husband and two sons passed into the spirit world in a makeshift shelter near the bank of the Mississippi River. Heartbroken, Whispering Woman joined with a handful of other refugees who had also remained to care for stricken relatives and fled back across Illinois to Potawatomi villages still scattered along the Kankakee and Iroquois Rivers.

Although she continued to grieve for her dead family, Whispering Woman eventually sought solace with Doga, her sister, whose husband had also passed away two years previously. Since their cousin, Massaw, had readily embraced Doga as part of her extended family, she also welcomed Whispering Woman into her household. During the past few years, the two sisters assisted Massaw with household chores and in managing her roadhouse and card room that hosted travelers along the Michigan Road.

Whispering Woman had been acquainted with Massaw before joining her cousin's household, but prior to her husband's death, their lives had followed different paths. Massaw's mother and the mother of Whispering Woman and Doga were sisters, and both women had been born in a Potawatomi village near the St. Joseph River, in southwestern Michigan. The village was one of several settlements scattered across the region that contained populations of Potawatomi people of both full-blood and mixed lineage. They also contained a significant number of Creole-French traders, many of whom had intermarried with tribal women.

Both Doga, born in 1788, and Whispering Woman, born five years later, been spent their childhoods in a village near the forks of the Paw Paw River. In 1808, Doga married Antoine LeClaire, a widower of Potawatomi and French descent. Twenty years older than Doga, LeClaire was an established trader associated with the Chevalier family, prominent merchants who had long centered their activities at Fort St. Joseph, the site of an old French post near the portage between the St. Joseph and Kankakee Rivers. After her marriage, Doga moved to LeClaire's cabin-warehouse at St. Joseph, and throughout most of her married life, she assisted her husband with his commerce, shipping goods back and forth between villages and even military posts within the Great Lakes and Mississippi valley. During the War of 1812, the community of traders at St. Joseph sold goods to both the Americans and the British, preferring commerce over bloodshed.

Whispering Woman's life had followed a different path. After her marriage to Flint Wolf, she had moved to his village at the junction of Rock Creek and the Kankakee River, in northeastern Illinois. Like many Prairie Potawatomis, her husband had fought with Tecumseh and Main Poc against the Chemokomon, and when the war ended, they had continued to follow a traditional life of hunting and raising small crops of corn, beans, and squash in gardens near their villages. Flint Wolf was not a trader, although he occasionally bartered pelts and deer hides to frontier merchants or other tribesmen for trade goods and other commodities. Whispering Women dressed the pelts and hides, but unlike her sister, she was not active in the trade. Before Flint Wolf's death, Whispering Woman had tended her lodge and garden, cared for their sons, and assumed the customary duties of a Potawatomi wife and mother.

After her husband's death, Whispering Woman's life changed. Yet in retrospect, her reunion with her sister and her acceptance into Massaw's household seemed a natural thing, a reintegration into an extended family structure where women played leading roles in widespread commercial activities that provided for their family. As young Potawatomi women growing up in southwestern Michigan, both Whispering Woman and Doga had known several tribal women who were active in the trade and readily participated in the commerce.

Whispering Women was well aware that through the years, the fur trade had changed. Although most of the beaver had been trapped from the streams that emptied into the eastern watershed of Lake Michigan, the market for other pelts had increased. Most certainly, the demand for the very dark, thick raccoon pelts taken from English Lake, the swampy region just south of the

St. Joseph-Kankakee portage, had burgeoned. Whispering Woman also remembered how she and Doga had assisted their mother in preparing bales of furs for shipment back to trading fairs at Michilimackinac or on to markets at Detroit. But she also recalled that as a child, she had observed several of her aunts and cousins performing different tasks. Even then, these women had managed the accounts, kept on rolls of buckskin, that monitored the trading activity of their husbands. Whispering Woman laughed to herself. Potawatomi and Creole men may have paddled their canoes up rivers and across lakes to secure the pelts, but their wives kept track of their profits and losses.

Lost in her memories, Whispering Woman was surprised to find that Doga had left the kitchen-storeroom and crossed the porch. Her sister's quiet moccasined footfalls were drowned out by night sounds—cicadas, crickets, and other insects and a cacophony of frogs from nearby trees and the shallow marsh where the stream joined Lake Keewawnay.

"What bothers you, sister?" Doga asked. "You seem upset. Are you angry that the government men want people still living along the Wabash and Yellow Rivers to leave and join our relatives in the west?"

"Yes. I've already been as far as the Great River, and I'm not going back. But I also was thinking about happier times, about our childhood in the village on the Paw Paw and how we helped our mother prepare the pelts. Do you remember how some women kept trade accounts on rolls of buckskin?"

"That was long ago," Doga replied. "After the Burnett's came to St. Joseph, most people working in the trade kept all their numbers on paper, especially their records of corn and maple sugar. My husband and I kept our accounts with a quill pen in a ledger book."[16]

"'I enjoyed the sugar making," Whispering Woman said. "I liked to help with all of it: tapping the trees, boiling the sap, and packing the sugar in the mukucks [wooden kegs]. Remember how grandmother taught us to weave the mukucks from the strips of black ash? We pounded sugar down in those baskets then closed them with a wooden lid. Grandmother said that some of them were taken as far as Detroit. I also remember how we wove other baskets, larger, looser ones, to ship apples and dried peaches to Michlimackinac. I had almost forgotten how those heavy trade canoes floated low in the water when all those kegs and mukucks were loaded in them. Grandmother worried that they might sink, but they always returned in the following year, so I guess the sugar and fruit reached Michilimackinac."

"Those were happy days," Doga replied. "After I was married and moved to St. Joseph, my husband traded in maple sugar, but he also assisted Burnett with the corn shipments, and that seemed to take much of his time."

In retrospect, Whispering Woman wasn't surprised. When Whispering Woman first visited Doga at Fort St. Joseph, she had been amazed at the size of the cornfields near the village. As a girl, Whispering Woman had helped her mother and aunts plant the traditional plots of corn, beans, and squash near their village on the Paw Paw River, but these small parcels of cultivated land shrank in comparison to the large fields of corn and wheat planted near the villages on the St. Joseph's River. Whispering Woman remembered how she had marveled at the huge fields which held many large gardens, divided into separate plots by paths, which made them accessible. The fields had been carefully cultivated by village women, and she also had been amazed at the number of baskets of corn, and even wheat (the latter grown mainly by Creole farmers), stacked into storehouses, awaiting shipment to Detroit.

Turning again to Doga, she asked, "Did you ever work in those large cornfields?"

"When I was first married, I did," her sister replied. "But after the first winter, I helped my husband with his accounts. I'd had enough of the cornfields."

"What about all the corn that was harvested?"

"We traded that to Sauganash [British] merchants who arrived on big sailing boats from Michilimackinac and Detroit. We paid my husband's relatives and other men in trade goods to carry the baskets of corn in canoes downstream to the [St. Joseph] river's mouth. Men from the big boats—I think they called them schooners; I think one was named the *General Hunter*—anyway, they loaded the baskets of corn onto their boats, and carried the corn north up the lake. Sometimes they paid us in trade goods. Sometimes they paid us in silver."

"Did they also take the maple sugar?" Whispering Woman asked.

"Not very often. We usually shipped the maple sugar down the Kankakee to the Illinois Country, to Creoles from St. Louis. I think they then sold it down the Great River to other people, near the river's mouth—but I'm not sure. The Creoles from the Illinois Country paid well. Sometimes they paid in silver. Sometimes they paid in trade goods."

Trade goods always had been plentiful among the Potawatomi villages in southwest Michigan, even when Whispering Woman and Doga had been girls. Whispering Woman recalled the heavy red woolen blankets that had warmed

Mas-sa, by George Winter. Courtesy of Tippecanoe County Historical Association, Lafayette, Indiana. Massaw operated a prosperous inn–trading post–gaming house a short ride west of the old Michigan Road, near Bruce Lake in modern Fulton County, Indiana.

her during the winters of her childhood, and she could remember her mother and aunt dressed in loose garments, sometimes fashioned from deerskin but also sewn from woolen strouds or bolts of flannel. All her relatives cooked in copper or iron pots and kettles, and her father and uncles carried trade muskets, not bows and arrows. Thirty years later, as she and Doga worked at their daily chores in Massaw's household, both regularly dressed in loose blouses and long skirts of cotton or wool trade cloth and wore plain, but comfortable buckskin moccasins. When she wasn't entertaining guests at her roadhouse or negotiating with other traders or merchants, Massaw dressed in a similar manner. But tonight, while she was hosting Pepper Grinder and that fool healer, Massaw was arrayed in her best.

Whispering Woman smiled to herself. Her cousin certainly made a striking impression. When Whispering Woman delivered the last jug of whiskey, she looked back at Massaw, sitting with her "tonic" at the head of the table and admired the broad gorget of German trade silver covering her chest and draped back over both her shoulders. Massaw's dark hair was oiled and parted from the center of her forehead, then pulled back into two log braids that were joined together in a silk scarf that fell down her back. Her ears were adorned with heavy silver earrings She was dressed in a conservative, dark blue, knee-length smock sewn of expensive cotton fabric, but she also wore a long silk shawl wrapped loosely around her upper torso and had added a matching silk scarf tied around her neck, which fell forward, over part of the silver gorget on her chest. Although Massaw's other garments were not visible beneath the table, Whispering Woman knew that she wore a pair of elaborately embroidered cotton leggings and heavily beaded moccasins. It was obvious that Massaw was projecting an image of authority. She was a woman of means — not to be taken lightly.

Whispering Women knew that many other Potawatomis had also prospered in the trade. When she first joined Doga in Massaw's household, she was surprised at how differently the tribespeople from the Tippecanoe and Wabash Rivers in Indiana dressed in comparison to her husband's people on the Kankakee and Illinois rivers. When many of the "Wabash Potawatomis" assembled to meet with government men in Keewawnay's village, they arrived on fine horses, wearing clothing crafted from expensive trade cloth. Like Massaw, many of the women were bedecked in silver jewelry. Some of the men wore frock coats, with fashionably wide lapels. Others wore ruffled shirts or handsome sashes, and many wore brightly colored silk turbans. Both men and women wore leggings that were heavily embroidered or embellished with ribbons. Whispering woman smiled to herself. The silk clothing and silver jewelry differed markedly from the frayed and threadbare clothing worn by Pepper Grinder, Sands, that fool healer, and other government men. She also scoffed at the drab homespun worn by the growing number of Chemokomon settlers who now seemed to infest the region like crows to a carcass. But the newcomers kept coming, and they kept crowding her people out.

Looking up, Whispering Woman watched Doga return from the storeroom, bringing tea for both women.

"Sister, why did Massaw and her husband come here from St. Joseph's? Why did they build such a large house and storeroom? How did some of our people along the Tippecanoe acquire such fine horses and clothing?"

Sitting down on the bench, Doga poured two cups of tea, spooned in maple sugar, then replied, "It's the trade, sister. It's the trade."

"Eight winters ago," Doga continued, "at the treaty when both our people and the Miamis ceded lands north of the Wabash, Massaw learned that a road would be built along the old trail that stretched north from the White River to the St. Joseph. She also learned that the road would pass near Keewawnay's village and that many government men, their soldiers, and other Chemokomon would travel back and forth along the road between Lake Michigamea and the

Wabash. She knew that these travelers would want to sleep under a wooden roof and would pay good silver to do so. They also would want whiskey and to play at cards. Massaw always played at cards, even as a girl, and she usually won. She still wins. All men—Neshnabe, Creole, Sauganash, and Chemoko-mon—lose silver when they drink. They still do. Look at the table tonight. Who has ended up with most of the silver and paper money?"

"What's more," Doga added, "Gosslieu knew that there were no trading houses near Keewawnay's village, and if more and more Chemokomon built cabins north of the Wabash, they, too, would need a place to trade for supplies and to sell their bacon, corn, or other products."

"That's true," Whispering Woman mused.

Sipping her tea, Doga added, "Massaw's no fool. The trade here is much smaller than at St. Joseph's and at posts belonging to Miami traders such as Richardville, or Godfroy, but Massaw has been willing to advance goods to Potawatomi people on the promise of future payment, or to help people in need, and people like to trade at her storehouse."[17]

"But how have so many other people from the villages along the Wabash fared so well?" Whispering Woman asked. "Not all of them own trading posts."

"No, but prices for both crops and furs have been high," Doga replied. "Many have prospered. And most people live in much smaller cabins and have fewer fine clothes than Massaw, the Burnetts, or other village chiefs. When they come to trade or to meet with government men, they wear their finery, but on other days, they dress like you or me, in trade cloth or sometimes even in buckskin."

Whispering Woman had other questions for her sister, but their conversation was interrupted when the healer staggered out the back door of Massaw's house, then vomited off the opposite side of the porch from where the two women were sitting.

Doga glared at the man, then whispered, "Look at that fool! He's one of the healers that the government men hired to accompany our people to the west. Massaw says that when he plays at cards, he drinks like a hard-ridden horse, and when he drinks, he quarrels with everyone. Gosslieu asked that he be fired, but Pepper Grinder refused to let him go."

"I heard that even the Black Robe priests at Menominee's village wanted him dismissed, but other government men spoke up for him," Whispering Woman replied.

Abel C. Pepper. Courtesy of the Indiana Historical Society. A resident of Rising Sun, Indiana, the stern-faced Pepper ("Pepper Grinder") was closely associated with the Potawatomis throughout the removal period.

"That's part of the problem," Doga said. "The government men distrust the priests. They think the Black Robes tell our people not to go west of the Great River." Doga shook her head and sighed. "Some government men like that crowing rooster McCoy, at Carey Mission, even claim that the priests are loyal only to the French king or to the pope and work against the will of the government—but I know better. I know that McCoy is a Baptist who wants to half-drown all our people in the river, then take them west himself. McCoy hates the priests. He's envious of their medicine."

"Is that why Pepper and other government men speak evil toward Father Petit and other priests at Menominee's village?"

Before Doga could answer, the two women were interrupted by Massaw, who emerged from the house and hurried across the porch to where the sisters were sitting.

"Some new plans," she announced. "Pepper Grinder has asked Gosslieu and me to go with him to the village at Wzawjewen [Yellow River] and to meet with Menominee and several other okimas to talk about abandoning the remaining villages along the Wzawjewen and going west. I told him we preferred to remain here in our homes, but he offered to pay us well if we just accompanied him and interpreted his talks. We decided to take his money but to privately tell Menominee and the others to remain—but we need you two to go along in the wagon and speak privately to Menominee and others in his village before we sit with Pepper Grinder at the council. If Pepper learns we're speaking against removal, I don't think he'll pay us. I'll tell him that you have a sister who lives in Menominee's village and you plan to visit with her while the council takes place."

"When do we leave?" Doga asked.

"Well, Pepper wants to leave early in the morning, but both he and the healer have drunk so much whiskey that they will sleep late tomorrow. I think we should plan to leave sometime after mid-morning."

The two sisters exchanged knowing glances, then Whispering Woman replied, "We will go. We have childhood friends from our old village on the Paw Paw who now live with Menominee's people, and some of them are related to Menominee's wife. Tell Pepper Grinder we are visiting old friends. I'll be glad to tell them of my removal experiences. We'll also advise them to remain in their homes. The lands beyond the river have no trees. The soil is thin. There is little rain for corn and squash, and our people who have gone there must fight the Nadewesiouz, Panis, and Wasaasa.[18] Better to remain in their cabins on the Wzawjewen."

At about 10:30 the following morning, the party left Massaw's house for the Yellow River. A disheveled and bleary-eyed Pepper and "Doctor" George Jerolaman (the "healer") accompanied by two of the Ewing Brothers' traders rode north up the Michigan Road on horseback. Gosslieu, Massaw, Doga, and Whispering Woman followed in Gosslieu's wagon. They arrived at Menominee's village after nightfall, but with ample time for Whispering Woman and Doga to meet with Menominee and his elders.[19]

The council took place shortly after noon on the following day. Massaw and Gosslieu translated Pepper's speech, in which he warned Menominee and his villagers that unless they agreed to remove to the west, the president would send troops to their village and they would be forced from their cabins at gunpoint. Yet before Pepper could finish his warning, Menominee stepped forward, seized his arm, and exclaimed, "The president does not know the truth! He like me has been deceived! He does not know that your treaty is a lie, and that I never signed it. He does not know that you got my young chiefs drunk, and got their consent, and pretended to get mine." As Whispering Woman and Doga watched from the gathering of tribespeople who crowded the council ground, Menominee further declared that the agreement allegedly selling his reservation was fraudulent, a pact made by liars, adding that when the president finally knew the truth, "he will leave me to my own." According to Menominee, "I have not sold my lands. I will not sell them. I have not signed any treaty and will not sign one. I am not going to leave my lands, and I don't want to hear any more about it."[20]

Visibly shaken, Pepper ordered a recess, but when he tried to reconvene the proceedings, Menominee refused to attend. Angry over the refusal, Pepper paid Massaw and Gosslieu for their service as interpreters but then dismissed them and met privately with several state officials sent to the council by David Wallace, the governor of Indiana. Early the following morning, Massaw, Gosslieu, Doga, and Whispering Woman climbed into their wagon and started back toward Massaw's trading post, near Lake Keewawnay.

It was a solemn ride. None of the four people in the wagon was optimistic. Gosslieu was acquainted with two of the state officials who met with Pepper following the council, and he knew that they were proponents of removal. Massaw reminded her fellow passengers that just three days previously, Pepper had asked her to provide room and board for several agents and food for additional government men who might assemble near Lake Keewawnay in the near future. Massaw believed that such a group could only be part of a removal party and that the government men were finalizing plans to move all the remaining Potawatomis along the Tippecanoe and Yellow Rivers west of the Mississippi. In response, Gosslieu talked with her about gathering their personal valuables and converting as much of their trade goods into specie, gold, or silver that could be transported west if they were forced to leave their trading post under duress, or on short notice.

Doga and Whispering Woman listened to their conversation and were much involved in a quiet dialogue of their own. If Massaw emigrated to the west, Doga was determined to go with her. She had become closely tied to Massaw's nuclear family, and with the exception of Whispering Woman, she had few relatives remaining among the Neshnabe still residing along the Tippecanoe and Yellow Rivers. Moreover, if the government men or soldiers forced these villagers west, most of her relatives, including Massaw and her family, would be part of the removal party. Doga preferred to remain in Indiana, but if she would be forced to find a new home, she would find it in Kansas, among many of her relatives who also had removed to the west.

Whispering Woman had different plans. Her tear-stained memories of cholera, and the ill-planned Prairie Potawatomi removal in 1832 had so embittered her toward ever going west again, that she vowed she would flee to the St. Joseph Valley and seek refuge among several small communities of Neshnabe who had been granted titles to a series of small individual tracts of land near the old trading post at that location. Many of these people, led by Pokagon, had thoroughly embraced the Black Robes, and with the help of the priests, they had secured papers (similar to those used by the Chemokomon) with titles to their lands. After she married and moved to the Kankakee, Whispering Woman had strayed considerably from the Black Robes' faith, but she

Kee-Waw-Nay Village, by George Winter. Courtesy of Tippecanoe County Historical Association, Lafayette, Indiana. Winter's ink and graphite sketch of the council at Keewawnay's village, near modern Bruce Lake, depicts Keewawnay and other Potawatomi leaders meeting with Abel C. Pepper, Lewis Sands, and other federal officials to voice their opposition to Indian removal.

had few qualms about rejoining the flock, particularly if it meant remaining in her homeland.

Whispering Woman pondered her decision. Neither Massaw nor Doga had ever waited for weeks in a dusty, crowded embarkation camp. They had never been forced to secure rations from ill-tempered agents in a series of sweltering campsites on the mosquito-infested prairies near the Sangamon River in Illinois. They had never seen their loved ones sicken and die of strange new diseases after being left behind on the muddy banks of the Great River. Massaw and Doga could go west if they wanted. She would remain in her homeland.

During the century and a half that followed the sailing of the *Griffon*, Potawatomis and other tribal traders spread their commerce across the western Great Lakes. With the withdrawal of the Iroquois threat, the Potawatomis migrated back around the southern tip of Lake Michigan to occupy a broad swathe of territory stretching from Milwaukee, south into northern Illinois, particularly the Chicago region, then eastward across northern Indiana and southern Michigan to Detroit. Intermarrying readily with both the French and other tribal people (particularly the Odawas and Ojibwes), Potawatomi traders paddled their canoes through the interlocking watersheds that cover the region, visiting both tribal villages and French Creole settlements stretching from St. Louis to Detroit and Michillimackinac.

The intermarriage of Potawatomi and Creole French populations in the region facilitated Potawatomi commerce. Eager to gain access to the scattered network of Potawatomi villages, French Creole traders took Potawatomi wives, sometimes in Catholic rituals but more often in tribal ceremonies or à *la façon du pays* (in the manner of the country), the widely accepted arrangement through which tribal women and Creole merchants agreed to live together and raise families. Obviously, access to their wives' kinship networks facilitated the traders' acceptance into the burgeoning web of interconnected Potawatomi villages in the region, and the mixed-lineage, or métis, children resulting from these unions often continued in their father's footsteps. For Creole or métis traders, marriage also provided a willing set of hands to share the labors associated with the commerce, and although their wife's contributions may initially have been in preparing furs, harvesting crops, or other more mundane and traditional chores, evidence suggests that many Potawatomi or other tribal women quickly learned the more sophisticated or nuanced aspects of the business and often emerged as successful traders on their own. Like Massaw at her inn and trading post near Keewawnay's village, D'Mouchekeekeeawh, the wife of mixed-lineage Abram Burnett, prospered in the trade near St. Joseph, while Ozahshinquah bought and sold both pelts and agricultural products (particularly horses) among the Miamis on the Mississinewa River.[21]

Much of the early commerce initially focused on the south bend of the St. Joseph River and adjacent areas that straddled portages between the Great Lakes and rivers that provided access to both Lake Michigan and watersheds leading to the Mississippi valley. Potawatomis from the Green Bay region had reestablished villages in the St. Joseph valley by the 1690s, and the growing population attracted Jesuits, who founded a mission in the region. Led by Winamac (the Catfish), Potawatomi elders asked the French to establish a post near their villages, and in 1718, Fort St. Joseph was erected on the St. Joseph River, near the site of modern Niles, Michigan. Ostensibly placed to protect the St. Joseph-Kankakee portage, the post attracted additional French traders and tribespeople. Not surprisingly, the mixed-lineage population increased, and new Potawatomi villages proliferated along the neighboring river valleys. The burgeoning Potawatomi-Creole commerce was temporarily threatened by the Fox Wars, but by the middle decades of the eighteenth century, Potawatomi traders were again carrying both furs and trade goods to tribal villages throughout the region.[22]

Potawatomis from the St. Joseph region supported the French in their struggles against the Meskwakis (Foxes), and during the ongoing warfare between the French and British empires, they continued to send war parties to fight for Onontio (the governor general of New France), both in New York and in the West. But after the British gained the ascendancy, the tribespeople along the St. Joseph gradually withdrew from confrontational politics and focused their efforts on the trade. They participated in Pontiac's Rebellion, but during the American Revolution, their support for either side waxed and waned according to whoever seemed to hold the upper hand. And in the three decades that followed the Treaty of Paris (1783–1815), they dabbled in the internecine border warfare that plagued the Detroit-Maumee frontier, but they readily traded with all sides.[23]

Most of their kinsmen in Illinois and southwestern Wisconsin followed a different path. Although some Potawatomis residing at Chicago and Milwaukee traded furs and other commodities and attempted to remain neutral or aloof from the warfare that occurred during the Revolutionary and Federalist period, many others readily participated in these conflicts. In the early 1790s, war parties from Illinois fought against the Americans in Ohio or raided settlements near St. Louis and Vincennes. During the War of 1812, many readily listened to the Shawnee Prophet and Tecumseh, then followed leaders such as Main Poc (Crippled Hand), Nuscotomeg (Mad Sturgeon), and Shabonna (Burly Shoulders) in attacks against the Americans. Moreover, in contrast to their relatives on the St. Joseph or in the villages that had spread to the Tippecanoe and Wabash, these western or Prairie Potawatomis followed more traditional lifestyles. They continued to live by hunting, fishing, and raising small gardens. Like Flint Wolf, Whispering Woman's fallen husband, they followed the ways of their fathers. They believed in Wisaka. They prayed to the manitous. Very few were Catholics.[24]

Not so the tribespeople on the St. Joseph. As Susan Sleeper Smith has so persuasively illustrated, the "Catholic connection" in southwestern Michigan and northwestern Indiana was much more pervasive. The Jesuits maintained a mission near Fort St. Joseph from the 1690s through 1773, but even in the decades (1773–1830) after the mission was closed, priests from Detroit and Vincennes visited the region, holding mass and keeping many of the Potawatomis and their Creole neighbors Catholic in form if not in substance.[25] Although evidence suggests that during the 1820s, some mixed-lineage families temporarily enrolled their children in a school at Carey Mission, an institution founded in 1823 by Baptist minister Isaac McCoy, McCoy's emphasis on transforming their children into small yeomen farmers, his support of Indian removal, and his decision to baptize several students through the ice on the St. Joseph River on Monday January 17, 1825, while the temperature hovered at ten degrees above zero dampened their interest in Protestant evangelism. By the end of the decade, almost all the Potawatomis had withdrawn their children from McCoy's clutches, and Carey Mission had foundered. In 1832, McCoy packed up and moved to a new station, at Shawnee Mission in Kansas.[26]

While the Baptists declined, the Catholics burgeoned. Led by Pokagon, a village chief from the South Bend region, most Potawatomis in the region abandoned McCoy, and in July 1830, Pokagon welcomed Father Frederick Rese, a priest from Detroit, into his village. Within ten days, Rese baptized thirty-two tribespeople, including Pokagon and his wife, and also instructed other Potawatomis and Creoles in the Catholic faith. Upon his return to Detroit, Rese

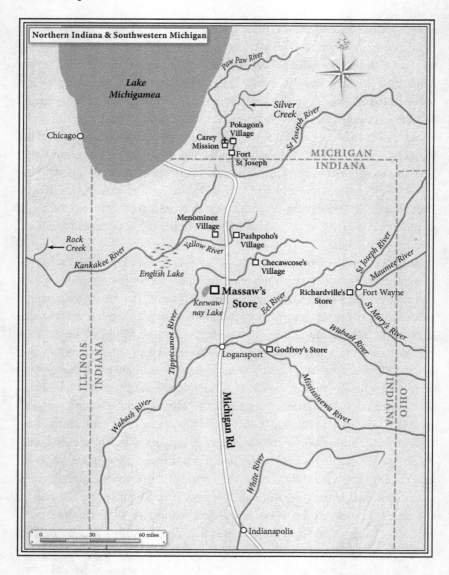

was followed by Pokagon and a party of Potawatomi and Creole spokesmen who pleaded with Catholic officials to send another priest to reside permanently on the St. Joseph River. In response, during mid-August 1830, Father Stephen T. Badin left Detroit and reopened the mission in the St. Joseph Valley. He was accompanied by Angelique Campeau, an elderly Catholic lay sister. After erecting a chapel in Pokagon's village, Badin labored at renewing the faith. Within six months, he had baptized over three hundred converts and brought numerous other lapsed Catholics back into the fold. Meanwhile, Campeau, who was fluent in both Potawatomi and French, opened a school for village children.[27]

Using the revitalized mission in Pokagon's village as a base, Badin expanded the Catholic influence throughout Potawatomi villages in northern Indiana. In 1831 he was joined by Father Louis Deseille and Ghisler Boheme, a novice training for the priesthood. Badin's efforts were also supported by the Creole population in the region, but the latter were distrusted by many Anglo-American settlers who questioned both the Creoles' close relationship to tribal people and their adherence to many French cultural patterns. American officials, particularly local Indian agents, shared in these suspicions and reported to superiors that neither the Creoles nor the priests supported Indian removal.[28]

The Indian agents' suspicions were valid. Many of the priests, including Badin, Deseille, and others, believed that the Potawatomis and other tribespeople should stay on their remaining lands in Indiana and Michigan, where they could continue as self-sufficient, Catholic Indian communities within the general mainstream of frontier society. Since most of the priests were from France or Belgium, they did not share in the widespread racial prejudice against Native American people held by many white settlers on the American frontier. Accordingly, Badin and his companions attempted to disassociate themselves from both Indian removal and federal Indian agents. They strengthened their ties to the Creole community and reveled in their French identity. Indeed, in addressing both the Potawatomis and the Creoles, Badin often referred to himself as "their affectionate father, the French Priest," and although the Catholics eventually received some federal funds for their mission, he was careful to distance himself from American Indian policy.[29]

Eager to "harvest additional souls for heaven's bounty," Deseille traveled among the Potawatomi villages that had spread to the Yellow and Tippecanoe Rivers. In 1834 he baptized Menominee, a village chief from the Yellow River, and one year later, accompanied by Father Simon Gabriel Bruté, the bishop at Vincennes, he visited Potawatomi villages on the Tippecanoe. At Checawkose's (Little Crane) village, near modern Tippecanoe, Indiana, the priests were met with crowds of Potawatomis, "donned (in their) best spring attire, mounted on horseback," who had assembled "to see the chief of the Black Robes" (Bruté).

After Bruté confirmed a number of new converts, Checawkose offered the bishop a half-section of land on which to build a chapel and a school. Bruté was hesitant to accept the tract, since he did not want to anger Pepper and other Indian agents, but he encouraged the assembled tribespeople to remain constant in their faith, then journeyed back to Vincennes. In contrast, Deseille rode back through Menominee's village, where he found that the Potawatomis on the Yellow River had already erected a chapel. They also offered him a half-section of land to establish a school for their children. Deseille, too, remained hesitant to accept the land, but he baptized about forty additional converts before returning to Pokagon's village near South Bend. Deseille was jubilant about the Potawatomis' renewed interest in the faith, but Bruté was less sanguine. In November 1835, the bishop wrote to his superiors that although he was "much touched by the piety and self-communing" of the tribespeople, Bruté reported that he was afraid their good works might soon be brought to an end. Worried about the Potawatomis' future, Bruté warned that "the policy of the United States is to shut them out from all civilized states and to drive all the savages to the other side of the river."[30]

Bruté's fears were well founded. During the previous fifteen years, the Potawatomis had already ceded large tracts of lands in Illinois, Indiana, and Michigan, but in 1830, Congress passed the Indian Removal Act, and by the middle 1830s, Indian removal was in full swing. Between 1832 and 1837, the Potawatomis signed twenty separate treaties with the government, ceding either large sections of land or in many cases much smaller tracts, sometimes no more than 640-acre reservations (one square mile) that had been awarded to individual tribesmen. Federal officials had originally awarded these small individual, or village, reservations (excluded from the larger land cessions) in return for the recipients' support in the government acquisition of the larger tracts of land. Indian agents had mistakenly assumed that the small village or individual reservations could easily be purchased in a piecemeal manner after the actual removals had begun.[31]

They miscalculated. Although large numbers of Potawatomis journeyed to the west through a series of removals (e.g., the removal of Whispering Woman's family in 1833), others remained in Indiana, simply moving onto the "village reservations" that survived or seeking shelter on the smaller reservations that had been awarded to individuals. When agents attempted to purchase these smaller tracts, they found that many of the tribesmen either refused to sell or demanded prices that the agents considered to be outrageous. Other tribesmen, grown familiar with the fast-and-loose practices of land claims on the Indiana frontier, readily sold the same tract to several different non-Indians, then took the money and quickly moved west on their own, leaving Indians agents and federal land office officials mired down in lawsuits between irate frontiersmen, all contesting claims over single, reservation acreages. Meanwhile, other Potawatomi leaders, men such as Menominee, steadfastly claimed that federal officials, such as Pepper and other Indian agents, mistakenly (or fraudulently) purchased individual or reservation lands from Potawatomis who had no title to the tracts.[32]

For Abel C. Pepper and other Indians agents, the resulting chaos was a nightmare. Not only were they now obligated to continually negotiate a series of separate treaties for a myriad of small reservations scattered across lands north of the Wabash, they were also forced to bargain with tribal people who already had decided that they wished to remain in Indiana; they didn't want to sell. In addition to Potawatomi recalcitrance, local Indian traders, such as the Ewing Brothers, Alexis Coquillard, and others became involved in these arguments. Since many of the remaining tribesmen were heavily in debt to these merchants, these traders vowed that they would use their influence to prevent any removals unless they were fully paid before the tribespeople left for the west. Adding to the problem was growing pressure by state and federal politicians such as Indiana governor David Wallace and US senator John Tipton who wanted all tribal people removed from their state and all remaining reservations, no matter how small, opened up to white settlement.[33]

Although all of the above complicated the removal process, federal officials continued to focus much of their resentment on the Catholics. Pepper denounced Deseille as a "foreigner," while Indian agent Anthony Davis complained, "I wish old Baddin and his Catholicism had been somewhere else than operating among the Indians for it ... makes them troublesome to the government."[34] Yet Deseille was undeterred. At the priest's suggestion, during the winter of 1835–36, Menominee and several of his headmen journeyed to Washington, where they obtained written promises from federal officials that they could remain on their reservation as long as they owned the land. Bureaucrats such as Secretary of War Lewis Cass and Commissioner of Indian Affairs Elbert Herring evidently assumed that Pepper would purchase all remaining village reservations during the following summer and that Menominee and his people would therefore be forced to remove.[35]

Cass and Herring obviously overestimated Pepper's persuasive skills, and underestimated Menominee's intransigence. Although Pepper spent the spring and summer of 1836 buying most of the reservations that remained in northern Indiana, Menominee refused to sell. Encouraged by Deseille, he repeatedly asserted that both the written and oral promises he had received from Washington superseded Pepper's authority and that he would remain in Indiana. Meanwhile, Deseille strengthened his mission at Menominee's village. After the Potawatomis gave him a section of land for a church and school, Deseille erected a residence on the property. Although Pepper forbade him from opening a school, Deseille did invite Angelique Campeau to move to the reservation. From Pepper's perspective, Deseille and Menominee threatened all his efforts. Frustrated by Menominee's recalcitrance, Pepper purchased Menominee's reservation from three other tribesmen.[36]

The illegal sale of Menominee's reservation created an uproar among many of the remaining Potawatomis in Indiana. Both Bruté and Deseille protested the transaction. In response, Pepper dispatched his assistant, Lewis Sands, to "investigate" the situation, and not surprisingly, Sands reported that Deseille again "was using his influence in opposition to the views of the government" and that the hubbub was all of the priest's making. In response, on May 13, 1837, Pepper ordered Deseille to leave Menominee's reservation and to cease holding any talks or councils with the Potawatomies." Two weeks later Sands also ordered Angelique Campeau to depart immediately. By June 1, 1837, both Deseille and his assistant had left the reservation.[37]

Deseille and Campeau retreated to the St. Joseph mission house, near Pokagon's village, at South Bend, but three months later, in September 1837, Deseille contracted cholera and died. In response, both Campeau and Menominee contacted Bishop Bruté in Vincennes, pleading for another priest, and in October, the bishop dispatched Benjamin Marie Petit, a newly ordained priest from Rennes, France, to continue Deseille's mission. Petit arrived in northern Indiana in October and spent the winter of 1837–38 traveling among the remaining Potawatomi villages. He was well received by both the tribespeople and their Creole relatives who took heart at what they envisioned as the church's continued support of their determination to remain in Indiana. Meanwhile, Petit reported that he had "nothing but the highest praise" for both the Creoles and "these Indians, who the Americans, with their hearts dry as cork and their whole thoughts [on] 'land and money' fail to appreciate and treat with so much disdain and injustice."[38]

But Menominee's and Petit's days in Indiana were numbered. During the spring, political pressure for Potawatomi removal from Indiana increased. Pepper sent several messages warning Menominee that he would have to go west, but the old chief refused, and when the two met at Menominee's village in mid-July (the council attended by Whispering Woman, Doga, Massaw, and Gosslieu), Menominee publicly denounced Pepper and other officials, charging that they had fraudulently purchased his reservations from other Indians who had little claim to the land. Angered, Pepper warned Menominee that he and his followers would have to vacate their village by August 6, but the tribesmen refused. Meanwhile, eager to gain access to Potawatomi land, white squatters began to build cabins on the reservation. Fearing bloodshed, Pepper took stronger measures.[39]

Contriving with Governor Wallace and Senator Tipton, Pepper arranged another council at Menominee's village on August 29, 1838, but when Menominee and his councilors assembled, they were surprised and surrounded by over one hundred armed Indiana militia, who seized Menominee and his headmen and forced the hapless villagers to enroll for removal. The tribespeople were confined to their village for a week, while additional Potawatomis from Michigan and Indiana were collected and escorted to the removal camp by armed volunteers and militia. Uncertain of their fate if they remained in Indiana, other groups of Wabash Potawatomis reluctantly joined the assemblage at Menominee's village. On September 4, they were forced west at gunpoint.[40]

Commemorated by historians as the Potawatomi Trail of Death, the 1838 removal from the Yellow River was a disaster. Food issued to both the tribespeople and the troops escorting them was so bad that many of the militia refused to eat it. In addition, both Indiana and Illinois were in the grip of a typhoid epidemic, and as the Indians trekked west, nearly three hundred of them contracted the disease. So many Potawatomis became ill and fell behind that a separate and smaller removal party collected survivors and other convalescents, then followed in the larger party's wake. In mid-October, after crossing into Missouri, the two parties merged. On November 4, 1838, 756 Potawatomis arrived at the Osage River subagency in Kansas. Forty-two of their kinsmen lay dead and buried beside the trail. Another sixty or so had slipped away enroute and had returned to northern Indiana.[41]

Father Petit accompanied the Potawatomis to Kansas. Petit survived the removal, but he, too, contracted typhoid, and his health was permanently impaired. Petit left his flock under the care of another priest in Kansas and attempted to return to Indiana but proceeded no farther than St. Louis, where he died of a respiratory ailment on February 10, 1839.[42]

Silver Creek, 1854

Sitting at her cousin's kitchen table, the aging Potawatomi woman placed the narrow splint of peeled black ash back on the heavily scarred tabletop and picked up her tin tea mug. She needed some hot water from the kettle. The tea in the mug, left over from her morning meal, had grown lukewarm, and the cup in her cradled hands no longer eased the pain in her fingers. She had fashioned black ash baskets since had been a child, but the years had taken their toll. Her fingers, once so deft in plaiting the dyed-ash splints, now ached like her hip, as did her lower legs, particularly during the cold months. A mug of hot tea not only warmed her insides; holding the warm cup also eased the throbbing in her fingers. As she aged, she grew to dread the long, cold winters. Here on Silver Creek, in the snow shadow of Lake Michigan, the winter seemed particularly long, and the snow seemed to fall too often this year. Many winters ago, when she and Doga were girls in their father's lodge on the Paw Paw River, the snow had delighted them. Now the snow and cold seemed only an added burden.

Yet she was glad to be here. Whispering Woman never doubted her decision. When Doga, Massaw, and most of the Potawatomis from villages on the Tippecanoe and Yellow Rivers had been forced to remove west in 1838, she had slipped away from the removal camp and had quietly made her way back to the St. Joseph Valley in southwest Michigan. She had been welcomed by her cousin, Zazbakwdoket Amo (Honeybee), who was married to Jean Pierre Levier, a man of mixed Potawatomi and Odawa descent. Like a scattering of other tribesmen in the region, Levier had secured papers to a small tract of land on Silver Creek. Staunch Catholics, her cousin's household and their Potawatomi neighbors followed the leadership of the Pokagon family and had been able to avoid the removals that had taken the majority of the tribe west. Whispering Woman knew that many of these remaining families continued to farm small acreages. The men also worked at an assortment of jobs, bringing in extra income and trade goods as part-time laborers. She and other women made and sold baskets. Since many of their small privately held tracts were on lands less desirable to the Chemokomon, they had been able to hold on to them. The government men had let them remain in Michigan. But they had paid a price. She learned that when the government men doled out the yearly payments to Potawatomi people for lands they had taken in Indiana and Michigan, they made the payments in the West. No funds were distributed to Pokagon's followers, the small community of Neshnabe people who remained near the St. Joseph Valley. The government men told them that they no longer were Potawatomis. They no longer were "Indians."

Pondering the payments, Whispering Woman shuffled over to the hearth and tossed a handful of leftover shavings and other debris from the black-ash splints into the burning logs. "Humph!" she spat. "Who were these hairy-faced drunkards to tell her people they no longer were Neshnabe!" Her people had built lodges along the banks of these rivers that flowed into Lake Michigamea before those fools had ever crossed the eastern mountains. "We were here then; we are here now, and our grandchildren will always be here." She knew that her days were numbered, but she planned to lay her bones beside her mother and grandmothers. She was a Neshnabe woman. She would be here forever.

Uniontown, Kansas, 1854

The June 9 issue of the *Western Watchman*, a weekly newspaper published by the Baptists in St. Louis, had been left behind by a party of emigrants who had ferried across the Kansas River at Darling's Ferry, then stopped for supplies in Uniontown. The newspaper, well-worn and dog-eared after passing through many hands, finally reached Uniontown in mid-July. Although the weekly's four-page format of religious tracts and secondhand news ordinarily would have attracted little attention, the paper's discussion of the recently passed Kansas-Nebraska Act found a welcome audience in Uniontown. For Maurie Gosselieu Taylor, the owner and operator of the Massaw House, a trading post and inn located near the center of the village, the paper brought good news. With Kansas now expecting more settlement, Maurie envisioned that traffic on the trail west would increase. Business, already brisk, would flourish.

Although the past decade had brought both good years and bad, at first the removal west seemed disastrous. In 1838, when Maurie and her husband, Henry Taylor, her parents, Massaw and Gosslieu, and Doga traveled from the Wabash valley to Kansas, so many people died that the Potawatomis now called the journey the Trail of Death. Things hadn't improved much when they arrived at the Osage River subagency in Kansas. Many of those, including her husband, who had survived the initial journey had been so weakened by typhoid that they died during the following winter, and although her parents tried to reestablish themselves as traders in the reservation on the Marais des Cygnes River, they encountered stiff competition from the Ewings Brothers, the Chouteaus, and other large trading houses.

Things improved after 1846, when both her people and other Potawatomis on the reservation in eastern Kansas joined with the Prairie Band people, who had been occupying a reservation near Council Bluffs, Iowa. During 1846, federal agents consolidated both bands of Potawatomis at a new reservation on the Kansas River, about seventy-five miles west of the Missouri state line. Uniontown, her current home, sprang up just south of the river, where the Oregon and California trails crossed the Kansas via ferries operated by Joseph Ogee, Lucius Darling, and other Potawatomi businessmen. The ferrymen had done a booming business. Maurie remembered that in the spring of 1849, Ogee charged up to $5 per trip (depending on the demand and the flood stage of the river) and that during May, as many as seventy wagons often lined up awaiting ferriage across the Kansas. She knew that other Potawatomis constructed toll bridges across many of the creeks that fed the river. They charged much less than the ferrymen, but they also turned a nice profit.

Even some of the Prairie Potawatomis participated in the commerce. While at Council Bluffs, prior to their arrival in Kansas, the Prairie people sold livestock and fodder to emigrants (particularly Mormons) who camped on their lands prior to proceeding west on the Oregon Trail. After their arrival in Kansas, many Prairie Potawatomis continued in the livestock business, trading in horses and mules with travelers crossing the new Kansas reservation and selling hay, fodder, and grain to both emigrants and the quartermaster at newly built Fort Riley. Massaw established a new trading post and inn at Uniontown, and business initially had boomed. Gold-seekers enroute to California often did not have much money, but many were willing to take a chance, and some readily wagered the little money they carried at the poker table in Massaw's new inn and gaming house. A quick learner, Maurie promptly learned her mother's tricks of the trade, and she, too, often sat at the head of a second gaming table in the inn's great room. Meanwhile, other employees at the trading post sold supplies to the emigrants or purchased (at greatly reduced prices) many items that the inexperienced travelers (after beginning their trek across the plains) now realized they would never be able to transport to California. Maurie was particularly fond of the small walnut clavichord, a former heirloom, that a family of emigrants wisely traded for extra supplies after hauling the instrument in the back of their wagon all the way from St. Louis. Doga soon learned to plunk out simple tunes on the instrument, and she sometimes played while the card-players made their bets at the poker tables.

Tragically, the concerts ended in 1850. During 1849 and 1850, the tribal villages and settlements scattered along the Kansas River were repeatedly struck with cholera, and Doga, Massaw, and Gosslieu all succumbed to the disease. Maurie had been spared and had continued to manage the inn and trading post, but late in 1850, the residents of Uniontown decided to burn all the buildings in the village to prevent cholera's return. Maurie agreed to the "cleansing," but she first removed all the merchandise and furniture from the inn, storing these items in a log barn while a new "Massaw House" was rebuilt in early 1851. She saved the clavichord, but no one in Uniontown knew how to play the instrument, so now it sat idle against the western wall in her inn's great room.

But they had survived. Standing now on the porch of the new Massaw House, Maurie pondered the news item that had been published in the worn copy of the *Western Watchman*. At two in the afternoon of the warm late-June afternoon, there were few customers in her establishment, but she wasn't concerned. Most of her mercantile trade came in the evening, when the emigrants camped for the night, or earlier in the morning, prior to their crossing the river. Her lodgers, or night trade, wouldn't arrive until late afternoon or evening. Since Uniontown's rebuilding following the cholera epidemic, business had been good, but she knew that the growing settlement of merchants and farmers at St. Mary's Mission, on the north side of the river about eight miles upstream, posed a threat to Uniontown's current prosperity. With the priests' support, Potawatomis who had settled near the Catholic mission began to raise large fields of hay, wheat, and other grain crops, and they readily traded them with travelers, luring potential customers from Uniontown.

Well, the article in the newspaper predicted that the recently passed Kansas-Nebraska Act would bring an influx of new settlers into Kansas. And if the market moved to St. Mary's, Maurie had no qualms about following it. All people—Potawatomis, emigrants, and settlers—needed supplies. She had no doubt that miners traveling west or soldiers stationed at Fort Riley would continue to play poker. She was confident that she could deal cards and sell merchandise as easily at St. Mary's as she had at Uniontown. Massaw had always told her, "Maurie, you do business where you can." Merchandise would be bought and sold. Meals would be served. Cards would be dealt. Both the trade and the cards would continue. So would the Potawatomis.[43]

Suggested Readings

Cooke, Sarah E., and Rachel B. Ramadhyani, comps. *Indians on a Changing Frontier: The Art of George Winter.* Indianapolis: Indiana Historical Society and Tippecanoe County Historical Association, 1993.

Edmunds, R. David. *The Potawatomis: Keepers of the Fire.* Norman: University of Oklahoma Press, 1978.

McConnell, Michael A. *Masters of Empire: Great Lakes Indians and the Making of America.* New York: Hill and Wang, 2015.

McKee, Irving E., ed. *The Trail of Death: Letters of Benjamin Marie Petit.* Indianapolis: Indiana Historical Society, 1941.

Sleeper-Smith, Susan. *Indian Women and French Men: Rethinking Cultural Encounter in the Western Great Lakes.* Amherst: University of Massachusetts Press, 2001.

White, Richard. *The Middle Ground: Indians and Republics in the Great Lakes Region, 1650–1815.* Cambridge: Cambridge University Press.

THREE

Crooked Legs Walk No More

Women, Buffalo, and Horses

Fat from the elk haunch dripped into the lodge fire, filling the tepee with the smell of roasting meat. The old woman awakened. She listened to the wind as it roared through the tops of the great cottonwoods that reached toward the river bluffs. Far above the fire, through the small open smoke hole, the woman could see cold, gray storm clouds that promised more snow. Crooked Leg smiled. Let the White Owl from the north spread his icy wing-beats across the great grasslands. The Inu-naina (Arapahos), her people, were below the river bluffs, protected amid the willow thickets that crowded the riverbank. Their lodges were warm, their cooking pots were full, and they possessed many buffalo robes. As she aged, she looked forward to these winter moons, when her people remained in their sedentary camps, surrounded by peace and plenty.[1]

Opposite the fire, on the other side of the lodge, Crooked Leg's daughter-in-law and her granddaughter talked quietly. The girl, Laughs in the Morning, stirred the fire and heaped the glowing coals under the elk haunch. Her mother, Wood Smoke Woman, repaired a parfleche. Their conversation seemed to focus on Iron Bear, Crooked Leg's son, the husband of Wood Smoke Woman and father of Laughs in the Morning.

Iron Bear was absent. Crooked Leg assumed that he had left the lodge to care for his horses. Earlier in the changing seasons, in the Moon of Falling Leaves, Iron Bear had led a war party against the Anihinin (Pawnees), the Wolf People, who lived in earth lodges on the Red Clay River. He returned with four new mares and a dark red stallion. Crooked Leg was proud when Iron Bear gave three of the mares to his relatives, but her son added the stallion and the other mare, a two-year-old buckskin, to his personal herd, which now numbered over a dozen animals. After the snow fell, Iron Bear and Rides Alone, Crooked Leg's grandson, spent more time caring for the horses, making certain they had adequate forage and that they remained in the protected river valley. Additional horses were a source of wealth, and they brought prestige to her family, but they also brought new responsibilities.

Huddled under the warmth of her buffalo robe, Crooked Leg could hear the footsteps of a horse as the animal's hooves broke the crust of the snow outside the tepee. She smiled, remembering how she had been so frightened when as a child of twelve winters, she saw one of these huge "elk dogs" for the first time. Now, over sixty winters later (December 1795), the "elk dogs," or horses, were an intricate part of her people's life.

In that far distant time, when Crooked Legs was a child, the lives of the Inu-naina were more difficult. Although the frail old woman now seemed to forget what happened yesterday, she could vividly remember her childhood, when the Inu-naina had walked across the grasslands, following hiitheinoon, the buffalo. Things were different then. They lived in tepees, but the lodges were much smaller, since the people could not transport long lodge poles from one location to another. Moreover, since the lodge skins that covered the poles were so heavy, the women in the family could carry only a limited number of them, and the Inu-naina were crowded into smaller, smoky lodges in which there was little room for people or their possessions.[2] Indeed, during her childhood, the people owned less of almost everything. Since they followed the buffalo herds on foot, the Inu-naina were forced to personally carry all their food, goods, and implements or to rely on the camp dogs to transport part of their possessions from place to place.

"The hethebi: the camp dogs! Four- legged tricksters! Chaos personified!" Crooked Leg shook her head as she remembered how her mother would pack parfleches containing part of the family's possessions on their dogs' backs in preparations for moving. Large dogs sometimes were fitted with travois on which bundles of clothing or other goods were tied and which the dogs dragged behind them as they were either led, coaxed, or herded forward by the camp's women and children. What a melee! The camp dogs were half-tame at best, and they were difficult to control as the people crossed the open prairie. Every rabbit or gopher flushed from a clump of sagebrush offered a potential meal to the ever-hungry pack, which predictably bounded forward, tangling travois and scattering goods and parfleches. The rabbits and gophers almost always escaped, and the still hungry dogs received only kicks and tongue-lashings for their rampage. But the dogs never seemed to learn. Parfleches were repacked, travois were reloaded, and the people continued on to their new camp. Crooked Leg remembered that her mother, Broken Knife Woman, had refused to pack the family's most prized possessions in the dog parfleche or travois. These goods, and many other items, were carried by Crooked Leg, her mother, her aunts, and her sisters. Men and older boys hunted as the column moved, scouted ahead for enemies, and protected the women, children, and elders. The women and dogs carried the burdens.[3]

In the old days, they carried them more often. As a child, it seemed to Crooked Leg that the camp was always on the move following the buffalo herds. In that far away time, when the Inu-naina traveled on foot, hunting was less successful. She remembered how her father and uncles donned wolf skins and attempted to creep close to the buffalo herds, their scent masked by the smell of the pelts. The hiitheinoon possessed powerful medicine. They were four-legged brothers especially blessed by the Great Mystery, but their eyesight was poor, and as long as the hunters did not stand, the buffalo often mistook them for wolves. Wolves preyed on the herds, but they usually took only calves, the injured, or the infirm. As long as the buffalo remained in the herd, healthy animals were not immediately threatened by the predators, and the buffalo often allowed the disguised hunters to get within easy bowshot of them. But the old herd bulls were unpredictable. They were not frightened by wolves, and they sometimes charged the wolf-skin clad Inu-aina, trampling and goring a hunter before his comrades could down the animal. When Crooked Leg was a girl, her father and uncles sometimes killed buffalo in this manner, but the hunting was dangerous, and one of her uncles died after being gored and trampled by an old bull intent on defending his herd from the "wolf pack."[4]

The Inu-naina had preferred to hunt buffalo in other ways. During the summer moons, when the great herds grazed across the plains, the Inu-naina camped near special places, low but steep bluffs overlooking river valleys. Crooked Leg's father, and his fathers before him, selected sites where the usual rolling river bluffs were broken by stretches of low but precipitous cliffs, hidden from the surrounding plains by irregular terrain and by the windblown prairie grasses. As smaller herds of buffalo approached the cliffs, grazing on the prairies above the river valley, several hunters from the village circled behind them and slowly approached the animals, herding them toward the river. Meanwhile, other members of the village concealed themselves in two loose lines, forming a funnel that pointed toward the hidden cliff overlooking the river valley. Most members of the village participated in this great hunt, although women, elders, and older children formed the outer edges of the lines, while younger men and seasoned hunters hid themselves near the mouth of the funnel, closer to the cliff edge.

Crooked Leg remembered that when the people were concealed in their places, the party of hunters behind the buffalo shouted and ran toward the herd, alarming the animals and driving them toward the river. As they passed within the two lines of concealed villagers, the Inu-naina jumped from hiding and also shouted, waving buffalo robes, bearskins, and other objects that funneled the panicked herd toward the river bluff. When the leading animals reached the cliff, they attempted to stop, but the pressure and weight of the animals in their rear forced many over the edge before the trailing animals stopped their headlong flight. As the remaining buffalo turned, the men and older boys near the end of the funnel ran back, away from the cliffs, fleeing from the buffalo's new path and allowing the surviving animals to escape. These hunters were forced to move quickly, for if they remained too long, they might be trampled as the stampeding herd fled, en masse, along the river bluff. Yet the buffalo drive was less dangerous than it appeared, since the panicked animals were so intent on escape that they fled away from the retreating men as rapidly as possible. Relatively few of the Inu-naina were even injured near the clifftops, and the hunters considered a buffalo drive to be less hazardous than hunting hiitheinoon with wolf-skins.

But not always. When Crooked Leg was fewer than six winters, the Inu-naina had concealed themselves near a cliff above the Cedar Bluffs River. Since she was such a small child, Crooked Leg did not take part in the hunt but waited with her grandmother and other older women and children behind a small rise a few hundred yards behind the open end of one of the lines of concealed women and older men, safely out of sight of the buffalo. When the drive started, Crooked Leg, her grandmother, and the women and children accompanying them heard the hunters on the prairie shout as they ran toward the small herd, forcing it into the mouth of the funnel and on toward the clifftop. Excited by the sounds of the hunt, Crooked Leg, her grandmother, and several

of the other women and children climbed to the crest of the rise to gain a better vantage point. But unknown to Crooked Leg and her grandmother, as the
buffalo entered the funnel, an old cow who had grown suspicious of the herd's
headlong flight toward the river turned to the rise and led her calf through a gap
in the line of frantically waving older men and women. Instinctively, a dozen
other members of the herd followed the old cow, and as Crooked Leg, her grandmother, and the older women and children neared the top of the rise, the unsus-
pecting animals thundered up the opposite side, then over the crest and into
their midst. One small boy was trampled to death as four animals passed over
his body. Crooked Leg's grandmother collided with a golden-haired calf but was
not seriously injured. Crooked Leg remembered only that she had been knocked
to the ground by an old cow, whose rear hoof struck her left leg, just below the
knee, breaking her leg.

Buffalo Walking, an old shaman, had placed her leg in a splint made from
elk ribs, and when her body had burned with a fever, he had placed ashes on
her forehead, brought forth his medicine bundle, and chanted powerful healing
songs. Afterward, he burned sweet-grass, bathed her in the smoke, and sucked
the malevolence from her body with the hollow bone of hawk's wing. Crooked
Leg recovered, but her leg remained bent. She could walk with little difficulty,
but she no longer could run as fast as the other children, and when the Inu-
naina made their long treks in pursuit of the buffalo herds, her crooked leg
tired easily. For three or four winters following her injury, her father or uncles
sometimes carried her on the long walks. But as she approached her tenth winter, she seemed to regain her strength. Her leg was often painful, but she was
Inu-naina. She learned to endure it in silence.

At least the buffalo drive, like many others, provided the people with meat.
Most of the two dozen animals that plunged over the cliff did not die in the
fall but broke legs and were immobilized. Hunters from the village quickly
killed the animals, and both men and women joined in skinning their carcasses.
And while the meat was fresh, and so very plentiful, they feasted. Although
Crooked Leg was too ill to enjoy the feasting that followed the drive in which
she had been injured, she remembered many others, and how the Inu-naina
delighted in such choice morsels as livers, kidneys, or tongues. After the initial feast, the women cut meat from the loins, hump, and haunches into strips,
and as a child Crooked Leg, helped her mother smoke some of the pieces of
meat over a fire or dry other strips in the sun. The smoked strips were stored

in parfleches, while much of the sun-dried buffalo meat was pounded between flat stones, then mixed with tallow and choke cherries to form pemmican, a sausage-like substance that her people could transport easily and that could be preserved, with little spoilage, for months.[5]

Yet Cooked Leg could remember her mother's frustration over her inability to preserve and utilize more from the buffalo kills. Although Broken Knife Woman smoked and dried as much meat as possible and also saved buffalo horns that were fashioned into spoons or sinew that she used as thread, she was almost always forced to abandon meat, hides, and other potentially useful products because neither she nor her people could transport them. Crooked Leg could remember how in the late moons of winter, when the snow lay deep and the wind howled across the plains, the Inu-naina sometimes went hungry. Their meager stores of dried meat and pemmican had been exhausted, and hunters who scoured the region within a day's walk of their campsite returned empty-handed. Crowded into their small, smoky lodges, the Inu-naina remembered the plenty of the previous summers, when buffalo fell at the killing cliffs and the people were forced to abandon the surplus meat to the wolves and coyotes. And Broken Knife Woman had lamented that she had not carried more pemmican on her back, but she and her sisters knew that their backs were so burdened with other necessities that the amount of food they could transport was limited.[6]

In the spring following Crooked Leg's twelfth winter, their lives changed. Her father and three of her uncles had journeyed far to the south, where they had met with the people whom the Kiowas and Cheyenne called Snakes but her people called the Catha (Comanches). Her father and uncles had carried packs laden with ermine pelts that they had laboriously snared during the previous winter, when the Inu-naina camped in the foothills of the great mountains. They also carried powerful, short, but rare and highly valued bows constructed of mountain-sheep horn, which had been crafted by the Shoshone cousins of the Catha, who lived in the region of stinking springs and foul-smelling waters. Moreover, one of her uncles had a parfleche filled with elk teeth, since he knew that the Catha valued these objects as ornaments and that few elk roamed the southern prairies.[7]

They returned shortly after the summer solstice, and they brought back four horses. Crooked Leg, her mother, and many others among the Inu-naina were terrified of the great beasts whom they first called "elk-dogs." But they found that the animals were tamer than many of the camp dogs and much more useful. Crooked Leg at first refused to be placed on her father's horse's back, but she finally mustered enough courage to ride double with him for a short distance. When the animal trotted, she clung tightly to her father's waist, afraid that she would be thrown from its back, but she screamed with delight when the mare broke into a gallop and she seemed to fly across the prairie. By the end of the summer, she was able to ride alone, but the new animal was so valuable that her father rarely permitted her to do so. During the next four winters, her father, like other warriors among the Inu-naina, acquired additional elk-dogs, and the people became accustomed to them. In the summer following her fifteenth winter, her father gave her a black-and-white horse — a paint mare — whom she kept with her father's small herd but that she rode as her own, particularly when the Inu-naina changed camps, following the buffalo herds.[8]

How their lives had been transformed! Crooked Leg remembered the first time the village moved that summer after her father had acquired his initial horse and how, when her leg pained her after walking, her father lifted her up onto the animal's back and she rode while her father led the mare, which also dragged a travois piled with lodge-skins. To Broken Knife Woman's delight, her mother no longer was forced to rely on the bedraggled and half-wild camp dogs to transport most of the family's possessions. Some dogs were still forced to drag travois, but with the coming of horses, the women in the village crafted additional parfleches and other skin bags that were packed on the horses' backs or piled on the much enlarged travois that the horses dragged behind them. Moreover, as the number of her father's horses increased, Crooked Leg and her sisters helped Broken Knife Woman prepare additional lodge-skins, since the horses could easily transport the heavy buffalo hides from camp to camp. Of course, enlarged lodges needed longer, additional lodge poles, but these, too, were dragged behind the horses, often serving as supports for the travois that carried the goods. Through the years, moving camp became much easier. Now when the Inu-naina moved their village, almost everyone rode on horseback. Although her winters numbered more than seventy and her back and hips ached after several hours on horseback, Crooked Leg could still ride. And she was glad that other elders from her village, those too ill or infirm to sit astride a horse, could be carried on travois. Obviously, bouncing around on a travois was uncomfortable, but it allowed the aged or infirm to remain part of the village community.[9]

Now good food was rarely abandoned. Unlike the far-away time, when her mother and aunts had been forced to leave meat at the buffalo kill sites, the Inu-naina now prepared great quantities of smoked meat and pemmican, which was also carried on the horses. Late winter no longer was the hungry time, for the Inu-naina stored and kept enough food to feed their hungry families. What's more, in the Moon of First Ice, the Inu-naina now carried surplus meat and buffalo robes to the Kananin, the People with Broken Jaws (Arikaras), where they traded their surplus meat and even a few horses for dried corn, beans, squash, and the wondrous things that the Kananin obtained from the Nihoohoo, the Mysterious People, men with pale skins who sometimes resided in, or passed through Kananin villages. The corn, beans, and squash were stored with roots, dried berries, chokecherries, and other foods that the people gathered as they moved their camps in search of the buffalo herds, and these fruits and vegetables were combined with both fresh and dried meats to produce the rich stews that Inu-naina women cooked and kept warm near their lodge fires. During most of her life, Crooked Leg had prepared these stews in skin bags into which stones heated in the fire were placed to boil the ingredients. As the food boiled and the stones lost their heat, they were replaced by other stones until the stews were finished. When Crooked Leg was a child, her mother expected her to keep a regular supply of hot stones available so that the food would cook properly, and when she had children of her own, she assigned similar tasks to her daughters.[10]

But Laughs in the Morning, her granddaughter, never learned such a method. Before the child was old enough to assist with camp chores, her father, Iron Bear, returned from the Kananin village with a wondrous item: a small but sturdy iron kettle that Woodsmoke Woman, Crooked Leg's daughter-in-law, hung directly over the cooking fire and that was kept simmering throughout the day with a broth or meat stew, available when any family member was hungry. The old flint knives and camp axes were replaced by iron and steel utensils, also obtained from the Kananin people, and her daughter-in-law now possessed a smaller, brass kettle in which she carried and kept water. Crooked Leg admitted that steel trade knives and needles were more durable than the similar tools of bone and horn she used as a younger woman, but she still preferred to decorate her family's clothing with dyed porcupine quills and elks' teeth rather than the shiny glass beads that some of the younger women had begun to sew on their family's garments. Hmpff! Far too gaudy for her tastes!

Crooked Leg disliked the beads, but she was terrified of the kokoyono, the thunder sticks that several of the warriors had also acquired in the Kananin villages. How foolish the young warriors were! The Kananin readily traded food, metal utensils, and other useful items in exchange for the Inu-naina's surplus meats, decorated shirts, and buffalo robes, but when the improvident young men from her village asked for the thunder sticks, the Kananin demanded horses, many horses. Rides at Night, a distant kinsman, traded two pregnant mares and a young stallion for one of these evil devices, but when he brought it back to the Inu-naina camp, he placed it too near his lodge fire, and the spirit in the long stick became angered and spoke unsummoned, sending the round lead ball into his uncle's shoulder. The old man recovered, but Rides at Night was shamed.[11]

Yet Rides at Night's humiliation only increased. Several days later, Iron Bear had caused all the members of their lodge to shake their heads and laugh when he returned from a hunt and described Rides at Night's awkward attempts to reload the weapon while chasing buffalo on horseback. Iron Bear told how Rides at Night had fired his weapon at a fat cow, but he missed, and the noise so frightened his horse that it reared up, causing him to spill most of his gray thunder powder. Rides at Night then dropped his leather pouch of lead balls (Woodsmoke Woman added at the time that she wagered he might even have lost his own—but then, Woodsmoke Woman had a sharp tongue), and before he could stop and retrieve them, the buffalo herd had fled into the distance. Meanwhile, Iron Bear, armed with his cedar bow and arrows, killed two animals, which he and her grandson subsequently brought back to the village.

As she watched the fat drip from the elk haunch, Crooked Leg adjusted her buffalo robe, pulling it further up over her shoulders. The teepee was comfortable. In the distance, she could hear a mare as it whinnied to its colt in the willow thicket. Horses were valuable and brought prestige to her family. Thunder sticks were both unwieldy and unreliable. She was glad that Iron Bear had not squandered any of his herd on such foolishness. What's more, Iron Bear needed no thunder sticks to provide for his family and relatives. Armed with his bow and a quiver of arrows, her son was a successful hunter who killed many buffalo, which he distributed among the people of the village. Astride his gray stallion, his "buffalo runner," he could easily single out individual animals. And while the stallion raced beside the fleeing buffalo, Iron Bull often downed fat cows with a single arrow, placed into the hollow just behind the animal's shoulder blade. Iron Horse's stallion had been trained to leap to one side when the cow fell, preventing both horse and rider from being tripped or crushed by the falling animal. Iron Bear's buffalo runner was well known throughout the Inu-naina camps, and Iron Bear sometimes raced the animal against other buffalo runners, often winning additional horses in the wagers that accompanied such contests.[12]

Crooked Leg knew that Iron Bear also hunted buffalo in "surrounds" but that he considered this method of hunting to be challenging only to young boys and inexperienced hunters. Unlike the pursuit of buffalo across the plains, when using a surround, mounted hunters drove a small herd of buffalo into a blind canyon or a specially constructed and concealed corral where the animals were trapped and then killed with arrows that the hunters shot safely from horseback. The Inu-naina had utilized surrounds when they were pedestrian hunters, before they acquired horses; when organized effectively, the surround proved to be an effective method of killing many animals. Iron Bear was proud when Rides Alone, his son, killed his first bull in one of these box canyons. But Iron Bear complained that it lacked the excitement of the frenzied chase across the prairie and that little honor could be gained in killing buffalo in a fenced, box canyon. Crooked Leg loved her son, but she considered such vanity to be foolish. She could remember when she had been a child and the Inu-naina spent the winter moons with empty bellies. Buffalo killed in surrounds provided meat for the long winter evenings. Honor filled few cooking pots.[13]

But in recent years, honor seemed to fill the heads of many young men in the Inu-naina villages. Crooked Leg recalled that when she was a child, young men occasionally warred against their people's enemies, but such activity had not been common. The search for food, their limited resources, and the long distances separating them from their foes discouraged young men from raiding enemy villages. She shook her head; now, with horses providing both the motivation and the means for such warfare, raids were more frequent. During the summer and fall moons, war parties of young men left the village to strike at the Anihinin (Pawnees), Soshniteen (Shoshones), and Nichihinena (Kiowas). Often they attempted only to steal horses, but sometimes they were discovered and forced to flee for their lives, pursued by the animals' former owners. Such encounters commonly led to bloodshed, as both sides maintained a running battle until the raiders either escaped with their stolen mounts or abandoned them to prevent their own apprehension.[14]

Sometimes the raiding escalated to greater bloodshed. Crooked Leg sadly remembered that twelve winters in the past, a large war party of Wootene-hithi (Utes), seeking revenge for raids that the Inu-naina had made against their camps, swept in on her village, surprising the encampment when many of the men were absent hunting buffalo. The older men and boys and a few warriors present in the camp resisted the attack and finally forced the raiders to retreat, but the Wootenehithi took almost one hundred horses. Tragically, many Inunaina people had been killed or wounded, including Mountain Wolf, her husband. Mountain Wolf had counted coup on one of the Wootenehithi as the man rode by on horseback, but another of the enemy had then struck Mountain Wolf in the temple with his war club, and her husband of forty winters fell, never to rise again. Crooked Leg had screamed at the Wootenehithi and run toward them with her skinning knife, but they only laughed at her and rode away before other Inu-naina could come to her assistance. Mountain Wolf never regained consciousness and died a few hours later.

To show her grief, Crooked Leg cut her hair, rubbed her face with ashes, and gashed her forearms with her skinning knife. Assisted by her husband's relatives, she buried Mountain Wolf on a small knoll on the prairie. His favorite horse, which had escaped when the Wootenehithi struck the village, was sacrificed and left beside his grave; he would ride into the afterlife in a manner befitting an Inunaina warrior. Crooked Leg burned cedar branches for several nights after her husband's death, and she gave away their lodge and her husband's possessions. Following her period of mourning, she cleansed herself, burned all of her old clothing, and accepted her son's invitation to live in his lodge.[15]

She still missed her husband. They had been married when Crooked Leg had just passed her twentieth winter. Mountain Wolf, eight years her senior and already a successful hunter, had spoken to her brother, asking if a marriage could be arranged. Crooked Leg knew that her father would not force her to marry the young man, but then he didn't have to. She was aware that Mountain Wolf had been watching her for several seasons, and Crooked Leg's heart warmed as she remembered how she had encouraged him, smiling at him as she brought water from the river or gossiped with the other young women in the village. Mountain Wolf had honored her by presenting her family with seven horses, and her father had reciprocated, bestowing buffalo robes, beautifully quilled shirts, and a bow made of mountain sheep horn given to Mountain Wolf's relatives. After a feast, she and her husband occupied a new lodge prepared by her family.[16]

Crooked Leg had been happy. She had given birth to two sons and to two daughters, both of whom were married many winters ago. One of her sons had died of a strange coughing sickness after only two winters. The other, Iron Bear, her oldest child, was a prominent warrior and had just become a member of the Dog Lodge, the sacred society of middle-aged men who provided leadership for the village. Her family was respected by the Inu-naina people. She could hold her head high. That was important.[17]

Sitting by the fire, wrapped in her robes, the old woman contemplated the richness of the life that surrounded her. Woodsmoke Woman and Laughs in the Morning had left the lodge to carry water from the river. Crooked Leg smiled, aware that Laughs in the Morning had recently exchanged glances with a young man of her own. She knew that Iron Bear would soon receive a gift of horses, that she and Woodsmoke Woman would prepare gifts of clothing for the young man's relatives, and that another wedding feast would be shared with friends and kinsmen. The patterns of their life continued. If the Great Power in the universe smiled on her, she would live to see her great-grandchildren playing beside the lodge opening.

The sounds of voices outside her lodge bought Crooked Leg back from her memories. Two village girls giggled as they led a horse, laden with firewood, back to their parent's lodge. In the distance, a camp dog barked. The mare in the willows whinnied again for her colt. Crooked Leg looked up from the fire at the tepee liner that provided added insulation during the winter moons. The tanned buffalo hides that composed the liner were covered with carefully drawn pictographs depicting the major events of her son's life. One scene pictured Iron Bear mounted on his buffalo runner, slaying many buffalo on the plains. Another scene featured her son in a skirmish with the Ainuns (Crows), mounted on his stallion and counting coups on enemy warriors. Other scenes mirrored other exploits, but throughout the pictographs, Iron Bear was always on horseback. Indeed, her son had never known a life without horses, and he had admitted to her that he could not envision a life without them.

But Crooked Leg still remembered her childhood. Again, she smiled. The liner in the lodge contained no pictographs of horses pulling heavy travois or transporting loads of freshly killed meat back to the village. There were no scenes of women tying bundles of wood on the horses' backs as they gathered fuel for the hearths in their lodges. No pictographs featured horses carrying women, children, or the elderly as the village moved to a new campsite. None showed horses dragging the many lodge poles that supported the larger tepees that made their lives more comfortable. The pictographs did not depict

Indian Women Moving, by Charles M. Russell, 1898. Oil on canvas. Amon G. Carter Museum of American Art, 19061.147.

Inu-naina warriors trading horses with the Kananin for metal knives, kettles, and other wondrous implements that made Crooked Leg's life much easier.

Of course not. Iron Bear had drawn the pictographs, and Iron Bear, her son, was a man. He understood the ways of men. He did not see the world through the eyes of a woman. Shaking her head, Crooked Leg rose from her bed and placed another piece of firewood on the coals beneath the elk haunch. Iron Bear's pictures chronicled the ways in which horses had changed men's lives. But Crooked Leg knew the pictographs failed to show that horses had had an even greater impact on other people. They had enriched and transformed the lives of Inu-naina women.

Horses brought profound changes to Native American people living on the Great Plains. In the pre-horse period, the plains were inhabited by small groups of wandering pedestrian bison hunters or enclaves of sedentary village tribes such as Mandans, Hidatsas, Arikaras, and Pawnees who inhabited earthen lodges in relatively isolated locations along the Missouri or Platte river valleys. The pedestrian hunters eked out a precarious existence. Afoot in a semiarid, windswept landscape, they hunted bison by driving them over low cliffs or river bluffs, or they attempted to corral isolated animals in box canyons or arroyos where the beasts could be trapped, surrounded, and prevented from escaping. Unfortunately for the hunters, the bison wandered freely on the plains, and the tribespeople were forced to follow the herds if they wished to remain near their food supply. Since they possessed no beasts of burden except their camp dogs, these wandering hunters had to carry all their personal items, so their material possessions were relatively few. They resided in bison-hide tents, but bison hides are heavy, and few hides could be transported; therefore, many people were crowded into a limited number of small shelters. Moreover, although meat could be smoked or dried, only limited amounts could be carried, and the hunters and their families were forced to abandon considerable quantities of potential food after butchering animals that they had driven over cliffs or downed at other kill sites. And finally, limited food and other resources markedly restricted the population of hunting groups. Most of the pedestrian hunting bands were no more than a few crowded lodges of extended families, patrilocal kinship groups in which fathers, uncles, brothers, and grown male children cooperated in the hunt. The villages were small. Pedestrian hunters on the plains could sustain only limited populations.[18]

The arrival of horses brought many changes. Almost all the animals originated from Spanish settlements in the Southwest. Tribespeople in Texas, New Mexico, and Arizona first gained access to animals, but horses were then traded northward through two primary routes. The first, and most logical, was a natural progression from tribe to tribe north across the plains from Texas and Oklahoma, through eastern Colorado, Kansas, Nebraska, and the Dakotas. The other, more western, advance followed an intermountain route from tribes such as the Navajos and Apaches to the Utes on the western side of the Rockies, then northward to the Shoshones, Nez Perce, and Bannocks. In turn, these tribes traded horses to their eastern neighbors, such as the Crows and Blackfeet, in northern Wyoming and Montana.[19]

Historians have documented horses among the Caddoan-speaking tribes of Texas during the middle decades of the seventeenth century, and evidence suggests that the Apaches had traded them to the Utes by at least 1650.[20] By 1700, most Plains tribes living south of the Platte River had some familiarity with horses, although the number of animals they possessed was not large. Ethnohistorians argue that the Arapahos and other tribes living in the Black

Hills region acquired horses in the 1730s, although the village tribes along the Missouri did not receive them for another decade. During the third quarter of the eighteenth century, the horse frontier expanded rapidly across the northern plains, reaching the Cheyennes, Lakotas, and eventually the Assiniboines. The Blackfeet probably acquired their first horses from the Flatheads sometime between 1730 and 1745.[21]

By the early nineteenth century, most tribes had amassed significant herds. On the southern plains, the Kiowas, and particularly the Comanches, grazed large herds that they regularly supplemented through raids on the American and Mexican settlements. Indeed, both tribes continued to trade large numbers of animals to Indians on the northern plains, and early European or Anglo-American travelers in the region were amazed at the size of the Kiowa and Comanche herds. In 1840, to commemorate their peace with the Southern Cheyennes and Arapahos, the Kiowas presented their former enemies with so many horses that the Cheyennes and Arapahos did not possess enough ropes to lead the animals back to their village. Six years earlier, in 1834, when artist George Catlin visited the Comanches, he found one band of the tribe surrounded by a herd of horses and mules numbering at least three thousand animals.[22] Meanwhile, the Nez Perce, Cayuse, and Flathead peoples of the plateau, whose homelands provided verdant, well-watered, yet protected pasturage, also bred and raised huge herds of animals. Both contemporary observers and modern scholars agree that the Nez Perce averaged at least fifty horses for every lodge in their village. The Crows, who often served as middlemen between the plateau tribes and the northern Plains tribes, also possessed large herds, although not in numbers to match the Comanches, Kiowas, or Nez Perce.[23]

Other northern tribes were less horse affluent. Among the northern Arapahos (Crooked Leg's people), a man who owned two dozen horses would have been considered wealthy, while the Assiniboines and Plains Crees, tribes on the northeastern borders of the plains, possessed the smallest herds of any Plains tribes. Horse ownership among the Sioux is difficult to calculate. The western Sioux (Teton Lakota) owned many horses, while the eastern Sioux, those bands residing east of the Missouri River, particularly those tribespeople residing in Minnesota, herded considerably fewer animals.[24]

Ironically, while horses entered the plains from the south and west, firearms generally arrived from the opposite directions. Spanish policies forbade the legal sale of firearms to Indians, and during the eighteenth century, tribes on the western and southern fringes of the plains (those tribes with horses) had only limited access to guns. In contrast, trade muskets were standard fare among those commodities offered to the tribespeople by British or French traders. By the last quarter of the eighteenth century, trade muskets readily found their way into the hands of the eastern Sioux, the Osages, and those tribes living on the eastern fringe of the plains, particularly in the region north of the Arkansas River.[25]

Firearms gradually replaced bows and arrows as weapons of choice, but initially many plains tribes continued to use bows and arrows for both hunting and war. Firearms often needed repair, and ammunition was expensive and in short supply. Moreover, while galloping on horseback, a skilled archer could notch and shoot a dozen arrows during the period needed to reload and prime a barrel-heavy trade musket. Consequently, many Plains warriors shortened the barrels of their muskets to make the loading process less cumbersome, but this also made them less accurate. Mounted hunters continued to hunt bison with bows until the 1870s, when the herds were decimated and the tribes were placed on reservations.[26]

Horses markedly improved the quality of Plains people's lives. Mounted on horses, Native Americans could easily traverse the open plains, keeping pace with the buffalo herds, or more easily find the animals as they moved to new grazing grounds. In addition, horses allowed Indian people to transport goods more easily. Horses could drag longer tepee poles and transport many more buffalo hides, enabling tribespeople to erect and move much larger tepees. Some items were still carried by the dogs, but pack horses carried most things, and the availability of animals to transport material goods meant that Indian people could amass and keep an increased number of items that enriched their daily lives and made them more productive.[27]

Since more items could be retained, many commonly used items were more carefully fashioned or decorated, and quillwork, beadwork, and other artforms flourished. Tepee liners were carefully painted to illustrate the major events in their owners' lives, while brass-studded backrests, carefully painted parfleches, and additional buffalo robes were carried from camp to camp by the family's horses. Greater quantities of food could be prepared and transported, and the people went hungry less often. Surplus meat and hides were traded to horticultural tribes for corn, dried squash, and other vegetable products. Accordingly, tribal populations increased, as the abundance in food and material comforts impacted tribal demographics. Meanwhile, as horses became more plentiful, they also became a symbol of wealth, and they soon emerged as the standard item of exchange when items were bartered among Plains peoples.[28]

But horses also had a negative impact. Most certainly, they increased the amount of warfare. Since horses were so valuable, young men sought to obtain additional animals by raiding the herds of neighboring tribes. Not surprisingly, these tribes retaliated in kind, and in the subsequent attempts to either steal or retain the animals, lives were lost and warriors were injured. By the early nineteenth century, disputes over horses probably were the primary source of conflict on the plains, although access to diminishing buffalo herds may have inspired more warfare later in the century. And the intertribal warfare fed upon itself. Lives lost in horse raids demanded retaliation, which in turn brought increased vendettas from one's enemies, and the cycle both increased and continued. Meanwhile, as warriors assumed a larger role in tribal life, the status of warriors also increased, encouraging young men who sought the esteem of their peers and kinsfolk to seek recognition in acquiring horses or in defending the village and its herds from enemy raiders. Older village chiefs still led many of the villages, but by the middle of the nineteenth century, many of these older men who had risen to positions of prominence through their skill as hunters or their reservoir of common sense and good judgement had been replaced by younger men whose claim to fame rested on their military leadership. Success as a warrior—not moderation, common sense, and political experience—became the key to fame and influence.[29]

And ironically, the adoption of horses for hunting may also have initiated the death-knell for the very resource upon which this rich culture was based: the buffalo. Recent scholarship indicates that as both feral and tribal horse herds increased, they depleted a considerable portion of the buffalo habitat. Meanwhile, Native American participation in the buffalo-hide trade in the decades following the 1840s also seriously reduced the size of the herds. Coupled with several other factors (the introduction of foreign bovine diseases such as brucellosis, climate change, and the intrusion of white emigration routes that discouraged buffalo migration), horses and Native American hunters mounted on horses initiated the demise of the great buffalo herds that had existed on the plains for thousands of years. This decline began before midcentury but was accentuated when white hide hunters slaughtered most of the remaining herds in the 1870s.[30]

The advent of horses was readily embraced by the wandering buffalo hunters, but it worked to the disadvantage of the more sedentary Mandan, Hidatsa, and Arikara tribespeople, settled farmers residing in large earthen lodges along the Missouri River in modern North and South Dakota. Although these sedentary farming peoples did eventually adopt and utilize horses for their seasonal buffalo hunting, they did not abandon their settlements of great earthen lodges for a nomadic existence on the plains. For generations they had stored and traded the surplus crops harvested from their extensive gardens, and secure in their comfortable lodges, their lives were surrounded by economic plenty and elaborate ceremonialism. Indeed, prior to the arrival of horses, their villages were the very center of trade and commerce on the northern plains. The wandering hunters had periodically visited the village peoples to barter for beans, squash, and sunflower seeds in addition to the European trade goods brought up-river after the arrival of the Europeans. From the village people's perspective, horses were an interesting innovation, but the Mandans, Hidatsas, and Arikaras refused to relinquish the comforts of their way of life and become "horse Indians" who followed the buffalo in tepees. They believed that they had too much to lose.[31]

And in the middle decades of the nineteenth century, they lost almost everything. During the 1830s, when smallpox was carried up the Missouri River, the village tribes, still resident in their earthen lodges, were devastated by the plague. The Mandans suffered fatal casualties of over 90 percent, the Hidatsas lost almost one half their population, and the Arikaras' death toll amounted to about three hundred people. In total, during 1837–38, the tribes lost almost three thousand people, over 50 percent of their combined populations.[32]

In response, many of their previous trading partners and "country cousins," the nomadic horse-mounted buffalo hunters, fell upon them with a fury. Mounted war parties repeatedly raided their villages and dwindling horse herds, then fled before the village people could retaliate. In 1858, after two decades of devastation, the three village tribes banded together to form one village, Like a Fishhook, near modern Fort Berthold, in North Dakota. A mere shadow of their former prominence, the survivors of these once dominant political, cultural, and economic tribes were forced to rely on the federal government for their protection. They persevered, and today they constitute the Three Affiliated Tribes of the Fort Berthold Reservation in North Dakota.[33]

Yet the appeal of hunting buffalo on horseback continued. After acquiring horses, other tribes who had lived adjacent to the plains for centuries ventured onto the region in growing numbers. Some, like the Pawnees, Omahas, Otoes, and Wichitas had always hunted buffalo, but they were also horticulturists living in semipermanent villages on the eastern fringe of the plains. They had annually left their villages of earthen or grass houses for a summer buffalo hunt, but buffalo did not dominate their food supply. Like the Mandans, Hidatsas, and Arikaras, they too had grown crops of corn, squash, and beans. But with the acquisition of horses, they became much more reliant on buffalo as a food source, focusing less on horticulture and more on hunting. They did not abandon their sedentary villages, but they did adopt many tenets of the nomadic tepee tribes.³⁴

Other tribes also joined the parade onto the plains to hunt buffalo on horseback. From the east, the Teton Dakota migrated westward, first in search of beaver to trade to French and British traders, but by the late eighteenth century, they too were adapting to a nomadic, buffalo-hunting life. On the west, the Shoshones or Snakes moved out of the Great Basin to occupy central and southern Wyoming, while the Nez Perce, originally a people dependent on salmon and camas bulbs for sustenance, increasingly crossed over into Montana, where they were attracted by the allure of nomadism and buffalo hunting on horseback. Competition between these newcomers and the Crows, Blackfeet, Arapahos, Cheyennes, and other tribes for control of the buffalo lands west of the Missouri and north of the Platte spurred the growth of intertribal warfare, but the lure of mounted buffalo hunting on the plains continued well into the last half of the nineteenth century.³⁵ Even the eastern tribes (Potawatomis, Shawnees, Cherokees, etc.) whom the federal government had removed from regions east of the Mississippi and who had resettled in eastern Kansas and Indian Territory repeatedly sent mounted hunting parties west onto the plains, where they, too, fell upon the buffalo herds and periodically clashed with the nomadic buffalo hunters. For a century and a half, the lure of mounted buffalo hunting on the plains reigned supreme.³⁶

Consequently, it is not surprising that the popular image of the Plains warrior has emerged as the standard stereotype of Native Americans held by much of the American public and by many non-Indian people around the world. During the nineteenth century, as most of the nation passed through the Industrial Revolution, Plains Indians and their culture offered a glimpse of what seemed to be a simpler, freer, less complicated life. For many Americans who were tied down to the grueling routine of an industrialized society or who found themselves enmeshed in a market dominated agriculture over which they seemed to have little control, the Plains tribes provided a romanticized, if forbidden, alternative: a people still living unshackled by the demands and responsibilities that fettered ordinary Americans' lives. Moreover, in the antebellum period, the Plains tribes had already received considerable exposure from painters such as George Catlin and Karl Bodmer, whose paintings and sketches added to the tribespeople's romantic mystique. Following the Civil War, as the public's focus turned to events in the Black Hills, battles at the Little Big Horn, and the heroic flight of Chief Joseph and the Nez Perce, the Plains tribes and their culture received even more press coverage. Playing to the public's interest, reporters and journalists accompanied military expeditions in the west and sent back descriptions of warriors bedecked in feathered splendor. Many of these reports were much romanticized, but they strengthened the image that much of the public already had embraced.[37]

Not surprisingly, as Native Americans became less a threat, they became even more popular. Crowds flocked to see Plains warriors (or Indians dressed as Plains warriors) pursue wagons around the arena in Wild West shows, while many accoutrements of Plains culture (tepees, war bonnets, buffalo hunting, etc.) became the standard symbols of Indianness throughout the country. Ironically after the Plains people were denied their former way of life and confined to reservations, they still swept across the plains in dime novels, pulp fiction, and later on the silver screen. Of course, such imagery either ignored or denied the desolation of reservation life and even minimized the warfare, hardships, and other suffering incurred by the Plains peoples before they were confined to the reservations.[38]

Yet as the nineteenth century came to a close, aging tribesmen on reservations in Montana, Wyoming, the Dakotas, and western Oklahoma probably agreed. Like Crooked Leg, they also remembered a time of plenty. Once buffalo had been many, horses raced like the wind, and people, unfettered by fences or Indian agents, roamed the plains and prairies. Once life had been good. Once people had been free.[39]

Suggested Readings

Calloway, Colin G. *One Vast Winter Count: The Native American West before Lewis and Clark*. Lincoln: University of Nebraska Press, 2003.

Ewers, John C. *The Horse in Blackfoot Culture*. Washington, DC: Smithsonian Institution, 1955.

Hämäläinen, Pekka. *The Comanche Empire*. New Haven, CT: Yale University Press, 2008.

Holder, Preston. *The Hoe and the Horse on the Plains: A Study of Cultural Development among North American Indians*. Lincoln: University of Nebraska Press, 1970.

Roe, Frank Gilbert. *The Indian and the Horse*. Norman: University of Oklahoma Press, 1955.

FOUR

Herons Who Wait at the Spelawe-thepee

The Ohio River and the Shawnee World

In early September 1795, a middle-aged Shawnee warrior stood on the north bank of the Ohio River, about ten miles upstream from the mouth of the Little Miami River and gazed across at the Kentucky shore. His heart was heavy. He could remember when he once loved the Spelawe-thepee, the Great River, which rose amid the tree-covered mountains to the east. When Heron Who Waits was a young man, his heart often leapt when he crossed the broad river to journey into the dark and bloody ground of Kaintuck, where methotho, the great shaggy beast, once grazed in the Blue Grass country and where young warriors like himself took scalps from the Flatheads (the Choctaws and Chickasaws) who also hunted on the southern borders of the Shawnee world. But now, in Pokamawii-gisis, the Moon of Plums, as he stood on the river's north bank, the broad stream no longer seemed to be a friend. Now the Spelawe-thepee, called the Oheeyo or Beautiful River by the Senecas, was like a steel-bladed skinning knife, cutting the world in two, providing a broad pathway that carried more and more of the Shemanese, or Long Knives, into the Shawnee homeland; and the graying warrior recalled that in the previous moon, in Miskwimini-gesiss, the Moon of Raspberries (July 1795), much of that homeland had been lost. Sadly, he and other Shawnees had met with Shemeneto (Black Snake), Mad Anthony Wayne, at the new Long Knife fort at Greenville. There, Black Hoof, Red Pole, Blue Jacket, and other leaders of his people put their marks on the treaty paper. Now the Shawnee lands along the Great River's northern bank would belong to the Long Knives.[1]

Once, the river had been a unifying force. In Heron Who Wait's childhood, the Great River carried canoes and dugouts of both French and British traders, merchants who had ascended the Muskingum and the Scioto, visiting Shawnee villages and bartering for pelts brought back to camp by Shawnee hunters. In that golden age, the animal brothers were plentiful, and hunting parties from Heron Who Waits's village at Chillicothe journeyed down the Scioto, crossed the Great River, and returned with the coats of amaghqua (beaver), kitate (otter), and ehepate (raccoon). Other hunters supplied their families with meat from peshikthe (deer) or methotho (bison), and Shawnee women crafted these brothers' skins into clothing or robes.

The women also planted large gardens abutting the villages, and during the warm summers, the earth pushed forth the Three Sisters—corn, squash, and beans. These sisters danced together across the fields, intertwining their stalks, stems, and vines, and by Binakwi-gissis, the Moon of Falling Leaves, the land had produced a bounty of crops. Meat from roasted bison humps or venison haunches was combined with shelled and pounded corn, beans, and strips of squash and pumpkins into hardy stews, which were served from copper or iron pots that that simmered over cooking fires. Families and friends gathered around the campfires for feasts, dances, and ceremonies. Old men smoked. People smiled. Laughing children had played tag among the lodges. It was a time of plenty.

Later in the autumn, after frosts had turned the trees that sheltered the Scioto to red and gold, the people tightened their wigwams, adding additional layers of bark or reed mats against the falling temperatures. But their storage bins were full, they had meat in their larders, and they looked forward to the cold moons as a time spent mostly indoors, a time spent with families, sewing and mending clothes, repairing tools and weapons, and telling stories around the lodge-fires. The snows came, but the cycle of life continued. Elders died, but children were born. They were secure in their village. The Master of Life had smiled. It had been good to be Shawnee.

But then things changed. The Great Serpent, the Matchemanitou, the evil power, gained the ascendancy. The Shawnees had originally welcomed the French and British traders, men who brought the goods (metal tools and implements, firearms, gunpowder and lead, trade cloth, and glass and metal ornaments) that had been luxuries. But by the middle of the eighteenth century, many of these things had become necessities. Then, the Men with Hairy Faces had fought among themselves, and many winters in the past (1763), when

Heron Who Waits was a boy, the Sauganash (British) defeated Onontio's soldiers and occupied the former French posts in the Great Lakes region.[2] After the Redcoats' victory, their unruly children began to cross the great wooded mountains to hunt in the Blue Grass country.

Although neither the Shawnees nor their Mingo or Lenape (Delaware) allies maintained any permanent villages south of the Great River, they had hunted in these lands for generations, and they had defended the area against incursions by the Cherokees, Chickasaws, and Choctaws. They did not want to share these bountiful hunting lands with the Long Knives. Shawnee hunting parties confronted the Virginians and asked them to go back across the mountains, but the Long Knives laughed — and they refused. In response, the Shawnees seized the intruders' pelts and weapons. Some of these "long hunters" fled eastward for their lives, but others resisted, so the Shawnees took their scalps and their horses.[3] Once started, the bloodshed proliferated. The Long Knives replied in kind, and the Virginians returned in greater numbers, erecting small settlements along the Big Sandy and Kanawha Rivers.

Warfare flared intermittently in the early 1770s, and as a young warrior, Heron Who Waits took his first scalp in the spring of 1772, during a skirmish against a party of long hunters near the mouth of the Little Sandy River. In the next two years, the fighting intensified, and Heron Who Waits remembered that the Shawnees, Delawares, and Mingos had sought to join together to stop the Long Knives from establishing new settlements west of the mountains. But forming a unified resistance had been difficult for tribal people who sometimes fought among themselves. And the Long Knives were persistent. By 1774, parties of settlers, accompanied by their families, trekked westward along the old Warriors Path through Cumberland Gap, intent on settling in the Blue Grass region, while others descended the Great River in canoes or flatboats, then attempted to survey and claim tracts of land on the Kaintuck shore

The Shawnees and Mingos struck back. Heron Who Waits joined a war party that surprised a surveyors' camp, seized their weapons, and destroyed all their equipment. But after warning them not to return, they released them when the frightened Long Knives promised to go back to their homes in the east. But in the meantime, a war party of Cherokees, also angry at the Long Knives, attacked a party of traders from Pennsylvania, killing one and wounding two others. Heron Who Waits knew that no Shawnees had participated in the second incident, but Long Knives at the Great River's Fork (Pittsburgh) blamed his people and killed three of his kinsmen in retaliation. And so it went. Blood begat blood. Vendetta begat vendetta.

In late April 1774, things intensified. During mid-morning on April 30, in the waning of Poosh-gissis (the Halfway Moon), two canoes carrying seven Mingos, many of whom were close relatives of Logan, a Mingo chief known for his friendship to Long Knife settlers, were lured across the Great River to a trading post on the eastern bank, just opposite Logan's village at the mouth of Yellow Creek, in Ohio. While at the post, all but one of the Mingos were murdered by a party of frontier militia led by Daniel Greathouse, a settler and land speculator who claimed land on the Great River's eastern shore.[4] Alerted by the gunfire, two canoes full of Mingo and Shawnee warriors hurriedly paddled across the river to investigate its origin, but Greathouse and his followers hid in the underbrush along the riverbank, then fired on the warriors as the canoes approached the riverbank. Although one of the canoes capsized, the second made it back to Logan's village, but when the carnage ended, a dozen Mingo and Shawnee tribespeople lay dead at the trading post or floated face-down in the river. Among the dead were Logan's father, brother, and sister. Greathouse and his companions scalped all the victims, then dangled their scalps from their belts. Logan's nephew, the infant son of his slain sister, was spared but was carried to Pittsburgh and later offered up (for a price) to other settlers for adoption.

Heron Who Waits recalled that he and other Shawnees at Chillicothe had learned the details of the murders from Absalom, a M'kateweini (African American) slave owned by the trading post proprietor. In the aftermath of the slaughter, Absalom fled across the river to a village of Moravian Delawares, then passed through Chillicothe enroute to the Glaize in northwestern Ohio, where he eventually married an Ottawa woman. Absalom also informed them that Logan was infuriated and had sought retribution for his loss by raiding several settlements in Virginia but had then notified officials at Pittsburg that the spirits of his kinsmen were satisfied; justice had been served, and there would be no more attacks against the Long Knives or their settlements.

Heron Who Waits remembered how he and other younger warriors had been eager to join the Mingo war parties, but Cornstalk, a respected village chief from the Shawnee town on the Hocking River, convinced them to remain at peace and even sheltered several Pennsylvania traders in his village from Mingos seeking revenge. Yet when Cornstalk permitted the traders to return to Pittsburgh and even sent several Shawnee warriors from his village to escort them safely back to their homes, these warriors were attacked by frontier militia from Pittsburgh, who fired on the Shawnees' camp as they returned to Cornstalk's village. The Shawnees suffered only one warrior wounded and escaped into the forest, but when they arrived back on the Hocking, even Cornstalk was incensed. Messengers were sent to Shawnee villages along the Scioto and Muskingum warning that the Long Knives had violated a truce and obviously wanted bloodshed.

The Shawnees had prepared for war—but so had the Long Knives. Messengers were sent from the Shawnee villages to the Senecas, Cherokees, Creeks, and Chickasaws, asking them to embrace the reddened wampum belt and to join in a war against the Long Knives, but British Indian agents, many of whom were married into these tribes, interceded, and their leaders refused. Meanwhile, at Pittsburgh, John Connolly, the militia officer whose men had recently attacked the Shawnee escort, wrote to Lord Dunmore (John Murray), the governor of Virginia, and falsely informed him that the skirmish had been initiated by the Shawnees. In response, Dunmore raised almost 2,700 men, planning to attack Shawnee villages on the Muskingum and the Scioto. In Binakwi-gisiss, the Moon of Falling Leaves (October 6, 1774), one thousand Long Knives led by Colonel Andrew Lewis marched to the juncture of the Kanawha and the Great River, a place the Long Knives called Point Pleasant. There they established a fortified camp just north of the Kanawha's mouth and awaited the arrival of Dunmore and another 1,200 militiamen who had assembled at Pittsburgh. The combined force then planned to attack the Shawnee villages along the Scioto, burn their lodges, and destroy their cornfields.

Cornstalk was informed of the Long Knives' intentions, and although he received little assistance from other tribes, he rallied three hundred Shawnees from the Scioto towns and from villages along the Hocking and Muskingum. Assembling these warriors in the thick forests that blanketed the Great River's western bank, just opposite the mouth of the Kanawha, Cornstalk decided to attack Lewis's force before Dunmore could reinforce them. Late in the evening on October 9, Cornstalk and most of the Shawnees ferried across the Great River on rafts and reached the eastern shore undetected. Landing several miles upstream (north) from the Long Knives' camp, the Shawnees then passed silently through the river bottom in the pre-dawn darkness, hoping to surprise their sleeping enemy.

Heron Who Waits remembered that as a young man, he joined a war party from Chillicothe organized by his uncle, Puckeshinwa (Striking Hawk), a war

chief who led a party of warriors from the Scioto to Cornstalk's camp. At that time, Heron Who Waits had seen the snows of nineteen winters, and he was eager to strike the Long Knives. He also felt honored when Puckeshinwa asked him to keep a close eye on Chiksika (the Musket), his oldest son (and Heron Who Waits's cousin), aged only fourteen winters, who had accompanied his father to Cornstalk's forward camp.

They crossed the river and started west, through the overgrown river bottom before dawn. Puckeshinwa and Heron Who Waits, with Chicksika following closely behind, were in the forefront of the Shawnee advance and approached to within a half mile of the American position when they were discovered by two Virginians who had arisen early to hunt turkeys. The hunters hurriedly fired at the approaching Shawnees, then fled back to their bivouac, warning their comrades. Puckeshinwa had hoped to surprise the sleeping Long Knives, but now they were awakened, so he halted the war party and told them to take positions on the far side of a ravine they had just crossed, since he knew the Virginians would soon march out against them. Shrouded by the underbrush, Heron Who Waits and Chicksika crouched down behind the trunk of a huge fallen walnut tree. Heron Who Waits told his younger companion to check the priming on his musket, to keep low, and to watch for the advancing Long Knives.

They did not wait long. Shortly after dawn, a loosely formed line of militia appeared among the trees beyond the ravine, then cautiously descended the far side of the gully, heading toward the Shawnees' position. Puckeshinwa gave the war cry, and the Shawnees fired from the underbrush. The Long Knives fell back, retreating behind tree trunks. Meanwhile, the jubilant Chicksika, full of boyhood adrenaline, echoed his father's war cry, and war club in hand, he leaped onto the fallen walnut trunk preparing to race after the retreating Long Knives. In contrast, the more experienced Heron Who Waits knew that the Long Knives would regroup behind the tree trunks, take aim, and pulverize his cousin as the boy recklessly rushed forward in their wake. Before Chicksika could clamber over the walnut trunk, Heron Who Waits grabbed him by the waist and pulled him back behind the downed tree. He no sooner had landed than both Shawnees heard the thud of musket balls striking the walnut log where Chicksika, only seconds before, had shouted the war cry.

The Virginians momentarily continued their retreat, but they did not flee, and although the Shawnees were able to pursue them for a short distance, perhaps the width of the Great River, the Long Knives fought back, and they were soon reinforced by other militia from Lewis's camp. The Shawnees were then forced to retreat to their previous positions in the thickets opposite the ravine, and the fighting soon turned into a pattern of limited sorties by both sides, interspersed by rifle and musket fire between the two lines. Heron Who Waits shot a militia officer wearing a leather coat in the face as he led a small party of Virginians who tried to cross the ravine in front of the fallen walnut trunk. Disheartened, the party immediately fell back, and Heron Who Waits watched as Chicksika sent a musket ball into the buttocks of another Long Knife as the man turned and scrambled back up the ravine toward the shelter of the tree line. Both men (one dead, one wounded) were carried by their comrades back to the Virginians' position, so Heron Who Waits and Chicksika took no scalps, but the boy had stood his ground, and Heron Who Waits was proud of him.

Yet things did not go well. The fighting raged throughout the morning, but the Long Knives outnumbered the Shawnees by almost three to one, and they had larger supplies of ammunition. Shortly before noon, Puckeshinwa crept up to their position and told them to prepare to fall back. Supplies of musket balls and powder were running low, and they needed to get to the rafts and cross the river before the Long Knives could approach and fire at them from the riverbank. During a lull in the fighting, Heron Who Waits and Chicksika slipped away from the walnut log and crept through the underbrush. After putting a small grove of sumac between themselves and their enemies, they hurried through the river bottom toward the rafts. Puckeshinwa remained behind to help cover the Shawnees retreat. He instructed them to cross the Great River and wait for him on the western bank.

Heron Who Waits and Chicksika made it back safely to the Ohio shore, but Puckeshinwa did not. While leading a small party of seasoned warriors who fought a series of rearguard skirmishes, he was struck in the chest by a musket ball. His comrades carried him to the river and rafted him across, but when Heron Who Waits and Chicksika hurried to his side, Heron Who Waits could see that he was dying. He watched in silence as the rapidly weakening Puckeshinwa asked Chicksika to care for his younger brothers and sisters. A teary-eyed yet stoic Chicksika nodded his head, then also promised to never make peace with the Long Knives. Initial plans to carry Puckeshinwa's body back to Chillicothe were abandoned when scouts reported that the Long Knives were making rafts, intending to pursue the retreating Shawnees across the Great River. Their ammunition depleted, the Shawnees and their Mingo allies knew they could not stop the Virginian advance. After burying Puckeshinwa in a hidden grave in the forest, they dispersed to their villages.

Heron Who Waits recalled that in the weeks that followed, the Long Knives invaded Ohio and burned Shawnee villages on the Muskingum. In the aftermath of the battle at the mouth of the Kanawha and the subsequent destruction of Shawnee villages on the Muskingum, Shawnee leaders met with Lord Dunmore, put their mark on the paper, and reluctantly ceded to the Virginians (temporarily, in many Shawnees' minds) their claims to Kaintuck. But Heron Who Waits and many other warriors had disagreed with the cession. Let Dunmore and his army go back over the mountains! If other Long Knives dared to enter Kaintuck, let them come! The Shawnees and their allies had always excelled at war in the forest. With their army gone, isolated settlements of Long Knives would be no match for Shawnee war parties.

Yet Heron Who Waits smiled to himself as he remembered what followed. Surely the man on the cross, the Long Knives' manitou, must be a trickster, for no sooner had the Long Knives built their log houses in the Blue Grass country than they turned on themselves. And when the Long Knives' Redcoat Father asked the Shawnees to punish his errant children, Heron Who Waits and his fellow warriors struck back with a vengeance. Led by Blackfish, a war chief from Chillicothe, the Shawnees and their allies laid waste to the settlements, burning cabins, pillaging livestock, and besieging the Long Knives who crowded into log forts full of the stinking sickness. Of course, the Long Knives retaliated, and military expeditions led by John Bowman, George Rogers Clark, and Benjamin Logan crossed the Great River to attack and burn several Shawnee villages. But Heron Who Waits and his kinsmen rebuilt their wigwams, their women replanted their cornfields, and the warfare continued.

Indeed, those had been halcyon days for young warriors. Their Redcoat Father had supplied them with muskets, lead, and powder, and the Long Knives had proven to be easy targets. Standing by the Great River, Heron Who Waits watched as two sakiwa (great blue herons), his namesake, passed overhead, flying south toward the Kaintuck shore. The two large birds, flying one behind the other, reminded him that he had once accompanied another bird, a British officer with the same name, on a raid into Kaintuck, a raid whose initial success had limited its ultimate outcome.

In Miskwimini-gissis, the Moon of Raspberries (late June 1780), Heron Who Waits joined with Captain Henry Bird, about 150 Red Coats or Sauganash (British traders) from Detroit, and almost six hundred other Shawnee, Mingo, Potawatomi, Odawa, Ojibwe, and Wyandot warriors who journeyed down the Miami River to the Great River, then crossed into Kaintuck to attack the Long Knives. Unlike previous raids, Bird brought several small cannon, which he floated across the Great River on rafts, then brought these field pieces to bear on frontier forts in the Blue Grass region.

As usual, the Long Knives had smugly taken shelter behind their log stockades, believing that the tribesmen did not have the firepower to breach the walls, but Heron Who Waits chuckled to himself when he remembered how their smugness vanished when they saw the Redcoats wheel the small cannon from the surrounding forest and train them on the stockade walls. They first attacked Ruddle's Station, firing the cannon only twice before the residents surrendered, and although he took no part in the slaughter, Heron Who Waits admitted that several women and children had been killed when the large war party entered the palisade. The survivors were taken prisoner and herded to Martin's Station, another log fort only five miles distant, which after seeing the cannon, surrendered without firing a shot. Heron Who Waits then joined a war party of sixty Shawnees and Mingos who quickly journeyed to Grant's Station, a small fort located nearby, but they found the post deserted except for two men and one woman barricaded in one of the small blockhouses. The defenders opened fire on the war party when it approached, so the warriors returned their fire, then set fire to the blockhouse. When the three Long Knives attempted to flee the flames, they were cut down by musket balls. The war party then returned to Martin's Station.

Now burdened by over 450 captives and also encumbered with a large herd of captured horses, Henry Bird, the Redcoat captain, could no longer conduct his raid. Although Heron Who Waits and some of the younger warriors had wanted to attack other forts at Bryant's Station or Lexington, Bird and the older war chiefs advised them to retreat back across the Great River with their captives and horses. Carry the spoils of their victories back to their villages before the Long Knives could rally and retaliate against them. Hadn't they proven to the Long Knives that their log forts could be taken? Retreat with their prizes and make plans to come back another day. It was good advice, and Heron Who Waits had gladly taken it. Moreover, he had taken one captive, a boy of seven winters, whom he later adopted into his family, and three fine horses, two of which he later sold to a Creole-French trader living on the Auglaize River.

Heron Who Waits again crossed the Great River in the following summer (1781) when he and other Shawnee, Mingo, and Wyandot warriors had ranged as far south as the Clinch and Holston Rivers in Tennessee burning cabins, taking scalps, and stealing horses. And in 1782, during Kiishthwa-gissis, the Moon of Blackberries (August), he returned to Kaintuck with the Redcoat captain William Caldwell and Simon Girty to attack Bryan Station (in modern Lexington).

The assault failed, but as the Shawnees and their allies withdrew, the foolhardy Long Knives followed them through the forest, and Heron Who Waits and his kinsmen lay in ambush near Blue Licks, on the Licking River. As the Long Knives noisily splashed across the shallow stream, Heron Who Waits and his kinsmen opened fire, and from the seventy Long Knives who fell, Heron Who Waits took two scalps, which he proudly carried back to his village. Good memories! At Chillicothe and Piqua and amidst the other Shawnee villages, old men smoked, women smiled, and warriors recounted their exploits and danced the victory dances. Scouts sent south across the Great River reported that many Long Knives had abandoned their farms and were returning to their old homes east of the mountains. With their Redcoat Father's help, the war had been won. Kaintuck would be returned to the Shawnees.

But the Redcoats had betrayed them. Although British traders, men like Matthew Elliott and Alexander McKee, men who had married into the people and had taken Shawnee wives, assured them that their Redcoat Father had not given up their lands, the Long Knives claimed not only that they still owned Kaintuck but that the paper that ended their war with the Redcoats had given the newly formed Thirteen Fires control of the region north of the Great River and that Shawnee villages such as Chillicothe and Piqua now belonged to them. Heron Who Waits and his kinsmen scoffed at such claims, but Long Knife emissaries met with Shawnee chiefs and informed them that their lands would be occupied by Long Knife farmers. In response, the chiefs warned that the Great River, which had served as the artery of the Shawnee heartland, would now serve as a boundary, and if Long Knife settlers dared to cross to its northern shore, their cattle would be killed, their cabins would be burned, and they would be thrown into the flames until they, too, were no more than ashes. And Heron Who Waits, Chicksika, and other Shawnees warriors stood before the council fires, raised their clubs and hatchets, and shouted the war cry in support of Blue Jacket, Black Snake, and other defiant Shawnee leaders.

Still, the Long Knives persisted. In the seasons that followed, they repeatedly asked the Shawnees to attend their treaties and to accept their settlements north of the Great River. Heron Who Waits and his kinsmen repeatedly refused, but Wyandot warriors, men who had courted the Long Knives' favor, as well as Ojibwes and Potawatomis from Detroit, met with these agents, and these northern warriors eagerly accepted the Long Knives' presents, drank their whiskey, and put their marks on the paper. But Heron Who Waits and other Shawnees scoffed at such council. These northern tribes had no claim to the Shawnee homeland! And in response, Heron Who Waits and other Shawnee warriors threatened the lives of those tribesmen who sat at the Long Knives' feet! And when the Long Knives sent their flatboats down the Great River, the Shawnees fired on them, but the Long Knives came in such numbers that they finally established a permanent settlement, which they called Fort Washington, near the mouth of the Little Miami River. Again, the Shawnees struck back, and although the Long Knives clung to their beachhead, Heron Who Waits's kinsmen took many scalps, and the Great River still formed a barrier to the Shawnee homeland.

And then the Master of Life smiled upon his people. Frustrated by their losses, the Thirteen Fires had sent two military expeditions against Shawnee and Miami villages along the Wabash-Maumee waterway. And Heron Who Waits again smiled when he remembered their outcome. The first one, led by the Long Knife general Josiah Harmar, reached the headwaters of the Maumee in Binakiwi-gessis, the Moon of Falling Leaves (October 1790). There, Harmer's soldiers were ambushed twice by a large war party of Miamis, Shawnees, Potawatomis, and Odawas led by the Miami chief, Little Turtle. Defeated, the Long Knives turned back and returned to Fort Washington.

Heron Who Waits had not participated in this first series of encounters, but one year later, when the Long Knives launched a second expedition, Heron Who Waits was there to welcome them. Shawnee scouts and Indian traders, traveling between Fort Washington and the tribal villages, had reported that during the summer moons in 1791, Arthur St. Clair, the man appointed by the Thirteen Fires to govern the lands north of the Great River, had established a camp at Fort Washington. There he had accumulated a force of over two thousand fighting men, including two small regiments of regular infantry (about six hundred men) plus another fourteen hundred assorted members of Kentucky militia units and "volunteers." In addition, the Shawnees learned that the encampment also contained many women. Some of the soldiers had brought their wives; other women sought work as cooks and laundresses, and there were considerable numbers of "painted women" who also plied their services to such a large assemblage of potential customers. As the summer dragged on, many of the militia and volunteers drifted away, but in Binakiwi-geesis, the Moon of Falling Leaves (October 1791), St. Clair started north, leading about fourteen hundred men, accompanied by many of the laundresses and camp followers. Shawnee scouts monitored their advance and reported that as cold rains drenched the column, the militia and volunteers continued to desert, but in Gashkaindo-gisiss, the Moon of Hard Frosts (November 1791), as the Long Knife army reached the headwaters of the Wabash, their numbers (regulars, militia, and volunteers) still approached fourteen hundred men.

Heron Who Waits still wondered at the Long Knives' ineptitude. They camped for the night in a small meadow in the forest, an open region through which a shallow creek flowed—a campsite providing them with water but an area with little natural cover, surrounded by dense woods and underbrush. Scouts watched as St. Clair sent out patrols from his perimeter, but they easily eluded the shivering, hungry Long Knives. One sentry fired at a Delaware in the forest, but the warrior fled and the sentry later reported that it was only a "single thievin Indin probly tryin to steal some bacon." The sentries pulled back to the camp's perimeter, and many spent a cold night, mostly huddled by their fires, ignoring the woods that surrounded them.

It was a serious mistake. Heron Who Waits recalled that in the cold pre-dawn darkness, he and hundreds of other warriors (Shawnees, Delawares, Mingos, Potawatomis, Ottawas, Ojibwes, Miamis, Kickapoos, and other tribes-men) completely surrounded the clearing. As dawn broke, they watched as the Long Knives awakened, picked up their arms, and laid them aside as they built fires to prepare their morning meals. Little Turtle, the great Miami war chief, sounded the war cry, and Heron Who Waits and other warriors opened fire from the forest, then charged into the militiamen who were camped on the west side of the stream, apart from the regulars and the supply wagons. Heron Who Waits dodged a heavy-set, homespun-clad volunteer who lunged at him with a pitchfork, and as the man stumbled past him, he pivoted and struck the man in the back of his head with his tomahawk. The man dropped like an over-ripe persimmon. He then turned, seeking another opponent, but an older Kickapoo war chief fighting at his side shouted a warning: "The Blue Coat soldiers are coming. Fall back to the tree line."

Heron Who Waits and the other warriors retreated to the shelter of the trees, but as the blue-coated regulars advanced with fixed bayonets, the warriors poured a murderous fire on them, and the blue line faltered, then fell back across the stream toward the center of the clearing. The Shawnee warrior watched as panicked militiamen and volunteers tried to hide under the supply wagons, but the painted women, many of whom had taken up muskets and were firing back at the tribesmen, became angry with the frightened Kaintucks and kicked the remains of the cooking fires under the wagons to force the cowards to stand and fight. But the fires then ignited the supply wagons, creating further chaos in the Long Knives' ranks. Meanwhile, still sheltered behind the trees, Heron Who Waits and other warriors sent a deadly fire into both the regulars and militia.

Frightened and confused, the Long Knives fired back into the forest, shooting blindly at assailants they could scarcely see. A small group of gunners attempted to train several small cannon on the surrounding forest, but tribal marksmen killed their officers, and when the enlisted men discharged the fieldpieces, the cannon were aimed so high that the cannon balls and shot struck the trees far above the warriors' heads. Meanwhile, Long Knives and Blue Coats fell before the warriors' muskets and arrows like autumn leaves in a windstorm.

Finally, at midmorning, the Long Knives broke through the Indian perimeter on the eastern side of the clearing and fled for their lives. Heron Who Waits laughed out loud when he remembered that many of the militia units had covered, in the first twenty-four hours of their flight, a distance it had taken ten days to march prior to the battle. Indeed, the rout was so complete that both the fleeing Long Knives and Bluecoats threw away most of their weapons and abandoned all their equipment. Almost seven hundred scalps were taken, and Heron Who Waits returned to his village with enough captured clothing and blankets to outfit his wife and children. He still wore the blue greatcoat he had taken from a fallen officer. Fires burned high, the Shawnees feasted, and the victory drums sounded along the Au Glaize, the Maumee, the Scioto, and the Wabash.

In the brief seasons that followed, the Thirteen Fires again tried to negotiate. But Heron Who Waits and his kinsmen were proud of their victory and answered that the Great River must remain a permanent boundary and the Long Knives must abandon Fort Washington and their settlements east of the Muskingum and return south to Kaintuck. And when Long Knife spokesmen warned that they would send other military expeditions, Heron Who Waits and his kinsmen laughed in their faces, scurrilously inviting them to please send news of their preparations, for the Shawnees wished to arm their women and children with switches so they could again drive the Long Knives back from their homeland. And Heron Who Waits recalled that their Redcoat Father had also been heartened by the Shawnee victories, and in addition to sending more muskets, lead, and powder, he had ordered his soldiers to build a new post, Fort Miamis, near Shawnee and other tribal villages on the Maumee River. Meanwhile, Redcoat Indian agents such as Matthew Elliott and Alexander McKee, men who had taken Shawnee wives and had long been welcome in the Shawnee villages, assured Heron Who Waits and his kinsmen that their Redcoat Father would never desert them.

But then Matchemanitou, the Great Serpent, regained the ascendancy. The Thirteen Fires had chosen a new war chief, a warrior so driven that his own followers believed him to be mad, and he had retrained the Long Knife army. Then slowly, moving like scoutelawamee (the tortoise), this stocky, barrel-chested, heavy-drinking war chief whom the Shawnees called Shemeneto, or the Black Snake, but the Long Knives knew as Anthony Wayne, had marched north from Fort Washington, building a string of fortified supply posts. Heron Who Waits remembered that just one year earlier, in Odeimini-gissis, the Moon of Strawberries (June 1794), he had joined with other Shawnees, Delawares, Ojibwes, Ottawas, and Potawatomis to attack a pack train as it left Fort Recovery, a new post that Shemeneto had built near the site of Little Turtle's great victory over St. Clair. The attack had been successful. The warriors had captured the pack train, but in the aftermath, they had quarreled over the spoils. In response, many of the Ojibwes and Potawatomis had become angry, abandoned the Shawnees and Delawares, and returned to their villages in Michigan.

In retrospect, Heron Who Waits now knew that the quarrel had proven disastrous. Two months later, in Mini-gissis, the Moon of Blackberries (August 1794), Shemeneto had led his Long Knife army to the Au Glaize valley where he burned several Shawnee villages and cut down their corn fields. The Long Knife army numbered almost three thousand fighting men, including artillery and mounted riflemen (dragoons). The Shawnees, Delawares, and Wyandots had convinced some of the Ottawas and Potawatomis to return, and buttressed by some Miamis, they had decided to make a stand near Roche de Bout, just west of the Maumee River, where a violent windstorm had felled a grove of trees, forming a natural barricade to any advancing enemy. In addition, the location was less than four miles upstream from Fort Miamis, so if the warriors were forced to retreat, they could easily fall back to the new British post and make a second stand behind the log palisades, reinforced by the British garrison and resupplied with British ammunition.

The tribesmen, numbering about fifteen hundred warriors took their positions among the fallen timbers on the evening of August 18, expecting the Long Knives to attack during the following morning. With battle imminent, the warriors fasted, preferring to enter the coming fray with empty stomachs, a decision made both for spiritual reasons and because they knew that any abdominal wounds would heal much faster under those conditions. But the wily Shemeneto hesitated and constructed a fortified supply depot. He did not attack on the following day, and when rain fell during the following night, many of the warriors left their positions to return to the British post for food and blankets. When the Long Knives advanced on the rainy morning of August 20, some of the warriors had not yet returned from Fort Miamis. The tribesmen remaining in the grove of fallen timbers numbered less than five hundred warriors.

Heron Who Waits had not gone back to the fort and had spent the night among the fallen trees amid a party of Shawnee warriors near the center of the Indian position. Shortly after dawn, they moved forward and momentarily concealed themselves in underbrush, about fifty yards in front of the tangled tree trunks. Before they could advance any farther, they discovered a party of mounted Kentuckians riding toward the Indian position. Firing from ambush, Heron Who Waits and his kinsmen felled seven of the horsemen, and the others wheeled and fled back toward the Long Knife camp. Remembering the chaos of St. Clair's defeat, Heron Who Waits sprang forward, shouted the war cry, and urged his kinsmen to follow in the horsemen's wake, but as the Shawnees started forward, they saw that the soldiers in the new Long Knife army were a different breed. Behind the horsemen, a long line of Bluecoats now advanced, their muskets fixed with bayonets, while to their left, away from the river, large numbers of other mounted horsemen swept westward in a great arc, intent on flanking the Indian position.

In response, Heron Who Waits and his kinsmen fell back to the protection of the fallen trees, where they fired repeatedly at the advancing Long Knives. During the first hour, they fought furiously. When the Long Knife infantry eventually reached the tangled tree trunks, the fighting was hand to hand, and Heron Who Waits received a bayonet wound in the palm of his right hand, but being left-handed, he sunk his hunting knife into his assailant's chest before the man could pull his bayonet free. Although his musket had misfired, the Shawnee used it as a club and knocked another Long Knife off his horse, clubbed him to death, and took the man's musket to use as his own. But around him, his kinsmen were falling, and the Shawnees and other tribesmen slowly fell back, retreating toward Fort Miamis. There they intended to seek sanctuary in the fort, and supported by the Redcoats, they planned to turn back Shemeneto's march up the Maumee valley.

They were betrayed! Standing on the north bank of the Great River, Heron Who Waits angrily spat into the green water that swirled at his feet and asked the broad stream to carry his rancor downstream to Fort Washington. Bitter memories! He remembered that when he and other Shawnees had retreated from Fallen Timbers back to the new British fort expecting to find Redcoat soldiers and Sauganash militia waiting to assist them, they had been mistaken. Instead, they found the gates of the fort closed and the Redcoat commander, Major William Campbell, unwilling to admit them into the stockade. Dumbfounded, they then retreated downstream to Swan Creek, where they joined their women and children before fleeing north and west, seeking refuge in the Potawatomi homeland. Scouts reported that Shemeneto had led his Bluecoat soldiers and Kaintucks upstream to the post, but he did not attack the palisade. Neither did the Redcoat commander order his troops to fire on the Long Knives. Instead, the pompous fools exchanged papers full of insults, then Shemeneto ordered his soldiers to burn the remaining Shawnee lodges and other tribal villages in the region and to cut down all the Indian cornfields.

In the moons that followed, during the recent winter, the Shawnees suffered through a time of hardship. Although other Redcoat agents from Detroit had provided them with small quantities of corn and bacon, his family often went hungry. Heron Who Waits accepted the foodstuffs, but he cursed the Red Coats. Like many of his kinsmen, he knew he no longer could trust them. During those winter moons, he and other Shawnees had no other choice but to accept the Long Knives' armistice. They ceased their raids, and when Shemeneto demanded that the tribes assemble at Fort Greenville, the new Long Knife post built near the site of their former victory over St. Clair, Heron Who Waits joined with many Shawnees and other tribal people who reluctantly agreed.

Heron Who Waits and his kinsmen spent much of Miskwimini-gissis, the Moon of Raspberries, in the treaty camp. They ate Shemeneto's pork and mutton (Heron Who Waits despised the latter), they drank his wine and whiskey, and they accepted the Long Knives' gifts of knives, hatchets, and trade cloth. They met repeatedly with Shemeneto and other Long Knife war chiefs, and they listened to their promises. Heron Who Waits believed that the Long Knives' promises were no better than their mutton, but in the end, when the speeches had finished, the Shawnees and their allies were forced to make their marks on new papers, and much of their homeland would be taken by the Long Knives.

And so Heron Who Waits had made this final pilgrimage to the Great River of his childhood, the Speleawee-thepee, the river the Senecas, and even the Long Knives now called it the Oheeyo. And on this warm summer day in early

September 1795, as he stood on the northern bank, gazing across at the Kain-tuck shore, he knew he would never again hunt the Blue Grass region. The bar-rier was gone. The Long Knives, the Spawn of the Great Serpent, would now occupy the Center of the Universe. The world was in chaos. The Shawnees had lost their homeland.

Heron Who Waits is, of course, a fictitious, composite character, but the events of his life form an accurate microcosm of the Shawnee experiences in the last quarter of the eighteenth century. For the Shawnees and other tribes in the Ohio River's northern drainage, the river served as a unifying force, a natural ave-nue for communication and transportation. Indeed, even in the pre-Columbian period, various complex, sophisticated cultures had flourished along its banks, and the river had served as the great warp in the fabric of these cultures' exis-tence. Between 500 BCE and 400 CE, the Adena people established towns, erected great earthen mounds, and tended their gardens along the Ohio and its tributaries. They were followed by subsequent cultures such as the Hopewell and the Fort Ancient manifestation of the Mississippian Complex. For all these peoples, the river served as an artery of their existence, facilitating trade and the spread of new ideas from the Appalachians to the Mississippi valley.[5]

But in the historic period, the river proved dichotomous for the Indian peo-ples whose villages graced its headwaters or dotted its tributaries. It contin-ued to serve as an avenue of commerce for both French and British traders who guided their canoes beneath the green hills that shrouded its banks. Yet the metal utensils, firearms, and alcohol carried by these merchants, items that made the tribespeople's lives easier or more pleasurable, also carried the seeds of economic dependency, and after two generations, trade goods that had once seemed luxuries now became necessities.[6] Moreover, from the Shawnees' per-spective, by the final quarter of the eighteenth century, the river had begun to serve as a fountain of bitterness, spewing westward a human tide intent on usurping the Shawnee homeland.[7]

During the American Revolution, the Shawnees struck back, and the tide temporarily turned in their favor. Supported by British officials at Detroit, the Shawnees and their tribal allies swept south across the Ohio, creating havoc within the future Bluegrass State. Known to the Kentuckians as "the bloody year," 1777 witnessed the flight of numerous settlers back across the

Appalachians as war parties plagued the frontier settlements, burning cabins, destroying crops, stealing horses, and slaughtering livestock. In response, George Rogers Clark invaded the Illinois Country in 1778, then seized Vincennes, but lack of logistical support precluded his march on Detroit, and although John Bowman and Clark later led expeditions into Ohio and burned several Shawnee villages, they killed relatively few tribespeople. From 1780 through 1782, those settlers still in Kentucky remained tied to their forts, while the Shawnees and their allies continued to range across the Bluegrass country. As Heron Who Waits believed, for all practical purposes, the British and Indians won the Revolution in the Ohio Valley.[8]

That victory was not reflected at the Treaty of Paris. Eager to end the conflict, in 1783, at the treaty negotiations, the British gave up their territorial claims to the Ohio valley. In response, the Americans argued that the transfer of political hegemony over the region also included the "ownership" of the land; that is, that the very soil on which the Shawnees had built their villages, planted their fields, and used as hunting grounds now belonged to the new United States. Indeed, the Shawnees and other tribal people were only tenants, occupying the region through the grace of their new Great Father. In contrast, British Indian agents such as Matthew Elliott and Alexander McKee assured the Shawnees that the treaty was not meant "to deprive you of an extent of your country, of which the Soil belongs to, and is in yourselves as Sole Proprietors."[9] Accordingly, the stage was set for the ongoing confrontation that would plague Indian-white relations throughout the late eighteenth and nineteenth centuries, and even into the present. Both sides initially believed they possessed a viable and just claim to the land. After 1789, the federal government reluctantly waived the "right of conquest" and agreed that the tribes had the "exclusive right of occupancy, but not the ultimate ownership." Since that time, both sides have continued to dispute just where the boundary between these contesting realms should be drawn.[10]

Initially, however, the government seemed willing to compromise. Faced with overwhelming financial problems and possessing insufficient military forces, officials in Philadelphia (several of whom who had invested in land companies planning to speculate in Ohio real estate) announced that if the Shawnees and other tribespeople surrendered their claims to the region east of the Muskingum River, the government would allow them (at least temporarily) to occupy their homelands in northern and western Ohio. Between 1784 and 1789, government officials conducted a series of questionable treaties (Fort Stanwix, 1784; Fort McIntosh, 1785; Fort Finney, 1786; Fort Harmar, 1789) with a handful of representatives from several tribes, but most Shawnees denounced the agreements and threatened the lives of both the treaty negotiators, and those tribesmen who signed the documents. Meanwhile, American settlement gained a beachhead north of the Ohio River at Cincinnati, near Fort Washington, and at several other locations on the river's northern shore.[11] In addition, filibustering expeditions from Kentucky attacked Shawnee villages along the Great Miami River, but Shawnee, Miami, and Kickapoo warriors retaliated, raiding American settlements, stealing horses, and firing at flatboats on the Ohio. And so, for Heron Who Waits and his kinsmen, the Ohio River became a border, a great divider, and those settlers who persisted did so at their own peril, clustered around a series of small forts that hugged the north bank of the river.[12]

Shawnee resistance was buttressed by the Crown. In the aftermath of the Revolution, Shawnee spokesmen met with leaders from other tribes in Ohio, Michigan, and Indiana and attempted to form a loose confederacy to oppose American aggression. Since the British feared American ambitions toward Canada, they supported the concept of a red confederacy; yet the British found themselves in a quandary. They were eager to retain the loyalty of the western tribes, and British Indian agents at Detroit promised to supply the warriors with arms and ammunition, but higher-ranking British officials at Montreal or London did not wish to become involved in another war with the United States. Therefore, the Crown encouraged the tribes to stand fast against American expansion north of the Ohio River, but they tried to restrain the Shawnees and their allies from attacking settlers traversing the river in flatboats, or from raiding the growing settlements in Kentucky.[13]

The British policy failed. Armed with British weapons and encouraged by British traders and Indian agents whose private promises of assistance overstated the Crown's commitment of support, war parties repeatedly struck at traffic on the Ohio and at the Kentucky frontier. Angered by the Indian intransigence, in 1790 federal officials sent military expeditions against tribal villages along the Wabash and Maumee. In October 1790, Major John Hamtramck led a force of 330 troops from Vincennes up the Wabash valley toward Miami and Potawatomi towns on the Tippecanoe. He destroyed some abandoned Wea (Miami) and Kickapoo villages near the mouth of the Vermilion but then returned to Vincennes before encountering any substantial number of Indians.[14]

In contrast, during the same month, General Josiah Harmer marched north from Fort Washington with an army of 320 regulars and 1,133 Kentucky militia, intent on destroying Miami and Potawatomi villages clustered around the head-waters of the Maumee River, near modern Ft. Wayne, Indiana. Since most of the Miamis and Potawatomis had abandoned their villages and sent their women and children westward to temporary camps along the Elkhart River, Harmar initially encountered few tribesmen, but he burned several abandoned villages. After established a military camp, Harmar sent out several large parties to scour the surrounding countryside. On October 19, 1790, a poorly led force of over two hundred militia and regulars led by Colonel John Hardin was ambushed by a war party comprised of about one hundred Shawnees and Potawatomis. Most of the militia promptly fled, and after a brief firefight, the other Americans also retreated back to Harmar's camp. American casualties numbered almost one hundred, or about half of Hardin's original command. Two days later, in a subsequent battle, another war party of Shawnees, Miamis, Odawas, and Delawares inflicted similar casualties on a force of regulars and militia led by Major John P. Wyllys. After mustering his troops, Harmar learned that since arriving at the forks of the Maumee, he had lost 183 men. With one-fourth of his regulars dead and the militia entirely unreliable, Harmar had had enough. On October 22, he abandoned his camp and retreated back toward Fort Washington.[15]

Embarrassed by Harmar's defeat, federal officials planned another punitive expedition. In March 1791, Congress appropriated over $300,000 to build a series of new posts north of Fort Washington, and to send another military force against the tribal villages along the Maumee and upper Wabash valleys. During the summer of 1791, Arthur St. Clair, the governor of the Northwest Territories, assembled an army of approximately 2,300 men at Fort Washington. The force consisted of two small regiments of regulars and large numbers of six-month volunteers and militia units from Kentucky. The volunteers and militia were poorly trained, and the entire expedition suffered from inadequate and shoddy provisions. In an outstanding display of poor judgement, St. Clair allowed about two hundred women, described as "cooks and laundresses," but also many prostitutes and camp followers to join the expedition. Some of the women were accompanied by their children.[16]

St. Clair left Fort Washington on September 17, 1791. Traveling at a snail's pace, it took the expedition six weeks before they reached the headwaters of the Wabash River, in far western Ohio. Enroute, they were plagued by continual rain, and more than nine hundred of the militia deserted. St. Clair suffered so severely from gout that he had difficulty riding his horse. Late in the afternoon of November 3, they established a campsite, and wary of an attack, St. Clair sent out several patrols to search the immediate area. One of the patrols found "considerable Indian sign" but failed to report this discovery to their commander. Still apprehensive, an hour before sunrise on November 4, St. Clair roused his sleepy men from their blankets and ordered them to be on the alert against an attack at dawn. When no attack occurred, the American officers dismissed the men, and they began to prepare their breakfasts.[17]

Unknown to the Americans, while they slept, over one thousand warriors, including many Shawnees, Potawatomis, and Miamis, had surrounded the encampment and lay watching the troops, concealed by the trees and the underbrush. As the troops were kindling their cooking fires, the war cry sounded, and the underbrush exploded with musket fire. Panic stricken, the militia fell back on the six-month volunteers and regulars, who attempted to form ranks to meet the Indians. Although the warriors' initial assault was repulsed, the Shawnees and their allies continued to fire from the cover of the forest, taking a terrible toll on the soldiers. The battle raged throughout the early morning, but by 9:30 A.M., the American position was untenable. Native American marksmen had killed or wounded hundreds of American soldiers, and the remaining troops huddled together in the middle of the encampment, seeking shelter under the baggage wagons. Finally, St. Clair and his remaining troops broke through the warriors' ranks on the eastern perimeter and fled south toward safety. In their panic, the Americans abandoned their wounded comrades and most of their equipment. By noon, the battle was over.[18]

Ironically, the wholesale abandonment of arms, ammunition, clothing, food, and other supplies may have saved some American lives. So much equipment was abandoned that many of the warriors stopped to examine and collect such material, and it prevented them from mounting an effective pursuit of the fleeing and disorganized Americans. Still, St. Clair's defeat was the greatest Native American victory over an American military force in all of American history. Casualty figures for this encounter remain uncertain, but the United States lost at least 647 men killed, with hundreds more wounded. About one-quarter of the standing army of the United States suffered fatal casualties in this single encounter. The number of women and children killed is unknown. The Indian confederacy lost fewer than 125 warriors.[19]

In the wake of St. Clair's defeat, American officials again turned to diplomacy. In September 1792, they signed a Treaty of Peace and Friendship with some western Potawatomis, Weas, and Piankashaws (Miami) chiefs from the lower Wabash, but the treaty had little meaning since these tribesmen had remained peaceful and had not supported the anti-American confederacy.[20] Further east, federal commissioners met with delegates from the Shawnees and other tribes near Detroit, where the tribesmen argued among themselves over what position to take against the Americans. Some of the more northern tribes, people whose lands were not immediately threatened by American expansion, were willing to give up their claims to lands in southern Ohio and Indiana, while the Shawnees, Miamis, Kickapoos, Delawares, and others demanded that the Ohio River remain a viable boundary. Rejecting federal offers to buy more land in Ohio, the Shawnees suggested that federal officials take the money they had offered to the tribes for lands in Ohio and use it pay American settlers to resettle south of the Ohio River. According to the tribesmen, such payments would be considerably less than "the great sums you must expend in raising and paying armies" in the futile attempts to force the tribespeople from Ohio.[21]

Admitting that negotiations had failed, the federal government again looked for a military solution. This time they were more successful. In late March 1792, Secretary of War Henry Knox appointed Anthony Wayne as a major general in the United States Army and gave him the task of extending American control over the Ohio country. Although Wayne awaited the outcome of the negotiations between federal officials and the tribes before taking any overt action, he spent considerable time and effort in rebuilding the army and instilling discipline among its ranks. Moreover, in preparation for an upcoming campaign, during the fall of 1793 he built two new posts in western Ohio: Fort Greenville, about seventy-five miles north of modern Cincinnati, and Fort Recovery, at the site of St. Clair's recent defeat. Meanwhile, he stockpiled supplies and made careful preparations to attack the tribal villages along the Auglaize and Maumee during the following summer.[22]

Aware of Wayne's preparations and concerned over American aspirations toward Canada, British officials took pains to assure the confederacy of the Crown's support. In February 1794, Lord Dorchester met with Indian leaders in Quebec and rashly implied that the British would assist them. As proof of that commitment, during April, Royal Engineers began construction of a new post, Fort Miamis, on the lower Maumee, near modern Toledo. When news of the British actions reached the tribal villages, even tribesmen who had been tempted by the American peace offers now rejected any compromise.[23]

Assuming that an American campaign against tribal villages along the Maumee and Auglaize was imminent, in June 1794, large numbers of warriors assembled on the Maumee River, just upstream from Fort Miamis, and on June 30, a large war party left their camp and journeyed to Fort Recovery, where they launched an unsuccessful attack on the palisade but captured over three hundred horses. In the aftermath, a split developed in the Indian ranks. The Potawatomis, Odawas, and Ojibwes had led in the assault on the fort and had suffered most of the casualties. In contrast, the Delawares and Shawnees had surprised a pack train approaching from Fort Greenville and seized most of the horses. In consequence, the three northern tribes accused the Delawares and Shawnees of cowardice and demanded a greater share of the captured livestock. When the latter refused, the Potawatomis, Odawas, and Ojibwes abandoned the siege and returned to the Maumee, where many then withdrew from the assembled Indian army and returned to their villages in Michigan.[24]

Wayne marched north from Fort Greenville in early August, then halted at the mouth of the Auglaize where his troops built a new post, Fort Defiance. After destroying several tribal villages in the region, in mid-August Wayne proceeded down the Maumee toward Fallen Timbers, a site near Roche de Bout where a tornado had previously felled a stand of trees on the bluff overlooking the river. Although several hundred Potawatomis, Odawas, and Ojibwes had defected after the dispute at Fort Recovery, the Indian ranks still numbered over twelve hundred warriors, and on August 18, they took defensive positions amidst the fallen trees, expecting Wayne to attack. Wayne approached to within three miles of the Indian position but then stopped to build a small supply depot (Fort Deposit) before moving forward. Within the tangle of fallen trees and underbrush, the warriors fasted and waited for two days (August 18 and 19), but by the evening of the nineteenth, many grew restless, and when thunderstorms swept through the region in the evening, many left their positions and returned downstream to Fort Miamis to seek food and shelter.[25]

It was a serious error in judgement. When Wayne attacked on the morning of August 20, many of the warriors had not yet returned, and of the original twelve hundred tribesmen who originally had opposed his advance, fewer than four hundred, in addition to a small contingent of British traders, were waiting to meet him. In contrast, Wayne's army numbered just under three thousand. The battle began at mid-morning. The tribesmen pushed the initial advance by a party of mounted Kentucky volunteers back into the ranks of the regulars, but the latter held their lines, then advanced forward. Attempts by the tribesmen to outflank the American advance were turned back by mounted volunteers and dragoons, and as the warriors fell back, Wayne ordered his infantry to fix their bayonets and push forward. Overwhelmed, some warriors fought on, but after about ninety minutes, others retreated toward Fort Miamis, where they expected the British garrison to give them sanctuary.[26]

They were mistaken. Afraid of sparking a war with the United States, Major William Campbell refused to open the fort's gates. Stunned, the tribesmen hesitated below the fort's walls, then retreated down the Maumee to Swan Creek, where many gathered their families, then fled north into Michigan. Others scattered eastward into northern Ohio. Meanwhile, Wayne and Campbell traded veiled threats and guarded insults, but both were wary of igniting a much larger conflict. Campbell remained behind his fortress walls, while Wayne spent the next few days burning the remaining Indian villages in the region and destroying their adjoining cornfields. He returned to Fort Defiance on August 27. Losses on both sides were similar. The Americans suffered forty-four killed and eighty-nine wounded. Indian casualties are harder to ascertain, but probably ranged somewhere between fifty to sixty killed and wounded. But the number of casualties was overshadowed by the warriors' retreat and Campbell's refusal to give them shelter. Fallen Timbers was a major American victory. It illustrated to the tribesmen that although the British were generous with their promises, they were faithless in honoring them.[27]

In October 1794, the United States established a new post, Fort Wayne, at the headwaters of the Maumee, and Wayne sent messages to the tribes, reminding them that the British "had neither the power nor inclination to protect you." He also invited the tribesmen to make peace and to negotiate a new treaty with the Americans. British agents at Detroit attempted to counter Wayne's diplomacy by sending food and other supplies to the Indian winter camps, but their efforts failed. The hungry tribesmen accepted the food, but they wanted no more British promises. A few war parties of Kickapoos and western Potawatomis continued to make desultory raids against settlers in southern Illinois, but they were the exception, not the rule.[28]

In mid-July 1795, over five hundred Shawnees, Miamis, Delawares, Wyandots, Potawatomis, Odawas, Ojibwes, Kickapoos, and other tribesmen assembled at Greenville, and after two weeks of feasting, alcohol consumption, fireworks displays, and negotiations, tribal leaders made their marks as signatories to the Treaty of Greenville. The tribes ceded all claims to lands in the southeastern two-thirds of Ohio and a small tract of land in extreme southeastern Indiana. They also gave the federal government permission to construct new military posts at several strategic locations, including Chicago, Fort Wayne, Michilimackinac, and Peoria. In exchange, the government promised to provide the tribesmen with annuities (annual payments of cash and trade goods) and assured them that they could occupy and "enjoy" their unceded lands north of the Ohio, "hunting, planting, and dwelling thereon so long as they please, without any molestation from the United States."[29]

The Battle of Fallen Timbers and subsequent Treaty of Greenville (August 3, 1795) sounded the death knell for any meaningful attempts by the tribes to retain their homelands north of the Ohio River. From the colonial period through the end of the eighteenth century, the tribes had used their position as middlemen, valuable economic and military assets, to leverage their own independence within the broader and continually shifting balance of power between contesting colonial empires. The Shawnees and other tribes had repeatedly played the French against the British, then the British against the new United States. Their ability to provide sufficient military force to tip the fulcrum in favor of either side enabled them to gain access to European weapons and to retain hegemony over their homelands.

After Fallen Timbers and the Treaty of Greenville such leverage ended. The balance of power shifted dramatically in the Americans' favor. In the decades following the Treaty of Greenville, white settlement poured into the lower Midwest. In 1790, Kentucky's population was 73,677; in 1800, it surged to 220,959; in 1810, 406,511. Census reports for the three states just north of the Ohio River are unavailable for 1790, but their populations also expanded during the first decade of the nineteenth century. In 1800, five years after Greenville, Ohio's population reached 45,356; by 1810, it had burgeoned to 230,760. Indiana increased from 2,632 in 1800 to 24,520 by 1810, while Illinois grew from 2,458 to 12,282 during the same period. Census reports for Native Americans in this region are lacking, but evidence suggests that during the decade and a half following the Treaty of Greenville, due to emigration and disease it actually declined. The best estimate by modern scholars is probably less than twenty thousand. In any prolonged military contest, Native Americans faced overwhelming odds. The tribesmen's fate was sealed.[30]

In addition, they could no longer rely on the British as a counterbalance to the Americans. Following Jay's Treaty (November 19, 1794), the British agreed to withdraw from Detroit, Michilimackinac, and other American posts they had illegally occupied since the American Revolution, and their presence in the region was much diminished. They established a new post, Fort Malden, at Amherstburg in Ontario, across the river from Detroit, and they attempted to maintain their influence among the tribes, but it waned. During the War of 1812, those warriors led by Tecumseh accepted British assistance in their desperate, last-ditch, but futile attempt to repel the tide of American settlement pouring into their remaining homelands; and again the Redcoats proved unreliable. In September 1813, as the British prepared to flee before an impending American invasion of Canada, Tecumseh angrily confronted British officers at Fort Malden and denounced them. Reminding Colonel Henry Proctor that after Fallen Timbers, when the retreating warriors had sought refuge at Fort Miamis, "the gates were shut against us," Tecumseh demanded that the British either stand and fight or give their guns and ammunition to the warriors. In response, two weeks later, Procter and the British made a half-hearted stand, but in the resulting Battle of the Thames, the British troops fired three scattered volleys, then fled before even discharging their artillery. The warriors stood and fought, and in the battle, Tecumseh was killed. Afterward, Indian resistance faded. No longer envisioned as major allies in the colonial struggle for North America, the tribesmen were reduced to a secondary role, pawns to be used and discarded.[31]

The die was cast. In the decades following Fallen Timbers and the Treaty of Greenville, white settlement flooded into the tribal homelands. During the first decades of the nineteenth century, the Shawnees and other tribes were forced to sign over fifty treaties ceding their lands in Ohio, Indiana, Michigan, and Illinois. Although some tribal communities were able to retain reservations in more northern regions (Michigan and Wisconsin), during the 1830s and 1840s, most other tribal people were removed west of the Mississippi River. After 1850, most non-Indian residents of this region associated Native Americans only with a romanticized past, people whose languages provided interesting place names or exotic folk encountered on vacation trips to northern Michigan

Tecumseh, by Brenson J. Lossing. This composite portrait of Tecumseh comprised sketches made by Pierre le Dru during his lifetime and is considered to be the most accurate portrait of the Shawnee leader. Titled the le Dru–Lossing portrait, it was first published in Benson J. Lossing, *Pictorial Field Book of the War of 1812* (New York: Harper and Brothers, 1869).

or Wisconsin.[32] Their cultural footprints remained, but most tribal people (at least temporarily) were gone from their homeland.[33]

As the afternoon lengthened and a summer thunderstorm darkened the river bluffs over the distant Kaintuck shore, Heron Who Waits ended his reverie and prepared to begin his journey back up the network of trails that traversed the Little Miami River valley to his village in northwestern Ohio. He propped his musket against a fallen log and descended the riverbank to fill a brass flask that served as his canteen, but as he glanced upriver, he was surprised to see two flatboats, floating downstream, less than thirty yards offshore. He stood quietly as the vessels, laden with settlers and their possessions, neared his vantage point. Their untrained helmsmen (settlers themselves, not river pilots) were intent on reaching the new settlement of Cincinnati, less than ten miles downstream, and had carelessly approached too close to the forested Ohio shore.

Heron Who Waits marveled at their inexperience. For over two decades, he and other Shawnee warriors had often waited amid these forests, lying in ambush for the flatboats that carried Long Knives down the Great River to Kaintuck, and he had rarely seen these ungainly, flat-bottomed vessels so near to an uninhabited shoreline. Well, Red Pole, Blue Jacket, Black Hoof and other Shawnee leaders had made their marks on the treaty, and the days of the hatchet were past, but he also knew that if the two boats continued to follow so closely to the Ohio riverbank, they would run aground on a series of hidden sand bars that stretched out from the northern bank less than two miles downstream from his current location. Indeed, as he remembered, the heavily thicketed riverbank adjacent to the sand bars had once been a favorite place for war parties to waylay flatboats—but again, those days were over. The treaty had been signed. He would live with it.

Deciding to warn the flatboats of the hazard, Heron Who Waits stepped into the open and shouted (in Shawnee), "The Great River ahead is shallow! Go back to deeper water." He watched as the Long Knives on the flatboats, obviously alarmed, scrambled like frightened quail, then peered over the low sides of the rafts or hid behind the small huts built in the vessels' midsections. Now realizing that they had no knowledge of Shawnee and did not understand his warning, Heron Who Waits stepped closer to the riverbank, faced the boats, held both arms aloft over his head, and waved his arms forward, as if he were trying to force the boats away from the Ohio shore and out into deeper water. He again shouted that the water ahead was too shallow, and he moved his right hand down to his knee, then repeatedly pushed his open palm down toward his foot, which any Shawnee boy in his village would know meant "shallow water."

The Long Knife reply was not what he expected. While the helmsman on the second boat turned his long steering oar to guide the boat away from the bank and toward the middle of the river, the frightened farmer steering the leading boat abandoned his oar and took shelter behind a large barrel. Meanwhile, another passenger, an older man with shaggy gray hair, peered over the siderail of the leading boat and shouted, "Injun attack! Injun attack! I've heard that war cry before when I fought 'em on the Kanawha."

An older woman, also a passenger on the first boat answered, "Well look Henry, he don't have no musket. He's just waving at us." But the gray-haired man behind the siderail angrily barked, "I've spent my life fightin' these devils. He's a bad one. He's tryin' to push us away from our new lands in Ohio." The man then called back to the cowering helmsman, "Shoot him Lucas, you got the musket. He's standing right there on the riverbank."

Surprised by the passengers' response, Heron Who Waits first paused, but when he saw the helmsman reach for a musket, he scrambled up the riverbank and dodged behind a Sycamore tree. He then heard a gunshot, followed by the sound of a musket ball striking the tree trunk. Although his own musket was primed, and the passengers were easy targets, he didn't return the fire. He watched in silence as the flatboat, which had now lost its steering oar, floated on down the river, heading for the sand bars. Heron Who Waits scowled. Let the Great River take care of these intruders. Like all Shawnees, he believed that large bodies of water held Matche-manitou, the Great Serpents, and that these beings were eager to spread evil in the world. They lay in wait for people who upset the order of things. Sometimes they carried them to the river bottom. Shawnee shamans had warned that these serpents often lurked in the Great River. Hmphh! Let these Long Knives continue on downstream. The sandbars were waiting.

Yet as Heron Who Waits left the Great River and journeyed back toward his village, he had second thoughts about the recent treaty. Although Shemeneto and the other Long Knife spokesmen who had met with the tribes at Greenville had talked of peace and friendship, Heron Who Waits doubted if such harmony could ever be achieved. Perhaps too much blood already had been spilled. Perhaps Shawnees and Long Knives were not meant to live together. He knew he had little interest in planting crops like the Long Knife settlers. He had listened as Moravian, Quaker, and other Long Knife Blackcoats had long encouraged his people to "settle down," raise stinking pigs, and grow fields of corn and other vegetables, but he still believed that scratching in the dirt and similar labors were for women or white men—not warriors. He had also listened to the promises of Long Knife spokesmen at Greenville, and he had made peace, but he had not agreed to give up all the old ways.

And not all the Shawnee leaders had attended the treaty proceedings. At Fallen Timbers, he had fought beside a younger Shawnee war chief who encouraged his followers to stand and fight, had been reluctant to flee, and then had attacked and stolen horses from the Long Knife artillery. This chief had refused to attend the treaty proceedings and had established a new village in the Maumee valley. The village was not large, but its residents were conservative Shawnees, people like Heron Who Waits, people who would honor the treaty and keep the peace but who wanted to follow the traditional Shawnee way of life. Heron Who Waits knew that the young warrior came from good stock. He had fought beside the man's father and his brother at the great battle (Point Pleasant) near the mouth of the Kanawha. Puckeshinewa had died from wounds he received during that battle, and tragically, Chicksika had been killed several winters later, while fighting against the Long Knives in the South. Meanwhile, this younger son of Puckeshinewa and brother of Chicksika had grown to manhood. He had emerged as a respected younger war chief, a man known for his bravery, and he was wise beyond his years. Recently, the man had moved his village to a new site on the Mad River. Heron Who Waits planned to join him at the village.

The man's name was Tecumseh.

Suggested Readings

Edmunds, R. David. *Tecumseh and the Quest for Indian Leadership.* Boston: Little, Brown, 1984.

Hinderaker, Eric. *Elusive Empires: Constructing Colonialism in the Ohio Valley, 1673–1800.* New York: Cambridge University Press, 1997.

Lamomaki, Sami. *Gathering Together: The Shawnee People through Diaspora and Nationhood, 1600–1870.* New Haven, CT: Yale University Press, 2014.

Sugden, John. *Blue Jacket: Warrior of the Shawnees.* Lincoln: University of Nebraska Press, 2000.

Sword, Wiley. *President Washington's Indian War.* Norman: University of Oklahoma Press, 1985.

Warren, Stephen. *The Shawnees and Their Neighbors, 1795–1870.* Urbana: University of Illinois Press, 2005.

FIVE

Westbrooks Awash on a Trail of Tears

Tragedy and Tenacity in the Cherokee Nation

Snow flurries whipped through the barren branches that crowded the wagon trail, and the horses' breaths formed small clouds of ice crystals that were swept away by the wind gusting down the mountainside. Huddled in her multilayered cocoon of petticoats, a dress, woolen shawls, and a heavy blanket, Ida Westbrook still shivered from the cold as the wagon jolted along the frozen ruts that stretched on through the forest. She was hungry, but during the past six months, she had grown accustomed to such an emptiness, and she prayed that when her party finally arrived at Fort Gibson, in Indian Territory, they would be furnished with adequate supplies of corn meal and bacon. Perhaps their hunger would be ended. She was less certain that the great darkness that shrouded her heart would be so easily brightened. One year ago, in February 1838, Ida had believed that the Cherokee Nation had reached the nadir of its existence. Since then, she had learned that she had been mistaken.

For Ida Westbrook and the other Cherokee people who trudged southwestward across Arkansas in early February 1839, the world was full of uncertainty. Thirteen years ago, when Ida was nineteen, she had married Jonathan Westbrook, whose family, like her own, was of Cherokee-English descent. Since both families were Christians, the wedding took place in the Congregational Church, near her father's grist mill and farm, on a tributary of the Conasauga River in northwestern Georgia. Her father, William Harris, had been born in Pennsylvania but emigrated to the Cherokee country in 1805, where he had met and married her mother, the half-blood daughter of a prominent Scots-Irish trader. Her mother's mother, Ida's maternal grandmother, had been a full-blood Cherokee woman and a member of the Deer Clan. Settling down in the Conasauga valley, Ida's parents raised a family of five children (two others had died as infants), but since her father had been born in Pennsylvania and her mother's father also was of non-Cherokee descent, Ida's family were associated with the small but growing community of other mixed-lineage tribespeople.

Yet both her mother and her grandmother endeavored to maintain their ties to their (and her) clan, and Ida was fluent in Cherokee, for when she was a child, these women spoke only in their native language when they conversed with her. In addition to her mother and grandmother, she was surrounded by maternal aunts who also took particular pains to instruct her in the ways of a Cherokee woman and who took her to the Green Corn Dance and other traditional ceremonies. Sweet memories! They warmed her heart. As a young mother, she had promised that she would do her best to ensure that Sarah, her own daughter, would also be surrounded by loving grandmothers and aunts, but now those promises were gone. Like the old Cherokee homeland, those happy sunlit days had been left behind, buried beneath a trail of tears.

In contrast, her Anglo-American father had wanted his children to obtain at least the rudiments of a formal frontier education, and he had hired an itinerant schoolteacher from Baltimore to instruct both Ida and her brothers and sisters. The teacher wandered away after only one year, but encouraged by her father, Ida learned to read and write in English, and when she was twelve, her father enrolled her and her older brother in the school at Brainerd Mission, a Congregational institution just north of the Georgia border, on Chickamauga Creek in Tennessee.

At first, Ida had been reluctant to leave her home in the Conasauga valley. She initially had difficulty in adjusting to the school's strict rules and regulations and in scheduling her day to the missionaries' strange obsessions with time and punctuality. Yet she remained at the school for three years, eventually adapting to a regimen that resembled boarding schools in other frontier communities. She lived in a cabin with six other girls and a matron and followed a curriculum that combined "domestic arts" with religious instruction and more academic subjects. The students arose at sunrise, attended a prayer service, then worked at various chores until eight o'clock when they ate breakfast. During most of her enrollment at Brainerd, Ida was assigned to the kitchen, where she helped to prepare much of the food consumed by the missionaries and the two dozen students in residence. Ida remembered that following breakfast, she looked forward to the classroom instruction, and although she disliked mathematics, she did enjoy reading from the Bible and from other volumes at the school, such as Milton's *Paradise Lost* or books of poetry by Robert Burns and William Cowper.

Ida recalled that after the noon meal, she assisted with cleaning the kitchen and dining area, then resumed her studies until later in the afternoon. Since the school followed the Lancasterian method, Ida sometimes assisted in the instruction of younger students, and in retrospect, she valued the experience, for after her own children were born, she was able to provide them with similar training. Like most other Cherokee girls in attendance, Ida already was familiar with spinning, weaving, and sewing, but late in the afternoon, before again assisting in food preparation, she enjoyed the forty-minute period during which the missionaries' wives instructed the girls in such fine arts as quilting or embroidery. After the evening meal, Ida helped clean the kitchen and attended vespers, and at nine o'clock, following the school's regulations, she went to bed.

Ida never remembered her years at Brainerd with the same fondness that she always associated with her interaction with her grandmother and aunts, but she did admit that her enrollment at the mission school had markedly changed her life. She made several good friends at the institution, including Effie Westbrook, a girl one year older than she, whose family lived near Oothcaloga, south of the Coosawatie River. Through her friendship with Effie, she had met Jonathan Westbrook, her friend's older brother, who was not enrolled at Brainerd, but who earlier had attended the Reverend John Gambold's school at Spring Place. Nine years older than Ida, Jonathan had already established himself as a successful planter, and she remembered the first time that she saw him, a tall, handsome man dressed in a dark blue frock coat, a white shirt, and a waistcoat, but also wearing a dark red turban, comfortable broadcloth trousers, and beautifully tanned deerskin moccasins. They were married two years later and settled down on Jonathan's farm on the Coosawatie River, near New Echota, where Jonathan soon opened a store.

At first, things had gone well. As the demand for upland cotton increased, Jonathan had increased the size of his fields, purchasing four slaves to assist in his farming. He also had planted an additional acreage of corn, and buttressed by the small but growing business at their trading post, the Westbrooks prospered. In 1828, after only two years of marriage, they built a large, two-story log house as a new residence, converting their former single-story cabin into a larger store and warehouse. Their farm (or as Jonathan preferred, their "plantation") contained about one hundred acres of cultivated lands, a pasture, and a small woodlot. The farm also included their new home, their converted store/warehouse, two small slave cabins, a smoke house, a large barn, sheds for their hogs and poultry, a large garden, and a small apple and peach orchard.[1]

Her husband's standing in the mixed-blood community reflected his economic prosperity. In 1819, after ceding over four million acres of land in Georgia, North Carolina, Alabama, and Tennessee, those Cherokees who still resided on their homelands had assumed that both the federal and state governments would allow them to remain on their lands in the east. Accordingly, her husband and the other members of the planter elite who dominated the Cherokee National Committee passed a series of laws that strengthened the central authority of the Cherokee Council and created a "national" Cherokee government. That government was funded by annuity payments made to the tribe for lands previously ceded to the federal government. It was also financed through a series of limited internal taxes, enacted by the National Committee. In 1827, the committee passed a constitution that created a new tribal government modeled after the federal government of the United States. The constitution established a legislative branch, or National Council, composed of representatives elected from eight geographic-political districts within the remaining Cherokee lands in Georgia, Alabama, North Carolina, and Tennessee. The constitution also created a judicial branch and provided for a principal chief to be elected to a four-year term of office by the National Council. Lands within the Cherokee Nation were still held communally by the tribe, but improvements on the land were the property of those Cherokees who made them, and these individuals were given the right to occupy farms or plantations which they improved.[2]

Ida remembered that those had been exciting but sometimes trying times. Jonathan had been much involved in drumming up support for the new constitution, and in the decade following their wedding, he had spent so much time away from home on Cherokee National Committee business that she had often been forced to step in and supervise the production of corn or cotton on their farm when he was gone. Ida sometimes resented his absence, but she grudgingly admitted that she had been forced to learn the ins and outs of growing corn and cotton. She had also gained valuable experience in managing and supervising their four slaves (three men and one woman), and unlike some of their neighbors, she soon learned that her slaves responded more favorably

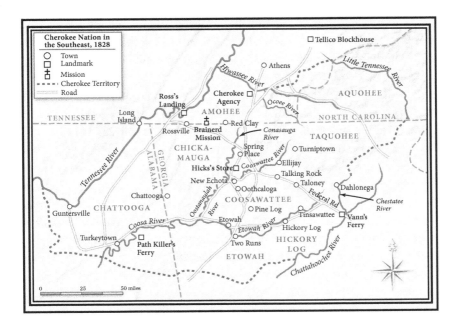

to good food and decent treatment than to intimidation and punishment. Yet their marriage was strong, she remembered. They weathered the short separations. She was convinced that her husband's efforts were necessary. She believed that such endeavors would provide her people with a progressive, civilized political system, a more centralized government that would ensure that the Cherokees would be able to maintain control over their homeland in Georgia, Tennessee, and Alabama.

Ida knew that many members of her mother's family disagreed. Still subscribing to more traditional ways, most of her aunts, cousins, and their husbands feared that the Cherokees' age-old adherence to clan and local villages was being threatened by the planter-merchant elite's emphasis on statutory laws and political centralization. In addition, many of these more traditional tribespeople had grown suspicious of the Protestant missionaries whom they argued had led the mixed-bloods astray. Her cousins particularly resented the missionaries' opposition to the yearly cycle of tribal ceremonies, dances, and ballgames, and they sometimes asserted that the missionaries' influence over the mixed-bloods had become so pervasive that the two groups (missionaries and mixed-bloods) had formed an alliance to radically transform just what it meant to be Cherokee. In contrast, her husband and his friends argued that they didn't wish to leave all the old traditions behind but that their people must make some changes if they wished to acquire the economic and political means to defend the remaining Cherokee homeland.

During the mid-1820s, in the years immediately preceding the passage of the new constitution, the traditionalists rallied around the loose leadership of White Path, an elderly, highly respected village chief from Turniptown, near Elijay in the Coosawatee District of the nation. Ida remembered that most traditionalists' complaints had been loosely focused but seemed to center around the consolidation of political power in the National Council and away from the influence of local village chiefs. In contrast, her cousins had been particularly resentful of the Congregational and Moravian missionaries who openly criticized Cherokee religious leaders and who tried to discourage tribespeople from practicing the old rituals and ceremonies still central to many Cherokees' belief systems. The traditionalists had attempted to organize a tribal council in opposition to the National Council, but their efforts failed. White Path's influence declined. But Ida knew that many of her mother's family still consulted the didahnesigi, the sorcerers, and still believed that the Creator had made the man Ksanati to be a hunter and the woman Selu to grow corn and that the Cherokees still should follow the ancient ways of their fathers.

Yet the mixed-bloods, the progressives, the party of her husband, had prevailed, and following the passage of the new constitution, John Ross, a close personal friend of Jonathan, was elected as the principal chief of the Cherokee Nation. Those were exciting times. The new constitution strengthened the Cherokees' central government, and Ida occasionally accompanied Jonathan when he visited New Echota, the Cherokee capital.

Established in 1825 at the site of Gansagi, a smaller Cherokee village, New Echota stood at the headwaters of the Coosa River and featured a large council house, the Cherokee supreme court, an inn, several general merchandise stores, a ferry, a growing cluster of private homes and cabins, and the office and press of the *Cherokee Phoenix*, the official newspaper of the Cherokee Nation. The village usually was relatively quiet, but when the National Council was in session it filled with council members, sometimes accompanied by their wives. Ida enjoyed the hustle and bustle of Cherokee politics, an opportunity to make or renew old acquaintances, and a chance to shop for merchandise unavailable at the smaller, more rural general stores near their farm.

She particularly enjoyed visiting with Susan Hicks, a former classmate from Brainerd, whose husband owned a grist mill and the largest retail merchandise establishment in the village.

Ida also remembered that she initially had enjoyed visiting the offices of the *Cherokee Phoenix* and chatting with Elias Boudinot, the editor of the paper, and his wife, Harriet, whom Boudinot had met and married while attending a Congregational boarding school in Connecticut. Written in both Cherokee and English, the *Phoenix* was published weekly, and in addition to reprinting excerpts from eastern newspapers, legislation passed by the National Council, legal documents, biblical tracts, and editorials, it also contained classified advertisements and even occasional items of gossip. Ida found the Boudinots to be an interesting couple, but after 1832, their friendship ended as the Boudinots sided with the Ridge family and other proponents of removal in outspoken opposition to her husband and John Ross. She found the political views of Elijah Hicks, Ross's brother-in-law, the new editor of the *Phoenix* to be more palatable than Boudinot's, but Hicks was a boring conversationalist, and after Boudinot resigned, she rarely visited the paper's office.

But events beginning in 1828 changed their lives forever. Thinking back over the past decade, Ida realized that both she and her husband had been naïve when they trusted in the federal government. They had believed that the government would never betray them, deprive them of their property, or drive them from their homeland. But they had been wrong. First, in 1828, came the election of Andrew Jackson (Jonathan still called him Gadohi Advsiqua, the "land hog," the devil who gobbles up people's farms and cabins). Then, in the spring of 1829, gold was discovered along the Chestatee River, near Dahlonega, just inside the eastern boundary of the Cherokee Nation in Georgia. Inspired both by the lure of sudden riches and the opportunity to expand its hegemony, in December 1829, Georgia arbitrarily asserted state sovereignty over the Cherokee homeland, and when John Ross, her husband, and other members of the National Council protested to federal officials, they were informed that the federal government would not protect them.

Those were dark days, and Ida remembered how white squatters first crossed over from the gold fields near Dahlonega into the Coosawatie valley, initially erecting their shanties on unclaimed land, then usurping fields that had been cleared and even planted by her husband and other Cherokees. Jonathan, neighboring planters, and many smaller Cherokee farmers joined together and attempted to drive the squatters away, but then the Georgia state militia intervened, and although the intruders had temporarily withdrawn from lands the Cherokees had already cleared or fenced, they remained on adjoining "unimproved lands" within the Cherokee Nation. Meanwhile Jonathan and other Cherokee landholders were warned by state officials that if they took further actions against the squatters, they would be arrested and imprisoned by the state of Georgia.

At least the crisis had reunited her family. Many of her more traditional cousins who earlier had questioned the mixed-blood planters' policies now rallied behind "the new Cherokee patriots": John Ross, her husband, and other members of the National Council who were determined to defend the Cherokee homeland. Supported by Samuel Worcester and other missionaries, the National Council fought the state of Georgia in the federal courts. First, the United States denied their status as an independent nation. And then, although the Supreme Court had decreed that the federal government should protect the Cherokee people against the state of Georgia, President Jackson—Gadohi Advisqua, the great land hog—refused to enforce the court's decision.

Meanwhile, in 1830, Congress passed the Indian Removal Act, and state and local politicians in Georgia, encouraged by such federal legislation, grew increasingly aggressive. Ida shuddered as she recalled how the Georgia state legislature had passed laws forbidding the Cherokees to mine any of the gold that might be discovered on their land, forbidding the Cherokee National Council to even assemble, and forbidding Cherokees from testifying on their own behalf in any lawsuit involving a white man. The Georgia legislature had also commissioned a survey of all the acreage on remaining Cherokee lands within the state, then authorized a subsequent lottery through which the Westbrook's plantation and other Cherokee farms eventually would be raffled off to white Georgians. Attempting to circumvent Georgia's aggression, in 1832 the National Council moved the nation's capital from New Echota to Red Clay, just across the state line in Tennessee. Red Clay was still within the Cherokee Nation, and Jonathan had assured her that regardless of Georgia's recent legislation, the Council could safely meet there; the state of Georgia had no jurisdiction in Tennessee. But the pressure on her people continued. The Georgia militia rode roughshod over the Cherokee Nation, occupied the former council house at New Echota, and forced both mission and tribal schools to close. In August 1835, they confiscated the printing press at the *Cherokee Phoenix*.

Eventually, part of her people succumbed. Convinced that the Cherokees no longer could remain in Georgia, a minority party in the National Council led by Major Ridge, his son, John Ridge (whom Ida had known as a student at Brainerd), and Elias Boudinot, the former editor of the *Cherokee Phoenix*, broke with her husband and other members of John Ross's party, and in 1835, they negotiated a separate agreement, the scandalous Treaty of New Echota, which provided for the removal of the Cherokees to the west. The majority of the National Council denounced the treaty, and John Ross, her husband, and a delegation of other council members journeyed to Washington urging its rejection. Ida remembered that many United States senators, men from New England and several northern states, and other politicians who disliked Gadohi Advsiqua, had supported the Cherokee cause, but in the end, they had failed. On May 23, 1836, the United States Senate, by a single vote, ratified the document. The Cherokees were given two years to "settle their affairs" and remove west of the Mississippi.[3]

Of course, the Ridge family and their followers started for the west almost immediately, for her husband and many other members of the Ross party had declared them to be traitors and had threatened their lives. Huddled deep inside her blanket, Ida spat at the wagon ruts as she remembered the Ridge family. They and their followers were utsonadi—rattlesnakes! The Treaty of New Echota would not be forgiven! Reckoning would come! She feared blood would flow when they reached Indian Territory.

At the time, their final years in Georgia had seemed like a nightmare. But now she knew that some nightmares only deepen and continue. Her family, the Rosses, and those Cherokees opposed to removal (the majority of whom had been conservative traditionalists) had steadfastly refused to emigrate, but they were subjected to harassment by citizens of Georgia. Border riffraff, and even some units of the Georgia state militia, repeatedly trespassed on Cherokee lands, and since the militiamen had seized many of the Cherokees' firearms, her people were hard-pressed to defend themselves. Many of the federal troops stationed in the nation were sympathetic to the Cherokee's plight, but their numbers were so small that they could not adequately protect the victims. During 1837, when some of the smaller Cherokee farmers along the Cooswatie and its tributaries had their crops cut down and their houses burned by white intruders, the Westbrooks offered them refuge at their plantation. These additional mouths to feed strained the Westbrook's resources, but Jonathan rearmed the refugees with muskets, powder, and lead from their store, and Ida had been grateful that the increased number of armed Cherokee men residing on their farm temporarily discouraged the intruders from destroying their crops or stealing their livestock.

But in May 1838, even this respite ended. Two years earlier, federal officials had informed the Cherokees that they must vacate their homes by May 1838, yet John Ross and his followers, including the Westbrooks, remained recalcitrant, and in turn, the government acted. Ida remembered that on Wednesday May 23, as she and her family were eating their noon meal, Matthew, her oldest son, jumped up from the table and bolted out the front door, then quickly returned, announcing, "There's soldiers outside! There's soldiers outside! I knew I heard horses."

Before her husband could reach the front porch to investigate, a squad of blue-coated soldiers surged into their home. Thank goodness they had been federal troops, for the young lieutenant in command, embarrassed by his task, allowed her family and their slaves two hours to pack up the most precious of their personal belongings and load them into a wagon before they were forced onto the road and escorted toward the emigration camp at Ross's Landing.

Enroute, the Westbrooks joined a caravan of other Cherokee families also being conducted to the emigration camp on the Tennessee River. Ida had been both frightened and infuriated by the invasion of her home, but at least she and Jonathan had been allowed to gather some of their possessions, including the broad money belt full of gold and silver coins that Jonathan still wore beneath his shirt. Many of the other Cherokees were much less fortunate. Still panic stricken, Elizabeth Rogers, whose family owned a plantation just east of Pine Log, told how her husband's farm had been seized by an ill-disciplined contingent of Georgia militia who pilfered their log house as the Rogers were forced to stand and watch the looting. All the Rogers's livestock, tools, household goods, silverware and jewelry, and even part of their clothing had been carried away before their very eyes, and when her husband had protested, he had been beaten. Other refugees told tales of thievery, rape, and even the looting of Cherokee graves from which drunken militiamen scavenged wedding rings and other jewelry that had been interred with the corpses. Meanwhile, as the column had passed through northwest Georgia toward the emigration camp, they had been followed by other frontier hoodlums who had tried to steal both their wagons and their horses.

Things only got worse. Their emigration camp of the banks of the Tennessee River consisted of five acres of sweltering, barren ground surrounded by a log palisade. After she pleaded with the officer in charge, he allowed her husband to pull their wagon inside the enclosure, and it provided better shelter than the makeshift brush and canvas tents erected by most of the other refugees. Indeed, shelter was in such short supply that Jonathan draped the canvas sheeting supplied by the government to their family over one side of their wagon and stretched it to the ground, fashioning a three-sided canvas lean-to tent that opened back under their wagon. The shelter served as a sleeping area for their four slaves, and because of the heat, the ends of the tent could be folded up to catch any wayward breeze but folded back down when it was raining. The shelter proved so successful that other refugees who owned wagons followed suit, and Jonathan even permitted a wagon-less family of full-bloods to pitch a similar tent-like structure off the opposite side of the Westbrook wagon to provide shelter for their family.

The army and local contractors supplied the camp with salt pork, flour, corn meal, and coffee. Because Jonathan had saved his money belt, Ida was able to purchase a limited supply of fresh fruits and vegetables, which they shared with friends and family members, but such commodities were in short supply, and some of the refugees contracted scurvy. Meanwhile, sanitary conditions were so primitive that two uncovered slit trenches dug at opposite ends of the enclosure and protected only by filthy canvas screens served as latrines. As the summer wore on, first dysentery, then whooping cough, and finally measles spread through the encampment.

The federal government had hoped to transport most of the Cherokees down the Tennessee River via steamboat and barges, and in June, three separate contingents totaling almost twenty-seven hundred Cherokees left the emigration camps near Ross's Landing, but the river was so low that the emigrants were forced to travel much of the distance on land, and they were plagued with critical shortages of food and other necessities. Many deserted, and when both refugees and rumors of such hardships returned back up the Tennessee valley, those members of the National Council still remaining in the camps convinced General Winfield Scott to postpone any further emigration until cooler weather in the fall and to allow the Cherokees themselves to manage the removal.

Ida remembered the feelings of relief that spread through the camps when the emigrants received news of the postponement. In addition, they were encouraged that federal officials had also agreed to permit the Cherokees to contract for their own rations while in the camps and on the journey west. At first it had seemed like welcome news; the federal rations had often been delayed, and many refugees often went hungry.

Yet the opportunity or responsibility to provide their own food supply also created problems. Angered over the sudden intrusion on May 23, when federal troops forced them from their plantation, both Ida and Jonathan hurriedly agreed that they would scatter their livestock into the woods rather than abandon them in their pens to be seized or slaughtered by white Georgians. Consequently, Jonathan ordered Quincy, one of their slaves, to open the gates to all the pens and pastures and to quickly drive their hogs and their single dairy cow into the surrounding forest. Ida doubted that the dairy cow would survive long in the wild, but she and Jonathan both knew that hogs readily adapted to life in the woods, and they both believed that most of the hogs probably still wandered in the forests near their former plantation. Hoping to acquire a supply of fresh meat, Jonathan had procured the six horses (four pulled their wagon) they had brought with them from Georgia, which had been pastured (and guarded) by federal troops outside the stockade. Accompanied by two of their slaves, Quincy and Noah, on Monday, August 20, her husband set out to travel the fifty miles back to the Coosewatie, intending to hunt, kill, and dress several of the hogs, and quickly transport the meat back to the emigration camp.

Things did not go as he expected. Two days later, when he arrived on the Coosewatie, Jonathan rode past his former plantation and was surprised to find his former home now housing two separate families. Two other families resided in what had been his combination store and warehouse, and a fifth family evidently lived in the barn. The stock pens and pastures were empty of livestock, but he spotted the hide of his dairy cow, stretched out and drying in the sun, now nailed to the side of his former smoke house. After a slight pause to take in the spectacle, he continued down the path that led through his former orchard to the river, about a mile away. There Jonathan and the two slaves dismounted, tethered their horses, and set up camp, intending to hunt the hogs that they believed were wandering through the river bottom.

They had just pitched their two small tents when they heard a voice call out, "Hold on there, Redskin! What you think you doin'?" Looking up, Jonathan saw three white men, who seemed to range from twenty-five to forty-five years of age, emerge from the path leading back to his former plantation. They were afoot and out of breath, but all were holding muskets or rifles that were leveled at Jonathan. As the men advanced forward, their weapons still trained on him, the youngest of the trio, a dark-haired man in his mid-twenties, moved away from the others and walked toward the tethered horses. Meanwhile, the leader of the group, a tall, gangly, sandy-haired man with the stubble of a beard, queried, "What you doin' here? This ain't Indin land no more. You crossed over into white man's land now. This here land, and everything that you can see. now belongs to us Georgians."

"Look at them horses," added the younger man. "Them's good horses. Too good for a worthless Indin! He won't have no need for them. The damned government'll give him new ones when they git him, his squaws, and his little nits out past the Missisip, where civilized people don't live nohow. What's more," the young, dark-haired man continued, "them blue-coat soldiers gonna carry 'em all out West and feed 'em for free, all at the same time. He don't need no horses."

"And lookit there," chimed the third Georgian, an older, heavyset man with a dirty, sweat-stained slouch hat, "He's even got a couple of slaves. If we had them slaves, we sure as hell wouldn't be bustin' our asses doin' chores or chopping all that cotton. No sir! That's slave' work, not white man's work. Them slaves sposed to be doin' it. That's what God intended, sure 'nuff."

Surprised by the intruders, Jonathan at first had not responded, but after a moment's silence, he slowly replied in English. "This land used to be mine. These slaves are mine. The horses also belong to me. When we were forced from our home, we left a milk cow and some hogs running free in the woods." Then, remembering the cowhide nailed to the shed, Jonathan added, "It looks like you already found my cow. She gave good milk. Only a fool would butcher a good milk cow in these parts. They're hard to come by." And finally, he pointed out, "We plan to look for the hogs here by the river. This is bottom land. It's no man's property. It's covered with canebrakes and willow thickets. Nobody lives here. Nobody will claim it because it floods and can't be farmed. My slaves are here to help me. We'll only be here for a day or so. We mean no trouble. We're authorized to be here. We've got a pass signed by both General Winfield Scott and John Schermerhorn, the agent in charge of removal. I can show it to you."

Jonathan then asked Quincy to get the pass from his saddle bag, but as the slave started toward the horses, a shot rang out, and as Jonathan turned back toward the tall, sandy-haired man, he saw that the latter had fired a warning shot over their heads. The man then declared, "Stop right there! Them papers don't mean nothin'! Yer tresspassin'! You got no right to be here! You got no right to slaughter them hogs. They belong to us. Matters be, everything that was on that plantation now belongs to us, even them horses and slaves."

"That's right," chimed in the older man with the dirty hat. "I'm claimin' them two slaves as my own." Then looking at his companions, he added, "You two can have them horses. If that Injun don't give em up, kill him."

The older man then laid his musket aside, picked up a heavy canvas sack he had brought with him from the plantation, and started forward toward Quincy and Noah, who were standing near the horses. As he walked toward the slaves, he momentarily paused, dumped the contents of the bag on the ground, then picked up two sets of slave shackles, intending to attach the heavy chains to Quincy's and Noah's ankles.

Encouraged by his older companions, the younger man who earlier had commented on the horses now stepped forward, obviously intending to seize the animals. He didn't get far. Infuriated, Jonathan raised his rifle, which he had loaded and primed in preparation for the hog hunt, and shot the gangly, sandy haired man through the heart. Surprised by Jonathan's actions, the younger man hesitated, but before he could raise and cock his weapon, Noah, following Jonathan's example, sent a musket ball through the man's forehead. A look of surprise frozen on his face, the man pitched backward like a top-heavy, falling cornstalk. Meanwhile, the older man, his hands full of shackles, had almost reached Quincy, but as the shots rang out he dropped the slave chains and turned to hurry back toward his discarded musket. He never made it. Although Quincy's musket was unloaded, he grabbed a small hand axe he had been using to set the tent stakes, leapt forward, and buried the axe blade into the skull of the lumbering, heavy-set man before he could reach his weapon.

Jonathan quickly reloaded his musket, then looked back at the two slaves. The two men were terrified. They had each just killed a white man, an unspeakable act in Georgia in the 1830s, and they knew that regardless of the circumstances surrounding the deaths, they would never escape with their lives. In contrast, Jonathan was determined to protect them. Turning to the two Black men, he first thanked them, then stated, "I've never freed a slave. I'm not an abolitionist. But you both just saved my life," then added, "I'm giving you your freedom, but you've got to get to Florida. The Seminole people down there have welcomed runaway slaves into their homeland, and although some of the slaves share their crops with Seminole miccos, they generally live as free men. Many even have fought with the Seminoles against the troops or state militia trying to remove the Seminole people to the West. On the other hand, if you return to Ross's Landing with me, I'll speak on your behalf, but I don't know if either I or even the federal troops can protect you from being sent back here to Georgia where you're sure to be hanged, if not worse."

"But Mr. Jonathan." Quincy replied, "How we ever gonna get to Florida? It's many long miles away, and we'd need to walk cross most of Georgia to get there, and they'd catch us both, for sure, yessir."

"You both have served me well," Jonathan replied. "I'll give you each a letter of emancipation. I've got some paper and ink in my saddlebags. And I'll also give each of you one of these horses, your musket, and some ammunition, most of the food we brought from Ross's Landing, and three dollars apiece in silver coins to take with you. Follow the back trails. Travel only at night. Hole up in thickets or canebrakes during the day. Steer clear of towns and farms. Keep to the hilly, broken country, and keep going south. Remember, always south. If your luck holds, you should reach Florida in a week or so."

Quincy asked if he and Noah could talk it over for a spell.

"Yes, of course,' Jonathan replied. "But don't spend too much time. I want to hide these bodies and get back to Ross's Landing before they're missed."

Less than ten minutes later, the two men returned and announced, "Mr. Jonathan, we're done talkin'. We're goin' to the Seminoles."

"Good," he replied, "but first help me hide these bodies deep in that willow thicket." The three men put the bodies on the backs of two of the pack horses and led the animals about sixty yards into the thicket. They dumped the corpses on the ground, then Jonathan asked Noah, who previously had looked after the hogs on his plantation, to call the hogs as he regularly had done when they filled their feed troughs with slop from the plantation kitchen. In response, Noah spent the next five minutes repeatedly shouting, "Sooey! Sooey! Hogs sooey." They never saw the hogs, but they heard them moving forward in the thicket.

The three men then led the horses back to the site of their camp. Quincy and Noah first packed Jonathan's possessions and his share of the remaining food on one of the three pack horses, then packed their food and bedrolls on the two remaining horses. Before they mounted, Jonathan shook each man's hand and wished him well. It was the first time he had ever shaken a Black person's hand. The two men then rode away, following a little-used trail south through the river bottom.

Mounting his horse, Jonathan took the reins of the three remaining pack horses and rode upstream to a nearby ford, where he crossed the river. He then turned westward, and after a day and a half of hard riding, on Friday, August 24, he reached Ross's Landing. In the aftermath, he told Ida what had happened but then admitted that he found the outcome of the failed trip to be sad—but also sinfully amusing. It was ironic. He had ridden back to the Coosewatie to hunt the escaped hogs, hoping to convert the poor beasts into additional food. Instead, just the opposite had happened. He had returned to the removal camp empty-handed. In contrast, the newly feral hogs in the river bottom had come out on top. They had escaped all harm, and in turn, it was the hogs who had gained the most from the ill-fated hunting trip. In the end, after answering Noah's call, they had been provided with a banquet.

During the weeks after Jonathan's return, the Westbrook's disillusionment deepened. In late July, when measles swept through the camp, Sarah, their only daughter, contracted the illness, and although she survived the malady, the disease left her frail and vulnerable. On October 14, when their party of eight hundred emigrants finally departed for the West, their two sons, Matthew, aged ten years, and Thomas, two years younger, frolicked with the other children as the column of Cherokees slowly started westward, but four-year-old Sarah, pale and sickly, rode quietly in their wagon.

They traveled slowly. Jonathan and other Council members supervising the removals used tribal annuity funds to buy additional teams and wagons and to purchase a small herd of cattle that followed in the wagon's wake, and as the removal party, stretching for two miles along the road, left Ross's Landing, Ida had thought that it resembled a disorganized, bedraggled army. Because the cattle continually strayed and many of the wagons were of inferior quality, the emigrants traveled only seven to ten miles a day, and during the first two weeks, the Westbrooks were forced to cover their faces with bandanas to protect themselves from the thick clouds of dust that rose from those wagons and animals that preceded them.

"Thank God for Simon and Tassie!" Ida thought. Their two remaining slaves had become indispensable Simon, a stocky, well-built man of forty, herded the Westbrook's spare horses, who ordinarily were not used as draft animals and who followed in the wagon's wake. Since good riding or pack horses were in short supply, Jonathan relied on the slave to feed, water, and protect the livestock, and Simon kept a close eye on them. Tassie, his wife, assisted Ida in procuring firewood, cooking, looking after the children, and other camp chores. Sometimes Tassie walked beside the wagon; at other times, particularly in inclement weather, she rode inside with Ida and the children.

In November, as the emigration passed from Tennessee into Kentucky, the weather turned colder, and they were plagued with rain. Previously dusty roads now became muddy quagmires, further delaying their progress. Twice in one day, their wagon mired down as far as its axles, and they were forced to stop until Simon and her husband could bring up their other horses and then solicit additional help to extricate the wagon. Meanwhile, the small herd of cattle became depleted. Some animals were butchered, others strayed into the canebrakes, while other animals were stolen in the night by cattle thieves who sold them in the frontier settlements. Early in December, the weather became even colder, and as they waited just opposite Cape Girardeau to be ferried across the Mississippi, the rain turned to sleet, and much of the emigration party grew cold and hungry.

Sarah fared poorly. The choking dust caused her to cough and gag, and when the rains came, the child huddled in her blanket, hollow-eyed and shivering. Ida took special care to keep her warm and to be sure that she had at least one good, hot meal every day. During mid-November, Sarah rallied, even spending several warmer afternoons walking beside the wagon as they trudged through Kentucky. But the drop in temperatures and the accompanying sleet storm as they waited on the eastern bank of the Mississippi did not bode well. After they arrived in Missouri, Sarah first developed a hacking cough, then a fever.

When they camped for the night four days west of Cape Girardeau, Sarah's condition rapidly worsened. Ida gave Tassie money, and the woman purchased an old hen from a frontier farmer, then made a pot of chicken soup, complete with boiled hominy, carrots, and dried peas, but the little girl had little appetite. Instead, she asked only to drink cool spring water and nibbled at a few corn dodgers that Tassie had prepared earlier for the family's breakfast. Dr. Collins, the frontier physician accompanying the emigration, applied poultices, but he possessed neither the skill nor the medicine to treat her. Ida had never known such agony! In desperation throughout that night of terror, she held her little girl inside her own blanket, as the child first shivered from the cold then burned with a fever, but by daylight, Sarah was gone, and Ida knew that if she lived for another century, she would never again know such anguish as when she

The Trail of Tears, by Robert Lindneux. Courtesy of the Woolaroc Museum, Bartlesville, Oklahoma. At least four thousand Cherokees, about one in every four Cherokee tribespersons placed in a removal camp, died before reaching Indian Territory.

dressed her daughter, her beloved little Sarah, for the final time, in a little gray woolen dress and small calico bonnet, then had wrapped her in a blanket and laid her in a shallow, unmarked grave by the side of the trail. Following the burial, when their wagon was forced to join the rest of the removal west toward Indian Territory, she kept tear-filled eyes fixed on Sarah's grave until the trail turned, the forest seemed to close in, and the gravesite no longer was visible.

The following three weeks passed in a grief-stricken haze of first muddy, then frozen roads, icy winds, and continual hunger. The Cherokees had contracted for food to be supplied to the emigrants at various stopping places along their journey, but when they arrived at several designated supply depots in Missouri, they found the food to be contaminated. Ida remembered that barrels of flour left by contractors swarmed with weevils, while the salt pork and bacon, even in frigid weather, was so rancid that the smell of the "bacon wagons" nauseated her. The Cherokees learned that corn and grain that some of the contractors provided for their livestock had previously been condemned and discarded as unfit for use by army mules by quartermasters at frontier military posts. Johnathan and several other Cherokee leaders who could afford the price purchased other supplies with personal funds, while groups of white settlers, moved by the emigrants' plight, also donated food and provided some of the ailing or elderly tribespeople with food and shelter in their barns and other farm buildings.

Ida knew that she and her husband did not grieve alone. Many other members of the emigrating party, both young and old, also had lost loved ones. But the removal continued, and three days ago, they passed into Arkansas. Tomorrow night they would reach Fayetteville, then they would turn westward through the hills to Fort Gibson. Surely, within the next week, or so, this ordeal would end.

Huddled in her blankets, a ragged shawl wrapped around her head, Ida felt her body shaking. Glancing to her right, she watched as her husband, sitting on the wagon seat, urged the exhausted horses up the steep trail through the mountains. The turmoil and anguish of the past ten years had aged him. His handsome face, once so smooth, was now lined, and he had dark circles under his eyes. His hair, once so raven black, was now streaked with gray. "Why?" Ida wondered. "Why has this happened? Why have my people who have tried so hard to walk the white man's road—why have we been so betrayed by them? For two generations, their missionaries and agents have promised us that if we would accept their God, their way of life, there would be a place for us. Why have they taken almost everything?"

"Why have they turned on us?"

"Why does my only daughter lie dead beside the trail?"

"Why have we been driven into this godforsaken, windswept wilderness?"

Although Ida Westbrook and her family are composite characters, the saga of their lives provides a rather accurate and poignant reflection of the plight of many Native American peoples residing in the region east of the Mississippi during the second quarter of the nineteenth century. Inspired by Rousseauan concepts of the "noble savage" and imbued with the optimism of the Enlightenment, the founding fathers of the new republic originally implemented an Indian policy based on the assumption that the tribes who resided on the trans-Appalachian frontier would eventually be acculturated and assimilated into the mainstream of American life. In consequence, both the Federalists and the Jeffersonians collaborated to pass the Indian Trade and Intercourse Acts, a series of statutes designed to regulate trade, control the liquor traffic, and administer justice between the tribes and the non-Indian settlers. Subscribing to a vision of rural communities and small yeomen farmers, Thomas Jefferson, particularly, championed agriculture and animal husbandry as catalysts for the tribespeople's assimilation.[4]

But the founding fathers' policies of supposedly benign, if often naïve, benevolence was overwhelmed by socioeconomic changes and the rapidity of the westward movement following the War of 1812. Although Eli Whitney had invented the cotton gin in 1792, it was not in widespread use until after 1815, but with its adoption, the cotton kingdom spread across the southern Appalachians into the Gulf plains. Surging westward from coastal regions in Georgia and the Carolinas and out of the long upland valleys and foothills on the eastern slopes of the Smoky and Blue Ridge Mountains, white settlers initially bypassed much of the hilly, more mountainous, Cherokee lands in northwest Georgia in favor of the fertile, more level lands in the southern part of the state, and in Alabama and Mississippi. Pressure mounted on the Creeks, Choctaws, and Chickasaws, but at first, the Cherokees seemed less threatened.

Each of the Five Southern, or "Civilized," Tribes (Cherokees, Creeks, Choctaws, Chickasaws, and Seminoles) varied in the extent of their acculturation, and as Ida Westbrook's differences with her aunts and cousins illustrate, the degree of acculturation within an individual tribe also encompassed a broad spectrum of diversity. Yet by the 1820s, all these tribes, with the possible exception of the Seminoles, were led by a mixed-blood elite who were acculturating toward social, political, and economic patterns modeled after their white neighbors. In most of these tribes, this elite leadership remained a numerical minority, but like the white planters who dominated the South, the tribal mixed-blood elite held an influence far in excess of their numbers, and most saw themselves as role models for their more traditional kinsmen.[5]

In many ways, the Cherokees seemed to lead in this acculturation. By the 1820s, significant numbers of Cherokee men were prosperous farmers, plantation owners, and small businessmen. Many dressed in clothing and resided in houses very similar to those of white Georgians. Many had attended either mission or tribal schools and were well educated by frontier standards. In 1821, Sequoyah (George Guess), a mixed-blood but very traditional Cherokee already living in Arkansas, formulated the Cherokee syllabary, and by 1824, missionaries reported that even among the more traditional full-bloods, "a great part of the

Cherokees can read and write in their own language . . . letters in Cherokee are passing in all directions," and nothing "was in so great demand as pens, ink, and paper." (The literacy rate for the Cherokee Nation would remain higher than that of the white South through the Civil War.) On February 21, 1828, a tribally owned press began publication of the *Cherokee Phoenix*, a four-page weekly newspaper printed in both Cherokee and English. The press also published pamphlets, religious tracts, hymnals, and the Cherokee constitution and laws, in addition to private items such as political announcement, sale bills, and so on.[6]

The Cherokee political system underwent a similar transition. Traditionally, the Cherokees had been a village people with political power diffused among the local communities. Held together by language, kinship, and ceremonial ties, inter-village relationships were tenuous; each town chose its own leaders and usually acted as an autonomous entity. But in 1798, in an effort to control horse thievery, the tribe formed the Cherokee Light Horse, a tribal police force, and ten years later, Cherokee leaders met to form a National Council, which formulated the tribe's first written laws. Political consolidation was disrupted by the War of 1812, but in the years following the conflict, the council reasserted itself, and in 1820, the remaining Cherokee homeland was apportioned into eight separate districts, each electing four delegates to the council for two-year terms.[7]

Throughout the 1820s, power was centralized in the National Council, which became a bicameral legislature with the establishment of a National Committee, or upper house. A national capital was established at New Echota, tax legislation was passed to finance the new government, and by 1822, the nation supported a judicial system, complete with judges, sheriffs, marshals, clerks, and written records. On July 26, 1827, a convention of delegates ratified a new constitution patterned after the federal system of the United States, and mixed-blood John Ross was elected to a four-year term as principal chief of the Cherokee Nation. Unquestionably, these political changes came too quickly for some of the more traditional full-bloods, and also for many Cherokee women who saw their political influence diminish in the tribe's embrace of more misogynous, Anglo-American political structures. In contrast, for missionaries and those federal agents who still championed acculturation, the Cherokees (at least the "progressive mixed-bloods") epitomized the goals of American Indian policy.[8]

The Cherokees also emulated Anglo-American economic development. After 1825, the National Council loaned tribal funds to planters and entrepreneurs such as Jonathan Westbrook for the construction of turnpikes, ferries, trading posts, and other enterprises. By 1828, the Cherokees owned over one thousand slaves, seventy-five hundred horses, and twenty-two thousand cattle. Almost every family possessed a plow and a spinning wheel, and one-quarter of the families owned a loom and a wagon. The Cherokees operated and maintained thirty-one gristmills, fourteen sawmills, six powder mills, nine saltpeter works, eight cotton gins, and eighteen ferries. At least sixty-two tribal blacksmiths and fifty-five silversmiths operated within the nation, and the Cherokees funded a nineteen-school educational system. Sophisticated financiers, the Cherokees refused to accept federal annuity payments when the government attempted to pay them in depreciated state bank notes. Instead, they demanded either US National Bank notes or coins. Once again, not all Cherokees walked the white man's road, but those who did were widening it into an avenue. Both they and the missionaries believed that their more traditional kinsmen would soon follow.[9]

But the federal government broke its promises. During the 1820s, political power in the United States passed from the more gentile Federalists and Jeffersonians, politicians at least ostensibly dedicated to Native American assimilation, into the hands of the Jacksonians, a new political force much less influenced by Enlightenment ideology and much more interested in uncontrolled economic growth and exploitation. Composed of small businessmen, displaced eastern farmers, and frontier opportunists, the Jacksonians were more responsive to western and local interests, and if potentially valuable resources lay within the realm of their grasp, they believed these resources should be developed. Gradualism and long-term planning were not their forte. Indians were Indians, whether mixed-blood or full-bloods, acculturated or savage, and if they occupied lands that might more profitably be used by white men, they should be forced to relinquish them. Such a philosophy had always been part of the Anglo-American frontier, but it burgeoned in the years following the War of 1812, and in 1828, with the election of Andrew Jackson, one of its champions captured the presidency.[10]

The Westbrooks and their kinsmen were not the first tribal people forced westward across the Mississippi. As early as the American Revolution, groups of Shawnees and Delawares had fled to Missouri and Arkansas, and during the three decades that followed, they were joined by bands of Kickapoos, Choctaws, Chickasaws, and Cherokees. Fleeing the American juggernaut, in the 1790s some Cherokees earlier had established villages on the St. Francis River in southeastern Missouri and northeastern Arkansas. Between 1809 and 1811, they were joined by fifteen hundred of their kinsmen. Ten years later, following a series of major land cessions, these "Old Settlers" welcomed an additional two thousand other Cherokees into their villages. Meanwhile, growing numbers of Kickapoos, Shawnees, and Delawares attached themselves to their camps. By the mid-1820s, many of these Native American refugees had established villages throughout western Arkansas, but like the Cherokees in Georgia, they too were continually harassed by white settlers. Consequently, in 1819, after the Adams-Onís Treaty established the border between American and Spanish territories, many of these Indian peoples sought a logical refuge, beyond the Sabine and Red rivers, in Texas.[11]

In Indian Territory, the Cherokee saga continued. The Westbrooks and other emigrants of 1838 joined with the Old Settlers and members of the Ridge-Oowatie Treaty Party who were already settled on lands set aside for the Western Cherokees in Indian Territory by earlier treaties signed in May 1828 and supplemented in February 1833.[12] Although these Western Cherokees had previously established a government in the region, they were outnumbered by the newcomers, many of whom bore bitter grudges against Treaty Party members who had negotiated the infamous Treaty of New Echota, providing for Cherokee removal. In retribution, on June 22, 1839, Cherokees who had opposed removal assassinated Major Ridge, John Ridge, and Elias Boudinot, three leaders of the Treaty Party. Stand Watie, another member of the Treaty Party, escaped unharmed.[13]

Although the assassinations threatened to plunge the Cherokee Nation into a civil war, federal troops intervened. Order was restored, but periodic revenge murders plagued the nation through the mid-1840s. Meanwhile, John Ross's followers, now a majority in the West, gained control of the Cherokee government in Indian Territory and implemented a constitution similar to the one they had passed in Georgia in 1827. The Cherokee Nation was divided into nine districts, a bicameral legislature was established, and a new judicial system was created. John Ross was reelected as principal chief, and a new capital was founded at Tahlequah, a growing town, near the Illinois River, about eighteen miles east of Fort Gibson. Although a tribal police force struggled to maintain law and order and some lawlessness continued, the nation was relatively stable, particularly when compared to other regions on the American frontier during these years.[14]

And the Cherokees prospered. Unlike in Georgia, where the Cherokees had remained primarily a village people, in the new Cherokee Nation in Indian Territory, they spread out across the land. They still retained their sense of kin, family, and community, but land was plentiful, and like many frontier whites in Missouri and Arkansas, they established rural homes on small plots of land where they planted modest fields of corn or cotton and allowed their livestock to graze in roughly fenced pastures or to free-range in the neighboring forests. Most people subsisted on what they grew, herded, or hunted, and their limited surpluses were traded for materials they could not manufacture themselves. The vast majority lived in one- or two-room log cabins, the latter separated by covered but open "dogtrots" or breezeways. Furniture was sparse but adequate for their needs. Food was cooked over an open hearth, which also provided heat in the winter. Moccasins were usually used for footwear, but most people dressed in trade-cloth clothing. In retrospect, during the 1850s, most Cherokees in Indian Territory did not live lives of luxury, but when compared to other rural Americans in the mid-nineteenth century, they enjoyed a life of rude, if rustic, plenty.[15]

Some lived more lavishly. Composed of both full-bloods and people of mixed lineage, the planter or merchant elite never numbered more than 10 to 15 percent of the tribe's population, but they dominated tribal politics and set the standards (at least in their own minds and in the opinion of neighboring whites) for fashion and gentility in Cherokee society. Emulating wealthy planters in Arkansas and Louisiana, many members of the planter elite maintained farms or plantations holding large fields of cotton, corn, and tobacco. Although most plantations were smaller, some Cherokee planters operated plantations of from six hundred to one thousand acres. Moreover, almost all Cherokee planters with large farms or plantations also owned slaves. By 1860, almost twenty-five hundred slaves labored on farms and plantations or in businesses within the Cherokee Nation. Most Cherokee planters or farmers owned no more than a handful, but some of the larger planters owned many more. Lewis Ross (brother of Chief John Ross), a planter, merchant, and businessman, utilized slaves not only on his plantation near Park Hill but also at his saltworks and in other businesses. He was reputed to own over three hundred adult slaves, plus dozens of children. Like the larger southern society that surrounded them, Cherokee slaveholders encompassed planters who, like the Westbrooks, attempted to treat their slaves well, but it also included some planters whose treatment of their slaves was harsh and inhumane. Indeed, although evidence suggests that Cherokee slaveholders generally treated their slaves kindlier than most white planters, Cherokee attitudes toward slavery closely mirrored the perspectives held by non-Indian (white) planters.[16]

The planter-merchant elite's lifestyle reflected their affluence. Prosperous planters and merchants lived in comfortable (sometimes large) frame clapboard houses furnished with carpets, books, fine china, and furniture brought up the Arkansas River from Memphis. Men wore frock coats or even top hats on formal occasions, while women wore calico or gingham dresses on a daily basis, but they dressed more elegantly when the occasion demanded. Unlike less prosperous Cherokees, the wives and daughters of the elite did not labor in the fields but sewed, crocheted, or did fine needlework. Others learned to play the piano and provided accompaniment to songfests after guests had formally dined in their home. Many planters or merchants raised or kept fine horses. John Ross regularly traveled the four-mile journey between his home at Park Hill and the Cherokee capital at Tahlequah by carriage, complete with liveried driver and attendant. Of course, material wealth within the Cherokee Nation was not evenly distributed, and few Cherokees could afford liveried footmen, but by the 1850s, most Cherokees were "doing well."[17]

The influence of the planter-merchant elite was particularly evident at Tahlequah and Park Hill. In 1850, Tahlequah numbered sixteen hundred residents and boasted that it contained the Nation's legislature, supreme court, chief's office, office of the *Cherokee Advocate* (the nation's newspaper), a post office, eight general merchandise stores, five hotels, three blacksmith shops, a tailor shop, a saddler, a tannery, a shoemaker's shop, a dentist, several law offices, and a brick Masonic temple. Park Hill, located about four miles southeast of the capitol, served as the center for Methodist and Congregational missionary activity within the nation and was favored by John Ross and many of the wealthier merchants as a place of residence. Smaller than Tahlequah, Park Hill fancied itself as the cultural center of the Cherokee Nation and was locally famous for its fine shops, social life, and seminaries.[18]

By the 1850s, over fourteen hundred students were enrolled at thirty separate schools throughout the nation, but the Cherokee male and female seminaries located at Park Hill were the planter-merchant elite's pride and joy. Opened in 1850, both schools were imposing, three-story brick structures that contained classrooms, dormitories, dining facilities, and formal parlors. Each seminary

Cherokee women at the gates of the Cherokee Female Seminary, 1892. Courtesy of Northeastern Oklahoma State University Archives, Tahlequah, Oklahoma.

was designed to house one hundred students, and twenty-five were admitted each year into the four-year program. The National Council provided teachers, tuition, textbooks, food, and lodging; the students furnished their own clothing and other expenses. Admission was supposedly open to any Cherokee student, but in reality, the student bodies comprised primarily the sons and daughters of the planter-merchant elite.[19]

In retrospect, the institutions resembled finishing schools more than institutions reflecting traditional Cherokee values. The curriculum at the male seminary was modeled after the Boston Latin School, and the female seminary's curriculum mirrored that of Mount Holyoke College in Massachusetts. Few traditional Cherokee values were either taught or espoused, and darker complexioned, more traditional students who enrolled in the seminaries sometimes faced disparaging remarks and other prejudice. Still, many of the graduates of these institutions fared well. Some went on to attend colleges in the East, and in the decades to come, many leading figures within the Cherokee Nation, and even later in the new state of Oklahoma, were products of these seminaries.[20]

Yet the patterns of increased acculturation came with some costs. In traditional Cherokee society, women exercised considerable power. Not only had their horticulture dominated Cherokee food production, but maternal-based clans interlacing the Cherokee villages also wielded considerable influence in tribal politics and ceremonialism. But by the middle decades of the nineteenth century, these institutions and networks (at least among the planter-merchant elite) had been replaced by more formal, statutory structures resembling those used in state and federal governments. In addition, succumbing to pressure by both Protestant missionaries and federal officials, most female members of the planter-merchant elite had recast themselves in secondary political and economic roles, as supporting figures within an emerging capitalistic, male-dominated, hierarchal society. Unquestionably, the wives and daughters of the planter-elite performed less strenuous physical labor than had their grandmothers, but they also exerted less influence. Yet ironically, in many venues, they still fared better than white women in neighboring states. Cherokee women of all classes and traditions could inherit, hold, and dispose of their own property separately from their husbands. They could sue their husband or other men in the Cherokee courts. And although all land was held in common by the Nation, Cherokee women could own houses and farm buildings. They could also own livestock and own and operate businesses, such as stores, mills, and ferries.[21]

Obviously, not all Cherokees approved of the ongoing changes. Although the acculturation continued, undercurrents of resistance emerged and flourished among the tribespeople who still wished to follow more traditional ways. Although they were often discounted by missionaries and federal agents, they continued to influence many Cherokees' lives. Formed in the mid-1850s, the Keetowah Society was a semi-secret organization composed mostly of fullbloods who opposed many policies of the planter-merchant elite, particularly efforts by the latter to emulate the lifestyle of white society in the American South. Although they were labeled as "abolitionists" by their detractors, many Keetowahs were initially ambiguous about slavery. They disliked the institution since it formed part of the elite's acculturation process, but the Keetowahs' primary focus was to return the Cherokee people to traditional patterns of government, economic activities, and ceremonialism.[22]

After 1860, intra-tribal arguments regarding acculturation were submerged by the deluge of the Civil War. The format of this essay is far too limited to adequately discuss the circumstances and impact of the conflict on the Cherokee Nation, but to briefly summarize these events, there is a single term that best describes the episodes and outcome: *devastation.* Principal Chief John Ross preferred to keep the Nation neutral in the conflict, but many of the planter-merchant elite, including most members of the old Treaty Party, favored the South. To prevent a civil war within the Nation, Ross reluctantly agreed to support the Confederacy. But in 1862, after defeating Confederate forces at Pea Ridge in Missouri, the Union Army invaded the Cherokee Nation and occupied Tahlequah. Ross surrendered and was sent into exile in Philadelphia, where he claimed that the Nation had been forced to support the Confederacy; he spent the remainder of the war supporting the North. Civil War then broke out within the Cherokee Nation, and old feuds, engendered by memories of the Treaty of New Echota and the removal debacle, fueled bloodshed that spread across the Nation until the end of the war. Confederate Cherokees were led by Stand Watie, the last Confederate general to surrender when the Civil War finally ended. Watie's Cherokee Rifles attempted to maintain military discipline, but much of the internecine warfare was plagued by old grudges and vendettas that devastated the Nation.[23]

In 1865, when the warfare ended, farms, plantations, businesses, and homes had been burned. Crops had been destroyed, livestock had been butchered or stolen, and many of the Nation's institutions, schools and churches were closed or suspended. By the war's end, one-third of all married Cherokee woman had been widowed, and one-quarter of all Cherokee children were orphans. About one-third of all Cherokees had died from violence, starvation, or war-related illness during the conflict. Indeed, the casualty rate for all tribal peoples in the Indian nations during the war was higher than that of any other state or region in the United States.[24]

Reconstruction brought other challenges. Both pro-Union and pro-Confederate Cherokees sent delegations to Washington to negotiate a peace treaty after the war, and the resulting document left much to be desired. The treaty, signed in July 1866, supposedly reunited these opposing factions, but Stand Watie became so disgruntled that he returned to Indian Territory before the negotiations were completed, and John Ross was so ill he could not sign the final document. Ross died on August 1, 1866, less than two weeks after the treaty had been signed. In the treaty, the Cherokees agreed to free their slaves, relinquish former claims to lands in Kansas, allow "friendly" Indians to settle on unoccupied lands in the "Cherokee Outlet" (a strip of lands extending westward from northern regions of the Cherokee Nation), and to allow several railroads to build rights of way through the Nation.[25]

In actuality, the treaty made regions within the Cherokee Nation available as settlement sites for the removal of tribes from Kansas and other locations. In the decade following the treaty, federal officials relocated Osages, Pawnees, Kansas, Poncas, Otoe-Missourias, Tonkawas, and other tribes on lands within former Cherokee territory. The railroads provided avenues of commerce for Cherokee farmers and businessmen, but they also served as avenues of penetration for non-Indian business interests. By the 1870s, economic growth had rebounded, but so had an influx of railroad camps, gamblers, hucksters, and prostitutes. The Cherokee Light Horse and legal system was hard pressed to handle many of the resulting problems, and non-Indian emigration into the Nation increased.[26]

Yet the Cherokee Nation, ever resilient, emerged from the ashes. New cabins and houses were erected. Fields were plowed anew, and crops were replanted. Growing herds of livestock spilled across the pastures. Cherokee entrepreneurs reopened their businesses. In addition, the cultural life of the Nation, although devastated by the war, also recovered. By 1875, there were sixty-five public schools (fourteen for the children of new Black freedmen) financed by the Cherokee Nation. Both the male and female seminaries reopened, and Tahlequah reestablished itself as the political, economic, and cultural center of the Nation. Yet many of the old ways persisted. The Keetowahs maintained their influence and took pains to insure that traditional ideals, values, and ceremonies endured. The Cherokee Nation persevered through 1907, when it became a cornerstone of the new state of Oklahoma. Today, both the Cherokee people and the Cherokee Nation continue.[27]

Ida found the familiar sound of the cicadas singing in the soft maples and cedar-elms that shrouded her son's Fort Gibson home to be comforting but also somewhat sad. They reminded her of the hosts of cicadas that sung in the trees surrounding the removal camp at Ross's Landing, during the late summer of 1838. Bittersweet memories! Bittersweet indeed! That was the last summer that she had been able to look across a campfire into the eyes of all her children or sit by a hearth and enjoy the company of all her family. Poor, sweet Sarah, her dark-eyed little angel, had died during that horrible trek from Tennessee to Indian Territory, and her body still lay buried in an unmarked grave somewhere along the route in southern Missouri. In 1841, Jonathan, their slave Simon, and Matthew, her older son, had ridden back along the trail, intending to disinter

Sarah's body and bring it back to the family plot in the new cemetery near Park Hill. But so many wagons had passed along the route and so many herds of livestock had traipsed beside them that her burial site had been obliterated. They had returned to their new home in the Cherokee Nation empty-handed.

And tragically, both her husband and son, the two members of her family who had searched in vain for Sarah's grave, now lay in the cemetery where they had hoped to re-bury the remains of their daughter and sister. Bitter memories indeed! Poor Jonathan! He had established a new farm near the Illinois River, southeast of Tahlequah, and had opened a fancy dry goods emporium in Park Hill. By the mid-1840s, they had prospered. Although he continued to support John Ross's political party, Jonathan had opposed the assassination of Major Ridge, John Ridge, and Elias Boudinot in June 1839, during the "days of reckoning." But his close association with Ross had engendered hostility among remaining Treaty Party members. Then, in 1845, the growing success of his mercantile business in Park Hill encouraged him to open a second store in Fort Gibson, which also seemed to threaten several established Treaty Party merchants. On October 25, 1845, as he journeyed back to Park Hill from his new store at Fort Gibson, he was shot and killed by "unknown assailants." Although the *Cherokee Advocate* described the crime as a "robbery," neither his gold watch nor his money belt had been taken. Robbery be damned! She knew that the roots of his murder lay deep in Cherokee politics.

Cherokee politics had also taken Matthew, her oldest son. After Jonathan's death, Ida had hired an overseer to manage their farm and stores until 1851, when Matthew reached the age of twenty-three and Thomas turned twenty-one. Her sons had then assumed the responsibilities for the farm and other family businesses. Matthew married and continued to live in the family home in Park Hill, while Thomas built this new house at Fort Gibson, where he managed the store and began his speculation in the growing lumber business. Because of their father's murder, both sons were wary of the quagmire of tribal politics, but when the Civil War spread into the Nation, Matthew became entwined in it. In 1863, he reluctantly joined the pro-Union Indian Home Guard in an effort to push pro-Confederate Cherokees south of the Arkansas River and to restore law, order, and some stability to the Tahlequah and Park Hill region. But in April of that year, he was killed in a minor skirmish near Webbers Falls, near the junction of the Illinois and Arkansas rivers. Now he lay next to his father, in the Park Hill Cemetery.

At least her younger son had survived all the bloodshed. In a remarkable feat of political dexterity, her sweet, affable, garrulous Thomas had kept the family's store and warehouse at Fort Gibson open throughout the conflict, trading openly with Cherokees from both sides. Because his store was one of the few remaining sources of needed supplies and because he was generous in extending credit to all Cherokees in need, particularly war widows or orphans (regardless of their family's politics), both Confederate and Union armies, when they alternately controlled the Fort Gibson region, had allowed him to operate without interference. He came through the war unscathed, and in 1866, he married Eunice Cornsilk, a Confederate war widow with three small children, one son and two daughters. Then, in proper Cherokee fashion, he promptly sired two children (one son and one daughter) of his own.

In 1867, Thomas sold the improvements and livestock on the Westbrook family farm near the Illinois River (the land, of course, belonged to the Nation) and used the proceeds from the sale to open an additional store and warehouse in Tahlequah. Meanwhile, he had enlarged his lumber business at Fort Gibson, hiring additional workers, many of whom were Black freedmen, to cut and haul timber from tribal lands to his sawmills on the Grand River, near its juncture with the Arkansas at Fort Gibson.

During Reconstruction, Thomas (and the entire Westbrook family), profited from the sale of lumber to rebuild the Cherokee Nation and from shipping boatloads of lumber down the Arkansas by steamboat to a much larger non-Indian market, but the arrival of railroads into the nation in the 1870s created a phenomenal demand for railroad ties. The lumber mills on the Grand River were readymade to meet the demand, and Thomas secured lucrative contracts from both the Missouri, Kansas, and Texas Railroad (the MKT, or Katy), which was bisecting Indian Territory from Kansas to Texas, and from the Arkansas Valley line, which entered the Nation from Arkansas but intersected the MKT at Wagoner, just northwest of Fort Gibson. The family's Park Hill store had suffered some damage during the war, but by the mid-1870s, her family had recovered, and Ida felt that their economic future was more than secure.

In 1867, following the war, Ida moved to Fort Gibson. Matthew and his wife had no children, and she encouraged Alice, her dead son's widow, of whom she was very fond, to remarry. She also believed that Alice's chance of finding a new husband would be considerably enhanced if she, Ida, were not sharing her home. Moreover, Alice's maiden name was Hicks, and many members

Cherokee Nation, Indian Territory, 1879

of the Hicks family still lived in Tahlequah. Ida knew that Alice would have ample companionship from her sisters, aunts, and cousins if she needed advice or moral support. The old clan system may have been frayed but it remained. Cherokee women took care of their own.

And she also believed that Thomas and his new family would benefit from her oversight and experience. In addition, many of her former cousins and nieces from Georgia also had settled in the Fort Gibson region. She looked forward to rekindling her old family ties and spending some time with them. Ida also had to admit that she had enjoyed interacting with and telling stories to her grandchildren. Two of her step-grandchildren were now grown, married and starting families of their own. Her youngest step-grandchild, Mattie Cornsilk, was enrolled at the Cherokee Female Seminary, where she was being instructed in those things that the "grand dames" of the nation and Florence Wilson, the principal of the school, deemed important. [28] Her other children, John Bernard and Lucille (Tomas's biological children) still attended local tribal schools, but she assumed they, too, would be enrolled in the seminaries in the next few years.

Lots of memories. Some brought joy; others brought sadness. Sitting in the rocking chair on the porch of her son's home at Fort Gibson, Ida listened again to the cicadas singing in the trees. They reminded her of her childhood and the quiet times when her grandmother told her the old Cherokee story that the cicadas' song was a warning that summer, the days of plenty, soon would pass, and that winter would follow. Like her grandmother, Ida also had tried to pass along the old stories and the old traditions to her grandchildren. And she ruefully remembered that as a younger women, when she had been a new wife with young children of her own—particularly before they had been forced from their home in Georgia—Ida had once believed that many of the old ways, the stories, the traditions of their fathers, were things of the past and that the Cherokees should embrace the ways of the white society that seemed to surround them. She had taken pride that the Americans had referred to her people as one of the "civilized tribes," and she had privately scoffed when some of her aunts and cousins and other more traditional tribespeople had cautioned against abandoning all the old ways and had warned that the white man's "civilization" was a hollow promise. Its emphasis on acquiring and hoarding wealth violated many of the precepts that the Cherokee people had always held dear. Some of the white man's ways were good, but others were shameful. As her grandmother had warned, "White men have large grasping hands, but they have no hearts."

The cicadas sang on, and in her seventy-second year, as Ida slowly rocked in her chair, she now saw the truth in her grandmother's warning. Although her people had been the most "progressive" of all the tribes, had followed the precepts set forth by the government and the missionaries, and had readily subscribed to many of the white man's ways, it had made little difference. Their efforts had been ignored. Her family and other Cherokee people had been rudely uprooted and forced west to Indian Territory. Moreover, the barbarism of the Georgia militia and the frontier riffraff who followed in their wake reflected the dearth of "civilized gentility" among those white Georgians who overran Cherokee lands and seized their belongings. And she knew that they had tried to kill Jonathan and steal his property. Civilized Indeed! And God bless Quincy and Noah. They had saved Jonathan's life. She prayed that they both had found a good life among the Seminoles.

The Civil War years had only confirmed her prejudices. Both her sons had tried to remain apart from the bloodshed. Neither had any particular affinity for slavery. Poor Matthew had joined the Home Guard not through any great loyalty to the Union but in an attempt to restore some sense of law and order to the Tahlequah region. It had cost him his life—a Cherokee life squandered in fighting a war fomented by white men. Although legitimate Union and Confederate forces had campaigned across the Cherokee Nation, during the war the region also had been overrun by armed bands of irregular forces, non-Indian outlaws and cutthroats who had robbed, burned, and pillaged at will, cloaking their crimes in their pretended allegiance to the Union or Confederacy. When the war ended, many of these bandits continued their thievery, earning both the Cherokee Nation and all Indian Territory an unhappy reputation for lawlessness. The Good Lord knew that she harbored no great affection for Stand Watie, but Ida had to admit that in comparison to those predatory bands of "civilized" white men who plagued the nation during the war and afterward, Stand Watie's disciplined force of Cherokee Rifles stood out in marked and positive contrast.

The fourteen years that had followed the war had only strengthened her opinion. It made no sense! During the war, her people, the Cherokee Nation, had borne the brunt of the fighting. The nation had been the only member of the Five Civilized Tribes to muster any significant support for the Union. But when the war ended, the Nation had been forced to surrender large tracts of land to the federal government, who then settled other tribes on the former Cherokee acreage. In contrast, both the Choctaws and the Chickasaws, who had staunchly supported the Confederacy, had retained all their territory. Why? In addition, the Cherokees had been forced to surrender rights-of-way to railroads that now began to crisscross the Nation, and although she admitted that these new routes brought in useful products and wealth to some members of the tribe (her family included), she also envisioned them as avenues of penetration through which questionable members of "civilized society" gained access to her nation and her people. Although Thomas had discouraged her from accompanying him to either the MKT or Arkansas Valley line camps where he regularly checked on the delivery of ties from his sawmill, he had mentioned that in addition to the many construction workers who labored at these locations, the ramshackle shed and tent communities that housed workers at the end of the lines also contained a hodgepodge of other individuals. Some sold whiskey, some ran gambling dens, and others, ladies of the night, offered additional services. Just where all these people would go when the rail lines were completed remained uncertain, but she was frightened by the prospect. Recently, she had noticed that several new saloons and an emporium had opened near the large livery stable, adjacent to the steamboat landing in Fort Gibson. The emporium, which also included a restaurant and a hotel, seemed to employ a large staff of painted, powdered, and gaudily dressed "maids and waitresses." From Ida's perspective, none of this boded well.

Sitting in her rocking chair sipping a lemonade that Tassie, once her slave, now a maid employed in her son's household, had just brought her from the kitchen, Ida pondered how the events of the past four decades had revamped her thinking. As a young woman in Georgia, she had taken considerable pride in the subscription of the Cherokee planter-merchant elite to the values and cultural patterns of white Americans. Indeed, according to missionaries and Indian agents, her people were the most "civilized" of the Five "Civilized" Tribes. She had looked forward to the day when all the Cherokee people would subscribe to such measures and would serve as a shining example to other Indian nations that they, too, could achieve a civilized status. They, too, could become civilized tribes whom white people would accept as equals.

But after surviving the past forty years, her appraisal had markedly changed. She now knew that many of the old ways taught by her grandmother remained valid. Some of the white man's methods were useful, but they needed to be tempered with the traditional ways of her people. Wealth and comfort had merit but so did ceremonies, tribal stories, a kinship with the land, and most importantly, family. And Ida smiled when she considered the most ironic part of her reevaluation. She had once been proud when whites, whom she had respected, had referred to her people as a "civilized tribe" when compared to many other Indian nations. Well, civilization be damned! Oh, Ida still believed the Cherokees were a "civilized" people, but not in relation to other tribes. Now she knew they were civilized in contrast to the greedy, violent, and dishonest white nation that continued to surround and threaten them.[29]

Suggested Readings

Denson, Andrew. *Demanding the Cherokee Nation: Indian Autonomy and American Culture, 1830–1900*. Lincoln: University of Nebraska Press, 2004.

McLoughlin, William G. *After the Trail of Tears: The Cherokee Struggle for Sovereignty, 1839–1880*. Chapel Hill: University of North Carolina Press, 1993.

———. *Cherokee Renascence in the New Republic*. Princeton, NJ: Princeton University Press, 1986.

Mihesuah, Devon. *Cultivating the Rosebuds: The Education of Women at the Cherokee Female Seminary, 1851–1909*. Urbana: University of Illinois Press. 1993.

Miles, Tiya. *Ties That Bind: The Story of an Afro-Cherokee Family in Slavery and Freedom*. Berkeley: University of California Press, 2005.

Perdue, Theda. *Cherokee Women: Gender and Cultural Change*. Lincoln: University of Nebraska Press, 1998.

———. *Slavery and the Evolution of Cherokee Society*. Knoxville: University of Tennessee Press, 1979.

SIX

Jumping Deer and New Badgers Still Walk in the Smoke

Perseverance in California

Finds Deer

Smoke from the smoldering lodges veiled the canyon. Downstream, several lodges that had housed his extended family still burned, sending embers into the chaparral overhanging the brook that tumbled through the boulders. He thanked Earth Maker that the season had been rainy and the thicket was still green and dense. It hid his wife and grandson on the hillside above and refused to ignite when the embers drifted down into the leafy shadows. But below, near the stream side, his lodge had been burned and his possessions pilfered, and many of his relatives lay dead. He watched as the Wolé diggers (American miners) rummaged through the ruins of his campsite, searching for anything they could salvage. His life, like his family and his village, lay shrouded in ashes.[1]

How he hated them, the Wolé, the crazy newcomers from over the mountains whose obsession with the soft yellow stones make them different from other human beings. Even the Panwyli (Spanish speaking people), the older newcomers who previously had brought their cattle and plows to the great valley despised the Wolé. His people, the Maidus, had not welcomed the Panwyli, since their livestock, especially their hogs, swarmed across the valley displacing deer and killing and eating newborn fawns. But the Panwyli remained in the valley by the big river (the Panwyli called it the Sacramento), where they planted their crops and herded their animals. They had little interest in the high wooded foothills and the mountains to the east, where Finds Deer and his people continued to live, following a traditional life that harvested deer, salmon, acorns, roots, and berries.[2]

Yet some of Finds Deer's relatives had come to terms with the Panwyli. Unlike Finds Deer and his village, mountain people who continued to follow the lifestyle of their fathers, many of his more distant kinsmen, the Nisenans, walked a different path. The Nisenans had chosen to live lower in the foothills, closer to the junction of the Kummayo (the American River) with the Sacramento, which drained the great valley to the north. Many of the Nisenan people had first traded with the Panwyli, then moved their lodges closer to their ranches, working with their livestock, assisting with daily chores, and finding temporary jobs near the Panwyli settlements and missions. In addition, some of his Nisenan kinsmen had also labored for the strange man who had built a fort of logs and adobe bricks near the junction of the Kumayo and Sacramento rivers, but as this man's settlement grew, his treatment of his Nisenan laborers hardened, and many fled back to their Maidu kinsmen whose villages in the higher foothills and eastern mountains offered sanctuary from the strange man's search parties.[3]

Both the Panwyli and the Wolé diggers called this man Sutter, but the Nisenans privately named him Yakan Sim, or Spit on His Tongue, since his speech sounded as if he spoke through a mouth full of saliva. The Nisenan refugees in the scattered Maidu settlements told strange tales of their interaction with both the Panwyli and Sutter. As they sat beside the campfires, the Nisenans admitted that they had first been lured to the Panwyli ranches by the seemingly endless supply of new foods and trade goods available in the Panwyli settlements. The Nisenans previously bartered with Panwyli and even Russian traders for metal objects and trade cloth, but many of the larger ranches had resident blacksmiths, men who fashioned things from iron, and even the scrap metal from their forges at first seemed like a treasure trove to the wide-eyed Nisenans. When they first labored for the Panwyli, they built their lodges in small settlements near the Panwyli ranches, but as the winters passed, many of the Nisenans moved onto the ranches seeking shelter in small adobe brick outbuildings the Panwyli had erected near their barns, stables, and large houses. These new homes, clustered adjacent to the haciendas, enabled the Nisenan laborers to more easily tend livestock and assist with the chores of the ranch and even prompted some of the Nisenan women to work in the hacienda cooking and serving food, sweeping and cleaning the broad verandas, or performing other domestic tasks.

In the past, other, more distant Nisenans and people of other tribes also sought safety around the fire pits of Finds Deer's camp; some of these refugees had fled from different villages, communities of tribespeople who had settled around the great stone and adobe buildings that the Panwyli considered to be holy places, where their shamans practiced strange magic and sang their medicine songs. Finds Deer had never entered one of these huge lodges, but he had viewed it from a distance and had listened as the peculiar chants sung by both their shaman and his followers wafted through the open doorway. Refugees from these shaman-led villages arrived less frequently than those who fled the ranches, but their stories of closely knit communities where brown-robed shamans supervised the production of crops and the tending of small herds of animals fascinated Finds Deer. In addition, these shamans also seemed to serve as village chiefs, adjudicating disputes and encouraging their followers to erect mud-brick buildings. Stranger still, from Finds Deer's perspective, were the shamans' demands that their followers participate in what seemed to be an endless series of communal religious ceremonies that honored a distant dead but living god and his never-aging mother. According to the refugees, if they failed to attend these ceremonies, the shamans forced them to leave the village. Finds Deer had wondered why any tribal people would ever submit to such arbitrary decisions. Why didn't their relatives intervene? The old ways were better. As refugees from both the shaman-led communities and the Panwyli ranches had admitted, life within these settlements offered some security, but it was also confining. Amid the sedentary adobe villages, strange men with strange ways governed tribal peoples' lives. Finds Deer preferred to walk the path of his fathers.

He also was bewildered by the tribal people who had cast their lot with Spit on His Tongue. Fourteen winters ago (1839), this haughty, heavyset man had arrived at the juncture of the Sacramento and Kummayo rivers accompanied by a small party of Kanakas, tribal people from a group of islands in the western sea. At first, Spit on His Tongue recruited nearby Nisenan, Maidus, and other tribespeople to assist him in clearing land, planting crops, and erecting buildings, and initially, this strange newcomer had been generous in his rewards of food, clothing, and trade goods. But when the seasons changed and many of these tribespeople tried to leave to gather acorns or to harvest the annual run of salmon up the Sacramento and the smaller streams that fed the great river,

John A. Sutter, 1850. Taken from *Harper's Weekly*, July 10, 1880. The discovery of gold at Sutter's Mill, on a branch of the American River in California, proved disastrous for many of the California tribes.

Spit on His Tongue grew angry and separated men from their families, using the women and children as hostages to keep the men from leaving. Those who escaped told frightening stories of refugees being hunted down like animals and of hostage women and children suffering at the hands of both Spit on His Tongue and some of his men.

Finds Deer also had been amazed at the growth of Spit on His Tongue's fortified village at the mouth of the Kummayo. The Wolé who had trickled through the mountain passes in their canvas covered wagons had flocked to the settlement (New Helvetia) like camp dogs to a skinning site, but at first. this relatively small influx of newcomers posed no immediate threat. Like both the Panwyli and Spit on His Tongue, these initial Wolé settlers seemed only interested in the broad river valleys. They avoided the rocky foothills and higher mountains where Finds Deer and his people continued to hunt deer and gather acorns and other foodstuffs. Finds Deer had resented their arrival, but he and his people easily avoided them.

But then things changed. Five winters ago, a Nisenan refugee seeking shelter in Finds Deer's camp bought news that a Wolé man had found a handful of the yellow stones in the Kummayo River at Spit on His Tongue's village, and the Wolé men in the settlement had gone crazy, grubbing through the river-bed and digging in smaller streams that joined the river near its juncture with the Sacramento. At first, Finds Deer had scoffed at such foolishness; the Wolé seemed like children, scurrying to gather blackberries. But within two winters, swarms of Wolé and other strange new people arrived in such numbers that the Maidus and neighboring tribal people were overwhelmed. Unlike the Pan-wyli and earlier Wolé settlers who had huddled in the lower river valleys, these newcomers, also were crazed by their hunger for the yellow stones, had clam-bered up into the higher foothills where Finds Deer and his people built their lodges. The Maidus fled before the invasion, seeking shelter in higher, more dis-tant mountain valleys, but even there, the Wolé diggers followed, forcing Finds Deer and his remaining kinsmen to flee from campsite to campsite, scrambling to escape these magpies.

Yet the Wolé onslaught increased. They climbed over windswept, rocky ridges, places where only mountain sheep wandered, and they scraped and dug at talus slopes inhabited only by marmots. The Maidus avoided such game-poor regions, but the Wolé diggers, in their frenzied search for the yel-low stones, crawled all over them. Finds Deer despised them. Their numbers and noise frightened deer and other game animals, and the Wolé readily shot any deer or other animals they encountered. Finds Deer had hunted all of his life, but he had never witnessed such slaughter. He, too, killed animals for food, but the Wolé killed indiscriminately, often leaving the carcasses to rot or taking only a few choice cuts of the slain animal while abandoning the rest. Foothills and mountain meadows where Finds Deer had once found abundant numbers of deer and elk were now almost devoid of animals. Moreover, even smaller animals such as beavers, otters, and rabbits had grown fewer in number as they, too, fell before the Wolé or retreated to more remote regions.[4]

At least the salmon still ran in the Sacramento, but the Wolé had dug up the banks and so muddied many of the other rivers that the yearly runs of salmon up these smaller streams, a special gift from Earth Maker once so welcomed by the Maidus, now had dwindled. He remembered how his people once had feasted during the salmon harvest and how his mother and aunts had dried and smoked the rich, savory slabs of fish that had helped to fill their cooking pots well into the cold moon. But now those days were gone. Great numbers of salmon now were harvested by Spit on His Tongue and his workers. They dried the fish, then sold them to the influx of foreigners, and those salmon that escaped their nets seemed reluctant to enter the muddy, polluted tributaries. Wolé digging for yellow stones built dams and other barriers that discouraged the fish from reaching their spawning beds, and the headwaters of the smaller streams, once so rich in spawning salmon, were now deserted.

Walks in Smoke

Finds Deer also knew that some of his more distant relatives, people who had once labored for Spit on His Tongue and were more familiar with both Pan-wyli and Mole' ways, also dug for the yellow stones. Amazed at how foolishly the Wolé craved the stones and at the large amount of trade goods they would barter for them, Walks in Smoke, Finds Deer's cousin who had assisted with Spit on His Tongue's cattle, joined with other Nisenan workers at Spit on His Tongue's village and fled from the settlement. Walks in Smoke and his companions recalled that they had glimpsed some of the yellow stones scattered along the upper reaches of the Kummayo River, and well, if the Wolé were foolish enough to trade metal tools, blankets, and other valuable things for the stones, then they would find them. They initially gathered some of the stones in several locations near the riverbank and exchanged them for trade goods in the new Wolé settlement (Sacramento) that had rapidly overshadowed Spit on His Tongue's village. But when word of their discovery spread through the settlement, parties of Wolé diggers followed them back up the Kummayo, overrunning their camp and forcing them to abandon their campsite. One of Walks in Smoke's companions had shown the Wolé a paper that a Wolé headman in the settlement had promised would allow them to dig for yellow stones at the camp, but the mob of Wolé diggers seized the paper, tore it in pieces, and threw it in the river. The mob then forced Walks in Smoke and the other Nisenan stone hunters to abandon the site and seek safety elsewhere.

Walks in Smoke told Finds Deer how he and the other Nisenan miners had joined with other refugees in small scattered villages in the lower foothills, but these small settlements soon eroded into swamps of desperation. Wary of returning to Spit on His Tongue's settlement and driven from the gold fields by the burgeoning horde of Wolé and foreign miners, Walks in Smoke and his family scratched for an existence on the brink of a maelstrom, a world that had changed around them. Game was so scarce they could hardly find anything for their cooking pots, and although they still harvested acorns and tried to gather roots and berries, they now competed with large numbers of half-feral hogs that roamed the oak forests and fouled the mast. Walks in Smoke related a sad tale of living on the edge of starvation, unwelcome or even forbidden from entering the Wolé settlements.

Then the sickness fell on them. With the arrival of the diggers, strange new diseases swept through the tribal villages. Even Finds Deer's people, isolated in the mountain villages, suffered from some of these maladies, but deep into Nempombok, the Full Moon Month (late winter, 1851) a virulent coughing sickness broke out among the Nisenans and other tribal people in the valley and lower foothills. Young children and the elderly seemed particularly vulnerable. Walks in Smoke described how victims, including his mother and uncle, seemed to burn with fever and gasped for air as they struggled to breathe, then lapsed into fits of coughing that seemed to fill their lodges. Two of his nephews, one born during the previous autumn, also fell ill and turned glassy-eyed with fever. Healers, trusted grandmothers with a lifetime's knowledge of plants and traditional potions, hurried to the sufferers' lodges, but they seemed helpless against the sickness, as were the shamans, whose songs, ceremonies, and medicine bags also proved ineffective. Many died like salmon after the spawn. Others survived. But when the sickness ran its course, numerous lodges stood empty and abandoned.

In the aftermath, according to Walks in Smoke, he had tried to feed his remaining relatives by tracking cattle that had strayed from the Panwyli haciendas or other ranches, receiving small rewards when he returned the animals to their rightful owners. His previous experience working for Spit on His Tongue had served him well. He had learned the cattle's ways, readily found them in the forest, and brought them back to their ranches every few days. In return, he had been paid in trade goods, or sometimes with an old or emaciated beast that he had then driven back to the refugee camp and had shared with other tribespeople. Walks in Smoke's twelve-year old son, Badger Boy, often helped his father track the wayward cattle, sometimes remaining at a temporary site with a steer that had been recaptured while Walks in Smoke searched for additional animals. Occasionally even Willow Basket, Walks in Smoke's fifteen-year-old daughter, joined the tracking party, particularly when Walks in Smoke anticipated that there were several cattle in the neighboring forest and they all could be caught and then driven, as a small herd, back to their owners.

As Walks in Smoke later lamented, it was his attempts to collect and return multiple cattle that caused much sorrow. Yet his heart had been true; he was trying to feed his village. Two summers in the past, he indeed learned of several stray cattle missing in a neighboring aspen forest, and accompanied by both Badger Boy and Willow Basket, he journeyed to the region, knowing that the density of the aspen grove and the beaver ponds and willow thickets adjoining the crowded aspens would make finding the animals difficult. Walks in Smoke initially found one cow and calf, grazing near a beaver pond, but tracks near the pond indicated that at least three other cattle were in the vicinity and had strayed off into the forest. He left Willow Basket to watch the cow and calf while he and Badger Boy each followed separate tracks left by the other cattle who had wandered off in different directions.

As he later learned from Willow Basket, while his daughter waited with the cow and calf, she was surprised by two Wolé diggers searching for yellow stones in the stream that flowed from the beaver pond. Finding her seemingly alone, they first shared a flask of the fiery liquid to which they and a growing number of the Maidu and Nisenan tribespeople seemed addicted, then demanded that she remove her dress and lie with them. Willow Basket refused, and the older of the two men then seized her, forced her to the ground, and partially removed his heavy canvas trousers. As he knelt over her, tearing at her dress, the girl seized a skinning knife she carried in a small buckskin pouch hanging across her back and had buried it into the left side of the man's neck, repeatedly slicing away until blood spurted out, covering both her hand and her assailant.

The heavy Wolé man had gasped in surprise, then fallen forward on her, trapping her against the ground. Willow Basket sensed that he was dying, but his weight prevented her from springing up and fleeing. The second man, a cousin to the Wolé stabbed by Willow Basket, had anticipated a voyeuristic pleasure in watching his relative rape the girl before he, too, took a turn, and had already dropped his trousers, which were now wrapped around his ankles. When he saw Willow Basket defending herself, he turned and tried to waddle toward a musket the men had left on their pack mule tethered to a willow branch about twenty yards away, but he tripped and fell, and as he regained his feet, he stopped, wide-eyed, as he saw a grim-faced young Indian boy who trained the musket directly at him.

Walks in Smoke had owned no firearms, but Badger Boy had seen these weapons, and earlier in the summer, in Yomen, the Moon of Blossoms, one of his father's friends had permitted the twelve year old to fire an old musket several times at a pine stump near their village. At first, he overshot the target, but after two or three trials, he hit the stump, blowing a chip from its side. Badger Boy knew that he had only one shot, so as the Wolé digger, now cursing both the boy and girl and all tribal people in general, struggled to pull up his trousers, Badger Boy ran toward him, and when the man finally stood, still tugging at his suspenders, Badger Boy shot him point blank in the face with a load of ball and buckshot—blowing the back of his head off.

Still tracking two cattle in the aspen grove, Walks in Smoke heard the gunshot and raced back to the beaver pond. There he found both of his children safe and unharmed. But he also found two dead Wole.' Willow Basket recounted the events leading to the death of the first digger, and Badger Boy told his father how he had returned with a steer only to see his sister being attacked. Walks in Smoke and his children buried both bodies and most of their tools in the aspen grove, but Walks in Smoke kept the musket. He wrapped the firearm in an old saddle blanket that was part of the mule's pack and sent his children home, instructing them to wait until nightfall before carrying the bundle back into the village. He also instructed them to hide the weapon in his lodge and to tell no one except their mother, Wren's Song, what had happened.

Walks in Smoke then drove the three captured cattle and the mule down the valley toward the ranch from which the cattle had wandered. He spent the night with the animals, in a thicket on the ranch's outskirts, then freed the mule so that it might wander into the ranch on its own—and hopefully not be associated with the tragic events of the previous day—and then returned the stray cattle to the ranch's foreman. He received his reward for recapturing the missing cattle and journeyed back to his village.

Two days later, when the mule was found grazing in one of the ranch's pastures, neither the foreman nor anyone else at the ranch associated the animal with Walks in Smoke or his village. But the Wolé digger killed by Badger Boy had a brother back in a mining camp near Sacramento, and when the dead man and his companion failed to return, the brother searched for them, following their general trail up the Kummayo (American River) toward the stream that joined the river from the beaver pond. He failed to find either the bodies or their gear buried in the aspen forest, but he eventually wandered down into the valley, where he stumbled into the ranch. Recognizing his brother's mule, he questioned the foreman about the animal and was told that it had been found in the pasture, about six days ago. The foreman had no knowledge of the missing miners and did not associate their disappearance with Walks in Smoke, whom he described as both friendly and as asset in retrieving lost cattle, but the brother, originally from the Springfield, Missouri, region, hated Indians in general, particularly those he had encountered in California, since he believed the "red devils" knew of gold deposits in the mountains that they refused to share with "regular human kind" (like destitute miners from Missouri). Demanding that the foreman surrender the mule, he then led the animal back to the mining camp.

He arrived just at sundown and loudly proclaimed that the "red devils" had killed his relatives, stolen all their property, and then sold their pack mule to the "greasers." Since the camp was full of destitute Wolé miners whose pipe dreams of quick riches in California had dissolved in failed claims, backbreaking labor, and bitter disappointment, his focus on Maidu and Nisenan scapegoats fell on fertile grounds. Maybe the missing men had found one of the Indians' treasure troves. Maybe they had discovered the bonanza lode that the red heathens had kept for themselves, and the murderin' savages had killed them accordingly. As night fell, rumors spread through the camp that justice must be done; the savages should be taught a lesson. And who knew what might be found? Maybe they could force them red heathens to give up the location of their bonanza. Lubricated by frontier whiskey, the mob decided to meet at dawn, march on the refugee village, and mete out justice. Murderin' savages should be punished! If those damned Indians had anything of value in their village, that would be justifiable payment for all their red-skinned crimes. And if Indian women were available, well, they too had a payment to make.

The mob's drunken decision to wait until dawn saved many lives. Word of the planned attack had spread throughout the mining camp, but it also spread to some miners who were appalled by the mob's intentions. One miner from Ohio, a staunch Catholic, informed a priest at a neighboring mission, and the Brown Robe, who had limited ties to the Indians but despised the drunken miners for their anti-Catholic rants, dispatched a rider to Walks in Smoke's village. The man arrived shortly after midnight and warned the tribespeople of the mob's intentions. In the hours that followed, almost everyone abandoned the camp, fleeing up into the foothills toward the mountains. An hour after dawn, when the mob had arrived, they found the campsite abandoned. Most escaped, although a few miners on horseback pursued one family that had chosen to flee toward the aspen forest where Walks in Smoke and his children

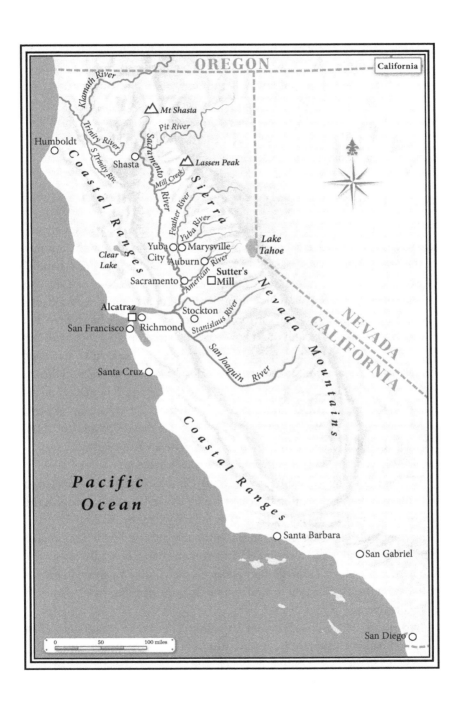

had hunted the cattle. Three hours after sunup, the family was overtaken by seven men on horseback. Four adults (two men and two women, one an aged grandmother) were shot and killed, their bodies then mutilated and thrown into the beaver pond. Three children (a boy aged ten and two girls aged nine and seven) were carried back to the mining camp. Children were profitable. Everyone knew there was always a demand for Indian children, either in the mining camps or down river in San Francisco.

Finds Deer and Walks in Smoke

Following his flight from the abandoned village, Walks in Smoke sought refuge in Finds Deer's village. Located in a secluded canyon high in the foothills of the Sierras, Finds Deer's small settlement consisted primarily of a handful of extended families housed in lodges scattered along the banks of a shallow, chaparral choked brook. Wandering miners who had stumbled into the area consistently ignored the small canyon since the stream bed seemed devoid of any gold-bearing quartz, and the thorn-laced chaparral on the brook's borders appeared to be impenetrable. Finds Deer welcomed his cousin but questioned him about his flight from the refugee camp. He also cautioned Walks in Smoke and his family to hide their exit or entrance into the canyon. Finds Deer and his followers had resided there since the previous summer, but recently, they had watched from the chaparral as three parties of Wolé diggers passed along the hillside. The village remained hidden, but the Wolé now seemed to be searching for yellow stones in places they had previously avoided.

During the following winter, the two men and their families remained in the village, entering or exiting the canyon only by walking on boulders in the stream bed. Small parties led by Finds Deer fed the village by hunting the dwindling number of deer that now ranged in the foothills, and by taking smaller game such as rabbits and raccoons. Their wives and daughters collected acorns and berries in season, although they gathered such food only in small groups of twos and threes, reluctant to stray too far from the canyon's mouth, wary of being discovered.

In contrast, Walks in Smoke used his captured musket to occasionally kill a steer that had wandered far from its pasture, but aided by Badger Boy, he disguised the kill site, leaving ample evidence to indicate that the animal had been killed by Wolé. From previous hunts through the foothills, Walks in Smoke knew that Wolé diggers regularly shot and butchered cattle they found wandering in the forest, and after studying their kill sites, he learned to leave much of the carcass behind, abandoning part of the meat and mimicking their wasteful techniques. Walks in Smoke, Badger Boy, and Willow Basket carried only the meat Wolé favored (loins cuts from the rear quarters, the heart, tongue, etc.) back to the village, but other cuts or organs, like the liver, that his people considered desirable were left to rot. Moreover, the cowhide containing the wound from the musket ball was always conspicuously abandoned at the site — and a clumsy trail of footprints, leading from the site toward the mining camps, was laid out by Badger Boy and Willow Basket, who both wore a pair of heavy (and uncomfortable) mining boots that Badger Boy had taken in the early morning hours from outside a tent pitched by drunken miners near Sacramento.

The ruse had worked. Few Wolé diggers possessed any tracking skills. and if the kill site was discovered by Panwyli ranchers looking for lost cattle, hide fragments with bullet holes, clumsily butchered carcasses, and readily apparent boot tracks only confirmed what the ranchers faced on a regular basis: cattle illegally killed by Americans. At winter's end, the people in Finds Deer's village had survived. They sorely missed the rich taste of salmon, and sometimes their cooking pots were not full, but venison from fallen deer, beef from poached cattle, and stews made from rabbits and raccoons added to rich acorn meal were available. They did not go hungry, and they remained hidden from the Wolé.

Walks in Smoke even rekindled his ties with the hacienda. Twice during the winter, he brought a strayed cow back to the hacienda to which he previously had returned cattle, and the foreman had again rewarded him with trade goods, although he questioned Walks in Smoke about the location of his current village and if he had found the remains of other cattle butchered in the forest. Walks in Smoke had replied that he and his family had fled to a distant village, much higher in the mountains, a site where they would be free of the Wolé. He also claimed that when he first returned to again look for cattle in the ⸱ aspen grove, he discovered so many butcher sites that he fled back to the village. In response, the foreman angrily cursed the Wolé diggers as cattle thieves and promised Walks in Smoke more trade goods if he would bring in additional cattle. Walks in Smoke returned later in the spring of 1853 with two more cattle but had narrowly avoided a small party of diggers enroute. The foreman, much alarmed, again paid him for the cattle but also warned him to use care in returning to his village. According to the Panwyli, the new Wolé government had made plans to remove all tribal people to distant lands or to force them to labor in the Wolé settlements. In addition, some Wolé settlements had recently offered bounties on tribal people and had sent out parties of unemployed diggers to search for them.

On the following day, when Walks in Smoke returned to the village, he sought out Finds Deer, and the two men pondered their future. The late spring of 1853 was in full bloom, and the women had collected plant foods from the forest. But the number of deer browsing in the forest continued to decline, and Finds Deer warned that he believed their numbers would continue to dwindle. Walks in Smoke replied that stray cattle also had become more scarce and that he had been forced to journey farther from the canyon to find them. He also relayed the information that the Panwyli ranch foreman had given to him at the hacienda. Supposedly, the Wolé had set aside regions in which the Maidus and Nisenans could live in peace, but they also were sending parties of unemployed diggers into the foothills to hunt down tribal people and carry them back to labor in the settlements. If people resisted, they would be shot, and a bounty would be paid to those Wolé who killed them.

The new information alarmed Finds Deer. Unlike Walks in Smoke, he had always avoided the Wole,' and he wanted no part of them. He wished to live as a Maidu should live, following the path of his fathers. Perhaps they should abandon the canyon village and move higher into the eastern mountains, to places where the Wolé still rarely ventured. But as Walks in Smoke reminded him, high mountain campsites brought only hardships in the winter: bitter cold, deep snow, and poor hunting. After pondering their options, the two men decided to remain in the canyon village for the time being. Fewer diggers had passed through the region during the recent spring, and none had shown any interest in the small canyon. Deer, though diminishing, were still present; smaller game could always be taken, and the forests still offered acorns, berries, and other plant-foods. And who knew what Coyote, the trickster, had in store? Maybe after the Wolé found all the yellow stones, they would leave the foothills and the Maidus could live in peace.

At first, their decision seemed wise. In the weeks that followed, only one small party of diggers (three Belgians with a pack mule) passed by the canyon mouth, and after giving the streambed a cursory look, they ambled on, unaware of the armed Maidus watching closely from the thorny thicket. But in Ihlak, the Hot Month (late July 1853), Willow Basket, her mother, Wren's Song, and Blackberry

Woman, Finds Deer's grown daughter, left the camp to pick wild plums that had ripened in a small cluster of trees growing downstream, about one and one-half miles from the brook's exit out of the small canyon. The women filled three buckskin bags with the fruit, carefully erased or covered their moccasin tracks below the plum trees, and followed the brook back toward the canyon. But after a mile's journey, Wren's Song lost her footing, slipped, and left several faint moccasin prints in the gravel bar beside the creek bed. Accustomed to most diggers' lack of tracking skills and eager to get home, the women failed to eradicate the moccasin tracks from the gravel and returned to the village.

It was a grave mistake. Two hours after they crossed the gravel bar, the faint tracks were discovered by Ezra Shalhorn, an alcoholic middle-aged mountain man, originally a member of Jim Bridger's company, who had abandoned trapping beaver for what had proven to be a fruitless search for gold. Filthy, bedraggled, and destitute, Shalhorn still had "plenty of trackin' deft," and he decided to try his hand at "Injun huntin'," hoping to earn enough money to pay for a new start in Colorado, where he heard that both "gold and whores" were more plentiful, and liquor was "considerable less chuck." He waited for dusk, then followed the stream up to the canyon mouth, where he spent considerable time crawling through the chaparral until he found the village. Estimating that there were about thirty people in the encampment, he retreated back through the thorns, then hurried down to Sacramento. There, he quickly recruited two dozen men, mostly miners down on their luck and eager to pocket some dollars regardless of how they earned them. He promised them that for $20 (about 85 cents apiece), he would lead them to the village, and then it was every man for himself. "If you can't catch em—well, just kill 'em and bring in their scalps." He boasted that there were about three dozen people, including many women and children, in the village. Or, as Shalhorn sneered, "Easy pickins."

The Wolé diggers struck the village shortly after dawn. As usual, Finds Deer had posted a scout in the chaparral near the canyon mouth to warn of any overnight intruders, but the fifteen-year-old boy had fallen asleep and was discovered by Shalhorn, who slit his throat before he could sound any warning. The other Americans, however, some on horseback, avoided the thick, thorny chaparral and splashed up the stream bed, providing a brief alarm to the three lodges at the lower end of the village. Both Finds Deer's and Walks in Smoke's lodges were located upstream, at the other end of the village, but Finds Deer's grown son, Antler Knife, his wife, Blackberry Woman, and their seven-year-old

daughter, Jumper, lived in the lodge farthest downstream, and as the Wolé noisily approached the village, Antler Knife, armed with a bow, ran out to meet
them. Blackberry Woman sent Jumper up the streamside, telling her to warn
the others that the diggers were attacking their village then to flee to her grandfather. Antler Knife got one arrow off, sending the shaft into the thigh of a
burly, red-bearded man on horseback, but another mounted miner lifted a long
flintlock rifle and sent a lead ball through the middle of Antler Knife's chest.
The Maidu staggered, then fell back over the ashes of his family's cold campfire.
Enraged, Blackberry Woman ran screaming past her husband's body brandish-
ing a small hand axe, but she, too, was shot down amid comments by one of the
leering diggers that he hated to see such a "nice turned-out woman go to waste,
even if she was only an Injun.'"

Upstream, both Finds Deer and Walks in Smoke seized weapons and emerged
from their lodges. Finds Deer immediately sent both his wife, Horn Spoon, and
Jumper, who now stood shaking beside her grandmother, into the chaparral that
crowded the canyon wall. The woman was familiar with a narrow but passable
game trail that spiraled upward through the thorns, and Finds Deer instructed
them to climb the canyon wall and hide in the underbrush until he came for
them. He then hurried down toward the lower end of the village, taking shelter
behind boulders near the creek bed, where he shot arrows at the Wolé. One of
his arrows struck a digger in the face as the man turned to shout to a friend, slicing downward through his right eye and then protruding out his opposite cheek.
The man screamed and several other diggers accompanying him all took cover
behind burning lodges or boulders. Finds Deer smiled. He knew that the wound
probably wasn't fatal, but he also knew that the Wolé would spend his remaining years viewing the world from a one-eyed perspective.

Yet things were going darkly. His son and daughter-in-law lay dead outside their burning lodge, and the residents of the other lodges located at the
lower end of the village were either dead or captured. Finds Deer turned and
scrambled back up the creek bed where Walks in Smoke had first mustered a
handful of other survivors then sent them climbing up the game trail through
the chaparral to safety. Walks in Smoke and Badger Boy remained behind, but
they had been searching for Willow Basket. Shortly after the attack had begun
and the family had heard the firing, both Wren's Song and Willow Basket had
rushed outside to observe what was happening. Since the stream bed curved
toward the lower end of the village, they had crossed the brook to gain an

unobstructed view, and when Wren's Song climbed on a boulder to momentarily see farther downstream, she was struck in the neck by a stray bullet. Willow Basket had raced back to her father's lodge to seek help, but when she and
Walks in Smoke ran back to the streamside, they found Wren's Song dead in a
pool of blood, her jugular severed by the rifle ball.

Walks in Smoke had instructed Badger Boy to remain behind until they
returned with Wren's Song and to tell any additional survivors who might appear
to climb the trail up the canyon wall, but the young Nisenan was incensed that
his mother had been shot by the Wolé diggers. Although unaware that she had
died, he still wanted to avenge her, and while his father and sister hurried to the
streamside, Badger Boy picked up the old musket that his father had left behind
in his haste to reach his wife. The young Nisenan then ran down the canyon
toward the approaching diggers. The weapon had medicine! He had used it once
to protect his sister; now he would use it avenge his mother's injury.

Ahead, Badger Boy could see the Wolé as they splashed up the stream bed.
They moved cautiously, aware that the Maidus had bows but secure in the
knowledge that their quarry obviously had no firearms. No shots had been
fired at them. They had already killed several of the "red devils," but there
seemed to be a few more lodges upstream. Those who had escaped had run in
that direction. The miners believed they had the survivors trapped in the nar-
rowing canyon, hemmed in on both sides by steep walls covered with thorn-
trees. Those they didn't kill they would capture. Money to be made!

At the head of the advancing miners, Ezra Shalhorn was less optimistic. He,
too, believed that the Indians possessed no firearms, but he was well aware
what arrows tipped with obsidian, flint, or iron could deliver from the bows
of skilled archers, and he knew that "some of these damn Injuns had spent
their lives huntin' deer—they ain't no hang-around-the-fort whiskey soppers."
What's more, he knew that the chaparral that seemed so impenetrable to the
miners would seem less formidable to the Maidus. Afraid that their quarry
would somehow escape, he kept hurrying the miners on, ranging ahead of
them by forty yards, beckoning them to catch up with him. "Don't let 'em git
away!" he urged. "Easy pickins when we catch 'em!"

But it was also an easy shot for a Nisenan boy determined to avenge his
mother. Hidden behind boulders at the edge of the stream bed, Badger Boy
watched as the man he believed to be the Wolé chief encouraged the other diggers to move forward. He nestled the musket between two boulders, and while

the man trudged up the stream bed, both the boy and the musket remained well hidden, motionless amid the huge rocks. As Shalhorn approached, Badger Boy trained the weapon on the middle of the Wolé's chest, waited until he could see the grease and tobacco stains on the man's filthy buckskin shirt, then fired from about ten yards. Shalhorn never saw the young man who killed him. The big, smoothbore musket ball, after shattering a rib, plowed through Shalborn's heart, knocking him backward into the creek. The miners in his wake all dodged down behind what cover they could find, alarmed that "them sneaking Injuns" had waited to use their firearms after luring them into an ambush. Meanwhile, Badger Boy seized the musket, darted behind other boulders, then raced, mostly unseen, back to his father's lodge.

There he found his sister and his father carrying the body of his dead mother, frantically searching for him, while Finds Deer stood guard near the mouth of the game trail. Anguished over his mother's death, Badger Boy wanted to charge back down the brook and attack the Wolé, but the two older men convinced him that since their leader had been killed by a firearm, the diggers now would advance even more cautiously. Better to retreat up the game trail and live to fight another day. And Walks in Smoke was eager to bury his wife's body above the canyon, where it wouldn't be desecrated by the diggers. With Finds Deer leading the way, the party ascended the game trail. Badger Boy helped carry his mother's body out of the canyon.

Both Finds Deer and Walks in Smoke overestimated their enemies. The miners had relied on Shalhorn to lead them to the village. After all, he was the seasoned mountain man with a "good reckoning of fightin' Injuns." But after he fell, they were hesitant to proceed farther up the canyon. Who knew how many Indians were hidden in the chaparral, and who knew how many of "them devils" were armed with muskets? The miners had arrived at dawn planning to attack a small village inhabited primarily by women and children, not warriors who might offered a stiff resistance. Better to collect their prisoners (they had captured seventeen, primarily women, children, and two elderly men), cut the scalps or other parts (as souvenirs) off the five "bucks" and one "squaw" they had killed, and "git outa there." It had been a profitable morning. There was a market for Indian women and children—and folks over at Maryville paid bounty money for scalps. The two elderly Maidu men had little market value, but if they couldn't be sold or indentured—well, they, too, had scalps. At least that was something. After hurriedly searching through the remaining lodges, they set all the dwellings afire, then retreated down the shallow stream bed and out of the canyon.

Concealed in the chaparral high above the burning village, Finds Deer watched them leave. Ten residents of the village had survived—finds Deer, his wife, Horn Spoon, and granddaughter, Jumper, a childless middle-aged couple (the woman was a sister of Horn Spoon), two younger men, both unmarried, but nephews of Horn Spoon, and Walks in Smoke and his two children, Willow Basket and Badger Boy. On the following day, Walks in Smoke and his children buried Wren's Song in the forest.

The survivors sought temporary shelter in small, hastily constructed lodges hidden in the chaparral above the canyon, but ten days later, Finds Deer and Walks in Smoke sat beside their small shared campfire to discuss what paths to take. Sickened by the loss of his son, daughter-in-law, and other relatives, Finds Deer had decided to lead his surviving kinspeople north and to seek sanctuary in lands that a visiting Yana man had informed him had been set aside by honorable men among the Wolé, men who were not diggers, men whose promises tribal people could trust. The Yana messenger had related that these protected tribal lands lay south of the Pit River, adjoining the high, broken country the Wolé called Lassen Peak. Finds Deer put little faith in Wolé promises, but the Yana had been so swayed by the new Wolé chiefs that he had agreed to inform other tribesmen of the refuge, and he had assured Finds Deer that the Wolé chiefs were determined that the region would remain tribal land, free from trespass by the diggers. Finds Deer had decided to go to these lands that the Yana called a "reservation." If the Wolé chiefs broke their promises, he could always retreat to more distant places. But he still wished to live as his fathers had lived: as an honorable man, a man who hunted and fished for salmon. He was not Wolé no Panwyl. He wished to live as a Maidu.

Walks in Smoke chose a different path. He, too, hated the Wolé, but he and his family had learned to live among the Panwyli. Both he and Badger (his son, now an experienced warrior who, having killed two enemies, was no longer called Boy) had considerable experience working with cattle, and Walks in Smoke believed that he, Badger, and Willow Basket would be welcomed by the foreman of the hacienda to which he had previously returned cattle. Moreover, all three Nisenans had some familiarity with Spanish and could readily blend in with the herders and other workers on the hacienda. Neither Walks in Smoke nor his children had any intention of relinquishing their tribal identity—they would remain Nisenan—but they believed they could live within the Spanish-speaking community, still interacting with other Nisenan workers but protected from the Wolé. Old Nisenan ways, old stories, old traditions would be kept and cultivated—no bounty hunters, no forced labor, no drunken diggers preying on their women and children. But amid the Spanish speakers, they could hide in plain sight.

Both men knew that their people had always occupied the big valley and the foothills. They had lived beside the Big River for countless generations. Their numbers had diminished, but like other tribal peoples, they would bide their time. They and their children would persist through these dark decades. They were Maidu! They were Nisenan! They would remain! And they knew that one day, their grandchildren, or their grandchildren's grandchildren, would reemerge to reoccupy their homeland!

California

The saga of Finds Deer, Walks in Smoke, their families, and their people offers some poignant insights into the struggle by tribal people in California to retain their homeland and way of life. Most scholars agree that prior to the European entrance into the New World, the region now defined as the modern state of California contained one of the largest Native American populations of all the regions included within the current United States. Pre-Columbian populations are difficult to ascertain, yet in 1800, at the beginning of the nineteenth century, the Native American population in California numbered over 200,000, but by the 1830s, following the end of the mission system, it had tumbled to about 150,000. Twenty years later, at the onset of the gold rush, it had shrunk to about 130,000, and during the next fifty years, it fell precipitously. In 1900, the official US census report listed only 15,377 Native Americans living in the state of California.

Obviously, the Native American population decline in California had started prior to the Spanish entrance into the region, but Spanish colonization, which began in 1769, and the subsequent transfer of political hegemony to Mexico in 1820 accelerated the process. As Franciscan missions spread north from San Diego to the Bay area and both the Franciscans and their converts penetrated into the lower Sacramento and San Joaquin valleys, their intrusion markedly changed Native American life. The Franciscans were accompanied by small Spanish military garrisons and by traders who readily interacted with the tribespeople, but they also introduced new diseases that spread from village to village, decimating large numbers of Native Americans. Traditional village life was disrupted as some tribespeople fled to the missions for help, while others retreated to more distant tribes, further spreading the maladies.[5]

Tragically, the missions, presidios, and Spanish settlements along the coast became the centers for much of this pestilence. Dysentery, diphtheria, measles, typhoid, smallpox, malaria, pneumonia, tuberculosis all took terrible tolls during the Spanish and Mexican periods, and these diseases continued to infect tribal people after the gold rush and into the American period, when they were joined by outbreaks of Asiatic cholera and various strains of influenza. More pernicious, perhaps, was the spread of venereal disease. Carried north by Spanish soldiers, sailors, and traders from Mexico, both syphilis and gonorrhea spread into the mission and tribal communities along the coast. At San Diego, Franciscan Junipero Serra lamented that because these newcomers routinely forced themselves on tribal women, the general "plague of immorality" had undermined his efforts to spread the gospel. As historians have pointed out, many of the victims of these rapes were married women, who then, unknowingly, carried these diseases back to their families. Family members were infected, and the diseases proliferated, afflicting even fetuses who were either stillborn or brought forth as diseased newborns, often doomed to a short life span. Other tribespeople, who survived the initial infection, became sterile, and the birth rate among the tribes plummeted.

With the onset of the gold rush, the loss of life to disease continued. After several generations, tribespeople may have gained limited natural immunities to some of the Spanish borne diseases, but new maladies carried over the Sierras or imported with the horde of gold-seekers who flocked to the region from Europe and the Pacific basin also claimed many victims. In addition, the destruction of villages, separation of families, devastation of traditional food sources, and general disruption of tribal life created cataclysmic conditions that both weakened the Native American population (both physically and emotionally) and nurtured an environment in which disease ran rampant. For example, cholera, carried by miners from the east, reached tribal villages in 1850, while influenza ravaged several tribal communities during the 1870s. By 1900, those Native Americans in California who had weathered this biological holocaust had developed natural immunities similar to many other Californians. Their numbers were much diminished, but they persisted.

They also persevered against concerted attacks by outsiders trying to destroy their way of life. In 1769, the Franciscans established San Diego, the first mission in California, and in the decades that followed, other missions spread up the coast to the Bay Area, where San Francisco Solano, the northernmost of the missions, was founded near modern Sonoma in 1823. Implemented earlier in other parts of the Spanish Southwest, the missions were designed to transform tribal people into an agricultural laboring class resembling peons or peasants in Spain. In exchange for economic security, "the mission Indians" were required to labor in the mission fields or to learn trades that would make the missions self-sufficient economic communities. They were also instructed in the Spanish language and required to relinquish their traditional tribal religions and accept Roman Catholicism (or so the Franciscans believed). Life in the missions was often heavily regimented, and many mission converts resented the corporal punishment meted out by the Franciscans. Both the Spanish and later the Mexican governments attempted to ameliorate conditions within the missions, but efforts to appoint administrators or *alcaldes* from among the mission Indian ranks proved unsuccessful, since the latter often proved to be as oppressive as either the Franciscans or local Spanish officials.[6]

In 1833, Mexico secularized the missions and decreed that half the mission lands, livestock, and implements were to be distributed to the neophytes, but much of this property soon fell into the hands of local Mexican citizens, who then established haciendas. Meanwhile, former mission Indians sought employment on these estates or drifted into coastal towns where they eked out an existence as day laborers or in other menial positions. In the lower Sacramento valley, Nisenans and other tribespeople labored for Jacob Sutter at New Helvetia, Sutter's estate on the American River. Many of these tribespeople, people like Walks in Smoke and his family, eventually grew weary of the regimented life in the Spanish missions, on Mexican ranches—or even at New Helvetia—and fled back to the diminished number of villages still inhabited by their kinsmen. They brought back an exposure to new ideas, but also a warning that while life with the Franciscans, the Mexicans, or John Sutter offered access to wondrous new things, it often came at a high price for tribal people who still honored the old traditions.

Not surprisingly, this conflict between old and new ways fomented violence. Many tribal people were reluctant to join or remain within the mission system, and when the Franciscans, or Spanish and Mexican officials attempted to prevent them from leaving the neophytes took matters into their own hands. In 1774, Tipai-Ipai tribesmen rose up and burned the mission at San Diego, killing three of the Franciscan missionaries. Eleven years later, in 1785, an armed rebellion broke out at San Gabriel, and in 1812, neophytes assassinated an abusive priest at Santa Cruz. Miwok warriors and a Spanish military expedition skirmished over stolen horses in 1819, and during the Mexican period (1824), Chumash people, still loyal to their old gods, rebelled against authorities at Santa Barbara, then fled to neighboring Yokut tribesmen who lived in the San Joaquin valley. Five years later, Yokuts led by ex-neophytes fought Mexican troops to a standstill near the Stanislaus River, east of modern Modesto.

Armed conflicts between Native Americans and Spanish-speaking invaders occurred frequently while California remained under Spanish or Mexican hegemony.[7] After the coming of the Americans, they markedly increased. There were several reasons. In 1848, the year in which the Treaty of Guadalupe-Hidalgo transferred political control of California to the United States, gold was discovered near Sutter's Mill, on the American River. Within four years, the resulting gold rush transformed the demographic profile of the region. Several thousand gold seekers arrived in the Sacramento and San Joaquin valleys during the fall of 1848, but in 1849, the number of prospectors increased by 100,000. By 1852, it had surged to over 250,000. Some of these gold seekers came from Asia, Europe, and Latin America, but most arrived from either Oregon or the eastern United States. Native Americans were overwhelmed.[8]

The sheer numbers of newcomers permeated Native American hunting and fishing grounds, killing game and polluting salmon streams. But more importantly, the character or nature of the newly arrived Americans differed markedly from the Spanish-speaking emigrants who had earlier settled in the region. Unquestionably, many tribal people suffered under the Spanish and Mexican regimes, but both the mission system and the secular Mexican government attempted to incorporate Native Americans into the economic and social systems that they espoused. The Franciscans needed Native American neophytes as laborers within the mission system, and Spanish or Mexican ranchers and merchants needed tribal people to work on their haciendas and in their vineyards or to perform the menial tasks associated with their trades. The Spanish and Mexican systems may have consigned tribal people to the lower echelons of their socioeconomic system, but it did have a place for them. Moreover, the Catholic Church, through the mission system, also deemed Native Americans to be actual "people": they were men and women with souls. They were worthy of salvation.

Most of the newly arrived Americans saw tribal people much differently. They envisioned them primarily as a barrier, an obstacle to progress and an impediment to the miners' feverish hunger to share in the get-rich-quick fantasy of fortunes to be made in the gold fields. Several factors contributed to this Americans' bias and their subsequent violence toward tribal people. First, many of the newly arrived miners carried anti-Indian prejudices with them from the East. Many of the miners were products of Texas, the lower Ohio valley, or the Middle Border, regions that had experienced recent clashes between Native Americans and whites: former hide hunters from Texas, lead miners from Dubuque, or roustabouts from Missouri and Kentucky, who had nurtured negative feelings toward Indians for decades. In addition, many of the gold seekers who flocked to California arrived with expectations of riches that were totally unrealistic. Fueled by grandiose rumors of streambeds awash with gold nuggets, their descent into the harsh reality of endless digging in rocky soil or icy-cold streambeds, coupled with outrageous prices for supplies and mining equipment, was not what they had expected. Their subsequent discovery that some of the more promising sites were already being mined by Native American miners only added to their bitterness.[9]

As a result, the mining camps descended into virtual wellsprings of violence. Most miners were unattached males between the ages of eighteen and forty, ready tinder for social unrest and chaos under the best of circumstances. They wished to strike it rich, then move back to civilization. Unlike farmers or ranchers, they had no intention or remaining in the region, and they were not motivated to develop lasting peaceful relationships with neighboring Native Americans. The miners were not encumbered with wives or children, family members who might be endangered if tribespeople retaliated for acts of violence or injustice. Indeed, there were few women at all in the mining camps, and many of them, like tribal people—like the land itself—were objects of exploitation. In retrospect, the camps were sadly lacking in many of the institutions (families, churches, functioning governments) that helped maintain order in more settled regions. Often, vigilante law prevailed, and lubricated by a plentiful supply of cheap whiskey, such "justice" did not bode well for tribal people.

Violence erupted in 1849. In March, prospectors from Oregon kidnapped and raped several Maidu women near the American River, then shot and killed

PROTECTING THE SETTLERS.

Attack on an Indian Camp. This sketch, taken from the August 1861 issue of *Harper's New Monthly Magazine*, is one of the very few contemporary illustrations of whites attacking an Indian camp in California.

their male relatives when the latter tried to rescue them. In response, the Maidus killed five miners, which in turn triggered a retaliation by the Americans, who slaughtered seven neighboring Miwoks and Nisenans who had not been involved in the previous violence but whose proximity to the Americans made them convenient targets. In 1850, Pomo tribesmen from the Coastal Range were forced to leave their families and labor in mines near the Feather River. When the mine owners withheld their food then refused to pay them, the Pomo conscripts killed two of their "employers." In response, the US Army attacked the Pomo village at Clear Lake, killing over sixty Pomos, including many women and children. Angered over some pilfered livestock, in 1852 miners near modern Auburn attacked a village of Maidus, initially killing over thirty tribespeople then fatally knifing the wounded survivors. And the slaughter continued. Among other accounts, Theodora Kroeber's biography of Ishi poignantly chronicles the campaign against the Yahis near Mount Shasta and Mill Creek in the late 1860s and early 1870s. These incidents are tragically typical of the violence that swirled through the gold fields during these years.[10]

The separate and repeated accounts of bloodshed and loss of life are too numerous to delineate in this limited space, and Native Americans fared better in some parts of California than in others, but demographic records indicate that tribal people living in or adjacent to mining areas east and north of the Bay Area fared the worst. Historians estimate that in 1849, just prior to the gold rush, whites in California outnumbered Native Americans by about two to one. Within the next thirty years, the numbers changed markedly. By 1880, census records from California indicated a new ratio of thirty whites for every Indian. Of course, part of this increase resulted from the influx of white population during the gold rush, but it also illustrated the dramatic decline in the number of Native Americans. There had been no official census of tribal people in 1850, but historians have estimated their numbers at approximately 130,000. In 1880, the official United States census listed the Native American population of California as 23,000.[11]

In the midst of this holocaust, both local and state governments in California formulated or passed legislation (both surreptitious and official) that they hoped would alleviate their "Indian problems." Some of it, particularly at the local level, reflected the most racist and depraved currents in nineteenth century American society. For example, in 1855, after Shasta City offered $5 for every Indian head, one party of "Indian hunters" led a packtrain of several mules to city hall, each mule carrying the heads of eight to twelve decapitated Indians. Four years later, a small town near Maryville offered bounties "for every scalp or some other satisfactory evidence" that a tribesperson had been killed, but they ended their program when it became apparent that many of the miners were turning in "several different and disturbing parts" from the same Indian victim. In 1861, Tehama County also offered payment for Indian scalps, and in 1863, Honey Lake established a similar bounty system. If searching for gold proved futile, unsuccessful or unemployed miners could always hunt Indians.[12]

The gold rush took a particularly heavy toll on Native American women and children. Some tribal women found employment performing menial tasks amidst the mining camps, but most associations with the miners were fraught with danger. Although Anglo-American miners repeatedly described tribal women in negative terms ("degraded ... dwarfish beings ... repugnant in all ways"), they readily sexually assaulted them. Newspapers published in California during the period contain numerous accounts of such rapes and the violence that often flared in their aftermath. Because Indians had little legal recourse, rapists generally were immune from prosecution, and since many miners considered the California tribespeople to be less than human, the stigma associated with rape in more "civilized" areas was rarely applied in the mining districts. And even those tribal women who willingly entered into legal or common-law marriages with miners often found themselves abandoned when their erstwhile husbands pulled out of the gold fields to seek a living elsewhere.[13]

Children fared even worse. During the Mexican period, children occasionally had been kidnapped and clandestinely forced to work on ranches or for tradesmen, but in 1850, after legislation passed in California legitimized the apprenticeship and indenture of Indian children, Native American children could be legally removed from their families. Supposedly, children could not be apprenticed without a parent's or relative's approval, but professional "apprenticers" systematically kidnapped Indian children then forged their parent's signatures, obtained them from dishonest law enforcement officials, or followed in the wake of frontier vigilantes who killed the children's parents then seized the children as "orphans." Boys were usually apprenticed until they were twenty-five years of age, girls until they reached twenty-one. Prices for the children ranged from $30 to $2,000 (older, more handsome girls brought the highest prices), but most sold for around $50 apiece. As the elevated prices for attractive teenaged girls suggest, some of this market was driven by a sex trade that preyed on these children, both female and male, and evidence illustrates that that on occasion, younger, physically attractive preadolescent boys also brought high prices. The entire apprenticeship program was so flagrantly abusive that in 1860, it was essentially repealed, but historians estimate that before its demise, at least four thousand tribal children fell victim to its brutality.[14]

Recoiling from the most glaring abuses and facing harsh criticism from the eastern states, in 1850, the new state of California passed "An Act for the Government and Protection of Indians." Unfortunately, although the legislation gave lip service to reform, it did little to curtail many of the abuses mentioned in the preceding paragraphs. The act prohibited non-Indians from forcing tribal people to work against their will, but it legalized other employment practices that ensured that many Native Americans would serve as convict laborers or indentured servants. For example, able-bodied tribespeople could be arrested for loitering or "strolling about," and if declared a "vagrant," he or she could be hired out to the highest bidder for up to four months. In addition, any Indian fined by a court for any offense was liable to work for the non-Indian paying the fine until the value of the Indian's labor matched the fine payment. Non-Indians paying the fine were required to feed and clothe tribal people working for them, but since the 1850 act also provided that "in no case shall a white man be convicted of any offence on the testimony of an Indian," almost all allegations of abuse by Native Americans were summarily dismissed. As noted historian Albert Hurtado has sardonically pointed out, the act of 1850 "protected them [Native Americans] very little and governed them quite a lot."[15]

Officials in Washington attempted to regulate the chaos. Relying on a system that had been implemented in the East, in 1851, federal commissioners negotiated a series of treaties in California to establish eighteen separate reservations totaling about 7,500,000 acres, or approximately 7.5 percent of the total land in the state, which would serve as homes for about twenty-five thousand tribespeople. But when the treaties arrived in Washington, politicians from California intervened, arguing that the lands to be set aside were far too large and too valuable. If all these lands were enclosed in Indian reservations, they would be "wasted." Bowing to the pressure, the United States Senate refused to ratify the treaties, and in response, Indian agents were instructed to renegotiate for smaller tracts. During the following decade, federal agents created a series of much smaller "reservations" or "farms" on federal land, but these tracts, totaling no more than two hundred thousand acres, attracted fewer than ten thousand Indians.[16]

Yet like Finds Deer, Walks in Smoke, and their grandchildren, tribal people in California weathered the storm. Although the Native American population in the state continued to decline, census takers in California during the latter half of the nineteenth century unquestionably failed to enumerate many tribal people. Focusing their efforts on the few remaining reservations, rancherias, or former mission communities, they overlooked people such as Walks in Smoke and his family who sought employment on the ranches in the lower Sacramento valley. Other tribal people worked on farms, in vineyards, and as laborers in a broad spectrum of jobs, learning both Spanish and English but living amid the Spanish speaking population. Many adopted Spanish surnames, which further confused Anglo census takers, and since they lived in proximity to Spanish speaking communities, both local officials and the growing "white" population in the state assumed that they were part of the Mexican American community.

Ironically however, like displaced tribal people in parts of the American South and Midwest, many Native Americans in California hid in plain sight. They might have adopted Spanish or even Anglo surnames, and they might have been fluent in Spanish or English, but they remained Maidu, or Nisenan, or Pomo, or Yahi, or Miwok, or Yokut, or Chumash, or Cahuilla, or one of more than one hundred other indigenous tribal communities that continued to exist. They came together regularly, sometimes yearly, sometimes more often, and they told the old stories, sang the old songs, and practiced the old ceremonies that their ancestors had celebrated for generations. Sometimes, their gatherings were private; sometimes they shared their traditions with other people. But they cherished them and passed them on to their children. And they persevered.

And in the twentieth century, they were joined by an influx of other Indian people. As the fertile valleys of the Sacramento and San Joaquin Rivers blossomed into agriculture meccas that fed both the state's growing urban areas and also the nation, the demand for agricultural labor drew many tribal people from throughout the western states. In the 1930s, the Great Depression brought an infusion of Native Americans among the "Okies" displaced by the Dust Bowl—Cherokees, Choctaws, Potawatomis, Delawares, and other tribespeople from the Great Plains. Then, ten years later, the lure of good-paying defense jobs in the aircraft factories of the Los Angeles basin and the shipyards at Long Beach and in the Bay Area also attracted an influx of tribal people from across the United States. When World War II ended, many of these relatively new Native American residents remained, and California, once the region most closely (and accurately) associated with catastrophic population decline, was transformed. To the surprise of many non-Indians, by 1960, the state's Native American population had skyrocketed. In addition to the more recent emigrants, the members and descendants of the indigenous California tribes, people whose ancestors had weathered the holocaust, and who had quietly persevered, reappeared and took their rightful place among the burgeoning Indian population in the state. In 2010, there were one hundred and nine federally recognized tribal communities functioning in California. Another seventy had applied for such recognition. The Native American population in the state was officially numbered at over 360,000 individuals, the largest such population for any state in the union.[17]

Perseverance

In November 1969, a group of young Native American activists, embittered over federal Indian policy, living conditions on both reservations and in urban areas, and the lack of economic opportunity in the Bay Area, stormed ashore on Alcatraz Island, located in San Francisco Bay, about one and a quarter miles offshore from Fisherman's Wharf. Declaring the island "Indian Country," the activists established a radio station, published a newspaper, and entertained Hollywood notables such as Anthony Quinn and Jane Fonda. They received considerable news coverage from across the nation and the world, and although they abandoned the occupation after six months, the Alcatraz seizure both attracted and energized younger Native Americans, such as Wilma Mankiller and George Horse Capture, who would go on to become successful leaders, both among their tribes and at the national level. Among the activists who landed on the island during the first day of occupation was a young Nisenan man, a truck driver, who had been living in Richmond, just south of Oakland. He had been active in support of the East Bay Indian Center, and after arriving at Alcatraz, he joined the security detail that monitored the Coast Guard vessels that repeatedly circled the island. His name was Carlos Tej'on. *Tej'on*, of course, is the Spanish term for badger.[18]

Three years later, in May 1973, during the midst of the news media's coverage of the American Indian Movement's (AIM) occupation of Wounded Knee, an eighteen-year-old girl of mixed Maidu and Irish lineage graduated from a small rural high school northwest of Yuba City, in the Feather River district of northeastern California. A conscientious student, the girl had won several writing contests with essays and poems that reflected her attachment to the region in which she lived. Although her parents had little education—her father like his father and grandfather before him had worked in the lumber industry, and her mother was a cook and a housewife—they had encouraged her to do well in school, and to the girl's surprise and her parents' great pride, she had been awarded a scholarship and financial aid to enroll at the University of California at Berkeley. She intended to enter the university's prelaw curriculum, and, proud of her Maidu heritage, which she inherited from her mother, she also planned to immerse herself in Berkeley's newly formed American Indian studies program. She had recently watched news footage that focused on a group of young Indian attorneys who had formed a new organization, the Native

American Rights Fund (NARF) to defend the legal rights of tribal people. The girl, Linda Jumper O'Reilly, whose middle name had been passed down from generation to generation, had been favorably impressed. She envisioned the NARF attorneys as "the new warriors." When she completed law school, she fully intended to join them.

Jumping deer and new badgers still walk in the smoke.

The struggle continues.

Suggested Readings

Bauer, William J. *We Were All like Migrant Workers Here: Work, Community, and Memory on California's Round Valley Reservation, 1850–1941.* Chapel Hill: University of North Carolina Press, 2009.

Hackle, Steven W. *Children of Coyote, Missionaries of St. Francis: Indian-Spanish Relations in Colonial California.* Chapel Hill: University of North Carolina Press, 2005.

Hurtado, Albert. *Indian Survival on the California Frontier.* New Haven, CT: Yale University Press, 1988.

Kroeber, Theodora. *Ishi in Two Worlds: A Biography of the Last Wild Indian in North America.* Berkeley: University of California Press, 1961.

Lindsay, Brendan C. *Murder State: California's Native American Genocide, 1846–1873.* Lincoln: University of Nebraska Press, 2012.

Rawls, James. *The Indians of California: A Changing Image.* Norman: University of Oklahoma Press, 1984.

Sandos, James. *Converting California: Indians and Franciscans in the Missions.* New Haven, CT: Yale University Press, 2004.

SEVEN

Flower Girls, Fires, and Sausages

Surviving the Boarding School Gauntlet

Most of the buildings were gone. Of course, Martin Luther Hall, which held the director's office, most of the classrooms, and the dining facilities attached to the building's rear, had burned in the big fire of 1898, but the dormitories at the Iowa Lutheran Indian School had been dismantled, and much of the lumber used in their construction had been sold by the Missouri Synod. The barn, bedecked in faded forest-green paint, like the other old school buildings, still stood, as did the director's cottage (now turned into a comfortable farmhouse), and she recognized some of the old workshops, which now served the farmer who lived on the acreage as smoke houses, poultry coops, and other farm sheds. The farmer obviously had purchased some of the lumber from the dismantled dormitories to build a series of fenced pens holding hog houses and farrowing sheds that crowded the area that had been the athletic field. Part of the west pasture remained, and she could see that it held a small herd of dairy cattle and four horses, but the rest of the old pastures had been plowed under and planted in corn and some other grain crop (she thought it was wheat, but she wasn't sure). She wasn't surprised. Prices for grain crops had soared during the Great War, and farmers throughout the Midwest had rushed to cash in on the profits. Even today, August 31, 1920, almost two years after the war ended, many farmers still hoped that the inflated prices for their cash crops would continue.

The trip back from Green Bay to Chicago, then across Illinois and Iowa on the Union Pacific Railroad to Marshalltown, had been challenging, since she rarely journeyed outside eastern Wisconsin. More recently, however, Rose Hill

Greenspring and her husband had traveled by train from the Oneida Reservation to Milwaukee on several occasions to visit her husband's relatives, so she had some familiarity with train schedules. And of course, she had traveled by rail to Marshalltown before. Twenty-four years ago, in 1896, when she was fourteen years old, she and four other students from Oneida, accompanied by a Lutheran minister, had journeyed from Wisconsin to Marshalltown when she and the other students had first enrolled at the school. Now, on this hot August afternoon, those events seemed like a lifetime ago, but she remembered those days—both the good times and the bad—and they had markedly shaped her life. In fact. even now, she was enroute to visit Lilly New Crow (Flint), who lived on the Omaha Reservation in Nebraska. She had stopped only briefly (for an afternoon) to visit the site of the old school where two decades ago both she and Lilly had been classmates. Later this evening, she planned to board the 8:40 train west to Ames, then on through Council Bluffs to Fremont, Nebraska, where she would catch a local line that ran north to Rosalie, a small depot on the Omaha Reservation.

Rose was eager to see her friend. Both she and Lilly had arrived at the school in the same year (1896), and although Lilly was one year older than she, both girls were enrolled at the "fifth year level," which the principal, the Reverend Wilhelm Holzhauer, believed matched their previous academic training. Both girls had sporadically attended day schools on their reservations, but like other rural students in the Midwest, bad roads, inclement weather, and the necessity to assist their relatives with everyday chores had caused them to miss many classes. Still, as Rose remembered, both she and Lilly read and understood the primers that were furnished to them at "Lu-Tern" (their nickname for the school), and although they found the texts to be boring and innocuous, they easily mastered them. Both Rose and Lilly had left the school in 1898, after the fire, and had returned to their respective reservations, but they had corresponded on a semi-regular basis, shared information about their husbands and children, and even sent a few photographs back and forth between Wisconsin and Nebraska. Rose knew that distance and the passing years, like wind on a cobweb, had frayed at their relationship, but she also knew that those bonds of friendship and sisterhood, forged in the years and companionship at the school, remained strong. They remained sisters in their hearts if not in their blood.

Rose remembered that their companionship initially had been kindled by both girls' arbitrary enrollment in the same classes and by their assignment to similar "domestic training," where they spent most afternoons supposedly learning to cook and prepare meals or to wash and iron clothes. In theory, the domestic training was designed to better prepare them to provide and care for their future families or to obtain a position as a productive domestic worker in the service of a non-Indian household after they graduated from the institution. In actuality, as both Rose and Lilly soon learned, they spent most of their afternoons assisting in the preparation of meals for the 140 students enrolled at the school or in washing, ironing, and occasionally mending their clothing.

It was in the kitchen, and later in the laundry, that both Rose and Lilly first met Iris Pipestem, a fourteen-year-old Otoe girl from Red Rock Creek, on the tribe's reservation in Oklahoma Territory. Iris's family were members of the Coyote Band of Otoes, a conservative people, and although she had been exposed to English, she had been raised by her grandparents who spoke only Otoe in their home. Iris's family called her Tho-ni-xramuxra, or Blue Water Flower, but when she was first enrolled at a Quaker day school, none of the Quaker missionaries could pronounce her Otoe name. Her teacher, a maiden lady from Delaware, had grown up amid spring gardens awash in iris blooms. Well, irises were also dark blue flowers that needed lots of water, so Tho-ni-xramuxra was officially enrolled as Iris, and the name stuck. Iris's attendance at the day school was sporadic at best, and she trailed many other Indian students of her age in her familiarity with a "white man's education." In response, Indian agents in Oklahoma sent her to the Iowa boarding school in an attempt to separate her from her family and other traditional Otoes.[1]

At the Lutheran school, Iris was both isolated and lonely. After listening to her quietly sobbing for several nights in the girl's dormitory, Rose sat on the foot of her bed and offered her an apple that she had saved from the evening meal. Neither Rose nor Lilly spoke Otoe, but all three girls worked in the laundry, and Rose and Lilly helped Iris learn the ropes in terms of washing, ironing, and the daily routine. Since there were some similarities between the Omaha and Otoe languages, Lilly also informally tutored her in the jargon-ridden "Indin-Enlish" that formed the vernacular of students. For her part, Iris despised her morning classes in which she was forced to spend time in classes with younger students, but she looked forward to the afternoons in the laundry, and later in the kitchen, where she shared stories about her family with the two girls her own age. By the end of the girls' first semester, in late December 1896, Rose remembered that the three girls had formed a close, but informal clique. They spent time together, they did their best to look after each other, and they privately named themselves the Flower Girls (Rose, Lilly, and Iris).

They had their hands full. Founded by the conservative Missouri Synod of the American Lutheran Church, the Iowa Lutheran Indian School was staffed by Lutheran clergy and laity dedicated not only to the education of Native American children but also to remolding them into late-nineteenth century "good American citizens." Following general guidelines established by the US Indian Office, Reverend Wilhelm Holzhauer and his board of directors designed a curriculum that required students to spend their mornings (8:00 A.M. until noon) enrolled in four classes of age-graded, traditional academics such as reading, arithmetic, grammar, and religion (after all, this school was a Lutheran institution). After an hour spent eating "dinner" and taking care of personal items, the students spent the afternoon learning vocations that supposedly would prepare them to become productive, useful American citizens.

Unlike the academic classes taught in the morning, the afternoon classes were divided by gender. Some of the girls joined the Flower Girls in the kitchen and laundry, but others were taught the rudiments of sewing, poultry raising, gardening, and housecleaning (particularly how to wash windows and mop and polish floors in large, institutional buildings). In contrast, male students were encouraged to pursue vocations or trades that flourished in rural Iowa in the decades that followed the Civil War. Most of the boys were funneled into mastering those skills needed to operate a small midwestern farm. They learned how to clear and plow fields and to plant, cultivate, and harvest crops such as corn, wheat, oats, and hay. They also learned how to raise, care for, and butcher hogs. Some worked with a small herd of dairy cattle. Others were taught how to string and mend wire fences and how to build small farm buildings. A smaller number of boys were shunted off into those trades necessary to a farm community: blacksmiths. harness makers, cobblers, carpenters.

Not surprisingly, although much of the afternoon's vocational training was supposedly designed to provide students with those skills they would need in the future, it also provided an important economic foundation that buttressed the school. Rose remembered that Reverend Holzhauer had hired Frieda Schwarzenheimer, his middle-aged second cousin, as the school cook to oversee the kitchen and supervise the girls who in reality prepared most of the meals. The school also hired two other German Lutheran women from Marshalltown; one oversaw the laundry, the other supervised the cleaning of the institution's buildings. Another woman, Irene Klaus, the spinster sister of one of the members of the school's board of directors, served as the official school seamstress, but in reality, Rose knew that girls from all the grades spent their afternoons in the "clothing building" darning socks, replacing buttons, mending rips and tears, and occasionally cutting and sewing new garments. All the school uniforms, however, were purchased from a Lutheran supplier in St. Louis. Rose also remembered that the dirty dishes and pots and pans in the kitchens were washed by younger girls assigned to the task. Dirty laundry was also washed and pressed by students, while younger girls were responsible for sweeping, dusting, and polishing the floors and furniture.

The local German American staff (most were immigrants or the children of immigrants), coupled with the predominantly German American Lutheran teachers, infused the school with a highly structured, conservative Lutheran character. Rose had encountered a few Lutheran children in Wisconsin, but most of the Christian Oneidas (the majority of the tribe) were either Episcopalians or Methodists, and she had been raised in a Methodist family. The German American farmers who lived near the Oneida Reservation were Catholics from southern Germany. They enjoyed a good time, generally avoided the Oneidas, and left all proselytization to their priests or other clergy. But the German Lutherans who staffed the school in Iowa were cut from a different, stiffer cloth. Most of the teachers—those who taught academic classes and many of the less formally trained staff who provided vocational "training" and supervised the students' daily rounds of chores, both in the school and on the farm, enforced a strict code of discipline and a series of rules that emphasized student adherence to what the teachers called "civilized ways."

During the morning classes, students were expected to be seated in their desks (actually, in their chairs quietly seated at assigned places at long tables) three minutes prior to the beginning of the class, and when the teacher entered or left the room, all the students were expected to rise as a token of their respect for the instructor. Rose recalled that when students were asked to read or to answer questions, they were required to stand, and if they were ever sent to the large slate blackboard at the front of the room, they were required to be careful not to break the chalk, and to clean the board with a rag that hung from a hook beneath the chalk tray when they finished. Any conversation between students was strictly forbidden during class time. Subject matter was learned by rote, not through informal discussions. And needless to say, all oral communication between students and between a student and the teacher was in English. Heaven help the poor child who forgot and replied to a question in his or her tribal language.

In comparison, the "vocational training" courses that took up much of the afternoon were less structured. Rose remembered that Mrs. Schwarzenheimer, who preferred to be called "Frau" Schwarzenheimer (ironically, although tribal languages such as Omaha, Otoe, and Oneida were forbidden, terms or titles in Teutonic tribal languages—such as German most certainly—were acceptable) regularly supplied the girls who worked in the kitchen with a list of foods to be prepared, after which she would sit on a tall stool in the kitchen drinking coffee and watching as the students peeled potatoes, boiled cabbage, and prepared whatever cuts of pork were to be roasted, fried, or boiled for supper (the evening meal). Sometimes the girls prepared soups that would serve as the following day's dinner (as the midday meal was called), and they regularly baked bread and other pastries that could be eaten over the next two days. Obviously, such activity necessitated conversation between the students involved in these tasks, but Frau Schwarzenheimer tolerated no frivolity among the girls under her care. Learning to cook (preparing meals for the students and the faculty and staff who also resided at the school) was a "serious task," and the girls were supposed to keep their noses to the grindstone.

Yet Rose smiled as she recalled how the students circumvented the cook's supervision. It was easy to carry on quiet conversations when the heavyset German American housewife was perched on her stool, drinking coffee and nibbling at sausage patties or pastries (the latter of which she brought from her home in Marshalltown and rarely shared with anyone), and it also was easy to slip items of food—apples, freshly baked bread—under one's apron to later share with friends in the dormitory. Rose also remembered how her friend Lilly delighted in purloining sugar, molasses, and spices such as cinnamon and nutmeg that were later added to apples or bread to produce late-night delicacies consumed by the Flower Girls and their friends. The Flower Girls and many other students had adapted quickly. They had learned how to get along.

Although the "Lu Tern" school faculty took pains to limit contact between male and female students (no "hanky-panky" allowed!), the Flower Girls made friends with many of the boys. Rose was well acquainted with Walter Swamp, an Oneida boy one year her senior who also had enrolled in the school in 1896, and their friendship had continued. Lilly's cousin, Russell Fontenelle, had been enrolled at the school since he was nine, and had spent two years on campus prior to Lilly's arrival. Iris was the lone Otoe at the institution, but she became acquainted with several boys from Oklahoma who were from the Pawnee, Ponca, and Potawatomi Reservations. From these friends and from other boys at the school, Rose learned that the afternoon "vocational" training provided to male students resembled, yet differed (in kind) from, that of the girls. Male students assisted two Lutheran school farmers with the cultivation and harvest of approximately seventy acres of corn, wheat, and hay, and in maintaining and repairing the school buildings. They also helped the farmers in the feeding and care of the draft horses needed for the farm implements and in caring for a small herd of dairy cattle and a considerable numbers of hogs, whose sheds and hog houses were located on the periphery of the school-grounds, strategically far downwind from the school and the dormitories.

Other boys spent the afternoons with local carpenters, cobblers, and harness makers. Most were semiretired, elderly men, all of whom worked at the school on a part-time basis. They supervised male students as the latter repaired school buildings and furniture, cobbled or mended shoes, or learned the skills of a blacksmith. Yet Rose had learned that the male students fared better in their afternoon training than did the girls. In retrospect, she realized that the boys were taught skills or trades in preparation for occupations that now were less in demand, but at least employment opportunities in some of these fields still remained. Moreover, she knew that the student-teacher relationships between the boys and their grandfatherly part-time teachers were much more cordial and open than those of the girls and their strict afternoon cooks, laundresses, and seamstresses. She remembered that many of the male students often spoke fondly of their supervisors, who regularly openly joked with the boys about the school's stuffy, stiff-necked faculty.

Not so the Flower Girls and other female students. Their relationship both with the women who supervised the kitchen, laundry, housekeeping, and seamstress programs and with the dormitory matrons, girls' disciplinarians, and female teachers (with a couple of notable exceptions) was much less cordial. Thinking back over her years at the school, Rose was convinced that the female faculty's overzealous determination to "civilize" their Indian students and to "free them from their tribal ways" prevented most of these straitlaced Lutheran women from accepting that the girls brought with them many worthwhile traditional values from their varied tribal backgrounds. Rose wondered

Eleven female Omaha students, circa 1882. Courtesy of the Carlisle Indian School Digital Resource Center, Cumberland County Historical Society. These Omaha girls enrolled at Carlisle are wearing uniforms that served as the model for similar uniforms at other Indian boarding schools across the United States.

why the women at the school had failed to understand that the institution offered a wonderful opportunity to blend the best of these tribal values with the admirable traits of late nineteenth-century American mainstream culture, but they had not. Instead, in addition to academic and vocational instruction, the women at the school took every opportunity to condemn any pattern of tribal culture that a girl continued to follow.

Rose remembered how quickly her friend Lilly had run afoul of "Freda Hammer" (the Flower Girls' secret nickname for Frieda Schwartzenheimer), the school cook. In mid-September 1896, about two weeks after their arrival at "Lu-Tern," Freda Hammer instructed both Rose and Lilly to cut up large slabs of meat taken from the front quarter of a freshly killed old dairy cow, to be used in the preparation of beef stew, which the cook planned to prepare in enough quantity to provide several meals for both the students and the faculty. Since the menu at the school rarely featured beef (German farmers in east-central Iowa raised pigs, not beef cattle), the girls welcomed the dietary change, especially Lilly, whose reservation in Nebraska regularly grazed cattle. Lilly had often helped her mother and aunts prepare beef stews and other meals, and as the Omaha women had cut the meat into strips for roasting or the stew pot, they would often nibble small tidbits of the raw meat as delicacies. The practice originated when the Omahas hunted bison on the plains, but when cattle were substituted for "buffalo," the Omaha women continued the practice, similar to the manner in which an Iowa housewife might have eaten a few juicy, fresh blackberries as she prepared to bake a blackberry cobbler.

Both Rose and Lilly were cubing beef at a large, oaken butcher block, and in the midst of a private, hushed, quiet conversation about how much they hated their school uniforms, Lilly periodically sliced off small fragments of raw beef and ate them, when Freda Hammer jumped off her stool, rushed across the kitchen, and grabbed Lilly by her apron, shouting, "Spit it out! Spit it out! We're not heathens! This is a God-fearing kitchen!" Rose remembered that she too had observed Lilly occasionally eating a small sliver of meat, but since her Oneida family did not follow the practice, she hadn't joined her friend, but she never considered the practice to be strange. Her grandfather had told her that Oneida hunters sometimes ate a sliver of raw venison after dressing a deer to thank the spirit of the animal for providing food.

The cook did not share Rose's tolerance. Still holding Lilly by her apron straps, she marched her out the kitchen door and down to the director's office. Rose and the other girls in the kitchen listened wide-eyed as Freda Hammer berated the poor Omaha girl about not appreciating the opportunity to leave her heathen ways behind in Nebraska and "make something of herself among civilized people in Iowa." When the cook returned, she was alone, but the girls were subjected to another twenty-minute tirade on how eating "good civilized foods" brought "good, clean civilized ideas." Poor Lilly was confined for several hours in the "atonement room" and then sent back to her dormitory. Because she had already "eaten her share of the beef," she was sent to bed without her supper.

Most of the students found the food at the school to be both monotonous and not to their liking. It certainly reflected the tastes and preferences of the institution's German American administration and faculty. Rose remembered that pork, in its various cuts, formed the basis for most of the meals that she helped prepare in the school's kitchen. Rose's family had regularly eaten pork on the reservation in Wisconsin, but never in the quantity or frequency it appeared on the menu at Lu-Tern in Iowa. Pork butts, pork shoulders, pork loins, "fresh side meat," ham, bacon, and most important, pork sausage, sometimes as links but more often as sausage patties, were doled out to the students on a daily basis. Although the faculty and staff regularly enjoyed pork chops and ham slices, the students more frequently received their daily rations in the form of ham and beans, pork and vegetable stews, or more commonly, greasy, fat-ridden patties of pork sausage. Part of this pork came from hogs raised and slaughtered on the school's farm, but much of it was purchased from Lutheran farmers in the region, who welcomed the opportunity to sell their surplus animals. From the school's perspective, pork was cheap and plentiful. Moreover, everyone knew it was a "civilized" food eaten by civilized people. There was nothing better than ham or pork sausage to teach "wild young Indians" what was best for them.

Recalling Lilly's experience, Rose remembered that two or three times a semester, the kitchen did prepare beef, and occasionally they would receive several large cages of scrawny chickens that the Flower Girls called "grasshopper chickens" since the birds were so tough and stringy from chasing grasshoppers around Iowa farmyards. Under threats from Freda Hammer, the girls in the kitchen were forced to kill, scald, pluck, dress, and then dismember the poor birds before boiling them in large pots with carrots and potatoes. Rose hated the process, but the resulting stew, served over bread, was a favorite dish of the school's students. She chuckled to herself when she also remembered that three Navajo boys, sent to the school from New Mexico, had approached Freda Hammer and asked why no mutton was ever on the menu. Freda had picked up a large spatula and chased them from the kitchen, loudly claiming that "decent people didn't eat sheep—only Jews, Arabs, and Spaniards."

Rose also recalled that the students disliked some of the regularly served vegetables. Most of the students tolerated the boiled potatoes that were a standard side dish at most meals, and almost all enjoyed the boiled corn when it was available. But corn was not a favorite of either Freda Hammer or the faculty, whose taste ran to beets and particularly cabbage. Rose and most other students found boiled beets not to their liking, but they absolutely detested cabbage, which even when picked fresh, smelled like an old outhouse when it was cooking, and they particularly hated it after it had been pickled in vinegar and transformed into something Freda Hammer had called "sauerkraut." Lilly renamed the slimy, foul-tasting concoction "rotten skunk-grass," and when she dared to ask Freda Hammer if perhaps it already had spoiled in its barrel, the cook angrily told her to "shut her mouth" or she would send her back to her "rightful place" in the atonement room. Yet Rose was well aware that most of the large bowls of sauerkraut regularly placed on the students' serving tables usually remained untouched, although the faculty and staff readily devoured the slimy pottage.

Fresh vegetables, even in the summer, were usually in short supply, although the students were treated to roasting ears and green beans in season. Since the green beans were always served with large chunks of ham hocks or bacon, Rose found them palatable. In contrast, the faculty and staff regularly ate some strange little red roots called radishes, which Rose found bitter and distasteful, and they also ate watery, green seedpods called cucumbers, although they doused them in a solution of sugar, onions, and vinegar. In the summer, watermelons were a treat for both the students and faculty, and bushels of apples from the school orchard were harvested in the fall and stored in a fruit cellar, available as a special treat during the winter months. Rose recalled that the students enjoyed the wheat bread served with most meals, and at Christmas and Easter, they relished the apple strudel, occasionally baked from the stored apples and from butter produced at the school's small dairy. They were less fond, however, of the lukewarm oatmeal that was served as breakfast, seven days a week, except on special occasions.

Rose and Lilly served in the kitchen during their entire tenure at the school, and she laughed out loud when she remembered how Lilly's ongoing quarrel with Freda Hammer had landed the Omaha girl "in Dutch" but how Lilly had retaliated. During the early winter of 1897, the Flower Girls made friends with two boys their own age, Robert Red Elk, a Sauk and Fox student from Oklahoma, and Nathan Jumps About, a Winnebago (Ho-Chunk) from Wisconsin. Nathan was enrolled in morning classes with Rose and Lilly, while Robert shared morning classes with Iris, but both boys spent their afternoon caring for the farm's draft horses. They had little opportunity to interact with each other during the day, but both groups sometimes sat near each other at chapel, which usually followed the evening meal, and they sometimes met in out-of-the-way alcoves during the evening, where the girls gave the boys food they had purloined from the kitchen. In return, the two boys regaled them with rumors and gossip that their mentors had shared with them about the faculty and administration. Since both Iris and Robert were from Oklahoma, they felt a particular kinship, especially since the Otoe and the Sauk and Fox Reservations were not far apart and since Iris had relatives living near Stroud, on the Sauk and Fox Reservation.

All the students were especially fond of apples, and once, while Rose distracted Freda Hammer with a question about boiling potatoes, Lilly slipped down the stairs into the fruit cellar and stuffed eight or ten of the stored apples into a small flour sack, then carried them back to the kitchen, hidden under her apron. The theft initially had been successful, but when she tried to divide the apples into two bundles so that she and Rose could conceal them inside their jumpers and take them back to the dormitory, Freda Hammer noticed the unsightly bulges inside Rose's clothing (Rose remembered that as a girl, she had been as skinny as a rail; alas, those days were gone) and stopped her, found the apples, and sent her to the atonement room. Since Rose had several apples, she was forced to spend three nights locked in the room, alone, sleeping on a rough blanket on the floor. Rose remembered that she had borne her punishment well. When Freda Hammer asked if other people had also taken any apples, Rose had said nothing. In consequence, Lilly made it back to the dormitory with her share of the fruit.

Rose accepted the punishment in silence, but Lilly, chagrinned that she had in fact taken the apples and Rose had been punished, sought revenge. Rose remembered that when they met with the boys two days later, Lilly and Iris had given the boys an apple apiece, but Lilly talked quietly with Nathan, who then laughed, replied out loud, "Oh, yes, indeed," then added, "Just give me a day or two." Two days later, when they again met after chapel, Nathan handed Lilly a small burlap feed bag, telling her, "Keep 'em somewhere cool, and use 'em in the next day or so," to which Lilly replied, "Don't worry, I've got just the place for them." Rose recalled that when she asked Lilly what was in the bag, Lilly grinned but refused to answer, telling her to come to the kitchen later that night at midnight, after curfew.

Shortly after midnight, when Rose stole back through the darkened hallways to the kitchen, she found both Lilly and Iris giggling in the dark. But illuminated by moonlight that trickled in through a window, Lucille showed Rose the carcasses of two large rats that Nathan and Robert had caught in traps in the horse barn and which they skinned and dressed as if the rodents had been squirrels or rabbits. Meanwhile, Iris had already retrieved the small sausage mill used to grind limited quantities of pork sausage, and to Rose's horror, Lilly dumped both rats—heads, bones, tails, and all—into the mill while Iris cranked away, turning the rodents into rat sausage. Rose asked what they were doing, to which Lilly replied, "Just wait till Freda Hammer gets a bite of this. She'll learn better than to mess with the Flower Girls."

On the following afternoon after Freda Hammer took her place atop her stool, Lilly carefully replaced the two fried pork patties on the plate sitting on the counter behind her with the special ones the girls had prepared the night before, complete with salt, pepper, a handful of ground oats, a little dirt, and some dried horse saliva from the horse's feed sack in which the boys had carried the dead rodents. Then the Flower Girls quietly went about their assigned chores, preparing potatoes and boiled cabbage for the evening meal. They watched from three separate locations as Freda Hammer reached back to the cabinet top behind her, picked up the first fat sausage patty, and bit off half of it. After momentarily chewing her mouthful, Freda stopped, looked back at the other half of the patty, took a swallow of coffee, then devoured the rest of the sausage on her plate. She then turned to Sarah Lafromboise, an Ojibwe student from the Red Lake Reservation in Minnesota, who usually oversaw sausage preparation and commented, "Well, Fraulein, I don't know what sort of spices you put in the sausage today, but that pig must have eaten some strange slop. Anyway, It's *sehr gut*! If you've got any more, I'd like to have them." Unaware that the sausage had been switched, Sarah looked back at the cook in amazement. But hidden behind the huge cook stove, Rose, who had watched Freda Hammer gobble down both sausage patties, then lick her chops, could hardly contain herself. She also could hear Lilly choking back laughter behind a large storage cabinet, but in the pantry, poor Iris had less control. She laughed so hard that she wet her bloomers and had to go back to the dormitory for dry ones.

Bloomers! Rose shook her head as she recalled how the girls had hated those things. In their attempts to remold Indian students into white children, the Lutherans subscribed to the widely accepted belief of the late nineteenth century that "civilized clothes could tame the wildest Indians," and both boys and girls were issued uniforms that they kept in storage lockers in the dormitories next to their beds. Although the uniforms differed slightly according to the students' age groups, when the Flower Girls arrived at Lu-Tern, they were issued several pairs of baggy cotton briefs, two cotton undershirts, four gray cotton blouses (two lightweight and two heavyweight; the fabric resembled dark gray denim), and ankle-length jumpers for everyday wear. Each girl was also given a single dark blue "Sunday dress" that buttoned up the front, complete with a detached white starched collar. They were also issued heavy dark blue woolen jackets. Rose remembered that the coats resembled US Navy peacoats worn by sailors in the recent war and wondered if the St. Louis firm that supplied these garments had purchased them as Navy surplus items from the government. Every girl was also given a short, dark blue, knit stocking cap. In contrast, knit woolen mittens and matching scarfs, in an array of bright hues and patterns, were regularly supplied to the school by women's missionary groups at local Lutheran churches in Iowa, and Rose recalled that the girls had welcomed the opportunity to add this small touch of individual color to their winter clothing.

The school's uniform also included long black cotton socks with garters and a pair of the most uncomfortable shoes that Rose had ever worn. Heavily influenced by the tastes and demands of rural Iowa farmers, the school yearly supplied both the girls and the boys with one pair of ankle-high, often ill-fitting, heavy black brogans. Rose remembered that these "clod hoppers," as the students called them, were manufactured in the school's cobbler shop, primarily by student apprentices who paid little attention to detail or sizing. Surplus pairs of these "clunkers" were then stored, supposedly according to size, on long shelves for future use. The girls hated the ugly rough shoes, which were identical to those issued to male students. Although both the school's faculty and staff were offered free access to this homemade footwear, almost all, except for the school farmers, wisely declined.

Like the girls, the male students at Lu-Tern also were issued uniforms. Boys regularly wore "union-suit" underwear, light gray cotton collarless shirts, and bibbed overalls of a dark blue heavy denim fabric. They received "Sunday clothes" consisting of gray trousers and a matching wool military style tunic, that like the girls' dresses, buttoned up the front. For everyday use, they wore dark brown canvas "barn coats" and gray caps with small front visors, although larger straw hats were available during the summer. For Sundays or special occasions, they were issued short gray wool jackets that matched their military tunics. They also wore the heavy, ill-fitting brogans manufactured in the school's cobbler shop, but the boys accepted them more readily than did their female counterparts.

Rose recalled that the students' primary complaints about their uniforms were related to the wide-ranging temperatures encompassed in the Iowa climate. The Uniform Selection Committee that ordered the uniforms from the

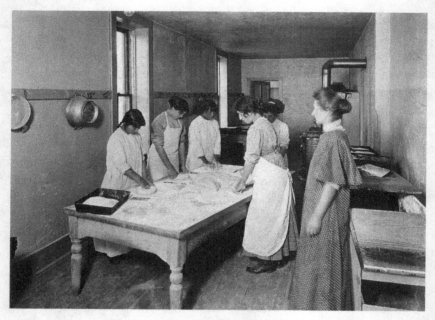

Native American students working in the kitchen at the Genoa Indian School, Genoa, Nebraska. Courtesy of Genoa US Indian School and Genoa Historical Museum. Similar to the "Flower Girls" featured in chapter 6 of this volume, these girls at the Genoa Indian School also prepared food under the supervision of a cook or teacher.

Lutheran supplier in St. Louis met and studied the catalog and made their selection in mid-January, when the high temperatures in Marshalltown were well below freezing for over a week, and they had ordered uniforms designed to keep the students warm. The uniforms amply served that purpose, but from early May through mid-October, and especially during the Iowa summer, when temperatures often spiked into the mid-nineties, many of the students sweltered.

And that's when the bloomers became a problem. The two female members of the selection committee (Irene Klaus, the school seamstress, and Alma Schneid, a Lutheran minister's wife from Cedar Rapids) had demanded that all the girls be issued two pairs of dark gray (to match their jumpers) ankle-length bloomers as a "garment of modesty" to "shield their nether regions" as they stooped, bent over, stored items on high shelves, or performed other tasks associated with their afternoon "vocational training." Discounting the fact that their full, ankle-length jumper skirts and their heavy cotton socks already draped the lower halves of the girls' torsos from any unseemly glances, the Lutheran women steadfastly maintained that the bloomers were necessary to protect the girls' virtue—and the girls were required to wear the bloomers all afternoon, regardless of the task or the temperature. Rose remembered that in the warm months, when hot ovens and stoves raised the afternoon temperatures in the kitchen into the upper nineties, the added layers of the bloomers were devastating. She sometimes felt faint from the heat, and even Freda Hammer, perched atop her chair drinking cold lemonade and frantically fanning herself with a church fan, complained mightily. "And she most certainly was not burdened with bloomers!" Rose recalled indignantly. The thought of Freda sweating away in a huge pair of bloomers still made Rose laugh out loud, even now, over twenty years since she had labored in that sweltering kitchen.

At least the school's "outing" program gave them some relief. Between mid-June and the first of September, most of the older students, both male and female, were farmed out to "good, God-fearing" Lutheran families in Iowa or eastern Nebraska. Both federal officials and Lu-Tern's board of directors believed that the students would benefit from spending time during the summer with a Christian family and experiencing "the fellowship of civilized family life." Most of the boys were sent to Iowa farmers, where they functioned as an additional hired hand on the farm, earning a small wage in addition to their room and board. Rose recalled that some of the boys were forced to work long hours and were treated very poorly, but she remembered that both Robert and Nathan seemed to enjoy the experience. Their work was hard, but they shared in the family activities and enjoyed trips to town on Saturdays, where they spent part of their small earnings on food or items of clothing.

Both Lilly and Iris also enjoyed their outing experience. Lilly was sent to the home of a Lutheran schoolmaster in Des Moines where she assisted his wife in the kitchen and in other housekeeping duties, but the kindly schoolmaster also spent time each day showing her his books and tutoring her in reading and geography. The schoolmaster and his wife treated her as a member of their family, and she grew fond of their two daughters, whom she supervised while their parents were absent from their home. Iris, in contrast, was sent to a small cattle ranch near Beatrice, in southeastern Nebraska, where she also initially assisted the rancher's wife with household chores. But when the rancher learned that her uncle had taught her to sit astride a horse and ride bareback on the Otoe-Missouria Reservation in Oklahoma and also had taught her how to move and

208 ❖ *Chapter 7*

water cattle, he had laughed and asked her if she would prefer to assist him and his son on the ranch rather than "help his missus." Iris readily accepted, and she spent most of the summer on horseback helping the rancher and his son herd cattle. The rancher warned her not to tell school officials about her change of jobs, and he sent her back to Marshalltown with the obligatory letter stating that she had "always lent a helping hand in the kitchen and with the washtub." But the rancher had been grateful for her assistance with the cattle, and when she returned to Lu-Tern, Iris carried twenty silver dollars and an invitation to return in the following summer.

Although Rose did not participate in the outing system, her summer duties at the school had also been changed. Because so many of the students were absent from Lu-Tern on their outing assignments, the kitchen prepared far fewer meals, and Rose was temporarily reassigned to the school's administrative office, where she served as an errand girl for Clara Braun, Schoolmaster Wilhelm's Holzhauer's unmarried twenty-three-year-old granddaughter. Although Clara worked as Holzhauer's clerk and secretary and admired her grandfather, she believed that many of the institution's strict rules regarding student conduct were archaic and counterproductive. Unlike her grandfather, Freda Hammer, and many of the faculty, Clara tried to develop a cordial, more open relationship with many of the students, and Rose remembered how pleasantly surprised she had been when she was first assigned to her office. Rose initially had few office skills, but she closely observed how Clara managed affairs in the office, and she willingly performed those tasks Clara assigned to her. Moreover, carrying notes and messages back and forth between the institution's office and the many separate academic or vocational units enabled Rose to learn the ins and outs of the school, both at an official and an unofficial level.

Sitting in her hired buggy on the gravel road at the site of the old school, still daydreaming about the past, Rose chuckled again when she remembered that the first news the Flower Girls were eager to share with each other when they reassembled in the dormitory at Lu-Tern in early September 1897 was not their summer adventures but the fact that they all had spent the summer without wearing their bloomers. Florence Schapmeir, the wife of the Des Moines schoolmaster, detested the garments and had forbidden her daughters to wear them. She readily agreed to Lilly's request not to wear bloomers while she resided with the schoolmaster's family. Rose had similar news. Aware of how uncomfortable the long, hot pantaloons were and eager to test the authority of stuffy disciplinarians such as Freda Hammer and Irene Klaus, the school seamstress, Clara, Rose's supervisor, informed her that she need not wear the garments while she worked in the office. Clara's declaration surprised Headmaster Holzhauer, but he doted on his granddaughter and reluctantly agreed. He received strong protests from both the school cook and seamstress, so he assured them that when the fall semester started, all female students would again be "dressed appropriately." Meanwhile, back from Nebraska, Iris informed both of her friends that she had not worn bloomers since she arrived at the ranch and that the rancher's wife had sewn two denim split riding skirts for her that she had worn, on horseback, all summer. In fact, the woman had given her the skirts when she left the ranch and she had worn one with her school blouse back on the train from Nebraska but had changed into her school-issued jumper in the train depot restroom at Marshalltown before returning to Lu-Tern. Later that evening, Iris modeled the skirt for Rose and Lilly in the darkened dormitory, but she kept both skirts concealed in her clothing trunk, afraid to wear them openly.

Yet in retrospect, Rose now realized that the temporary triumphs over the bloomers paled in comparison to what she learned after working during the summer in Clara Braun's office. She had previously suspected that the school relied on student labor to keep the institution functioning, and she knew that the school was supported by Lutheran churches and religious organizations from Iowa and parts of eastern Nebraska and northern Missouri. But Rose discovered that this financial support waxed and waned from quarter to quarter and from year to year, depending on harvests, crop prices, and other economic vagaries. More to her surprise, Rose also learned that the institution continually balanced the uncertainties of Lutheran financial support by contract payments from the federal government. Indeed, according to a letter that she found while retrieving some papers that had fallen from Clara's desk, she discovered that during 1895–96 (the previous year), the Office of Indian Affairs had paid the school $182 for the "keep" of each student enrolled in the institution. Humpff! No wonder the school tried to keep such a tight rein on the students. If too many left, Lu-Tern would falter.

Rose recalled that she also learned of other problems. During the summer, she overheard several conversations between Clara and her grandfather that indicated that not all the outings had gone as smoothly as had Lilly's and Iris's. One twelve-year-old boy, a Kickapoo from Kansas, had been forced to work at least twelve hours every day, had been poorly fed, and had been forced to sleep in an old chicken coop. He had fled the farm and had been arrested by the local sheriff, who after speaking with the boy had kindly returned him to the school, not back to the farmer. Another boy, a fourteen-year-old Quapaw from Oklahoma, had been outed to a farmer near Grinnell, but after suffering similar abuse, he had fled to the Meskwaki settlement near Tama, and the local sheriff, preferring not to tangle with the testy Meskwakis, refused to enter the reservation to search for him. Rose later learned that after a Meskwaki family gave him an old horse, he rode it back to Oklahoma. Nellie Washee, a Forest Potawatomi girl from Michigan's Upper Peninsula, was sent back to the school after only one month, when the mistress of a household in Waterloo claimed that she was lazy and refused to work. Yet an investigation by Clara indicated that the disgruntled housewife had demanded that Nellie prepare all meals for the woman, her banker husband, and their four children. In addition, the woman had ordered Nellie to clean and maintain a twelve-room house, do the family's laundry, and maintain the family garden.

Another girl, Marie, a pretty fourteen-year-old Ojibwe girl from the Lac Courte Oreilles Reservation in Wisconsin, had been returned to the school after only three weeks residency with a Lutheran minister and his wife in a small town near Waterloo. Rose had never learned all the details of the student's short tenure in the minister's home, but in retrospect, she was sure she knew what had happened. The poor girl had been brought back to Lu-Tern in tears, accompanied by a tight-lipped local sheriff's deputy and his wife, and had been consigned to the school's small infirmary for several days after her return. On the day following the girl's arrival, Rose had been filing papers in Clara's office when she overheard an irate Clara confront her grandfather with, "Something should be done about that man. I learned from a friend in Waterloo that he's tried that game before." The accusation attracted Rose's attention, and she hurried to the closed door between the two offices and listened while Headmaster Holzhauer replied, "Now Clara, we must remember that he's an ordained minister, a man of God. I can't believe that he would force himself on a young girl like that. Moreover, his church has been very generous in their support of this institution." To which Clara angrily retorted, "Grandfather, according to the deputy, his own wife lodged the complaint against him!" Rose then heard Clara stomp toward the closed door, so she scurried back across the room, where she quickly resumed her filing. In tears, Clara burst through the door from her grandfather's office, told Rose she was going to visit Marie in the infirmary, then asked her to finish filing and leave the office. Rose remembered that she quickly complied. She also remembered that a very subdued Marie remained at Lu-Tern for the remainder of the summer, but when September arrived, she went back to Wisconsin. Rose recalled a few other unhappy incidents involving the school's outing system, most of which she also learned during her summer internship in Clara's office, but they seemed to pale in comparison to the assault of the young Ojibwe woman.

Yet the institution had other problems that it also preferred to keep from the public. As Rose found out, Lu-Tern was hardly a bastion of robust good health. Rose recalled that during her enrollment at the school, the institution maintained a small infirmary (about two dozen beds) separated into two wards by gender and attached to a school nurse's office, located in a frame building just next to the dormitories. The infirmary was supervised by Hilda Wolter, the resident school nurse, and a cadre of part-time volunteer assistants, usually goodhearted, matronly Lutheran women from congregations in Marshalltown or the immediate area. More serious medical problems were addressed by Dr. Otto Schnortz, a country doctor also from Marshalltown. Nicknamed Dr. Snort by the students due to his allergies and sinus drainage, the physician was an older man who subscribed to conservative views of medicine and believed that if left alone, most patients might suffer but would heal themselves. "Keep them warm, give them fresh spring water and chicken soup, and don't feed them rich foods" was his usual panacea for most maladies. For more serious cases, he carried an ample supply of little gray pills (contents unknown) that caused many seriously ill students to sweat profusely and hopefully broke their fever, then induced them into a deep sleep. Subscribing to prevalent nineteenth-century beliefs about "vanishing redmen," Schnortz agreed that "the Indian race" was physically inferior to Anglo-Saxons and prone to certain diseases. When the school's board of directors had first contracted with him for his service, he had promised them he would do his best, but he warned them that that he had occasionally been called to the nearby Meskwaki Reservation, and his experience had taught him that "these swarthy-skinned heathen children sometimes resist all treatment." But Schnortz's fees were quite reasonable, he was an affable fellow—also a Lutheran—and he was willing to regularly travel the two miles from Marshalltown to the school, so the board hired him.

In retrospect, Rose remembered that the medical care was, at best, haphazard. She recalled that during the summer she worked for Clara, she had carried notes back and forth from the office to the infirmary containing instructions from Clara to the nurse regarding the widespread incidence of trachoma at the school. The eye disease infected many of the students, including the Flower Girls, and all three had undergone the rather painful eyewash treatment that Dr. Snort and Nurse Wolter prescribed as a remedy. Rose and Iris quickly recovered, but Lilly's condition, although much improved, never completely went away. Like many of the younger children at the school, she continued to be periodically plagued with the runny, swollen, red eyes and eyelids that characterized the disease. Frustrated, Clara lamented to Rose that despite the medical staff's efforts, trachoma flourished in conditions where children lived in close quarters. Eyewashes were successful in some cases (in Rose and Iris, for example), but trachoma was such a contagious disease and was spread so easily by commonly used towels, dirty hands, and other contaminated things such as toys, pencils, and kitchen utensils that the disease easily rebounded.

At least it did not seem to have threatened any students' lives. Other maladies, however, took a darker toll. Rose remembered that during her two years at the institution, in addition to students regularly suffering from severe colds, which sometimes deepened into pneumonia, the school was also plagued with several outbreaks of contagious diseases that swept across Iowa and the Midwest. Measles erupted throughout central Iowa in the late winter of 1896, spreading to the institution and taking four students' lives. Influenza, in its many forms, was a regular visitor during the winter months, and depending on the particular strain, also took a grim toll. And in spring of 1897, scarlet fever made a brief appearance, striking particularly hard at younger children but running its course more quickly than some of its lethal cousins. Still, it left three little girls dead and two Delaware siblings, a boy and a girl aged seven and eight, respectively, permanently deaf in its aftermath.

Looking back at those days, Rose now realized that all these diseases had been facilitated and transmitted by conditions at the school. Not only did crowded dormitories serve as fertile incubators for communicable diseases, but school administrators (particularly Freda Hammer) were reluctant to excuse student workers from their afternoon responsibilities, ensuring that newly infected students (those not yet seriously ill, just "under the weather") remained at their posts, further transmitting the maladies to their peers. In addition, the school's infirmary, which functioned adequately under ordinary times, was far too small when faced with a measles or scarlet fever epidemic. Rose believed that Nurse Hilda and her volunteers had done their best, and she remembered that Dr. Snort had promptly answered requests for professional assistance, but his reliance on spring water and chicken soup buttressed by his little gray pills were not always effective. To give the physician credit, Rose knew that in very serious cases, he regularly recommended that students be transferred to the Lutheran hospital in Marshalltown, but sometimes his recommendations were not followed. She learned from an irate Clara that both her grandfather and the board of directors were often reluctant to promptly send students to the hospital. Hospital care was expensive.

But the real killer—less obvious, yet more pernicious—was tuberculosis. As she matured and become more aware of the incidence of tuberculosis on her own Oneida Reservation, Rose now realized how often while enrolled at Lu-Tern she had unknowingly observed its symptoms within the school's student body. Crowded into dormitories, classrooms, and other workspaces, the students were in constant contact with one another, and coughs, or sputum on less-than-clean handkerchiefs, were seen as an accepted norm. Rose remembered that several of the girls who worked in the laundry were plagued with chronic coughs and that Eva Brinkerman, one of the two women from Marshalltown who supervised the facility, regularly coughed up blood-flecked mucus into a series of small flowered handkerchiefs that she then added to the linen being washed and ironed by the students. It always seemed strange to Rose that more girls than boys seemed to be "wan," underweight, and chronically suffering from respiratory problems. Maybe the boys' afternoons spent working outdoors on the farm or in the less crowded, open-aired workshops provided a healthier workplace, but for reasons unknown to her then, or even now, in 1920, the male students seemed to fare better. Well, good for them!

In contrast, Rose specifically remembered Annie Rain, a quiet fifteen-year-old Caddo girl from Oklahoma Territory who had arrived at Lu-Tern only a year prior to Rose. Annie had spent the previous two years washing dirty clothes and linen in the laundry but had been reassigned to the kitchen in the fall of 1897, where Rose first made her acquaintance. When Rose asked Annie why she had been moved to the kitchen, Annie had told her that during the past year, she had developed a nasty cough and lost weight. In response, the school nurse had requested she be assigned to the kitchen, where she might perform lighter tasks and perhaps have access to better food. Annie had welcomed the change, but her condition had not improved. Rose recalled that the Caddo girl seemed frailer as the year wore on, and her cough worsened. Rose, Lilly, and Iris tried to look out for the ailing girl and often helped her with her kitchen chores, but Freda Hammer intervened, scolding the Flower Girls and warning Annie that "My kitchen *ist* no place for slackers!" If Annie "couldn't keep up the pace," she would be transferred back to the laundry or maybe to housekeeping, "where *sie* can scrub *die Fussboden* [floors]." Annie struggled mightily, but her condition gradually worsened. By early January of 1898, Annie had lost additional weight. She also began to occasionally spit up blood into kitchen rags, which she hid in her apron pocket.

Annie desperately wanted to go home to her family at the Caddo Agency, near Anadarko, in Oklahoma Territory. Like many of the students at the institution, Annie sorely missed her family, and as her health failed, she feared she would never see them again. Rose remembered that many students at the school, especially the younger ones, also spent long lonely nights weeping in the darkness of the dormitory. Some of the students from neighboring states occasionally were surprised by short visits from family members, but such occasions were rare since most reservation families had no extra funds for travel, and the school administration discouraged such visits, which they believed disrupted or set back the institution's ongoing efforts to transform the students into "productive, patriotic Americans." Lilly's mother and aunt had visited her during her first year at the school, and Lilly had begged to return to Nebraska with them, but they convinced her to remain at the school for another year or until the schools on the Omaha Reservation could provide an adequate education. During her first summer at the school, Rose's father had also journeyed to Marshalltown and had been forced to sleep for one night in the school's horse barn when no hotel would rent him a room. He, too, promised her that if she spent three years at Lu-Tern, she could return to Wisconsin and finish her education at the Oneida boarding school on the reservation, which was currently being enlarged and adding additional classes to meet the growing demand by Oneida families. Rose remembered that her father's promises provided her with an achievable goal: there was light at the end of her tunnel.

Not so with Annie, Iris, and most of the other students from Oklahoma, New Mexico, and the Southwest. The long distances separating them from their families made visitations almost impossible, and the uncertainties of rural mail service to isolated reservation communities meant they had great difficulty communicating with their homes. Like Annie, Iris also felt shut off from her family in Oklahoma, and as Annie's health deteriorated, Iris developed a special kinship with the Caddo girl and her struggles. Moreover, Iris was thoroughly convinced that Annie's declining health was aggravated by Freda Hammer's heavy-handed tyranny in the kitchen. In February 1898, after Annie almost fainted after a fit of prolonged coughing, Iris confronted Freda, telling her that she was taking Annie to the infirmary. Freda Hammer coldly replied, "Well, go ahead. Go ahead! Next week, that one be scrubbing floors." Then, laughing, she said, "Maybe not so far for her to fall when she fall down, huh?"

Iris had escorted Annie to the infirmary, where Nurse Hilda put her to bed and called Dr. Snort. Annie later told Iris that after he examined her, he shook his head and told her, "Young lady, you need to go to the hospital," but after conferring with Schoolmaster Holzhauer, Annie rested for a day in the infirmary then returned to her classes—and her new "vocational training program," working in housekeeping. The Flower Girls could no longer assist her in the kitchen, but they saw her during the next week carrying a heavy mop and bucket cleaning the hallways and staircases. Incensed, Iris again confronted Freda asking why Annie had been given heavier work, but the cook told her to "mind your business or *sie auch* will get the mop."

In response, late in the afternoon on the following day, the Flower Girls took their case to Clara. Since she had worked for Clara the previous summer, Rose led Iris and Lilly to Clara's office, but before they could say anything, a red-eyed Clara told them to sit in the three chairs in front of her desk, then tearfully told them that Annie had collapsed earlier in the afternoon and that one of the school farmers, assisted by Robert Red Elk and Nathan Jumps About, had hitched a horse to a farm wagon and carried her to the Marshalltown Lutheran hospital. She told the girls that Annie was very ill, had hemorrhaged considerable blood from her lungs, and that Dr. Snort was very concerned about her. When Iris inquired why the school had waited so long before sending her to the hospital, a bewildered Clara replied that both she and her grandfather had been told by Freda Hammer and Eva Brinkerman, one of the school laundresses, that Annie was a troublemaker, a malinger, a student who continually complained about feeling poorly to avoid the rigors of her vocational training. Consequently, they had relied on the cook's and seamstresses' advice and kept her at the institution. When Rose, Lilly, and particularly Iris described the full extent of Annie's deteriorating health and the cook's and seamstresses' complicity in it, Clara grew steely-eyed and very quiet. She then thanked the girls, told them not to mention to anyone—students or faculty—that they had spoken with her, and promised them that she would get to the bottom of this.

The following morning, the Flower Girls returned to their classes. Shortly before noon, they learned that Annie had died during the previous evening. A funeral service was held for her two days later, and she was buried, among the unmarked graves of other students who had died at the school, in the Lutheran cemetery near Marshalltown.

One week later, Eva Brinkerman was instructed to report to the hospital, where after a physical examination, Dr. Snort and two other physicians certified that she was tubercular and therefore unfit for service at the institution. She was discharged. Freda Hammer also underwent a thorough physical examination, but fortunately (or unfortunately, from Rose's perspective), Freda was found to be quite obese but free from communicable diseases. She temporarily resumed her position as school cook, but her activities in that position were continually monitored by Clara Braun, who repeatedly dropped in on the kitchen to observe Freda's supervision of food preparation. Clara also strongly suggested to the cook that she get off her stool and actually move about the kitchen rather than spend her afternoons eating sausage. Indeed, to Freda's dismay (and to the Flower Girls' delight), after three days, the cook's stool seemed to disappear (although a careful inspection might have found it in the horse barn), and Clara's intrusions to the kitchen increased. More galling still, from Freda's perspective, Clara repeatedly intervened, countered her instructions, and permitted several of the older students to select items, which Freda personally disliked, for the school's menu. Aware that the students were now laughing at her behind her back, after two weeks of Clara's repeated kitchen visits, Freda stormed down to the director's office and demanded that her second cousin "do something about his granddaughter," who was ruining her kitchen and causing disciplinary problems among the students under Freda's charge. To her dismay, Headmaster Holzhauer replied that during the past two weeks, he had received several comments from both the students and faculty that the quality of the food being served at the school had been much improved. Indeed, he had wondered if Freda might consider taking a new position as an assistant housekeeper in charge of Martin Luther Hall's attic storage areas and the building's large basement. On the following morning, Freda blustered her way into Clara's office, accused her of "poisoning my cousin against me," then walked into Holzhauer's office and resigned. At 1:00 in the afternoon, when Clara informed the girls in the kitchen that they would soon be working for a new cook, the cheers rattled the dishes.

Sophie Zeitman, who took Freda Hammer's place, was cut from a different cloth. A friend of Clara's, the thirty-two-year-old widow (her husband had been killed two years earlier in an accident at the local lumber yard) enjoyed working with the students, and they appreciated both her attempts to learn more about their different tribal backgrounds and her tolerance of their good-natured pranks.

Both Rose and Lilly attempted to show Sophie the ropes, and Iris was quietly friendly, but the Otoe girl had been particularly close to Annie and still blamed the school for her friend's death. On a cold night in late March, Iris crept from her bed, dressed as warmly as possible, then warily stole from the dormitory and walked the mile a half to the Lutheran cemetery, which lay between the school and Marshalltown, where she visited Annie's grave, and in a traditional Otoe mourning rite, ceremoniously burned a small bundle of cedar.

Unfortunately, the flame was visible from the nearby road and attracted the attention of a sheriff's deputy who happened to be passing at the time. Iris was charged with trespassing and desecrating a grave and returned to Lu-Tern on the following morning, where was given a tongue-lashing by Reverend Holzhauer, then sentenced to three days in the room of atonement. When she returned to the dormitory, both Rose and Lilly found that she had changed. Good-natured, fun-loving Iris had grown quiet. The isolation had only made her more resentful. Iris had atoned for nothing.

That was the beginning of the end. Rose remembered that in 1898, Easter arrived in April, and following their usual practice, Reverend Holzhauer and the board of directors had made arrangements for the student body to attend Easter services at the two Lutheran churches in Marshalltown and at several smaller country Lutheran churches in the immediate vicinity. The 140 students, attired in their dress uniforms, were divided into six groups, and accompanied by faculty chaperones, they were transported via teams and wagons to the churches where the students participated (to a greater or lesser extent) in the church services. Following the services, the groups of students were treated to an Easter Sunday dinner before returning to the school. Holzhauer believed that the practice served two purposes. It gave the students an opportunity to dress up and travel outside the confines of the institution's campus, and it enabled the school to project an image of well-behaved Christian Indian children well on their way to becoming good citizens. The latter image, of course, was important to the school in its constant quest for more funding from Lutheran congregations.

Early on the morning of Easter Sunday, April 10, 1898—Rose most definitely remembered that date—the Flower Girls donned their dark blue Sunday dresses and their matching blue wool jackets and gathered by the wagon that was to carry them to one of the Lutheran churches in Marshalltown. In addition to about two dozen other students, they climbed into the wagon, but as the vehicle rolled out of the courtyard, Iris quietly slipped out over the back of the wagon, telling Rose and Lilly that she needed to go to the outhouse and that she would catch up with them before they reached the town. Busily talking with the driver, the chaperones did not see her leave. Neither did most of the students, who were excitedly chatting about going to a white man's church and about what they might expect in the upcoming dinner.

Iris never returned. Rose and Lilly kept watching for her, but the wagon reached the church, and everyone went in, bowed their heads at the appropriate time, generally ignored the boring sermon, and dutifully sung "A Mighty Fortress Is Our God." Following the service, the students assembled in the church's social hall and dined on Easter ham and assorted vegetables and big slabs of apple pie. But still no Iris.

Obviously, the chaperones were unaware that Iris was absent, and Rose and Lilly were determined not to tell on their friend. At 2:30 P.M., they loaded back in the wagons, but as they left the north side of Marshalltown and started up the road past the cemetery then headed back toward the school, they noticed that a column of gray-black smoke was rising in the distance. Alarmed that it seemed to be coming from the general area of the school, the driver hurried the horses forward, and as Rose and Lilly bounced north along the gravel road, they could tell that the smoke came from Lu-Tern. When they arrived, they found that Martin Luther Hall, the building that contained all the academic classrooms, the library, the administrative offices, and even the dining hall and laundry, was completely engulfed in flames. The local fire department, whose horse-drawn water wagon was woefully small to address such a fire, sat at the edge of the road, and a crowd of spectators watched while the large two-story wooden frame building was rapidly turned to ashes. Luckily, the dormitories and many of the "vocational classrooms" were spared. The students were ordered to return to their dormitories and to not leave until they were given permission.

When Rose and Lilly reached their wing of the dormitory, they found Iris, in her nightgown, in bed, with her eyes closed. When they asked her where she had been, she replied that she had felt unwell and had returned to the dormitory to rest, and "must have fallen asleep due to her sour stomach." Rose asked her why she hadn't been awakened by all the noise from the fire, to which Iris slyly smiled and answered, "What fire? Is something burning?" Rose then informed her that much of Lu-Tern was now in ashes, to which Iris replied, "Well, it's lucky that it caught fire while no one was in the building. I guess everyone must have gone to church this morning. I'm sure all the doors were locked tight." But Lilly, who had walked to the other side of Iris's bed, where Iris kept her storage locker, interrupted the conversation to state, "Iris, I think I smell coal oil." In turn, Iris replied, "Oh yeah, well I guess that's not surprising. After I jumped off the wagon and ran to use the outhouse, I accidently kicked over the coal oil can from the kitchen that someone must have left outside the outhouse door. I spilled some of it on my shoes — but they already smelled like coal oil, since we always use it to start our fires in the kitchen." Rose and Lilly exchanged long glances and left. But on the following day, Iris informed the school cobbler that she needed a new pair of shoes. According to Iris, somehow her shoes had become lost in all of the upheaval surrounding the big fire.

In the aftermath, the school struggled to complete a shortened spring semester, and students were forced to meet for academic classes in barns, cobbler shops, and stables. Plans were made to erect a new Martin Luther Hall, but wringing dollars from tight-fisted German Lutheran farmers proved difficult, particularly since newspapers in Des Moines and Cedar Falls both carried reports that the federal government was rumored to be planning a new federal Indian "school or sanitarium" near Toledo, Iowa, to service the local Meskwakis and other midwestern tribes.[2] To lighten the drain on their finances, the board of directors decreed that the school's "outing" program would extend from early May through mid-October, but when news of the fire reached reservation communities, parents and other relatives from tribal communities in Michigan, Wisconsin, Minnesota, Nebraska, and the Dakotas (although hard-pressed for cash) arrived in Marshalltown (some by train, others on horseback) and demanded that their children be released. Reverend Hollzhauer and some of his faculty members (but not Clara Braun) tried to dissuade them, but they were unsuccessful. Lilly accompanied her uncle back to Nebraska. Rose and her father returned to the Oneida Reservation in Wisconsin. But before Rose left, she and her father escorted Iris to the train depot, where Iris procured a ticket to return to her previous outing location, the ranch near Beatrice, Nebraska. Privately, she assured Rose that at the end of the summer, she planned to go back to the Otoe-Missouria Reservation in Oklahoma Territory, not to Lu-Tern. Needless to say, for her train trip to Beatrice, Iris had bedecked herself in one of her riding skirts and a new pair of highly polished black leather boots, which she had paid one of the students in the cobbler's shop to make for her in the fire's aftermath. She had paid for them with four shiny silver dollars.

As the summer of 1898 drew to an end, it became apparent that many of the students who had been enrolled prior to the fire would not be back for the fall semester. Most who returned to their reservation communities planned to enroll in other schools, and many of the students in the outing system refused to return to Marshalltown. Rose enrolled in the enlarged Oneida boarding school at Oneida, Wisconsin, while Lilly attended a small day school near the Omaha Agency near Macy. Following her second summer on the ranch near Beatrice, Iris returned to the Otoe Reservation, where she enrolled in the government school at Red Rock. Meanwhile, although Reverend Holzhauer and the board of directors labored mightily, they could not raise sufficient funds to rebuild the classrooms or pay the faculty. Finally, they decided that they would seek "more fertile, less stony fields to sow the seeds of God's good word." In October 1898, the Iowa Lutheran Indian School closed permanently.

Retrospect

The Iowa Lutheran Indian School and its faculty, like the Flower Girls and their classmates, are fictitious places and people, but they are representative of the Native American boarding school experience in the late nineteenth and early twentieth centuries. Boarding schools for Native American students first emerged in the colonial period, and sponsored by Christian denominations or missionaries, they proliferated across the eastern states during the antebellum period.[3] Aware that literacy in English would enable Indian people to read the Bible, the missionaries were convinced that if tribal people read "God's Holy Word" they would understand that God wanted them to settle down on small acreages and become yeoman farmers, similar to white settlers. By 1800, the Moravians were active among the Cherokees, Creeks, and Delawares, and they soon were joined by Quakers, Presbyterians, and other Protestants. In 1805, the

Presbyterians opened a boarding school among the Cherokees at Hiwassee, in eastern Tennessee, and during the following decade, the Moravians established a similar institution for other Cherokee students at Brainerd, near modern Chattanooga. In 1818, Cyrus Kingsbury founded a mission and later a boarding school among the Choctaws in Mississippi. Meanwhile, Moravian missionaries opened several small boarding schools among the Delawares in Ohio, while Quakers and Baptists ministers established day schools among the Shawnees, Miamis, and Potawatomis in Ohio and Indiana. Although the initial schools among these northern tribes were not officially boarding schools, many of the students who attended these one-room institutions often resided with the missionary's family.[4]

After 1820, the pace quickened. In 1819, Congress appropriated $10,000 annually to instruct tribal people in agriculture and "for teaching their children in reading, writing, and arithmetic." Officials in Washington decided to funnel these funds through "benevolent societies" such as churches or missionaries, and the race was on among various religious denominations competing for government dollars. Meanwhile as midwestern or southern tribes ceded lands to the government, many of these land-cession treaties stipulated that part of the funds paid to the tribes for their lands would be used to support schools and teachers. By 1830, over two dozen boarding schools were functioning in Indian Country, and in 1834, these institutions received over $34,000 annually in federal funds.[5]

These boarding schools could be found both north and south of the Ohio River. For example, in the South, both male and female Cherokee students enrolled at Brainerd Mission School, established by the American Board of Commissioners for Foreign Missions near Chattanooga, Tennessee, where they attended classes in mathematics, reading, writing, spelling, and geography. Girls were also instructed in the "domestic arts," while boys learned the rudiments of yeoman agriculture or trades such as carpentry and blacksmithing. In addition, all students were required to attend daily religious services, infused with the values of nineteenth-century Anglo-American culture, and warned that any adherence to traditional Cherokee beliefs, traditions, or ceremonies would retard their progress toward "civilization."[6]

Founded in 1818 by the Baptist Mission Society at Great Crossings, Kentucky, the Choctaw Indian Academy enrolled only male students and struggled until 1821, when it was able to secure financial support from treaty funds provided by the Choctaw tribe. Ironically, the school was erected on land owned by Richard M. Johnson, whose major claim to fame was that he had personally killed the Shawnee war chief Tecumseh at the Battle of the Thames in 1813. The school followed a mixed academic/vocational format similar to other institutions enrolling Indian students in these decades, but it was plagued by student complaints, truancy, and fires. It was also subjected to several government investigations during the quarter century of its existence. In addition to Choctaw boys, it enrolled students from several tribes including Seminoles, Chickasaws, Creeks, Potawatomis, and Miamis, but after the Choctaws were removed to Indian Territory, the tribe terminated the school's funding, and it closed in the mid-1840s.[7]

Typical of early boarding schools north of the Ohio River, the boarding school at Baptist Carey Mission, which operated near Niles on the St. Joseph River in southwestern Michigan between 1822 and 1831, also followed a strict regimen that included both academic and vocational training. Founded by Baptist minister Isaac McCoy, who boasted that his students "were not allowed to be idle" and that the school was dedicated to "taming the wild man," the institution enrolled Potawatomi, Ottawa, and Miami students who were awakened by a bugle at 4 A.M., promptly marched to morning religious services, then spent their day studying academic or vocational subjects, interspersed with agricultural and domestic "chores" necessary to maintain the mission. The evening meal was at 6 P.M., followed by "vespers," after which the students were required to retire to their beds. McCoy proudly stated that most students spent half of their "daylight hours" in the "manual arts" or working for the mission. Many of the students were of mixed Native American-Creole French lineage whose Catholic parents resented McCoy's Baptist proselytization of their sons. After 1828, the school declined, and McCoy became more interested in removing his flock west of the Mississippi where he claimed they would be free from the "machinations of Papists and whiskey peddlers."[8]

The passage of the Indian Removal Act (1830) and the subsequent removal of many tribes to new homes west of the Mississippi brought some important changes to Indian education. After their arrival in Indian Territory, some of the tribes established their own boarding schools or enlarged nascent school systems they had created prior to their removal. For example, the Cherokees had previously established a tribal school system in Georgia, and after adopting a Cherokee syllabary devised by Sequoyah (George Guess), the tribe's literacy rate surpassed that of white settlers who surrounded them in states such as Georgia, Alabama, and Tennessee. In Indian Territory, students enrolled in a tribally sponsored school system that funded thirty elementary schools scattered through the Cherokee Nation, and although most of these institutions were day schools, additional mission boarding schools also functioned. Some graduates of these elementary schools (particularly the children of an influential tribal planter or merchant elite) enrolled in the Cherokee Male Seminary at Tahlequah or in the Cherokee Female Seminary in neighboring Park Hill. These seminaries, modeled after New England institutions such as the Boston Latin School and Mount Holyoke Seminary, combined traditional academic subjects with instruction in "conduct befitting young gentlemen and ladies of quality" in mid-nineteenth-century American society. The young women were also taught those skills and techniques needed to manage a household in the Civil War era. All instruction was in English, and the Cherokee National Council provided for teachers, tuition, textbooks, and food and lodging. Students furnished their own linen, clothes, and other expenses.[9]

Other tribes followed a similar, if less elaborate, pattern. During the 1830s, Cyrus Byington, a missionary with the American Board of Commissioners for Foreign Missions, developed a written form of the Choctaw language. Utilizing Sunday schools and weekend camp meetings, both missionaries and Choctaw converts encouraged literacy through many members of the Choctaw tribe. After removal, a series of mission-sponsored elementary schools spread across the Choctaw Nation, and during the 1840s, the Choctaw National Council opened Spencer Academy, a secondary boarding school for "young Choctaw gentlemen" near Doaksville, while New Hope Academy, a boarding school for young Choctaw women, was established near Fort Coffee.[10] The Chickasaws followed suit by founding five boarding schools in the 1840s and 1850s, including the Chickasaw Manual Labor Academy for boys, located at Tishomingo, and Bloomfield Academy for girls near Achile, which later moved to Ardmore. Like the Cherokee Female Academy, the curriculum at Bloomfield was modeled after women's finishing schools in the East, and Bloomfield prided itself on its reputation as the "Bryn Mawr of the West."[11]

Following the Civil War, federal support for boarding schools accelerated. During the late 1860s and 1870s, as white settlement spread into the West, tribal people fought back, but they were eventually overwhelmed and assigned to shrinking reservations. Still intent on "Americanizing" tribal peoples and forcing them to adopt the cultural patterns of mainstream American citizens, both religious reformers and the federal government increased their reliance on "education." In 1877, one year after Custer's defeat at the Battle of the Little Big Horn, the total federal expenditure for Indian education was only $30,000. Twenty-three years later, in 1900, the annual appropriation of federal funds for Native American education had climbed to almost $3 million.[12]

Much of this growth resulted from the proliferation of boarding schools. During the late 1870s, some Native American children enrolled in Hampton Institute in Virginia, a federal boarding school for African Americans, and other Indian students would continue to enroll at Hampton in the decades that followed, but the primary poster child for Native American boarding schools was Carlisle Indian Industrial Training School, a coeducational institution located at an abandoned army barracks at Carlisle Pennsylvania. Founded in 1879 by Richard Pratt, an ex-army officer, Carlisle's administration, focus, goals, curriculum, student codes, and vocational-training programs soon became the model for other Native American schools, both federal and private. Opening on Indian reservations and also at off-reservations sites, boarding schools spanned the nation, although most were located west of the Mississippi River. By 1900, these boarding schools enrolled more than fourteen thousand Native American students. Another fifty-five hundred attended reservation or Indian Agency day schools that did not separate students from their parents.[13]

Most of the travails surrounding the Flower Girls at the fictitious Iowa Lutheran Indian School were modeled after actual experiences encountered by Native American students enrolled in existing boarding schools during these years. Like Iris, many students were taken from their parents or guardians and sent to distant boarding schools against their own wishes and the wishes of their parents. Sometimes these students were separated from their families because Indian agents believed that the student's close relationship with his or her family members prevented them from acquiring the "civilized ways" necessary to become "a cultured white person." In other cases, children were separated from their parents as hostages to control militant or recalcitrant parents or tribal leaders opposed to federal programs. But regardless of the motivation for the separation, their removal engendered considerable anguish. Letters and memoirs by both former students and their parents or relatives often reflect these emotions, and since some children were removed at a very young age, their agony was particularly heartbreaking.[14]

Other students, such as Rose and Lilly, were sometimes enrolled as a temporary solution to economic problems facing their families on their reservations, and although these separations may have been less traumatic than the forced enrollments, they were nonetheless disruptive to the students' lives. Many of these students envisioned these separations as a temporary necessity, and like Rose and Lilly, they made the best of it. But most were eager to return to their families and communities; they did not envision their enrollment as a catalyst to a new and different life.[15]

Similar to the Iowa Lutheran School, the curricula at most of these boarding schools resembled the plan formulated by Richard Pratt at Carlisle. For example, Haskell Institute, founded in Lawrence, Kansas, in 1884, featured a mixed program of academic subjects and vocational training. Both male and female students enrolled in elementary or intermediate classes in mathematics, reading, spelling, geography, handwriting, and English, while boys also trained to be farmers, blacksmiths, cobblers, and leather workers. Girls spent part of their day acquiring skills in cooking, sewing, and similar homemaking techniques. Like "Lu-Tern," the students raised much of the food consumed at Haskell on the institution's grounds. Other boarding schools followed similar patterns, and although some of the vocational training taught to male students provided them with trades that were marketable in the early twentieth century, others—harness making and blacksmithing, for example—were tied to an agrarian past and proved to be in much less demand as the United States embraced the industrial age of the twentieth century.[16]

Of course, both academic and vocational instruction at all the boarding schools was heavily infused with an effort to Americanize Indian students and eradicate traditional tribal values or cultures. As Carlisle superintendent Richard Pratt had once warned his followers, for boarding schools to succeed, they must "kill the Indian in him and save the man."[17] Many faculty members at these institutions followed Pratt's admonition with a vengeance. Although the Flower Girls had all been given "proper American names" (Rose, Lilly, Iris), before they enrolled at the school in Iowa, other students with more traditional tribal names were forced to choose a new Anglicized name or had one arbitrarily assigned upon their enrollment. For example, Plenty Kill, a Lakota boy from South Dakota, was forced to change his name to Luther after enrolling at Carlisle, then given his father's name, Standing Bear, as a new surname. Consequently he was known by non-Lakotas as Luther Standing Bear for the rest of his life. At Haskell, students were often assigned both new first and last names. Sometimes their new names were arbitrarily selected from an administrator's or a teacher's friends or acquaintances or from his or her familiarity with litera- ture or politics. Sac and Fox student Lucy Logan was renamed after Union gen- eral John Logan by a former officer who served in Logan's command during the Civil War. Ironically, enrollment lists at Haskell also indicate that Julius Caesar, Napoleon Bonaparte, Henry Clay, Henry Ward Beecher, and Grover Cleveland also attended the school.[18]

Nomenclature and language were focal points of the boarding schools' attempts to destroy tribal culture and transform Indian children into (slightly darker) mirror images of Anglo students. Although a few schools made some feeble attempts, particularly with younger children, to integrate some tribal vocabulary in their instruction, the vast majority of institutions insisted that students enrolled in their classes communicate only in English. As a result, students whose enrollment in these school stretched over several years often found that they lost fluency in their native languages, and when they returned to their reservations, they sometimes encountered difficulty in communicating with their families. Moreover, since language heavily influences cultural pat- terns, including assumptions regarding time, family structures, material well- being, and an individual's relationship with the larger society that surrounds him or her, fluency in English did bring changes to some tribal communities.

Ironically, this fluency served as a double-edged sword. English gradually emerged as the common, pan-tribal language for tribal communities across the United States, enabling Native American peoples from different reserva- tions and backgrounds to communicate and band together in support of Native American rights. In addition, English also became a medium through which tribal people educated at the boarding schools vented their displeasure and resentment at federal Indian policy and eventually made non-Indian Ameri- cans more aware of the general failure of American Indian policy in the late nineteenth and twentieth centuries.[19]

Federal policies designed to separate Indian students from tribal cultures were manifested in many other ways. All students were forbidden to practice traditional religious ceremonies, and like Iris, if they violated such proscrip- tions, they were promptly punished. As James Marvin, Haskell's first superin- tendent proclaimed, "Fear of the Lord . . . is the beginning of wisdom," while Hervey B. Peairs, who served first as a "disciplinarian" at Haskell, then later as the school's superintendent, proclaimed, "A really civilized people cannot be found . . . except where the Bible has been sent and the gospel taught." For administrators at Haskell and at other institutions, any adherence to traditional tribal religions impeded the civilization process.[20]

Traditional music, dancing, and other cultural celebrations were also seen as suspect since many teachers and administrators feared that they held hidden religious underpinnings or that they also reinforced students' ties with tribal communities. Most tribal ceremonies were strictly forbidden, and school administrators labored mightily to replace traditional dancing, music, and games with "civilized" substitutes such as social clubs, YMCA or YWCA activities, reading clubs focused on patriotic literature, marching bands, and particularly athletic teams and contests. Both Haskell and Carlisle took great pride in the athletic teams, and Jim Thorpe, a Sac and Fox student from Oklahoma, achieved fame as an Olympian, much to the pride of Carlisle, tribal people everywhere, and most other Americans across the United States. Both Haskell and Carlisle featured student bands and also presented pageants, plays, and other dramatic productions. Yet any portrayal of tribal culture was closely monitored by school administrators to ensure that it reflected the progress students were making toward the American ideal.[21]

The outing system originally initiated by Richard Pratt at Hampton Institute was expanded in 1879 after Pratt took charge at Carlisle. It soon spread to several boarding schools in the West. Pratt and other administrators believed that the system forced students to rely entirely on English and enabled them to learn the "subtleties of civilized living" apart from the rigid, "superficial atmosphere" of boarding schools. They also argued that the outing students would serve as attractive ambassadors for Indian education to the American public and would assist students to safely "break away from the tribal commune and go out among our people and contend for the necessities and luxuries of life." Generally, most sponsors enjoyed having the Indian students as part of their household, and the demand for outing students usually exceeded the number eligible for placement. In turn, most students, like Lilly and Iris, seemed to enjoy the temporary respite from boarding school life, although some, like Lu-Tern's Kickapoo boy from Kansas, Quapaw boy from Oklahoma, Potawatomi girl from Michigan, and particularly Marie, the Ojibwe girl from Courte Oreille, were abused by their sponsors. In retrospect, the outing system seemed to function more effectively in the East, the Midwest, and on the eastern fringes of the Great Plains. It was less successful for Native American students in regions where agriculture utilized "stoop labor" such as the beet fields of Colorado or the truck farms and orchards of California or Arizona. But in all regions, the outing system worked much more successfully in rural regions. According to Pratt, "In the city," outing students often floundered and "became the victims of some degeneracy."[22]

Years later, when graduates of the boarding schools were asked about their experiences, they readily complained about their meals. Similar to students everywhere, many complained about the selection of food served to them daily, but more important, evidence indicates that some students suffered from malnourishment. Estelle Aubrey Brown, a teacher and administrator who served at Crow Creek, South Dakota, and at several other schools in the West at the beginning of the twentieth century, admitted that "for sixteen years I was to see . . . children systematically underfed." Extensive federal investigations conducted in the 1920s confirmed Brown's charges. The Meriam Report, published in 1928, indicated that many boarding school children were underweight and that their diet suffered for decades from insufficient milk, fresh fruits, and vegetables. The students at Lu-Tern may have suffered from a lack of fresh fruit and vegetables, but they probably fared better than students at many other schools; they were not underfed. Thanks to the German farmers who surrounded Marshalltown, there were plenty of potatoes, sausage, and sauerkraut.[23]

Clothing was a different story. When asked about the clothing furnished to them during their enrollment, students almost universally complained about their uniforms. Obviously, the school uniforms differed markedly from the clothing they had worn within their tribal communities, and even those students who had worn "white man's clothes" before their enrollment were surprised at the itchy pants, baggy underwear, and rough, ill-fitting shoes. Some institutions, such as the Albuquerque Indian School, allowed female students to brighten their dresses with small adornments of ruffles or lace, and male students at Carlisle were allowed to decorate their dress uniforms with red stripes and braid, but generally, most students went through their daily routine in rather drab attire. Like the Flower Girls, most female students detested their bloomers.[24]

Both genders were expected to wear their hair "cut and styled in a civilized manner," which encountered relativity little opposition from the Flower Girls and most other female students since the regulation demanded few changes from the manner in which they had kept their hair in their home communities. In contrast, many male students resented boarding school haircuts. Most male students from the Great Plains and Southwest traditionally wore their hair rather long, and they resented the haircuts forced on them when they reached the boarding schools. Moreover, among these western tribes, closely cropped hair had considerable cultural significance. Along with several other physical symbols and gestures, closely cropped hair was adopted only in association with the death of a loved one. It was a sign of great personal loss and mourning.[25]

Unfortunately, personal loss and mourning shrouded the boarding school experience. The primary cause was disease. Like Lu-Tern, most boarding schools were subject to periodic outbreaks of the communicable diseases (measles, scarlet fever, influenza) that swept through the United States during the late nineteenth and early twentieth centuries, but the concentration of Indian children in stuffy, crowded classrooms and dormitories made them more vulnerable to these maladies. Cemeteries at the schools bear mute testimony to the eruption of these seasonal outbreaks, but they also indicate that a greater killer, tuberculosis, loomed as a more serious problem. Moreover, TB proved to be a more insidious illness since it sometimes lay dormant, then followed students back to their home communities, where it continued to debilitate its victims and brought their lives to an end. Almost all schools harbored tubercular students, but Haskell Institute provides a symptomatic example. In 1908, the school enrolled approximately seven hundred students, but during that year, Haskell sent home 104 students because of their tubercular condition. In addition, seventy-six other students were diagnosed with the disease but allowed to continue at the school because their TB had not progressed to the extent that the school physician and administrators believed it threatened other students. During this period, many of the children were forced to share beds with their infected classmates, and during the winter, they slept in basement rooms with little ventilation. Bedding used for tubercular patients was reassigned to other children without being disinfected, and band instruments (woodwinds and brass most notably) were habitually shared among many students without any attempts at sterilization. TB was widespread. It ravaged the student population at Crow Creek in South Dakota and also infected many students at Carlisle and at the Phoenix Indian School. In response, federal officials eventually erected several sanitariums, but the disease still took a heavy toll. Of the first 130 Southern Cheyenne and Arapaho students who graduated from Carlisle, twenty-five died of TB within two years after returning to Oklahoma.[26]

Yet students persevered. Like the Flower Girls, both male and female students carved out sufficient space, beat the system, and maintained their own identities. As Tsianina Lomawaima illustrates, both male and female students at Chilocco Indian School in Oklahoma formed age-graded, tribal or inter-tribal cliques and groups that met irregularly but often. Cliques of girls at Chilocco cooperated to defeat the schools bloomer policy, vied for control of kitchen privileges, purloined food from the kitchen back to their dormitories, and used peer pressure to control snitching by other students to teachers or administrators. Informal gangs of boys secretly concocted home brews and shared bootleg whiskey. They also met in secluded places on the wooded Chilocco campus and hunted squirrels and rabbits, prepared unauthorized outdoor meals, and sometimes battled with other groups for control of certain areas on the school grounds. At Haskell, informal groups of students of both sexes met regularly after hours in dormitories and at outside venues to converse in the tribal languages or to practiced traditional religious ceremonies or share information about the peyote faith.[27] Indeed, years later, when asked to recall their experiences at the boarding schools, almost all former students readily described their membership in these informal groups, which successfully contested or circumvented many boarding school rules and regulations.

During the early twentieth century, the role of boarding schools gradually declined. As a result of a squabble between several Protestant denominations and the Catholic Church, federal financial support for these schools after 1900 was curtailed. Many of the smaller schools that had flourished in the late nineteenth century closed. During the 1920s, following a federal investigation, the resulting Meriam Report concluded that boarding schools were disruptive to both tribal communities and family life. In response, federal policies changed, and in 1932, with the emergence of John Collier's Indian New Deal, the federal government turned to day schools located on or adjacent to the reservation communities as the preferred formats for Native American education. In addition, the passage of the Johnson-O'Malley Act (1934), which provided federal funds to individual states for the education of Indian students within the state's existing school system, supposedly facilitated the enrollment of tribal students in local non-Indian schools. Although the act produced mixed results, it continues as a keystone in federal policy. Some boarding schools (Haskell in Kansas, Riverside in Oklahoma, Sherman in California, Phoenix in Arizona, among others) continued, but most closed. The era of boarding schools as the backbone of Native American education ended.[28]

"Well," thought Rose, "enough of these memories." Her watch showed 4 P.M., and Rose needed to return her horse and buggy to the livery stable in Marshalltown. The owner had informed her he planned to close at five o'clock, on the dot, and there would be an extra charge if she returned after that hour. The drive back to town took only twenty minutes. She returned her rig, then walked to a small café near the depot, where the only item still available on the menu was a blue-plate special left over from the midday meal. Rose wasn't surprised to learn that it consisted of a sausage patty, a small slice of pork tenderloin, fried potatoes, cooked cabbage, and bread and butter. She hated to admit that it immediately brought back memories of Freda Hammer. Rose ate the potatoes, cabbage, pork tenderloin, and bread and butter. She left the sausage.

Following her early supper, Rose walked to the depot, retrieved her battered suitcase that she had checked in the luggage closet, then sat on a bench in the waiting room for the hour's wait until the train arrived. The waiting room was empty when she arrived except for a heavyset, fiftyish ticket agent who was cleaning the floor with a broom and dustpan. The agent recognized that she was Native American and asked her if she was from the Meskwaki settlement located about ten miles east of Marshalltown. When she replied that her people were Oneidas, from Wisconsin, but that she had attended the Lutheran Indian School, he became excited and told her that he remembered when it had burned. Rose assured him that yes, she, too, remembered the fire (although she did not share with him some of her suspicions about the event's origins), and as they talked, she learned that the man's sister was Sophie Zeitman, the young widow who had replaced Freda Hammer as school cook after Annie Rain's passing. He also told her that Reverend Holzhauer had died of tuberculosis in 1907 or 1908 (he wasn't sure which), but his spunky young granddaughter, Clara Braun, had upped and married a college professor of some sort at Drake University and now lived in Des Moines.

Rose asked about several other faculty members, than finally inquired about Freda Schwarzenheimer. The man scoffed, shook his head, then replied. "That old Battle-Axe! After she was let go by the school, she spent the next ten years complaining that Clara Braun got her fired, then blamed my sister for taking her job. Complaints, gossip, and lies! Complaints, gossip, and lies! On and on! For ten years! At church, at the quilting bees, at the ladies missionary society meetings! Never a good word for anybody!"

"Well," Rose asked, "does she still live here in Marshalltown?"

"Hah!" the stationmaster exclaimed. "Oh, she's here all right. But she got so fat from eating sausage and apple strudel that about four summers ago, she fell off her own back porch, hit her head against the cast-iron well pump, cracked her skull, and just laid there and died. Yep, right there next to her chicken coop. She's here all right! She's buried in one of the back lots out at the Lutheran cemetery."

At 8:45 P.M., Rose boarded the Union Pacific train, then spent the next twelve hours traveling through western Iowa, across the Missouri River, into eastern Nebraska, and on to Fremont, where she transferred to the Sioux City and Nebraska Railroad, whose tracks crossed the Omaha Reservation. Shortly after 1 P.M., when the second train made a brief stop at the small Rosalie depot, Rose spotted Lilly and a tall, lanky Omaha man waiting for her on the platform.

After giving Rose a big Omaha hug, Lilly introduced her husband, Walter Flint, who then drove the wagon as the party traveled east along a dirt road toward Macy, where Lilly and her family lived in a small frame house on the old Flint family allotment. Although they had intermittently corresponded, neither Rose nor Lilly had seen each other since they had left Lu-Tern, and they caught up on news about each other's family, children, lives, and other matters. Rose told Lilly about her recent visit to Marshalltown, how the school site had changed, and what she had learned about Reverend Holzhauer, Clara Braun, and especially Freda Hammer.

Lilly just shook her head and replied, "Well, I can't say that I'm sorry. That cook was one of the ugliest people I've ever known. Not in her looks, although she was fatter than a hog. But at her core. If she had a heart, it must have been full of cold, gray ashes. I'll never forget poor Annie, and how her passing affected Iris."

Thoughts of Iris brightened Rose. She no longer had Iris's address, but she knew that Lilly occasionally heard from her, so she suggested that when they arrived at Lilly's home they write a long letter to Iris to tell her that two of the

Flower Girls were plotting again, just like old times, and to pass on the gossip that Rose had heard in Marshalltown. But when she mentioned it, Lilly at first seem startled, grew momentarily silent, then stared at the distant Missouri River bottoms.

"Oh no," she replied. "You mean you never got a letter?"

"What letter," Rose asked.

And then a solemn, and much saddened, Lilly told her that three months ago, in early June 1920, she had received a letter from one of Iris's aunts informing her that Iris had died during the previous spring, when the Spanish influenza swept through the Otoe-Missouria Reservation. The woman had asked Lilly for Rose's address, and Lilly had sent it to her, but she evidently had failed to notify Rose, in Wisconsin.

The two women spoke very little during the final fifteen minutes of the wagon ride to Lilly's home, but as they approached the house, Lilly turned to Rose and commented, "Well, wherever she is, Iris obviously learned of Freda Hammers's death before either of us."

"I'll give her that," Rose replied. "That Otoe girl got around, and I'll bet she's still pestering that grouchy old cook, if she can get at her."

"Oh yeah," Lilly added. "You know, when Iris went back to Red Rock, on the Otoe Reservation, the Indian agents stuck her back in the Otoe boarding school, even though Iris wanted to work as a ranch hand." Rose replied that she had received a letter from Iris complaining about the Otoe-Missouria Reservation School, but it had been shortly after the Flower Girls left Lu-Tern and returned to their homes, and she hadn't given it much thought.

"Well," Lilly continued on, "did you know that the Otoe boarding school had a curriculum similar to what we were taught at Lu-Tern?

"No, I didn't, but I'm not surprised," Rose answered.

"And did you know," Lilly asked with a hint of a smile in her voice, "that the Otoe boarding school burned down twice after Iris returned to her reservation?"[29]

Rose laughed out loud. "I wonder where she got the coal oil. I hope she didn't ruin another pair of shoes."

Some things changed, but other things continued. Iris had passed, but Rose and Lilly endured. Lu-Tern, Reverend Holzhauer, and Freda Hammer were gone, but the spirit and determination of the Flower Girls persisted.[30]

Suggested Readings

Adams, David Wallace. *Education for Extinction: American Indians and the Boarding School Experience, 1875–1928.* Lawrence: University Press of Kansas, 1995.

Archeleta, Margaret, Brenda Child, and Tsianina Lomawaima, eds. *Away from Home: American Indian Boarding School Experiences, 1879–2000.* Phoenix: Heard Museum, 2000.

Child, Brenda. *Boarding School Seasons: American Indian Families, 1900–1940.* Lincoln: University of Nebraska Press, 1988.

Coleman, Michael C. *American Indian Children at School, 1850–1930.* Jackson: University Press of Mississippi, 1993.

Lomawaima, Tsianina. *They Called It Prairie Light: The Story of Chilocco Indian School.* Lincoln: University of Nebraska Press, 1994.

Newland, Bryan. *Federal Boarding School Initiative Investigative Report.* Washington, DC: Department of the Interior, 2022.

Vuckvic, Myriam. *Voices from Haskell: Indian Students between Two Worlds, 1884–1928.* Lawrence: University Press of Kansas, 2008.

EIGHT

Summer Hawks in Concrete Canyons

Relocation and Its Aftermath

Early on New Year's Eve 1957, a Lakota man sat sipping strong hot tea, laced with sugar, from a heavy ceramic coffee mug, in a tenement in Denver. The winter twilight brought a time of reflection for Roland Summer Hawk. The past twelve months had not been easy ones. Born on the Pine Ridge Reservation in South Dakota, Roland Summer Hawk had been raised among the Lakota people, and until the previous February, he had spent his entire life on the reservation or in neighboring communities. But in February 1957, encouraged by Bureau of Indian Affairs (BIA) officials at Pine Ridge, he had brought his wife and thirteen-year-old son to Denver to participate in the government's "relocation" program. Now, eleven months later, he had serious doubts about his decision.

At first, the move seemed like a good thing. BIA officials at Pine Ridge had assured him that there were plenty of good jobs in Denver, and they had even promised that the bureau would pay for their resettlement, find them housing, and provide Roland with expense money until he received his first paycheck. Since he was a skilled leatherworker, they indicated that he would have little trouble finding a job. They furnished him with colorful brochures showing happy Native American families, dressed in neat clothing, living in ranch style houses containing televisions sets, modern kitchen appliances, new upholstered furniture, and all the other conveniences owned by more affluent white people residing in the towns near Pine Ridge.

Roland had also been influenced by his cousin, Henry Two Birds, who had lived in Denver ever since the end of World War II. Roland didn't know Henry

236 ++ *Chapter 8*

very well, but he talked with him when Two Birds made his periodic visits back to the reservation, and although Henry seemed a little aloof, his new clothes and two-tone 1955 Pontiac Catalina (complete with white sidewalls) attested to his ability to provide for his family. Since jobs at Pine Ridge were "scarcer than hen's teeth," Roland had hoped that the move would provide economic opportunities lacking in South Dakota. Besides, as described in the BIA brochures, the entire relocation process had seemed like a grand adventure.

Their arrival in Denver had been traumatic for Roland and his family. Since they did not own an automobile, they rode from Pine Ridge on a bus, arriving in Denver late in the evening. BIA personnel met them at the bus depot and found them rooms for the night, informing Roland that on the following day, he should appear at the BIA office to meet with local officials who would assist him in finding housing and a job. They assured him that the office was just a few blocks away, and if he arrived early in the morning, they could get a good start on his processing. Roland, his wife, Mary, and his son, Robert, rose early the next morning and wandered along the street looking for the BIA office. Although Roland remembered the street name where the office was located, he had forgotten the exact address, and when he stopped several pedestrians to ask them where the BIA building was located, they looked puzzled and could give him no assistance. Confused and bewildered, the Lakota family walked for about an hour before a cab driver suggested that they look in a phone book. Finally, just before noon, the Summer Hawks reached their destination.

The BIA officials were somewhat rankled over Roland's late arrival, and since he had lost his appointment, they kept the family waiting until late in the afternoon before an agent drove them in a bureau automobile to look at prospective housing. Bewildered by the size of the city and uncertain of just what to expect, the Summer Hawks readily accepted the first apartment shown to them, a small one-bedroom flat in a mixed working-class/light commercial neighborhood, near Federal Boulevard. Two days later, accompanied by a BIA agent, Roland interviewed with a local saddle maker and accepted a job in a tannery. Mary also found work as a maid in a small motel located near their home, and Robert enrolled in the local junior high school. After a month, when Roland received his first paycheck, the BIA stopped their relocation payments, and the Summer Hawks seemed to be making a start in pursuit of the American Dream.

COME TO DENVER
THE CHANCE OF YOUR LIFETIME !

Good Jobs

Retail Trade

Manufacturing

Government-Federal,State, Local

Wholesale Trade

Construction of Buildings,Etc.

Happy Homes

Beautiful Houses

Many Churches

Exciting Community Life.

Over Half of Homes Owned by Residents

Convenient Stores-Shopping Centers

Training

Vocational Training
Auto Mech., Beauty Shop,Drafting,
Nursing,Office Work,Watchmaking
Adult Education
Evening High School, Arts and Crafts
Job Improvement, Home-making

Beautiful Colorado

"Tallest" State, 48 Mt. Peaks Over 14,000 Ft.

350 Days Sunshine , Mild Winters

Zoos, Museums , Mountain Parks, Drives

Picnic Areas,Lakes, Amusement Parks

Big Game Hunting,Trout Fishing ,Camping

"Come to Denver—The Chance of a Lifetime." Courtesy of the National Archives and Records Administration. This BIA relocation recruitment poster was designed to lure tribal people to Denver but portrayed an unrealistic image of what many Native Americans encountered when they arrived.

Yet the dream faded quickly. Although the Summer Hawks lived near the hotel where Mary was employed (her job paid minimum wages and had no health insurance or other benefits), Roland was forced to ride city buses and make a series of transfers to reach the tannery. At first, the public transportation system intimidated him. He had readily traversed muddy or snow-blocked roads on the reservation, but in Denver, all the buses looked alike, and the mad scramble by rush-hour passengers to get aboard and find a seat differed markedly from the pace of life at Pine Ridge in South Dakota. He finally mastered the time schedules and transfer systems, but he continued to dislike them. On several occasions, the buses were late, and he missed his transfers, arriving at the tannery late for work.

He also missed several days of work when he and his family returned to Pine Ridge to attend his brother Roger's funeral. Six years older than Roland, Roger had suffered from poor health for over a decade. Like many reservation residents, Roger's diet had been heavily laden with starch, sugar, and fatty meats, and the steady consumption of fry bread, salty chips, hamburgers, and french fries, all washed down with soft drinks, had taken took its toll. Coupled with a lack of physical activity and a genetic proclivity toward the disease, Roger developed diabetes. In 1954, surgeons at the Indian Health Service at Pine Ridge removed several toes on his left foot and warned him to change his diet and get more exercise, but he generally ignored their advice. In late May 1957, he suffered a massive stroke and died less than twenty-four hours later. It took the Summer Hawk family most of a day to travel from Denver to Pine Ridge by bus, then they spent three days participating in family business, attending Roger's funeral, and meeting with family members before spending much of another day returning to Denver. Fortunately, because Roger had died on a Wednesday evening, they had not left Denver until Friday morning, so the trip was completed over a weekend and Roland was absent from his job for only three workdays. Art Carson, his supervisor at the tannery, reluctantly agreed to his absence, but he docked Roland's bimonthly paycheck for three days on the following Friday.

Roland enjoyed his work at the tannery. He had been trained in leatherwork by his uncle at Pine Ridge, and the Lakota elder had taken great pride in producing beautifully tanned hand-tooled leather pieces. Roland often spent extra time preparing the hides for tooling, ensuring that each piece of leather was properly stretched and uniform in coloration. The supervisor admitted that

Roland "kept his nose to the grindstone" and that the hides that he prepared were "first class," but he also chided Roland to work faster, reminding him that he was now part of the business world and needed to meet schedules. According to Carson, a native of rural New Mexico, the business world waited for no one; it did not run on "Indian time."

Yet Roland continued to work at his own pace. His uncle had taught him that each hide, like the animal from which it came, had its own spirit. It must be treated with respect. A good tanner could not hurry the tanning process. Hides tanned in their own time. And Roland also knew that skilled leatherworkers needed sufficient time to measure, cut, sew, and shape the tanned leather into finished products such as saddles, scabbards, belts, and purses. In addition, it took considerable skill to design and then stamp in the intricate patterns that made these leather objects so handsome. He used floral and geometric patterns his uncle had taught him at Pine Ridge, and he carefully applied touches of dye to enhance the designs on the leather. He envisioned his leatherwork as an artist envisions his canvas. He took pride in his work. He refused to produce brusquely constructed, hastily stamped, slipshod saddles or other tooled leather objects.

Sitting at the small kitchen table in his tenement apartment, Roland remembered that Carson had continued to ride him, warning that he needed to work faster if he wished to make it in the white man's world. But Roland smiled down at the strong sweet tea cooling in his heavy mug as he recalled that although he initially had been worried by Carson's harassment, he also had made friends in high places. The tannery-saddleworks was owned by Peter ("Pete") Ventress, a former Oklahoman who had fled from Chickasha to Denver during the Dust Bowl. Although Ventress, who was semiretired, didn't oversee the employees in the tannery on a daily basis, he was well aware of the quality of work produced by the two dozen workers employed in his business. Moreover, he was much impressed by the artistic ability of his new Lakota saddle maker. Like many Oklahomans, Ventress had grown up among many people of Native American ancestry, and his uncle had married Lorraine Wright, a Choctaw woman from McAlester. Ventress was favorably impressed by the artistic quality of Roland's work, and to Carson's surprise, he had approached the Lakota and asked Roland to personally craft a saddle as a graduation gift for his grandson, a senior at suburban Wheat Ridge High School. Roland gladly accepted the assignment, and when he presented the finished saddle to Ventress, the older man marveled at the craftsmanship. He informed Roland that he wanted him to cut, craft, and tool leather purses for his wife and several of his female relatives for their birthdays, which would be coming up over the next few months, and Roland readily accepted the assignment. Ventress's open praise did not sit well with Carson, but Roland recalled that the supervisor generally left him alone after the owner's commendation.

Things went bad in July. At 10:15 on Friday morning, July 19, 1957, while driving from his home in Arvada to the tannery, Pete Ventress's Buick Roadmaster was hit broadside by a Coors beer truck that ran a stop sign on Wadsworth Boulevard, and the aging Oklahoman was killed almost instantly. Having little business experience, Mildred, his widow, decided to sell the tannery, but while the business was on the market, she abdicated responsibility for its management to Art Carson, since he was familiar with the tannery's everyday routine. In August, however, a business recession set in across the United States, orders for leather products fell, and attorneys for Ventress's estate suggested that the tannery should lay off some of its employees. In response, Mildred contacted Carson, who not surprisingly informed Roland that he would have to be let go. The job at the tannery ended.

Roland turned to the Denver BIA office for assistance, and they gave him the names of several companies (a large department store, a supermarket chain, and a gasoline bulk plant) that had agreed to hire responsible Native American workers. Roland followed the BIA officials' directions, bussed to the supermarket employment office, filled out forms, and even interviewed with a store manager about a job as a meat cutter. Things seemed to go well. The job paid decently and even offered a health plan, and the manager hinted that the position would be his just as soon as his job history could be checked out with Roland's previous employer. But to Roland's initial surprise, something then went wrong. He later learned that the call to the tannery was transferred to the acting manager, and Art Carson refused to give him a favorable recommendation. His applications and interviews at the department store and gasoline bulk plant followed a similar pattern, and after spending two weeks in frustration, Roland abandoned the BIA job procedure and looked for work on his own.

The recession continued, and he could find no other jobs related to his skills as a leatherworker, but in mid-August, he took a job in a lumberyard where he unloaded boxcars and loaded building materials onto customers' trucks. The other lumberyard workers and even a few of the regular customers called him "chief," and several of the men with whom he sat and ate his sack lunch kidded him about Cochise and Tonto. Compared to what some non-Indians had called him in South Dakota, Roland considered the lunchtime conversations to be relatively good-natured if ignorant banter, although he grew tired of their incessant questions about what it was like to be an Indian. In contrast, he strongly resented comments by the loud-mouthed manager of the lumberyard's paint department that he cut his braids and get a flattop, a "real" American haircut. After listening to the paint manager repeat his tirade, Roland finally silenced him by suggesting, "When we Lakotas decide to cut anybody's hair, we cut it shorter than any flattop. Just ask General Custer." Taken aback, the paint manager quickly retreated down the center aisle, past the paint and varnish, through the garden hose and sprinkler department, and into the men's room.

As the recession continued, it also took a toll on residential construction, remodeling, and other facets of the construction industry, and the lumberyard, like the tannery, also was forced to lay off part of their employees. Roland's boss at the lumberyard had been satisfied with his job performance, but since Roland was one of last hired, he was one of first fired, and in mid-September, he again found himself unemployed. Throughout the following three months, he worked at a series of odd jobs, periodically performing unskilled labor on a daily basis, but he had been unable to find a permanent position.

But the lumberyard job brought some important changes to the Summer Hawk family. Shortly after Roland started to work at the yard, a coworker helping him unload lumber from a boxcar mentioned that there was a vacant apartment in his building, and to save both time and transportation expenses, Roland moved his family into the new apartment, which was within walking distance of the lumberyard job. The neighborhood was less desirable, and the building was in poor repair, but the apartment was larger, and the rent was less. The new apartment contained a small second bedroom that enabled Robert to sleep somewhere besides the frayed secondhand living-room couch. In addition, Colfax Avenue featured several motor hotels where Mary had again secured employment as a maid, and in late August, Robert transferred into a nearby junior high. Roland earned less at the lumberyard than at the tannery, but their expenses were less. Mary, too, walked to work, and with her income, they managed to get by. But after Roland lost his steady job at the lumberyard, they were periodically short of cash and often hard-pressed to make ends meet.

242 ❖ Chapter 8

The series of moves and relocations were hard on his family. Mary found steady work as a maid, but she also found her life in Denver to be far from the happy existence pictured in the BIA brochures. At Pine Ridge, she had grown up amid a large extended family, maintaining relationships with sisters, aunts, and cousins on an almost daily basis. In Denver, she seemed isolated from her people, and she longed for the warmth and fellowship of family gatherings back in South Dakota. She also remained uncomfortable in her associations with non-Indians. A rather traditional Lakota woman, Mary was the product of a society in which relationships between people were more formalized than on the streets of Denver. She liked many of her coworkers at the motel, but she often found them to be too aggressive or pushy, and she was shocked at their familiarity with non–family members or even strangers. As the maids, clerks, and other domestic workers scurried around the large, two-storied motor inn, they readily shared information about their private lives, the personal problems of their families, or other gossip that Mary considered to be surprising and completely inappropriate. They often joked with, and even seemed to occasionally flirt with, coworkers and customers of the opposite sex, conduct that would have been reprehensible among her conservative family members back at Pine Ridge.

In turn, Mary's coworkers respected the hard-working, dependable Lakota woman, but they found her to be shy and reticent to enter into their ongoing, if somewhat raucous, conversations. When she had first joined the staff, the other maids had asked her numerous questions regarding her life and her family, but she had provided only brief, laconic answers, so they ceased their inquiries, assuming that she wished to be by herself. None of the other maids disliked the Lakota woman, but they privately agreed among themselves that maybe her reluctance to join their friendly banter was "just part of being an Indian," and as long as she did her fair share of the work, they would let her be. From Mary's perspective, she was glad to be free of all the questions. She just wanted to remain politely apart from all the banter, do her job, receive her wages, and return home to her family. She succeeded, but she continued to have few friends, and she felt very isolated.

On Friday, September 20, Mary's life temporarily brightened when one of her brothers, Bernard Valcourt, also relocated to Denver. Bernard, aged twenty-two, arrived via the BIA's relocation program with promises of employment as a carpenter's apprentice, but the BIA's promises had been based on the prerecession economy, and the bureaucrats in charge of the program had failed to check with the construction company participating in their program after the economic downturn. Consequently, on the evening of September 19, Bernard had been provided with a bus ticket from Pine Ridge to Colorado, but when he arrived at the bus station in Denver on the following morning, he learned that the job no longer existed. The BIA official who met him assured Bernard that the bureau would come up with something and informed him that the BIA would provide him $125 in pocket money to tide him over until he could get on his feet. After escorting Bernard to the BIA office, where the Lakota man filled out a series of forms (many of which were duplicates of forms he had already completed at Pine Ridge), Bernard received his stipend and met with another bureaucrat who had been assigned to help him find adequate housing.

When Bernard informed the official that he planned to live with his sister and her family and supplied the man with the Summer Hawks' address, the man seemed surprised. According to the bureaucrat, the BIA usually did not approve of new relocatees renting apartments in the Colfax neighborhood, but since Bernard had family members living there, they would make an exception. Obviously, living with his sister's family would save Valcourt rent expenses (but what the man did not tell Bernard was that he and other BIA officials in Denver currently were having difficulty finding adequate jobs for newly arrived relocatees and that the initial $125 provided to him earlier in the day might have to be stretched for a longer period than anyone had first envisioned). He then loaded Bernard and his battered suitcase into a bureau car and drove him to the Summer Hawk's apartment building. After instructing Bernard to call him on the following Monday, the agent drove back to the BIA office. Since Roland was at a temporary day job, Mary was at the motel, and Robert was in school, no one was home. Bernard eventually found his way, past the postal boxes, to the apartment building's dingy office, where he waited on a well-used wooden bench until he saw Mary coming home from work at 3:30 in the afternoon.[1]

Mary was both surprised and delighted to see her brother. Bernard had written to her in August, telling her that he had applied to relocate to Denver, but he had failed to inform her of his arrival date, and she was not expecting him. After lots of smiles, a hug or two, and a conversation in Lakota, Bernard accompanied Mary to the apartment, where she made a pot of tea and opened a bag of Oreo cookies. The renewed conversation turned to relatives and events back at Pine Ridge, but within half an hour, Robert returned home from school, and he also was overjoyed to see his uncle. Roland's day job (stacking sheet metal and large tubular heating ducts in a furnace repair warehouse) kept him tied to his job site until 5 P.M., but when he arrived home shortly after 5:30, he, too, was glad to see Robert. After a dinner of hamburgers, fried potatoes, and canned peaches, the Lakotas spent the evening catching up on all the news from Pine Ridge and talking about Bernard's plans for getting settled in Denver.

Since Robert had only a single rollaway bed in his bedroom, he gave up his bed to his uncle and spent the night back on the couch. On the following afternoon, Roland and Bernard walked to a nearby secondhand furniture store where Bernard bought a small used chest of drawers and another folding rollaway bed that they literally rolled along Colfax Avenue to the apartment building, where they then carried both pieces of furniture up the flight of stairs to the Summer Hawk's apartment. The additional furniture crowded the floor space in Robert's (and now Bernard's) bedroom, but no one complained. Bernard was glad to have a home and the support of family members in a strange new setting, while the Summer Hawks, particularly Mary, welcomed a familiar face who reminded her of kinspeople back on the reservation.

On the following Monday, after receiving some welcome advice from Roland, Bernard navigated the uncertainty of bus routes and transfers back to the Denver BIA office, where an employment counselor told him that because of the recession, construction had fallen off and the demand for carpentry had temporarily declined. He advised Bernard to put his plans to become a carpenter's apprentice on hold and to "just try your hand at something else" until the recession ended and the demand for carpenters returned. The counselor informed him that he currently had an opening for a "delivery associate" at Tucker's Department Store, which had been a fixture in Denver ever since the late nineteenth century. The associate would be required to assist the driver of the store's delivery truck haul heavy furniture or appliances to customers' homes and businesses in Denver and its suburbs, pick up the worn-out stoves, refrigerators, and old sofas they were discarding, and haul them to the city dump. The job paid little more than a minimum wage, but it would provide Bernard with an opportunity to learn about the geography and street grid of Denver and its suburbs, and since the driver of the truck would pick him up and also drop him off daily at his apartment, he would not have to ride the bus to and from work.

Bernard took the job. The driver, Carlos Avila, had been born in Trinidad, Colorado, but his parents had emigrated to the United States from rural Chihuahua in the late 1920s. Avila knew Denver and its suburbs well, and although lugging refrigerators, stoves, and freezers in and out of the warehouse, loading them into the truck, then hauling them (sometimes up two flights of stairs) into houses and apartments was hard work, the job introduced Bernard to a broad spectrum of people and neighborhoods. Bernard and Carlos got along well, and the work went smoothly for about a month, before they attempted to deliver a stove and freezer to a large house in the Cherry Creek region in south-central Denver. As they approached the address, Bernard asked Carlos about the people who lived in the obviously expensive neighborhood, and Carlos answered that the houses belonged to "rich gringos" who played golf in the summer, skied in the winter, and didn't seem to have much else to do. When they arrived, Carlos knocked on the front door and was instructed by a maid to pull the truck around to the back of the house and deliver the appliances through a utility-room door off the patio. After following the wide concrete drive around behind the house, they found a large paved patio stretching from the back of the house, where it met a well-watered lawn. The patio also enclosed a tiled swimming pool, complete with a diving board. The temperatures was in the lower sixties, so it was too cold to swim, but a heavyset man was sitting at a glass-topped table near the pool, pouring bourbon into a short, leaded-crystal glass from a half-full bottle.

Bernard and Carlos followed the maid into the house to the utility room, where they unplugged an older refrigerator, put the empty appliance on a hand dolly, and rolled it out to the truck that was sitting on the driveway next to the pool and patio. They unloaded the refrigerator, left it on the patio, and returned inside the house, detached the stove from its electrical outlet and ventilating system, then rolled it on the dolly out to the patio, where they placed it next to the used refrigerator. Both men then climbed into the back of the delivery truck and scooted both the freezer and the new stove to the open rear end of the truck, preparing to lift the heavy appliances down to the patio before loading them on the dolly and taking them into the house.

But to their surprise, the heavyset man, probably in his forties, walked over from the glass-top table and ordered them to "Get that filthy old stove off the patio and into that truck before it leaks grease or who-knows-what into my mom's swimming pool." Carlos replied that they couldn't put the used appliances into the truck until they removed the new ones — there wasn't any room — but that they would lift the old stove and refrigerator up into the truck just as soon as they could clear a space for them.

Obviously awash in bourbon, the man angrily spat back, "Just like a pair of greasers! Too stupid to do a job right." He then grabbed the dolly, wedged the lower end under the edge of the stove, lifted the handles and exclaimed, "I'll take this piece of crap where it should go—out to the curb in front of the house. You two greasers can load it on that truck out there."

Before Bernard and Carlos could get down from the truck and stop him, the bourbon guzzler had started across the patio, pushing the stove on the dolly, but he was so intoxicated he lost his bearings, and angled off to his right, away from the driveway and toward the pool. Bernard leapt down from the truck and rushed after him, but he was too late. Before he could reach him, the front wheel of the dolly tipped over the pool edge, and the stove went into the water. The drunken man teetered on the pool's brink and almost lost his balance, but at the last second, Bernard grabbed him by the waist and pulled him back, preventing him from following in the stove's wake.

To Bernard's surprise, the man erupted in a string of curses, screaming to Carlos, "Did you see that? Did you see that? This Mexican sonofabitch knocked that stove into the pool and then tried to push me in after it. I'm gonna sue Tuckers. Then I'm gonna sue both of your pepper-bellied asses. Get the hell off my mom's property! I'm gonna call an American company with real American workers to handle all of this." Then looking at the stove, which now sat at the bottom of the pool's deep end, he exclaimed, "But first pull that damned stove out of the water." Pointing at Bernard, he added, "That Mexican boy knocked it in. You both can get in there and fish it out."

As the tirade continued, Bernard became angrier. He wouldn't have put up with such insults at Pine Ridge, but he was new to Denver, and he wanted to keep his job. Consequently, he bit his tongue and said nothing. In contrast, Carlos had encountered situations somewhat like this before but never quite so bad. Finally, he had enough. Still standing in the back of the truck, Carlos stared down at the drunken windbag, who had staggered back to the glass table to get his bottle, and coldly replied. "Fish that fucking stove out yourself, you drunken son-of-a-bitch! You're the one who put it there. If Bernard hadn't saved your ass, you'd be down there with the stove in the deep end, probably drowned. My folks came here from Mexico forty years ago, and I'm proud of it. At least I'm holding down a job. I'm not a grown man sitting by my momma's swimming pool blubbering like a drunken fool. And Bernard's not from Mexico. He's a Sioux Indian from South Dakota, and he's also proud of his family and his people. So if you know what's good for you, you better get your sorry ass in that house before we decide to throw it into that pool and then stuff it in that old stove's oven."

The man beat a wise retreat toward the house, but before he entered and locked the door, he turned and yelled back, "A God-damned blanket-ass Indian! That's even worse than a Mexican! I'm surprised he didn't try to steal my Jim Beam. Everybody knows how they're hooked on it! Blanket-assed sons-a-bitches! My great-grandfather rode with Chivington when we ran their red-skinned asses out of this neck of the woods a hundred years ago. And we can do it again! Wait and see!"

Bernard and Carlos hoisted the new stove and freezer down from the truck, placed them safely under an awning that partially overhang the patio, loaded the old refrigerator back into the truck, and drove away. After depositing the used refrigerator at a scrap yard, they returned to Tucker's Department Store, where they were met by their supervisor. He informed them that he had received a ranting, almost incoherent phone call from Chester Scrump, the bourbon-drenched patio idler, but Scrump also had called Sylvia Tucker, the wife of the department store's owner and a member of Scrump's mother's bridge club. Carlos explained what had happened, and the supervisor shook his head and replied that he wasn't surprised. During the previous spring, another delivery crew had attempted to deliver a set of bedroom furniture to the same address and had encountered a similar, if less vociferous, reception from a tipsy Scrump, who ordered them to move furniture around from room to room for almost two hours before the driver and his assistant could get away from him. At that time, Scrump had also complained, but he had failed to call his mother's bridge partner. This time was different, however. Mrs. Bernice Tucker had intervened and had demanded that the "rude deliveryman who had tried to push poor Chester into the pool be fired," and the supervisor felt he had little choice. He admitted to Bernard that he believed the deliverymen's account of what had happened, and he assured Bernard that he would report back to the BIA that Bernard had been let go due to a shrinking demand for deliveries, not through any fault of his own. He also promised to write a favorable recommendation for Bernard if he applied for a job anywhere else in the Denver region. But according to the supervisor, his hands were tied. Bernard's job was terminated.

Bernard was devastated. Now back on his own, he joined with Roland and sought temporary work in the region near the Summer Hawk's apartment, and although he was able to wrangle a series of day jobs, most paid only a minimum wage (or sometimes less). By late November, Bernard was discouraged, and he began to spend his evenings drinking beer with several other young Native American men at a bar on Colfax Avenue. On two occasions, too much beer led to arguments with some non-Indian patrons, and the police had intervened. Bernard had said very little, but in the aftermath, he was rounded up with Richard Lame Bull, a Shoshone from Lander Wyoming, and Charlie Winter Kill, a Crow from Montana. On both occasions, the young men were held overnight, and although they were released early in the afternoon on the following day, they were subjected to racial slurs and threats of physical violence at the police station. The Summer Hawks readily welcomed him back into their household, but Bernard grew more depressed. His life in Denver seemed far removed from the happy, prosperous people pictured in the BIA removal brochures. Early in December, he hitchhiked back to Pine Ridge.

Bernard's departure saddened Mary, but it had a more profound effect on Robert. Prior to Bernard's arrival, Roland had often been concerned about his son. It had been hard enough to raise a teenager back on the reservation, but at least at Pine Ridge there had been a network of family and friends to provide some controls over the normal outbursts of teenage angst and exuberance, and on the reservation, Roland had known the families of most of Robert's friends. In contrast, Denver offered Robert and other adolescents the anonymity of numbers, and since both Roland and Mary were working, they were hard-pressed to keep track of the boy's whereabouts. During the summer, Robert had begun to associate with a small group of other Native American boys who spent considerable time on the streets, hanging out in parks and on playgrounds. In early September, when school started, Robert was truant on two or three occasions. He was reluctant to do his homework, and he was bullied in the school lunchroom and after school as he walked home. Since he had failed to turn in his homework, Roland and Mary received a warning slip from one of Robert's teachers informing them that their son was in danger of receiving a failing grade for the first six-week segment of the fall semester.

With Bernard's arrival, things had changed. Back on the reservation, Robert had always admired his uncle, and now, since they both shared the same address, Bernard spent considerable time with his nephew, serving an avuncular or big-brother role that Robert seemed to relish.[2] Roland admitted that Bernard had been a far better student at the high school at Holy Rosary Mission on

Pine Ridge than he himself had—Bernard actually graduated in 1952, whereas Roland dropped out after his sophomore year—and Bernard regularly encouraged the boy to do his homework, sometimes even helping him with math and reading assignments. Bernard also made several suggestions to help Robert deal with the lunchroom bullying, and he waited outside Robert's school on two or three afternoons when school was dismissed. In his own words, Bernard had "stared down" a couple of Robert's assailants and had "put the fear of God in the little bastards." Robert no longer was truant, and in mid-October, when he received his report card for the first six weeks of the term, his homeroom teacher reported that Robert's grades had "considerably improved over the past month or so," and that he was "doing well."

Mary was pleased. Bernard and Robert regularly went to the movies, shot baskets at a nearby playground, and sometimes played pool at a city recreation center. Her son seemed to be modeling himself after his uncle's (her brother's) image. Like Bernard, he decided to let his hair grow long, and to Mary's particular delight, Bernard convinced Robert to again converse in Lakota when the family was together in the apartment, a practice that the boy had refused to do following the Summer Hawks relocation to Denver.

Still sitting at his kitchen table, Roland took another sip of the now tepid tea and admitted to himself that after Bernard left, Robert spiraled downward. He again refused to do his homework, and in the weeks between Thanksgiving and the Christmas holidays, he had skipped (been truant) on three occasions. He now complained to both Roland and Mary that his teachers didn't understand him and that he wanted to move back to Pine Ridge, where he could go to school with other Indian students. Roland privately agreed that most of the teachers in Robert's middle school had little knowledge of tribal people or their problems, but he knew that Robert had done well at school before Bernard's departure, and he believed that he would recover and again get the hang of it. Just before the Christmas break, Roland and Mary were contacted by school officials, who suggested that Robert needed some counseling. Roland was wary of their advice. Sure, Robert was upset over his uncle leaving, but the boy seemed normal enough to Roland. Moreover, he resented their probing into his family's affairs. Lakota people took care of their own. They did not need the unsolicited advice of outsiders. Still, Robert seemed to have slipped back into some bad old habits, and Roland remained worried about what might happen to him in Denver.

Getting up from the table, Roland walked over to the sink and threw the remainder of the tea down the drain. He put the tea kettle back on the stove, lit the burner, and waited for the water to boil. He needed another cup. He wished he had something stronger—after all, it was New Year's Eve. He rarely drank, just a couple of beers now and then, but it had been a long December and he could use a Coors or two to tide him over into the New Year. He shook his head, remembering that the first time he had ever tasted Coors beer was three months ago, at his cousin's house in early September.

At that time, he had just lost his job at the lumberyard and had turned to Henry Two Birds for advice. Not much had come of it. He did not know his cousin very well, but Henry had lived in Denver since 1952, and Roland assumed that he would have some good advice on how Lakota people could make a go of it here in the city. Roland had telephoned his cousin, and Henry had asked Roland, Mary, and Robert to drive over to his house in Applewood. Henry offered to put some steaks on his new charcoal grill, and while the steaks grilled, they could have a couple of beers, catch up on things, and see how Roland was getting along. Roland readily accepted. He still owned no car, but after checking the bus schedule, he found that they could ride a series of three busses to within two blocks of Henry's house then walk to his home. So on a Saturday evening in late August, Roland, Mary, and Robert showed up at Henry's ranch house for dinner.

It had not gone well. While Henry grilled the steaks, he and Roland sat in lawn chairs on Henry's small concrete patio, where they each had a beer and Roland told Henry about his employment problems. Henry wasn't much help. During World War II, Henry had joined the air force, where he was trained as an aircraft mechanic. He remained in the service when the war ended and served through part of the Korean War, mustering out of the air force in 1952. When he returned from Korea to Edwards Air Force Base in California to pick up his discharge papers, Henry noticed a poster announcing "Help Wanted—Openings for Trained Aircraft Mechanics" posted by Frontier Airlines. Following instructions on the sign, he flew to the Frontier offices at Stapleton Airport in Denver, walked to the office adjoining the Frontier hanger, filled out an employment form, underwent an interview, and was hired later in the afternoon.[3]

Henry had worked for Frontier Airlines ever since. He had little knowledge of the job market outside the airport, and his suggestions for career opportunities in the aviation business demanded job skills or advanced training that

Roland did not possess. As Roland pointed out, he was a skilled leatherworker, but unless Frontier Airlines wanted new hand-tooled leather seats installed in their first class section, he had few specialized skills to offer.

The remainder of the evening had not gone much better. In 1943, when Henry was undergoing training as an aircraft mechanic, he was stationed at Lackland Air Force base in San Antonio, Texas. While at Lackland, Henry met and married Bernadine Cravens, an eighteen-year-old salesgirl at a nearby Sears and Roebuck store. One year later, in 1944, their daughter, Judy Anne, was born in the base hospital. During the period of Henry's enlistment, the family continued to live in Lackland's base housing, but after Henry hired on with Frontier Airlines, they moved to Denver. After living for nine years in base housing, Bernadine was proud of her new ranch-style house in Applewood, and while Henry and Roland grilled the steaks, Bernadine gave Mary an in-depth tour of the house and its kitchen. Uncertain of how familiar Mary was with modern appliances ("After all," according to Bernadine, "the woman had grown up on an Indian reservation"), Bernadine took great pains to show Mary her new Kenmore washer and dryer, her two Kenmore refrigerators — the one in the kitchen even had an automatic ice maker, although the one in the basement with the big no-frost freezer did not. She also pointed out her new Kenmore electric stove (with two ovens) and the icing on her Kenmore cake: her new Kenmore deluxe automatic dishwasher!

Bernadine also demonstrated that their living room focused on their two-year-old Kenmore console black and white television set, with its "Magna 24 inch Krystal-Clear" screen. She admitted that RCA had recently offered a new color set but stated that they planned to wait until more shows were broadcast in color and until Sears would offer a color set under their Kenmore brand, since they continued to get a nice discount on Sears appliances. By the time Henry and Roland brought the steaks in from the patio, Mary was more than glad to be free of her Kenmore tour guide.

At least the dinner was good. Bernadine served the steaks with baked potatoes, roasting ears, tossed salad, and French bread. Dessert was Texas pecan pie. Conversation at the dinner table was dominated by Bernadine, who spent much of the time describing Judy's triumphs and accomplishments in her middle school's drama, debate, and dance programs and how disappointed they (at least she and Judy) were that Judy had failed to make the cheerleading squad. After dinner, they retired to the living room, watched the second half of

252 ÷ Chapter 8

the *Lawrence Welk Show* (Robert later admitted to his parents that he thought he might vomit), and an episode of *Gunsmoke*. Following the television shows, Bernadine brought out a large bag of pretzels, a couple of beers for Henry and Roland, and Pepsis for everyone else. Bernadine prattled on about where to shop in Denver, while Judy reminded her mother that she chose her fashions from ads in *Seventeen* magazine, and some of the stores in Denver didn't carry those brands. Mary quietly commented that she and her family bought most of their clothes on sale at Sears. Judy made a strange face, but Bernadine quickly added that although they were sold on the quality of Sears's appliances, they preferred to buy their clothes at smaller, more specialized places. Unseen by any of the Two Birds, Mary looked at Roland and gave him her "I've had enough of this crap" stare. In response, Roland announced that it was getting late and that he and his family should be heading back to their apartment.

Henry was surprised that the Summer Hawks had taken the bus to Applewood and offered to drive them home in his Pontiac. Roland accepted, and the rather quiet drive home took much less time than the bus rides to Henry's house earlier in the evening. When they reached their apartment building, Henry dropped them off, declined an invitation to come in for a few minutes, then rolled up all the car windows, locked the car doors, and, in Robert's words, "hightailed it outa there."

It was after 11 P.M., and the Summer Hawks all went promptly to bed, but on the following morning, while they ate breakfast, Robert declared that he never wanted to go to the Two Bird's house again. Mary said nothing, although Roland knew that her silence was telling. He tried to be the peacemaker and commented that maybe Henry and his family had lived in Denver so long that they had adopted different ways and they were just trying to be friendly, but he could tell that his efforts to assuage Mary and Robert fell on deaf ears. He could tell that Mary disliked both Bernadine and Judy, and two weeks later, when Roland suggested that the Two Birds come to the Summer Hawk home for a traditional meal of Indian tacos, Henry answered that Judy had a mandatory dance club rehearsal and that they couldn't make it. A week later, they finally got together at Brentwood-Whitehall Shopping Center, where Roland paid for their meals in a cafeteria, but only the adults were present. Bernadine reported that Judy had to attend a drama club play practice, while Robert complained to his parents that he had contracted a case of "roaring diarrhea" and couldn't take a bus ride. The evening went better than the visit to Henry's home. Everyone was quietly polite, but the families did not get together after that.

Roland noticed that the water in the teakettle was boiling, so he filled his mug, added a tea bag and some sugar, and let it steep. Thinking back on his attempts to meet with Henry, he knew that Mary had little use for Bernadine, and he had to admit that he agreed with her. Sipping his fresh cup of tea, Roland realized that after the months in Denver, he had grown somewhat accustomed, and even inured, to being patronized by boisterous, pushy white people, but Bernadine had been hard to take. And he was even more bothered by Judy. Judy's lineage was one-half Lakota; she had been enrolled at Pine Ridge, but her conduct would have been embarrassing among her relatives on the reservation. She seemed to ignore or reject many traditional Lakota attitudes regarding family values, elders, generosity, and respect. Roland was worried. If the Summer Hawks remained in Denver, would Robert, or Roland's future grandchildren, do the same?[4]

Well, if Henry and his immediate family seemed uninterested in the Summer Hawk's problems, Roland eventually found other people who commiserated with his trials. Since mid-November, he had been meeting with other tribal people in a small storefront Indian center funded by a coalition of local Protestant churches (Lutherans, Disciples of Christ, Methodists, and others). Although the center held a paucity of furniture (just some folding chairs, a couple of used couches, a desk, and several old, beaten-up tables), it contained a job board on which employment openings were listed. It was staffed by volunteers from the various churches who answered the phone and attempted to help Roland and other visitors with their problems. Unlike the BIA office employees, the volunteers at the center relied on an informal network of personal contacts to find jobs that matched the specific needs and schedules of the individual Indian person who came to them for assistance, and Roland found that he could often land a temporary job through the center quicker, and with much less paperwork, than through the BIA office.

The center also sponsored small monthly powwows and bi-monthly hand games that drew increasing numbers of participants and allowed both Roland and Mary to enjoy the fellowship and companionship of other Indian people.[5] Through their growing association with the center, both Roland and Mary found that regardless of their tribal affiliation, almost all the people they met at the center had much in common. Indeed, after less than two months, Roland had become good friends with Emmet Begay, a Navajo from Many Farms, Arizona, whose family seemed to face many of the same problems confronting the Summer Hawks. Denver treated all Indians the same. People still remained tied to their reservation communities, but in the city, some of the tribal differences were eclipsed by urban problems that everyone who visited the center seemed to share.

Finishing his tea, Roland wondered about his future in the city. Although he currently had no permanent job, he continued to work at a series of temporary day jobs, and at the present, combining both his and Mary's earnings, the Summer Hawks were getting along, but just barely. Recently, one of the Lutheran volunteers at the center, a retired banker, had told him "to keep his chin up," that the economy was getting ready to rebound, and Roland felt confident that he would eventually get another steady job, maybe back as a leatherworker. But was the income from the employment worth the sacrifices? What would happen to his family? Would he ever be happy in Denver? Perhaps his wife's brother had chosen the right path. Maybe he also should pack up and take his family back to Pine Ridge. Surely they were not leading the happy life promised in the BIA brochures. Roland had been unemployed on the reservation, but wasn't he also unemployed in Denver? Now he seemed adrift, his life a shadow of shattered promises.

Roland Summer Hawk, his family, and his acquaintances are fictitious characters, but they are representative of many of the Native American people brought to the cities in the mid-1950s by the Bureau of Indian Affairs' relocation program. During the 1950s, the federal government attempted to sever its long-standing relationship with many tribal governments and to terminate tribal people's legal status as "Indians." Armed with Public Law 280 and House Concurrent Resolution 108, the federal government allowed, and sometimes encouraged, state governments to extend their jurisdiction over the reservations and withdrew federal services from several tribal communities. As part of the termination policies, federal officials hoped to disperse the remaining reservation communities and to scatter and blend the Indian population into the general mainstream of American life. Since the United States was rapidly becoming urbanized, the BIA encouraged reservation people to move to the cities, where the assimilation process would be accelerated by the anonymity of urban life.⁶

During the early 1950s, relocation offices were established in Denver, Los Angeles, Chicago, and Salt Lake City, with subsequent offices opening in Cleveland, Cincinnati, St. Louis, Dallas, Oakland, San Jose, and San Francisco. Indians in the reservation communities, whose populations had burgeoned since World War II, were encouraged to move to the relocation cities where they were assured they would find employment and attain a status of economic independence. The BIA promised to pay their relocation expenses, assist them in finding jobs and housing, and provide them with living expenses until they became self-sufficient. Since many of the reservations were economically depressed, the bureau believed that with BIA encouragement, many tribal people would voluntarily choose to make a new start.⁷

The program immediately encountered difficulties. Like the Summer Hawks and Bernard Valcourt, many of the initial participants were ill-equipped for urban life; they found their initial entrance into the cities to be overwhelming. To remedy this situation, in 1958 the BIA offered adult education and vocational training to Indians both on the reservations and in the cities. The bureau intended to better prepare future relocation participants for life in the city and hoped to provide unemployed urban Indians with skills to match the current job market. In addition, attempts were made to carefully screen applicants for the relocation program so that those who participated would have a greater chance of success. Meanwhile, the BIA's emphasis on encouraging relocation diminished. After 1960, when the termination program was ended, relocation remained an option for Indian people on the reservations, but it was no longer championed as a panacea for America's "Indian problem."⁸

The additional preparation led to greater success. After 1958, the BIA's screening process examined the applicant' health, educational, and employment records. Upon their arrival in the cities, the newcomers were given several days of orientation by BIA personnel, and social workers were assigned to periodically check each Native American family to assure that they were coping with the complexities of urban life. Relocatees also were required to attend group sessions during the first few months, where they shared their experiences with other Indian people, both newcomers and old hands on the urban frontier. These later emigrants seemed to cope with the city much more successfully, and by 1970, the federal government had relocated over 125,000 Native Americans into urban areas. Since that time, other Indian people have continued to move to the cities, and today, the exodus still goes on.[9]

Was the relocation of Native American people into urban areas during the latter half of the twentieth century successful? The answer remains as complex and varied as the different people who participated in the program. Unquestionably, those people who participated in the process after 1958 and who were better prepared for their urban experience achieved a higher degree of "success" than did many of the earlier participants. Indeed, a significant number of Native Americans from throughout the program's history have "made it" in the white man's world, and although many periodically revisit their former reservations communities, they have remained permanently settled in their urban surroundings, successfully supporting themselves and their families.[10]

Others were less fortunate. Like the Summer Hawk family, they were poorly prepared for life in the city and have continued to eke out a living in the fringe areas of the urban environment. Shackled by the realities of city life, many of these people existed in a limbo of poverty and frustration. Of course, poverty and frustration also existed back on some of the reservations, but within the tribal communities, individuals had the security of membership in an extended circle of family and friends. There were heavy burdens to bear, but on the reservations, the loads could be shared, and people like the Summer Hawks could take refuge in the security of kinship and time-honored traditions. In the city, however, they often were alienated and felt very much alone.[11]

It is not surprising that Bernard Valcourt, Mary's brother, returned to Pine Ridge. During the first few years of the relocation program, so many of the participants returned to the reservation communities (estimates run as high as 50 percent) that after 1958, the BIA discontinued its collections of such data, not wishing to give critics of the program any additional negative ammunition. In the decade following 1958, the rate of returnees dropped, but significant numbers still returned to the tribal communities. It should be added, however, that some of these later returnees were retirees, people who had spent up to two decades in the cities, succeeded in their jobs, raised their families, then, after they reached their sixties, returned to the reservations to spend a less hectic, rural existence in the final decades of their life. Indeed, this return to the reservation or to smaller cities abutting reservation communities remains an ongoing pattern of Native America residency, even in the early decades of the twenty-first century. This reverse migration also has been spurred by economic growth and better employment opportunities on some reservations during these years.[12]

For Native Americans who remained in the cities, there seems to be several general consensuses. First, the BIA's goal of using relocation as a key component in the federal policy of terminating the special relationship of tribal people to the federal government failed. The government originally had hoped to disperse the reservation populations into urban areas as part of its more comprehensive plan to terminate the tribes and blend Native Americans into the mainstream population of the United States. In response, some tribal people moved to the cities, found jobs, raised their families, and made some adjustments to urban life—but they did not become "white"; they still retained their Indian identity. Meanwhile, with a few exceptions, federal attempts to terminate the remaining reservations also collapsed as tribal leaders, allied with some state and local government, Native American Rights organizations, and other supporters, successfully thwarted the initial federal plans to do away with the reservations. The reservations, as distinct enduring Native American homelands and centers of tribal traditions, have remained.[13]

Unlike the idealistic scenarios portrayed in the BIA's relocation brochures, those tribal people who remained in the cities did not scatter across the broader urban landscape. In contrast, they formed Indian neighborhoods where Native American people from a broad spectrum of tribes settled near each other. Just as many of the relocates to Denver coalesced into a loose community around Colfax Avenue, other tribal people formed similar loose and unofficial Indian neighborhoods in other cities. In Chicago, relocated tribal people flocked to the Uptown region, renting apartments along Lawrence and Wilson avenues on the city's North Side. In the Twin Cities, an Indian neighborhood, sometimes derisively called a ghetto, emerged along East Franklin Avenue in Minneapolis. In the Dallas-Fort Worth Metroplex, many Indian people settled into neighborhoods in Grand Prairie and Arlington. Farther west, in the Los Angeles basin, relocatees established neighborhoods in the Skid Row/Winston Street region known as Indian Alley and in the Bell Gardens-Huntington Park suburban districts. In the Bay Area, relocatees established communities in the San Francisco's Mission District and in Richmond. Similar neighborhoods emerged in other relocation cities. Contrary to the BIA's initial design, those tribal people who remained in the cities created their own "cultural reservations," enclaves in which they found both companionship and familiar cultural patterns that they shared with other Native Americans.[14]

To the dismay of many BIA bureaucrats, the relocation of tribal people into the cities did not diminish their tribal identities. If officials believed that the separation of individual Native Americans and their immediate families from the reservation communities would eventually sever their tribal ties, they were sorely mistaken. Although they no longer resided on the reservations, the vast majority of urban Indians have continued to proudly identify with their tribal backgrounds. They have continued to live and work in the cities, but most regularly return to their reservations or tribal communities to visit friends and relatives and to participate in tribal festivities. A Pawnee man living in Phoenix Arizona remains Pawnee. An Ojibwe woman living in St. Paul is still proud to be Ojibwe. The tribal ties may sometimes by strained by the distance, but they continue.[15]

But another, coexistent identity also has emerged. Like the Summer Hawks, temporarily separated from old friends and family and set adrift in an urban wasteland, many of the relocatees gravitated toward new communities that emerged in response to the impersonality of city life. Often focused on residential patterns and urban Indian centers, new Native American communities arose in which the shared experience of city life added a new dimension to people's older ties to tribes and reservations. As pointed out above, all urban Indians still identify as members of tribal groups, but in the cities, as they face the challenges of a new urban environment, they know that on a daily basis, they have as much, or more, in common with other urban Indians as with many of their kinspeople back on the reservation. Since the relocation debacle, a nascent urban Indian identity has emerged and grown exponentially in relocation centers and other cities across the United States. People are still Oneida or Choctaw, but in their neighborhoods along Wilson Avenue in Chicago or in Richmond on the eastern side of the Bay Area, they also see themselves as "urban Indians."[16]

Finally, during the final third of the twentieth century, these urban communities, with their members sharing urban problems that transcended any tribal boundaries, have been wellsprings for the growth of Native American activism. Responding to poverty, prejudice, and questionable treatment by local law enforcement agencies, young urban Indian activists, both men and women, have banded together to fight injustice and to further urban Indian causes. It is from these initial coalitions that the Red Power movement emerged in the 1960s and 1970s. The American Indian Movement (AIM) was founded in Minneapolis in 1968, and Indians of All Tribes (IOAT), forged by Mohawk activist Richard Oakes, emerged in San Francisco in 1969. Similar organizations formed in other cities (Milwaukee, Chicago, Los Angeles, for example), but by the early 1970s, most of the smaller local groups had merged with AIM. At first, AIM had only limited support within the reservation communities, but after television coverage of AIM protests at Plymouth Rock (Thanksgiving 1971), at Mount Rushmore (1972), in the Trail of Broken Treaties (1972), and at other places, AIM's influence spread to the reservation communities.[17]

Two other events markedly shaped the Red Power movement. In November 1969, a party of urban Indians representing IOAT led by Richard Oakes, LaNada Means (Shoshone-Bannock), John Trudell (Santee Dakota), and others landed on Alcatraz Island and declared the island to be Indian Country, since under the 1868 Fort Laramie Treaty, the federal government was obligated to return to the tribes any federal lands it abandoned. They drolly offered to pay the government $24, the price (in trade goods) that the Dutch had once paid for Manhattan, but the federal government refused. The occupation lasted until June 1971 and attracted considerable media attention. The IOAT established its own radio station (Radio Free Alcatraz), which was rebroadcast on stations across the United States, and during the six-month occupation, IOAT spokespeople were hosted on late-night television shows. Meanwhile, the island was visited by journalists, movie stars such as Anthony Quinn and Jane Fonda, and many urban tribespeople from across the west. For example, relocatee Wilma Mankiller, who later returned to Oklahoma and served as the elected chief of the Cherokee Nation, and George Horse Capture (Gros Ventre), who subsequently assisted in the design and implementation of the Smithsonian's Museum of the North American Indian, both spent some time on the island. Although the IOAT's occupation of Alcatraz ended in June 1972, the protest was spearheaded by urban Indians, many of whom were the products of the BIA's severely flawed relocation program. Moreover, the occupation of Alcatraz forced the American public to focus on the rapidly growing urban Native American population and to reexamine the problems they faced on a daily basis.[18]

So did Wounded Knee. Reacting to the alleged miscarriage of justice in Gordon, Nebraska, and Custer, South Dakota, border towns in counties abutting the Pine Ridge Reservation, and to complaints by many Pine Ridge tribespeople

against the administration of Richard Wilson, who served as the tribal chairman, in late February 1973, some three hundred AIM members and local Oglala
Lakota tribespeople seized control of Wounded Knee, a small hamlet near the
site of the infamous massacre of Lakota tribespeople in 1890. While tribal
police, federal marshals, and FBI agents surrounded the hamlet and attempted
to seal it off from contact with the outside world, AIM leaders such as Russell
Means (Oglala Lakota) and Dennis Banks (Ojibwe) met with news reporters
and discussed conditions at Pine Ridge and among tribal people across the
United States. Both AIM members and their besiegers were well armed, and
the siege was punctuated by sniping and gunfire, particularly after nightfall. As
the siege continued, several people were wounded, and two Native American
men within the occupants' ranks were killed. Federal agents cut off electric-
ity and water to the village and tried to prevent food and other supplies from
reaching the occupants, but they were only partially successful. In addition to
food drops by small private planes that clandestinely parachuted canned food,
bottled water, and other supplies into the hamlet, individual couriers ("runners"), under the cover of darkness, also carried in backpacks full of ammunition and medicine.[19]

Even more than the occupation at Alcatraz, the Second Battle of Wounded
Knee catapulted the Red Power movement into public notice. Major television
networks in both the United States and Europe carried to their viewers nightly
reports of the events in South Dakota. Soviet newscasts repeatedly asserted
that Wounded Knee was symptomatic of the political and economic inequal-
ity in a capitalist society. In contrast, rightwing propagandists in the United
States argued that the "armed militants" (one was even portrayed with an
AK-47 assault rifle) were the forerunners of a communist plot to seize control
of the country (after all, weren't Indians "red" and many tribal societies "communal"?) Red Power, once seen as a novel political movement formerly associated with limited locations in the American West, became a focal point of
national interest.[20]

The siege lasted until May 8, 1973, when those occupants remaining in the
village surrendered to federal officers. While most of the AIM participants
returned to their homes, several others, including Dennis Banks and Russell
Means, were charged with conspiracy and assault, but after a lengthy trial, a
federal district court ruled that the charges should be dismissed due to "mis-
conduct by the government." A subsequent appeal by federal prosecutors was

also dismissed by a federal court of appeals, and the charges against Banks and Means were finally dropped. Obviously, the occupants of Wounded Knee included tribal people who were reservation residents, but much of the leadership, and many of the rank and file who stood together during the seventy-day siege, were individuals who had spent significant time in urban areas. The relocation program and its aftermath formed the nexus that gave rise to the Red Power movement.[21]

At 3 A.M. on a dark, windswept morning in late March 1973, while standing guard at a picket post on the northeast corner of the occupied region at Wounded Knee, two AIM members, thirty-one-year-old Wilson Velarde, a Jicarilla Apache man from Albuquerque, New Mexico, and his companion, Charles Rides Alone, twenty-eight, a Pawnee from Oklahoma City, watched as a small, intermittently flashing light descended a dry wash and warily approached their position. Both men were armed with deer guns, lever-action rifles chambered for 30-30 cartridges, which they had previously used to hunt deer and shoot coyotes, and they trained their weapons up the wash toward whoever was carrying the small flashlight. Challenging the intruder, Rides Alone ordered him to stop, or they "would blow your ass back up that arroyo."

In response, the newcomer answered back, "Don't shoot! Don't shoot! I'm AIM. I'm AIM. I'm coming in with a backpack full of medical supplies," to which Velarde replied, "Well, turn that damned light off before the feds or one of Wilson's goon squads opens up on all of us from that stand of cottonwoods over there."[22]

As the courier emerged from the darkness, the two men at the barricade saw a Native American man, in his late twenties or early thirties, dressed in blue jeans and a hooded brown canvas Carhartt work coat. He was carrying a large backpack. His shoulder-length hair fell below a dark blue stocking cap that had been pulled down against the icy high-plains wind that gusted in from the northwest. "Damn," he exclaimed. "I thought the wind blew hard off the mountains in Denver, but out here, it must get up a head of steam in Wyoming and doesn't stop till it hits Omaha. I wanted to put the hood up on my coat, but it shut off both my visibility and my hearing. I was afraid I'd run into the FBI or Wilson's police before I ever saw them, so I had to use that wool stocking cap. It helped some, but not much."

Wary that the stranger might be an FBI informer, Velarde asked, "Where did you say you're from?"

"From Denver," the newcomer replied, then added, "but I came in through Porcupine. I've got an uncle who lives there. He hates Dick Wilson. Spoke up against him in the last election, and when Wilson won, the sonofabitch fired my uncle from his job as district road supervisor. He'd been there for fifteen years. The new guy can't even drive a tractor let alone a road grader, but he's Wilson's cousin. Sits in his office all day drinking cokes and coffee. Everybody else on the road crew quit, and now the roads have gone to pot. A helluva mess!"[23]

"If you're Oglala, how did you end up in Denver?" Rides Alone asked.

"My family got relocated in the late fifties. My dad is a leatherworker. Got relocated, then lost his job and worked at lots of shitty jobs before getting back on as a saddle maker in the early sixties. My mom worked as a maid for a while, then got a good job in a candy factory. Jolly Rancher. She's still there. I went through the Denver schools and enrolled in a two-year course at Metro State. Trained to be an EMT. I've been working with ambulance and rescue teams ever since. My boss is a good guy. Mixed-blood Creek from Oklahoma. Hates the BIA and gave me a leave of absence to come up here. He also gave me the antibiotics, painkillers, and most of the other meds in this backpack. He and I go to AIM meetings and then usually have a few beers at this bar on Colfax. Called Three Coups. Run by this older Comanche woman—married to this white guy, Wasichu, named Buster.[24] Ex-marine. Served with some code-talkers in the Pacific. Likes Skins. Anyway, it's a good bar. AIM hangout."

No longer worried that the man was an informer, Rides Alone queried, "So what do you plan to do in the village?"

"Well, first I'm gonna see if anybody needs any medical assistance that I can help with, then I'll drop off the meds to somebody who will be responsible with them. In a couple of days, I plan to slip back out of the village and at night make it back to Porcupine, where my uncle will then drive me back to Denver. If you're still holed up here after another two or three weeks, I'll be back with another load of meds, or maybe even some ammo, if you guys are running short. You can get in touch with me through my uncle. He's a ham radio operator back in Porcupine. We'll work out some sort of half-ass code so that the feds can't figure out what's going on."

"Okay," Velarde replied. "As soon as it lightens up, we'll walk you into the village. We'll get some coffee—some breakfast—and we'll talk this over with whoever is in charge this morning." But we need to keep hunkered down out here until daylight."

Pulling the hood of his work coat up over his head, the stranger shivered and answered, "Fine by me. I'm hungry as hell, and I'm so cold, I think that the cheeks of my butt are frozen together. I sure could use some of that coffee."

"Oh yeah," Velarde added, "A couple of other things. What's your uncle's name, if we have to get ahold of him?"

"Bernard Valcourt," came the reply.

"And yours?"

"Robert Summer Hawk."

Suggested Readings

Blansett, Kent. *A Journey to Freedom: Richard Oakes, Alcatraz, and the Red Power Movement.* New Haven, CT: Yale University Press, 2018.

Fixico, Donald L. *Termination and Relocation: Federal Indian Policy, 1945–1960.* Norman: University of Oklahoma Press, 1986.

LaGrand, James. *Indian Metropolis: Native Americans in Chicago, 1954–1975.* Urbana: University of Illinois Press, 1986.

Smith, Paul Chaat, and Robert Warrior. *Like a Hurricane: The Indian Movement from Alcatraz to Wounded Knee.* New York: New Press, 1999.

NINE

Moving with the Seasons, Not Fixed in Stone

The Evolution of Native American Identity

On January 25, 1900, Edward Goldberg, the Indian agent at the Quapaw Agency in Northeastern Indian Territory, wrote to his superiors in Washington, DC, defending his performance as Indian agent to the Quapaws, Miamis, Seneca-Cayugas, and other tribes under his jurisdiction. Proud of the "advances" that some of the tribal people within his agency were making, he boasted that "progressives" such as Cayuga Amos Reed Bird were making great strides toward accepting the government's "civilization" program. Nine years earlier, in 1891, Reed Bird had accepted an allotment near the Neosho River, and unlike some of his kinsmen who continued to travel back and forth between the Seneca-Cayugas in Indian Territory and their relatives in New York and Ontario, Reed Bird resided permanently on his allotment. He raised pigs and chickens, grazed two horses, and periodically harvested small crops of corn and hay. He also buttressed his income through odd jobs for neighboring non-Indian farmers. As a boy, Reed Bird spoke only Cayuga, and he and his wife still spoke it at home, but he attended grammar school for four years and could read and write English as well as most of the non-Indian farmers in Indian Territory. Reed Bird and his family dressed in clothing similar to that of their white neighbors. Their diet also resembled that of other rural Oklahomans, although they relied more heavily on fish caught from the Neosho River and berries and wild greens gathered in the river bottoms. Reed Bird sent his children to the government school, but like many other Oklahomans of his time, he kept them home when the weather was bad or when extra hands were needed for the chores on his allotment.

A respected member of the Seneca-Cayuga community, Reed Bird sat on the Cayuga council, and he also led in the festivities surrounding the tribe's annual Green Corn Ceremony, held in the tribal longhouse each summer. Although Agent Goldberg attempted to discourage the Seneca-Cayugas from participating in such traditional ceremonies, he met with little success. The celebrations continued year after year, and by 1900, Goldberg admitted that they seemed harmless enough, particularly when compared to the new peyote faith that seemed to be spreading across Indian Territory. Like many other Indian agents, Goldberg was confused and uncertain about the new religion, but it seemed to threaten the government's authority. Both bureaucrats and missionaries were hard pressed to eradicate the old tribal beliefs; they did not welcome any new indigenous religions that might replace them.[1]

Yet Goldberg remained optimistic. If Reed Bird and other tribespeople seemed to be interested in peyote, they were also eager to embrace American technology. To the agent's surprise, Reed Bird and several other Seneca-Cayuga tribal council members had pooled their resources and purchased a small, open motor car that Reed Bird and other council members periodically piloted along the dirt roads that crossed the region. Reed Bird also delighted in providing rides to tribal children on Sundays at tribal gatherings, where he also instructed the children in Seneca-Cayuga tribal traditions.

As he concluded his report, Goldberg confidently assured officials in Washington that their Indian policies were achieving success. Progressives like Amos Reed Bird were literate in English, now dressed in "white-man's" clothing, resided on their own allotments, and even drove their own "new-fangled" automobiles. "Civilized ways" were coming to Indian Territory.

A century later, Reed Bird's great grandson, Garrett Red Bird (the surname had been changed when a principal at the Seneca Boarding School had first inadvertently misspelled the name, then refused to admit his mistake) sat drinking coffee in the community hall at the Seneca-Cayuga tribal complex, about nine miles north of Grove, Oklahoma. Red Bird was seated across the table from his sister-in-law, Lucy Reynolds, and they were discussing the tribal council's decision to pursue land claims in upstate New York. Lucy approved of the policies, but Red Bird was less certain.[2]

Red Bird had been born in 1937, still resided on his family's diminished allotment near Grove, and continued to subscribe to a series of cultural patterns that resembled those of his great-grandfather. Like his great-grandfather, he also farmed a few acres, harvesting hay that he fed to his three horses. He drove a battered pickup truck between his home and a marina on nearby Grand Lake, where he worked part time as a general handyman and as a fishing guide when customers were available. Like many other Native American men in rural Oklahoma, Red Bird regularly wore cowboy boots, jeans, and western shirts, although he replaced his worn Stetson with a baseball cap bearing the Seneca-Cayuga tribal logo.[3]

Red Bird spoke English in his home, but like his great-grandfather, he retained a good knowledge of the Cayuga language (he was one of less than two dozen tribe members who still possessed this fluency), and he was disappointed that two of his three children originally seemed to have little interest in learning the Cayuga tongue. Red Bird was a respected member of the Seneca-Cayuga community, and like his great-grandfather, he served as a "pot-hanger," or ceremonial leader at the tribes' annual Green Corn Ceremony. He also served as the source of considerable tribal oral tradition, and both tribe members and interested outsiders often relied on him to answer their questions regarding tribal traditions. Although the Native American Church had few adherents among the Seneca-Cayugas, Red Bird had become a member, often driving many miles to attend ceremonies among the Pawnees, who resided near Pawnee and Skedee, Oklahoma.[4]

During the 1970s, Red Bird served on the Seneca-Cayuga Business Committee, but more recently, he had become increasingly critical of the organization. Although he realized that modern Native American people needed to pursue employment in the non-Indian world and he himself worked at the marina, he opposed many entrepreneurial activities championed by the current business committee. Investments in smoke shops, gas stations, and convenience stores were bad enough, but Red Bird was particularly opposed to the tribe's bingo facility and the committee's attempts to expand their gaming enterprises into other locations. He feared the exposure to new economic endeavors and the potential financial returns that such activities might engender could potentially alter the nature pf the Seneca-Cayuga community.[5]

In the 1940s and 1950s, the Seneca-Cayuga people had struggled to make ends meet. But their lives seemed more focused on the old sense of community. Now things seemed to be changing too quickly. Red Bird knew that although many younger members of the tribe supported the changes, they still respected him for his knowledge of tribal traditions and language, but they now considered him to be a "traditional" elder, a respected senior adviser but dedicated to older ways. Red Bird sipped the last of the coffee from his heavy porcelain cup. He stared out the doorway of the dining hall toward the parking lot. Hmphh! Well, maybe he was traditional, but from his perspective, the council needed to slow down. Not all new and progressive ideas were good ones.

Although Indian agent Edward Goldberg actually served at the Quapaw Agency and the circumstances surrounding the Seneca-Cayuga community are based upon historical events, both Amos Reed Bird and Garrett Red Bird are fictitious composite characters based on Seneca-Cayuga history and culture.[6] The point, however, is that the two Seneca-Cayuga men subscribed to very similar values and cultural patterns, but during the twentieth century, Seneca-Cayuga culture, like almost all tribal cultures, continued to evolve. Within the context of their times, the two men exemplified two very different positions on the admittedly arbitrary, but widely accepted, spectrum of Native American adaptation.

Fluent in English and possessing the rudiments of a frontier education, Amos Reed Bird was described as "progressive" and "making great strides toward civilization" because he lived on his allotment, attempted yeoman agriculture, worked within the non-Indian employment market, and even drove a motor vehicle. A century later, things had changed. Reed Bird's great-grandson, Garrett Red Bird, subscribed to a similar lifestyle. He also resided on his allotment, raised hay and horses, worked part time for non-Indians, and drove a truck. He, too, spoke fluent Cayuga and was knowledgeable about Seneca-Cayuga history and ceremonies. But Red Bird was seen as "traditional" by many modern Seneca-Cayugas, who now possessed more formal education, did not speak Cayuga, worked full time in neighboring Grove, Miami, or Joplin, Missouri, and supported the business committee's efforts to expand business enterprises and gaming. Obviously, during the twentieth century (as in previous eras), Seneca Cayuga culture, and what it meant to be Seneca Cayuga, had continued to evolve. As Amanda Bearskin Greenback, a Seneca-Cayuga elder, has pointed out, Seneca-Cayuga people (like all Native American people), have always "moved with the seasons." What's more, as the Seneca-Cayuga elder also noted, Cayuga identity continues to evolve: "It has never been fixed in stone."[7]

Yet in the early twenty-first century, Native American identity, or "being Indian," faces some significant challenges. Questions continue to emerge as to definitions, particularly as to how the parameters of tribal membership are to be determined. Should enrollment in federally recognized tribes remain the sole criteria through which Native American, Native, indigenous, or Indian people are delineated? Each tribal government now has the legal right to determine that tribe's membership, and the spectrum of this determination varies from tribe to tribe. Currently, all federally recognized tribes rely, to a greater or lesser extent, on the principal of biological descent, but minimal blood quantums differ markedly from tribe to tribe.

In 2020, there were 574 federally recognized tribes. Obviously, it would be laborious to attempt to discuss the different blood quantum requirements of each tribal government, but focusing on Oklahoma and the tribal affiliation of many of the characters featured in the chapters in this volume, a series of phone calls to tribal enrollment offices, combined with a survey of tribal websites indicate that many tribes require that enrolled members possess a tribal blood quantum ranging from one-half to one-thirty-second. But there are growing and notable exceptions. The Five Southern Tribes, in addition to most other tribal governments in the eastern half of the state, rely primarily on biological descent, but all except the Creeks, who still require one-eighth lineage, have abandoned the blood quantum requirements.[8]

Of course, the irony of all of this is that the concept of blood quantum is not a Native American idea but was originated by the federal government. Blood quantums first appeared on removal lists when Indian agents enrolled the eastern tribes for removal to lands west of the Mississippi. Many of these newcomers to Indian Territory retained the blood quantum records during the territorial period, and the government then extended these criteria to other tribes who were allotted under the Dawes Act. Following the allotment period, the tribes' reliance on blood quantums became commonplace.[9]

But is a specific blood quantum a viable measure of tribal membership? The answer remains unclear. Undoubtedly, for the foreseeable future, all tribes will rely on some sort of biological descent, but as Native American people continue to intermarry with non-Indians, the blood quantums of tribal members will predictably decline. Currently, over half of all Native American people live in large urban areas, and within that urban Indian population, about 60 percent of young Native American women of "marrying age" will marry non-Indians. Indeed, in 1980, over half of all American Indians were already married to non-Indians. A far greater proportion of these people lived in urban areas, but since the proportion of Native Americans living in cities now also exceeds one-half and continues to increase, the rate of intermarriage probably will accelerate. Cherokee demographer Russell Thornton has pointed out that in 1980, about 87 percent of the Native American population possessed an indigenous blood quantum of at least 50 percent, but if current trends continue, by 2080, that number will shrink to 8 percent.[10]

Indeed, the percentage of people with less than a one-quarter blood quantum is projected to increase from about 4 percent in 1980 to almost 60 percent by the middle decades of the twenty-first century. Obviously, as this phenomenon proliferates, tribal governments will be forced to adjust their blood quantum requirements, or they will legislate themselves out of existence. Tribes whose members continue to reside primarily in rural reservation communities are just beginning to face this problem, but it certainly looms in their future. The number of "full-bloods" on almost all tribal rolls continues to decline.[11]

Yet the reliance on descent as the primary criterion in defining Native American identity may, in itself, raise valid questions. Are other factors, such as adherence to generally accepted cultural patterns, more important than biological lineage in ascertaining who really is functioning as a member of a tribal community? Can an individual adopted into a tribal community, and his or her descendants, be defined as part of the tribe? We know that historically, prior to the twentieth century, such was often the case. Individuals from other tribes, or non-Indians for that matter, were often integrated into tribal communities; they became, for all practical purposes, full-fledged members of the tribe.[12]

Today, these types of adoptions can cause considerable controversy. Regardless of the adoptee's adherence to accepted norms of tribal behavior, they often are not officially enrolled members of the tribe with whom they are associated. After joining the faculty of a large state university in the Midwest, the author served on a committee that examined the qualifications of applicants seeking admission into several graduate programs at that institution. Among the applicants for the graduate program in anthropology and linguistics was an individual living on a reservation on the northern plains who was not of Native American ancestry, but as a child had been adopted by a couple who were both enrolled members of the tribe. He had grown up within the tribal community, was versed in tribal traditions, took part in many tribal ceremonies, and was one of perhaps ten or twelve fluent speakers of the tribal language. When he was in his early twenties, his adopted father died, and as an expression of his grief, he severed part of a finger,, a traditional method of mourning among the tribe in the nineteenth century. He subsequently applied to the university and sought financial assistance through the institution's minority recruitment program but was informed (to the author's dismay) that he was ineligible, since he was not officially a member of the tribe and was (legally) not an Indian. He eventually enrolled in another midwestern university, but his rejection by the first institution vividly illustrates the conflict between differing definitions of Native American identity based on blood quantum and the adherence to cultural values in tribal communities.

So if both cultural patterns and blood quantum percentages have evolved through the twentieth century and into the present era, what will be the future of Native American identity? Will it continue to differ markedly among different tribal communities across the United States? No one can be sure, but some patterns seem obvious. Recently, some academics have written about the emergence of "urban Indians," individuals or groups claiming Native American descent but reticent or unwilling to claim any tribal identification, individuals, as Alexandra Harmon notes, who are "far from their indigenous forebears' various homelands, Indians [who] have found each other and have created new Indian communities, partly by sharing stories from their respective tribal pasts and partly by making their own urban experiences into a shared Indian story."[13] Sociologists refer to this phenomenon as "Indianness on the supra-tribal level," an ethnicity that may not completely replace tribal identities but that "encompasses and supplements them."[14]

Undoubtedly, Native American people living in large urban areas often band together, and many face problems different from those who continue to reside on reservations or near tribal offices and homelands. But as Susan Harjo has pointed out in *Indian Country Today*, urban Indians who are reluctant to reveal their tribal affiliations should be suspect, particularly if they have used their projected ethnicity for personal gain. It is difficult to believe that such a claim would be taken seriously in Oklahoma, New Mexico, Arizona, the Dakotas, or other regions in the West or in the upper Midwest where most Native American people are within easy driving distance of their tribal offices. Moreover, it is difficult to imagine that any Native American person would claim to be Native American and deprecate their tribal affiliation. Even unenrolled but legitimate tribally descended people's first claim invariably is to a tribal entity, not to the much more ambiguous claim of "being Indian."[15]

Throughout the United States, some form of biological descent from a state or federally recognized tribe undoubtedly will play the trump card in ascertaining tribal identity, but for most tribes, the blood quantum limitation will markedly decline or be eliminated. Indeed, conversations with tribal enrollment offices indicate that growing numbers of tribal members' children are currently ineligible for enrollment, and most tribes who still retain a one-quarter minimal blood quantum are now reconsidering their requirements. Although a few tribes have attempted to increase blood quantum, and others oppose lowering blood quantum restrictions, they seem to be swimming against a rising tide of intermarriage that is unlikely to ebb.[16]

In contrast to biological descent, if cultural patterns emerge as the criteria used to form the boundaries for both tribal and Native American identity, what cultural patterns will future Native Americans be expected to embrace? Will certain facets of modern Native American existence be privileged and singled out for protection and retention? In the early twenty-first century, modern tribal communities differ markedly in the variety of their cultural practices. These patterns differ not only from tribe to tribe but also within single tribal communities. As the opening vignette to this chapter hopefully illustrates, Garrett Red Bird's life in rural Oklahoma differs markedly from that of a Hopi farmer in Arizona, a Makah fisherman in Washington, a young Maidu woman working as an attorney for the Native American Rights Fund in Boulder, Colorado, or an Oneida woman currently stationed as an army nurse in South Korea. In addition, Red Bird's life and perspective differs from other members of his own Seneca-Cayuga community in Oklahoma. Agreeing on just what cultural patterns will define who "really is an Indian" will be a contentious and Herculean task, but some facets of modern Native American existence will probably be singled out for protection and retention.

Foremost among these institutions will be a tribal land base. During the twentieth century, those tribes that continued to possess reservations have assiduously defended them, and the tribes who lost their reservations through the termination policies of the 1950s have endeavored, with some success, to have those reservation lands restored. In Oklahoma and other places, tribes that held minimal acreage of land in the 1950s have steadily increased their holdings until many now have considerable lands in federal trust. The classic case is the Citizen Potawatomi Nation, which in the late 1950s owned only 2.5 acres and warehoused all their tribal records in a garden shed in one

272 + Chapter 9

member's backyard. Through hard work and dedicated leadership, the Citizen Potawatomis now own fourteen thousand acres in Pottawatomie County, Oklahoma. Although most other tribal governments have not increased their acreage as exponentially, many have added to their land bases.[17]

Why are these tribal land bases important? Because they remain the wellspring of tribal identity and enterprise. Across the United States, most Native American people consider tribally held lands or reservations to be "home," and they return regularly for ceremonies, homecomings, and family gatherings. For many Native American people living in urban areas and other off-reservation locations, the journey home helps to reaffirm their sense of community and provides opportunities to meet with family members and old friends. Kenneth McIntosh, the grandson of Chief W. E. "Dode" McIntosh, has referred to the Creek stomp dances held regularly across the old Creek homeland as the "heartbeat" of the modern Creek Nation. One only has to attend such a ceremony at the Creek Cultural Center at Okmulgee, or at smaller stomp grounds, or be present at the Pawnee Indian Veterans' Homecoming, or the annual Comanche Homecoming near Medicine Park to appreciate how important tribal land bases are in providing a geographic arena where a sense of tribal identity can be reaffirmed and replenished. The late Grace Thorpe, a prominent Sauk and Fox elder, once admonished future generations to "Hang onto the land. Hang on to the land. Don't give it up." Tribal people across the United States have continued to heed her advice.[18]

Yet tribal land bases offer more than spiritual replenishment. Since the passage of the Indian Self-Determination and Education Act of 1975, the liberalization of state gaming laws in the 1970s, and the Reagan administration's adoption of a "new federalism" in the 1980s, tribal governments have enlarged both sovereignty and its accompanying economic envelope to provide a wide range of both services and business opportunities. Gaming is the most publicized facet of this phenomenon, yet gaming runs the gamut from some casinos and associated tribal enterprises which are exceptionally successful, to others which are profitable, but less grandiose.[19]

As in real estate, "location, location, location" is usually the deciding factor. Those gaming facilities adjacent to or within easy driving distance of major population centers have a marked advantage. For example, Winstar World Casino and Resort, owned and operated by the Chickasaw Nation and located at Thackery, Oklahoma, just across the Red River from Texas and little more than an hour's drive north of the Dallas-Fort Worth Metroplex, is currently the largest single casino in the world. It offers over eight-six hundred electronic games, one hundred table games, and a poker room with fifty-five separate tables. Adjoining the casino is a luxury hotel containing fourteen hundred rooms, and the facility features nineteen separate restaurants. The convention center, attached to the hotel and casino, houses display centers, meeting rooms, and a large ballroom that can seat up to eight hundred guests for banquet functions. The resort site also includes two eighteen-hole golf courses. In 2019, the resort employed more than thirty-five hundred people. Slightly smaller, the Choctaw Casino and Resort at Durant, Oklahoma, is also located just north of the Red River. Similar to Winstar, the Choctaw gaming enterprise features a modern luxury hotel, eight restaurants, several bars and lounges, two noteworthy entertainment venues featuring major acts and concerts, a movie theatre, and a wide offering of slots, poker, and table games. The Choctaw Casino and Resort also draws heavily from the Dallas-Fort Worth metroplex, which lies less than an hour's drive south, in Texas.[20]

Other gaming venues, while smaller, have also proven profitable. The Inn of the Mountain Gods, a casino and resort located on the Mescalero Apache reservation, features a casino, hotel, and a bevy of outdoor activities that take advantage of the resort's scenic location in the mountains of south-central New Mexico. The facility's proximity to other vacation destinations, including horse-racing at nearby Ruidoso also enhances its attraction. In a similar vein, the Wisconsin Oneidas' Radisson Hotel, Conference Center, and Casino, situated across the highway from Austin Straubel Airport at Green Bay and conveniently close to Lambeau Field, provides the Oneida-owned enterprise with access to travelers, football fans, and residents of the Green Bay region. The Oneidas proudly proclaim that their casino is the "official casino of the Green Bay Packers." Unfortunately, many other casinos located in more isolated, sparsely populated regions in western states, while still turning profits, have been much less lucrative, and for many tribes, gaming has not been the financial panacea that some of its promoters promised.[21]

While gaming has attracted the most attention from the non-Indian public, other more mundane and less glamorous facets of tribal sovereignty may offer more long-term opportunities for economic self-sufficiency. Since tribally held land is not subject to many state and local taxes, businesses located on such real estate are free from state or local taxation usually levied on such items as gasoline and tobacco. In many instances, tribal governments have established retail outlets on tribally owned land and have marketed these commodities at lower prices than similar products sold from non-Indian owned locations. In turn, funds initially generated from gaming and other narrowly focused but profitable ventures can be invested in broader enterprises.

The Oneida Nation of Wisconsin (mentioned above) provides a good example. Through careful planning, they have combined income from their casino and hotel near Green Bay's Austin Straubel Airport with other funds to develop a broad spectrum of tribally owned and financed retail establishments. In addition to several gas station/convenience stores, the Oneidas have established retail centers where they have leased space to major retailers such as Wal-Mart and Home Depot. They also own and manage several fast-food outlets. In 2000, the Oneida Nation purchased the Bay Bank, a full-service financial institution that specializes in serving both Native American and non-Indian clientele. The only Green Bay area bank to offer US Department of Housing and Urban Development (HUD) Section 184 Indian Home Loan Guarantee Program loans to its customers, the Bay Bank has provided over $5 million in investments to Oneida entrepreneurs through the Oneida Small Business Project.[22]

The Oneida experience, although admirable, is not unique. Many other tribes have wisely taken a significant portion of the revenue gained from successful gaming enterprises and invested it into more diversified economic ventures. Like the Oneidas, the Citizen Potawatomi Nation has also successfully diversified its economic activities. John "Rocky" Barrett, the chairman of the Citizen Potawatomi Nation Business Committee, has likened gaming revenue to "seed corn" and has reminded Potawatomis that seed corn should be planted, not eaten (paid out in per capita payments). The Citizen Potawatomis have planted and cultivated their corn well. Like the Oneidas, they, too, own a bank, a supermarket, and a golf course. They also own and operate KGFF, an AM-FM radio station. Moreover, in 2021, they were the largest single employer in Pottawatomi County, Oklahoma.[23]

Regardless of its source, revenue from tribally based enterprises is critical for a tribe's control over its future. Like Garrett Red Bird, there are individuals in every tribal community who doubt the wisdom of gaming, and there is an ongoing debate over just which economic activities to embrace, but the tribal communities must become economically self-sufficient. Otherwise, they will be forced to rely on the federal government, which during the late nineteenth and much of the twentieth century provided tribal communities with annuities, some social services, and legal protection. Ironically, however, if there is one thing to be learned from an examination of the history of Indian-white relations during this period, it is that very often, "when push comes to shove," the federal government cannot be trusted. Throughout American history, when tribal communities have possessed resources that non-Indians have wanted (land, water, lumber, minerals, fish and game, and even children), they have taken them. Local, state, and federal governments in the United States remain vulnerable to influence by powerful pressure groups. These groups have access to considerable financial resources. If tribal communities hope to defend themselves, they, too, must assemble sufficient capital.

At first glance, this emphasis upon capital may seem peripheral to Native American identity, but such is not the case. As pointed out earlier in this chapter, a key factor in retaining a sense of tribal or Native American identity is the retention of a tribal land base that often serves as "the wellspring of tribal identity," a focal point for ceremonies and family gatherings, and a "geographic place where a sense of tribal identity can be reaffirmed and replenished."[24] Yet if these wellsprings of tribal identity are to be retained, it may become expensive. Within the past two decades, several reservation communities located in the Midwest, the Great Plains, and the far West have been assaulted by special-interest groups that have attempted to gain access to tribal lands by either "disestablishing" or (more commonly) "diminishing" the legal boundaries of reservations and opening large sections of lands within previously established and legitimate reservation borders to non-Indian economic development and to unbridled state and local legal jurisdiction. To defend reservation and tribal lands, tribal governments have been forced to rely on legal assistance. To give the federal government its due, in many cases, the US Department of the Interior and the Department of Justice have provided some legal assistance to the besieged tribes, but in many cases, tribal governments have used funds generated through tribal enterprises to pay for the legal fees. Thus far, in most cases, the tribes have prevailed, and the reservations have not been diminished, but the future remains uncertain, and tribal funds will continue to be needed if the remaining reservations are to be defended.[25]

Also endangered are the valuable mineral and lumber assets contained within the remaining tribal homelands. Huge deposits of coal remain on the Navajo Reservation in the Southwest and on the Crow and Northern Cheyenne

Reservations in Montana. The Navajo Reservation also contains significant deposits of uranium. Shoshone and Northern Arapaho lands on the Wind River Reservation in Wyoming and the Blackfeet Reservation in Montana both contain valuable petroleum resources, as do Ute lands in Colorado. Several reservations in Washington, Oregon, and the upper Midwest hold large stands of valuable timber.[26] Since many reservations are located in regions unsuitable for most agricultural development (Anglo-Americans had little use for these lands, therefore they were set aside for tribal people), these reservation communities have suffered from a lack of jobs and from high unemployment rates. Consequently, natural resources such as those mentioned above offer economic opportunities in the form of jobs and income for tribe members. They also offer avenues through which tribal governments can build the financial reservoirs to fund the defense of tribal homelands.

But the development and utilization of these resources can be a double-edged sword. For many tribal people, the natural resources contained within their homeland—indeed, the very land itself—is so intricately tied to their sense of who they are—their history, culture, religion, and identity—that they harbor considerable hesitancy about exploiting or depleting these assets. Many tribespeople hold bitter memories of decades in the past when federal officials supposedly "acting in the Indians' best interests" readily leased verdant timberlands, good grazing acreage, and valuable mineral deposits to non-Indian businessmen who then denuded the forests, over grazed the pastures, strip-mined the land, and drained the oil reserves. Tribal lands once blessed with these bounties were left depleted. Moreover, the very earth itself was often torn and permanently scarred in the process.[27] If the tribal homelands are to continue as viable wellsprings of tribal identity, the resources probably still can be developed, but their utilization must be closely monitored by well-informed and experienced tribal leaders.

Closely related to tribal lands is continued tribal access to water, and although this contest over water on reservation lands is just emerging, the growing water crisis in the American West has become acute. Access to the diminishing water in the Colorado River has already engendered nascent litigation in the Southwest, and since water is the lifeblood of both agriculture and the burgeoning urban development in the region, future conflicts over control of this resource that now flows through tribal lands are bound to increase. Conflicts have also arisen along the Klamath River in northern California and

Oregon. In addition, even rapidly growing urban areas on the periphery of the west, such as the Dallas-Fort Worth metroplex, are now utilizing water from Lake Texoma, on the Texas-Oklahoma border, but urban planners in the metroplex are already beginning to cast covetous eyes toward the large reservoirs within the modern Choctaw, Creek, and Chickasaw Nations. This chapter is too limited in scope and purpose to adequately explore this particular problem, but the upcoming battle in the West will be over water, and tribal governments must be prepared to defend it. Without adequate water, the reservation homelands will be untenable.[28]

Adequate water and tribally held lands are not the only pillars of tribal identity that are threatened. There is a general consensus among almost all the tribes that tribal communities should do their best to retain and propagate tribal languages. Some tribes currently have no members fluent in their native language, and in other tribes, the community of speakers already has shrunk below the critical mass that linguists argue is necessary for a language to continue. Even relatively isolated tribal communities who still possess a sufficient nucleus of fluency (Navajos, Lakotas, Hopis, Ojibwes) now find themselves bombarded by modern electronic media that threatens more than just tribal language. Envisioning their tribal languages as a key component to retaining their identity, many tribes have responded by channeling part of their newly generated resources into formal language programs designed to preserve tribal languages and provide their children with language enrichment programs in tribally based schools. Admittedly, for many tribes, this will be an uphill battle, but gains are being made. Colleges and universities are now offering formal instruction in tribal languages for teachers or other individuals who will serve in the communities, and linguists have recorded and produced extensive teaching materials in languages ranging from Arikara, to Cherokee, to Lakota, and Ho-Chunk. Funds generated from gaming and other businesses are helping to finance these efforts. In Mississippi, in addition to other tribal language programs, the Choctaws have used the profits from their tribally based Chahta Enterprises to purchase time on a local television station that broadcasts daily in Choctaw, providing newscasts, children's shows, and programs as diverse as advice on personal finance and microwave cooking. Approximately 60 percent of Mississippi Choctaws now have some fluency in their language.[29]

As the twenty-first century unfolds, there will be many other issues that will shape and impact the changing nature of Native American identity, and a single chapter is not the venue to speculate about or explore all of them. But there is at least one other issue that will remain critical if tribal people wish to maintain control over their land bases and their ability to adapt to the changes that undoubtedly will occur. We will need well-educated, highly skilled Native American people to confront and manage these issues. During the last half-century, considerable progress has been made. In the early 1970s, the author left the University of Oklahoma to accept a position at the University of Wyoming, where he initiated a program in Native American history. At that time, the ranks were so small that he personally knew almost every other academic of Native American descent in U.S. higher education, at least in the arts and humanities. Since that time, the number has increased to such an extent that, happily, he can no longer make such a claim. Moreover, the increase has not been limited to academics. During the 1970s, he participated in a series of lectures in Wyoming, Colorado, and surrounding states in which materials were presented regarding Native American land claims, the American Indian Movement, and Native American issues in general. At that time, the most frequently asked question from these town-and-gown (public and campus) audiences was What did tribal communities, or Indian people in general, need most to assist them in attaining their goals and protecting their interests? His rather trite reply was, "About a thousand young Native American lawyers." Well, their ranks do not number one thousand, but the emergence of a cadre of highly trained Native American attorneys, as exemplified by those associated with the Native American Rights Fund, certainly have made a big difference. In addition, growing numbers of Native American MBAs, accountants, computer scientists, social workers, and medical personnel have also helped transform and invigorate many tribal communities. They, too, are the cultivators who nurture and preserve the gardens of tribal identity.[30]

2018

Although she now lived in Tulsa, she had never missed returning "home" for the annual Strawberry Dance Ceremony. Katherine "Kate" (nee Red Bird) Tipton and her sister, LeeAnne, sat on the bleachers on the South Side with other members of her clan and extended family watching Kate's granddaughter, Brooke, and LeeAnne's youngest daughter, Emmaline ("Emmie"), circle the arena in their traditional tribal dresses. Since Brooke was only six but Emmie was fourteen, the younger girl watched her older "cousin" and did her best to imitate the teenager's measured steps to the drumbeats of the songs and dances that heralded the final part of the Strawberry Dance's ceremonies. Earlier in the day, adult members of the Seneca-Cayugas attending the festivities had formally shared the strawberry juice that symbolized the Creator's care for his people and his generosity in providing both the physical and spiritual substance for their lives. The Strawberry Dance and the ceremonies surrounding it had always been a favorite time for Kate, since it was an event when families came together; and this year, 2018, like almost all years, late spring in northeastern Oklahoma was a season of plenty, when everything was in bloom and full of promise.[31]

Kate, born in 1966, LeeAnne, born three years later, and Jason, born in 1974, were the three children who had been born to Garrett and Darlene Red Bird, and Kate and her siblings had been raised on the old Red Bird (Reed Bird) allotment, just off Highway 10, in northern Delaware County, Oklahoma. All three were enrolled members of the Seneca-Cayuga Nation. Their father, Garrett, who had died in 2015 (just three years previously), had been three-quarters Cayuga and one-quarter "white" (blood quantum), while their mother, Darlene, who still lived on the allotment, was a "full-blood," half Cayuga and half Wyandot. All three children had enrolled in local schools and graduated from Grove High School. Kate had gone on to Oklahoma State University in Stillwater, where she had majored in nursing, eventually earning her credentials as a registered nurse. Upon graduation, she moved to Tulsa and worked in the emergency ward at St. Francis Hospital, where she met and later married John Eagle, a mixed-lineage Ponca-Kaw physician whose total blood quantum from both tribes was somewhere between and eighth and a quarter. They had two children (girls) and two grandchildren. Her youngest granddaughter, Brooke, had accompanied her to the Strawberry Dance. Kate glanced back at the dance floor, checking again to see just where six-year-old Brooke and Emmie, Brooke's older cousin, could be found. At first she didn't see them, and it momentarily frightened her, but then she spotted the two girls, giggling over something, as they danced on the far side of the floor, partially hidden behind a group of other dancers.

LeeAnne, who had been checking something on her cell phone, had also lost track of the two girls. Before Kate could comment on their location, LeeAnne asked her sister if they had left the dance floor to go to the restroom.

"No, they're on the far corner behind the two women with the white and aqua colored shawls. See, now they've turned the corner, and there they are, grinning like they're up to something."

"Yeah, I see them now. I wonder what's so funny?"

"Who knows," Kate said. "When you're six and fourteen, you'll laugh at just about anything. It's one of the good things about being young, not having a care in the world, and being all dressed up in your special clothes, dancing after the Strawberry Ceremony."

"You're right about that," LeeAnne replied. "I remember when Mom and Dad brought us to these dances, and we couldn't wait to show off our new dance dresses and strut our stuff around that dance arena. What a good time! A chance to see our aunts and cousins and even to check out any cute boys who were back for the ceremonies. Do you remember that tall, good-looking Splitlog kid from Broken Arrow? He had a crush on you. I wonder what happened to him."

"After he graduated from high school, he joined the army. I talked to his sister at the Green Corn ceremonies several years ago, and she told me that they sent him overseas and he was killed in a helicopter crash in Germany, or somewhere over there. Never married or had a family of his own. What a waste. Seems like a long time ago."

LeeAnne watched her daughter and niece as they passed by in front of the bleachers. It did seem like a long time ago. She and Kate had danced together with their mother, grandmothers, aunts, and cousins in the summer dances at the Seneca-Cayuga ceremonial center ever summer during her childhood. They still danced together, and now her own daughter and niece were dancing to the same drumbeats.

"My God," LeeAnne thought. "How time had passed!" Like Kate, LeeAnne had also gone to college, but she had enrolled at the University of Arkansas in Fayetteville. Inspired by her mother, who had little formal training but who had "kept the books" at a local Ford dealership for over thirty years, LeeAnne majored in accounting. Upon graduation, she left Fayetteville and accepted a position in the mortgage department at a major bank in Springfield, Missouri. While in college, she met her husband, Gail Ordway, who laughingly admitted to being a "white-bread Irish-American." They married in 1992, shortly after both graduated from the university. Gail landed a job managing a large lake-front lodge and resort in Branson, Missouri, only thirty miles from their home on the southeast side of Springfield. The couple had two children: Andrew,

born in 1996, now also enrolled at Arkansas, and Emmaline ("Emmie"), who
was now dancing with Brooke in the arena.

LeeAnne nudged her sister and motioned with her water bottle at the
two girls who had stopped dancing and were talking with the tall, handsome
man standing at the far end of the dance floor. Jason Red Bird, both women's
younger brother (and the girls' uncle), smiled down at the girls and listened
with seemingly rapt (or so the girls imagined) attention as Emmie and Brooke
described the exciting events of their day. Listening to his nieces came easily
to Jason. He got along with just about everybody. Like his sisters, he, too, had
graduated from Grove High School, where he had been nicknamed "Jay Bird"
for his ability to "fly down the field" toward the goal line. Jay Bird had starred
as a lanky, sure-handed, All-District Honorable Mention wide receiver for the
Grove Ridgerunners and had even been awarded an athletic scholarship to
play football at Southwestern Oklahoma State University in Weatherford, but
he had "blown a knee" during his sophomore year and had been forced to
drop out of the program. He remained in Weatherford for two more years and
completed a bachelor of science degree in secondary education, then married
a Kiowa woman from Oklahoma City and attempted to teach high school history and coach track in Hobart, but it didn't work out. His wife disliked life in
the small western Oklahoma town, and Jason missed the "Green Country" of
northeastern Oklahoma.

The couple divorced, and Jason moved back to Grove. where he got a job
working as an instructor with the Seneca-Cayuga Historic Preservation Office.
In contrast to both Kate and LeeAnne, who as children had given little more
than lip service to learning the Cayuga language from their father, Jason had a
flair for language and had wholeheartedly embraced Garrett Red Bird's instruction. By the time he graduated from high school, Jason could easily converse
with his father and several of the other tribal elders fluent in the mixture of
Seneca and Cayuga, which served as their native tongue. After joining the Cultural Preservation Office, Jason secured several federal grants to enlarge the
tribe's language programs. He also lobbied with the tribe's business committee
and convinced them to apply part of the profits from the Grand Lake Casino,
the tribes major gaming facility, to expand other tribal cultural programs,
including additional classes in traditional arts and crafts, enlarged summer language camps for tribal children, programs focusing on Seneca-Cayuga history
and oral traditions, and support for additional activities in conjunction with

tribal dances and ceremonies. During the past decade, Jason had played a key role in this expansion, organizing and implementing these programs, but also relying on the expertise of his father and other tribal elders whose traditional knowledge ensured that the programs were presented correctly.

Kate remembered how her father, who had died in 2015, had been proud of Jason's labors and how he eventually admitted that if funds generated by casinos could finance cultural programs such as those championed by his son, then such money was well spent. She smiled to herself when she recalled how in his later years, her dad had been fond of using the old Oklahoma adage "I don't like paying those damned taxes, but I do like driving on these roads" to explain his change of heart. If the money from the casino and tobacco sales could be used to preserve those things that were Seneca-Cayuga (and that were close to his heart), then he was willing to make the best of it. Her dad had grudgingly admitted that things continued to change, but he found peace in his belief that the important things, the essence of being Seneca-Cayuga, still endured.

In retrospect, Kate regretted that when she was a girl growing up in her family's household, that she had not spent more time learning her tribal language or other facets of her tribal heritage. Both her parents and many of her aunts were familiar with the old ways, and both she and LeeAnne learned some of them, but when they were attending school in Grove, they both were swept up in the usual activities that surrounded teenagers in rural Oklahoma, and they failed to sit and talk with their older relatives about tribal ways and traditions. Both girls had always attended family gatherings and tribal ceremonies like the Strawberry Dance and the Green Corn Ceremony, but looking back on those days, Kate now wished that she, like Jason, had spent more time talking with her elders. After she married and had two daughters of her own, she took pains to ensure that her girls did not make the same mistake. She made certain that they spent time with her dad and particularly Jason, whom they both adored. She and the girls had faithfully returned from Tulsa to attend tribal ceremonies and get-togethers, and during the summer months, the girls spent several weeks visiting with their grandparents at their home on the old allotment. She also enrolled them in summer language camps sponsored by the tribe's Cultural Preservation Office and in several classes focusing on Seneca-Cayuga history and traditions taught by Jason and several tribal elders.

After her daughters were born, Kate resigned from her position at St. Francis Hospital, but she kept up with her training and retained her license as a registered nurse. Later, when her daughters were grown, Kate regularly returned to Grove for several days each month, where she volunteered her services as a nurse in the tribe's senior care program, providing advice and assistance with home health services and other medical issues. Her visits to Grove also allowed her to keep an eye on her parents' well-being, since she usually stayed overnight at their home when she was volunteering at the Senior Services Center. During the past two years she had become increasingly concerned about her mother. She had always been an outgoing, talkative woman, but since her father had died, her mom had seemed to retreat within herself. This year, for the first time in Kate's memory, her mom had declined to attend the Strawberry Ceremony. She was worried about her. Physically, her mom seemed to be much the same, but mentally and emotionally, she was a shadow of her former self.

Kate had discussed her mother's health with both Jason and LeeAnne. Jason continued to drop in on his mother almost every day but failed to notice any serious problems. In contrast, LeeAnne, like Kate, visited her mother less frequently and also noted her decline over a series of consecutive visits. Similar to Kate, LeeAnne regularly attended tribal ceremonies and dances, but in contrast to Kate, she was still employed full time at the bank in Springfield, and her job kept her from volunteering to help in any of the tribe's health or social services programs. But LeeAnne used her talents in other ways. An experienced accountant and investment officer, LeeAnne occasionally consulted with two members on the tribe's business committee about the investment of tribal funds and the distribution of income from the casino. Relying on her experience at the bank, LeeAnne gave good advice, but Kate knew that her sister was sometimes dismayed when the business committee ignored her counsel and invested tribal funds in several ventures that had been unprofitable.

Kate turned to her sister, still sitting next to her on the bleachers.

"Are you still thinking about running for the seat on the business committee as a councilperson?" she asked.

"Yeah, I think so," LeeAnne replied. "Gail and I've talked it over, and I could easily make it down to Grove for the monthly business committee meetings if they hold them regularly. What's more, it would give me a good excuse to check in with Mom more often to see how she's doing. So far, she seems to get along okay by herself out there at the home place, but I worry about her. I know Jason goes by to see her almost every day, but she's no spring chicken. I just worry about her, I guess."

Native American women in Oklahoma and across the United States proudly celebrate their identity through ceremony and dancing. Photo courtesy of Christopher Wetzel.

"But do you think the nation will elect someone to the committee who lives outside the Grove area?"

"Well, they have in the past. Sometimes it's worked—and sometimes it hasn't. Most of the time, when there've been problems, well, it's because the committee member couldn't get here for the meetings." "But," she added, "it's less than a hundred miles down her from the driveway at my house—and practically all interstate. I can get here in less than two hours."

"What's more," LeeAnne added, "we're well known here on the Old Rez. Our family is respected. Everybody loved our dad, and Jason has lots of good connections in the community. Both of us have remained active within the nation. And I really think that I could be of help on the business committee. Over the past decade or so, they've made some good investments, but not always. I think I've got the experience to help make good financial decisions and to protect tribal property. I think it's important that we build up a tribal nest egg to defend our remaining land base. We also need to hold on to those things that make us who we are. I've always been proud to be a Seneca-Cayuga. I want to ensure that our children and our grandchildren can be the same."

Kate reached over to her sister and gave her a hug. LeeAnne smiled back at her. Both women turned back toward the dance arena, searching again for their daughter and granddaughter. There they were. Still proudly circling the drummers and singers clustered in the center. Kate loved to hear the drums and the rattles and the old songs that accompanied them. Ever since she was a girl, she found the drumbeats to be transforming. She watched the girls pass by in front of them. The drums beat on. Kate felt as if time itself stood still. Brooke and Emmie were dancing to the same drumbeats and songs that their mothers had danced to before them, and their grandmothers, and their great-grandmothers in the past, stretching back for many generations. She knew that in the years to come, Brooke's and Emmie's daughters, too, would do the same. Kate's heart was proud. It was good to be Seneca-Cayuga.

Suggested Readings

Deloria, Phillip. *Indians in Unexpected Places.* Lawrence: University Press of Kansas, 2004.

Fixico, Donald L. *American Indians in the Modern World.* New York: Alta Mira, 2006.

———. *The Invasion of Indian Country in the Twentieth Century: American Capitalism and Tribal Natural Resources.* Boulder: University Press of Colorado, 1998.

Hamill, James. *Going Indian.* Urbana: University of Illinois Press, 2006.

Notes

Preface

1. See Institute of the American West, *Indian Self-Rule: Fifty Years under the Indian Reorganization Act* (Sun Valley, ID: Institute of the American West, 1983).

Chapter 1. City-States and Sleeping Serpents

1. Serpent Who Sleeps and his contemporaries are fictitious, composite characters who have been created to exemplify Mississippian society and life. They are entirely a product of the author's speculation but were inspired by the passage on pages 263–65 of Jesse Jennings, *Prehistory of North America* (New York: McGraw-Hill, 1974).
2. Charles Hudson, *The Southeastern Indians* (Knoxville: University of Tennessee Press. 1976), 226–29, 348. For a much broader discussion of the Black Drink, see the essays in Charles Hudson, *Black Drink: A Native American Tea* (Athens: University of Georgia Press, 1979).
3. Vincent B. Steponaitis and Vernon J. Knight Jr., "Moundville Art in Historical and Social Context," in *Hero, Hawk, and Open Hand: American Indian Art of the Ancient Midwest and South*, ed. Richard Townsend (New Haven, CT: Yale University Press, 2004), 166–81.
4. Christopher J. Peebles, "Moundville and Surrounding Sites: Some Structural Considerations of Mortuary Practices," in *Approaches to the Social Dimensions of Mortuary Practices*, ed. James A. Brown (Washington, DC: Society for American Archaeology, 1971), 68–91; John A. Walthall, *Prehistoric Indians of the Southeast: Archaeology of Alabama and the Middle South* (Tuscaloosa: University of Alabama Press, 1980), 216–27. Also see Gene S. Stuart, *America's Ancient Cities* (Washington, DC: National Geographic Society, 1988), 41–42; and Michael Coe, Dean Snow, and Elizabeth Benson, *Atlas of Ancient America* (New York: Facts of File Publications, 1986), 59.

5. William H. Morgan, *Prehistoric Architecture in the Eastern United States* (Cambridge, MA: MIT Press, 1980), xxvi–xxxvii; David Brose, James Brown, and David Penney, *Ancient Art of the American Woodland Indians* (New York: Abrams, 1985), 94–95, 108, 113–14. Also see Stuart, *America's Ancient Cities*, 37–41.

6. Brose, Brown, and Penney, *Ancient Art*, 97, 169–170. Also see Philip Kopper, *The Smithsonian Book of North American Indians before the Coming of the Europeans* (Washington, DC: Smithsonian Institution, 1986), 165–67.

7. The Hasinai were Caddoan-speaking people who erected villages along the Red River in Texas and Louisiana but more specifically along the Neches and Sabine rivers in Texas. They resided on the western fringe of the Mississippian cultural complex and formed part of the historic Caddo Confederacy. In the twenty-first century, many modern Hasinai people form part of the Caddo Nation, in Oklahoma. For additional reading, see Vynola B. Newkumet and Howard L. Meredith, *Hasinai: A Traditional History of the Caddo Confederacy* (College Station: Texas A&M University Press, 1988). Also see Russell M. Magnaghi, ed., *The Hasinais: Southern Caddoans as Seen by the Earliest Europeans* (Norman: University of Oklahoma Press, 1987); and F. Todd Smith, *The Caddo Indians: Tribes at the Convergence of Empires, 1542–1854* (College Station: Texas A&M University Press, 1995).

8. Hudson, *Southeastern Indians*, 240.

9. Descriptions and photographs of hundreds of ceremonial objects, burial goods, and trade merchandise associated with Spiro can be found in Larry G. Merriam and Christopher J. Merriam, *The Spiro Mound: A Photo Essay* (Oklahoma City, OK: Merriam Station, 2004). Also see Eric D. Singleton and F. Kent Reilly III, eds., *Recovering Ancient Spiro: Native American Art, Ritual, and Cosmic Renewal* (Oklahoma City, OK: National Cowboy Hall of Fame, 2021).

10. Merriam and Merriam, *Spiro Mound*; Singleton and Reilly, *Recovering Ancient Spiro*.

11. Merriam and Merriam, *Spiro Mound*; Singleton and Reilly, *Recovering Ancient Spiro*.

12. The Red River, which currently forms the border between Texas and Oklahoma.

13. For a discussion of Apache synonymy and nomenclature, see Morris E. Opler, "The Apachean Culture Pattern and Its Origin," in *Southwest*, ed. Alphonso Ortiz, vol. 10 of *Handbook of North American Indians*, ed. William C. Sturtevant (Washington, DC: Smithsonian Institution, 1983), 385–92.

14. James H. Gunnerson provides a good, broad discussion of the arrival of Athabascan-speaking people (Apaches, Navajos, etc.) into the Southwest; see "Southern Athapascan Archaeology," in *Southwest*, ed. Alphonso Ortiz, vol. 9 of *Handbook of North American Indians*, ed. William C. Sturtevant (Washington: Smithsonian Institution, 1979), 162–69. Also see Stephen Plog, *Ancient Peoples of the American Southwest* (London: Thames and Hudson, 1997), 188–89.

15. Turquoise was a common, but valued, trade item throughout the Southwest. Tribal peoples living in different regions of modern Arizona, New Mexico, and Nevada mined or gathered the stones, which were traded across the area and to other regions. See

Brian M. Fagan, *Ancient North America: The Archaeology of a Continent*, 2nd ed. (London: Thames and Hudson, 1995), 324–26; and Plog, *Ancient Peoples*, 24, 176–77, 184.

16. Plog, *Ancient Peoples*, 169–78.

17. Ibid.

18. An excellent, and very readable, overview of the Caddo villages in eastern Texas and Louisiana can be found in David La Vere, *The Caddo Chiefdoms: Caddo Economics and Politics, 700–1835* (Lincoln: University of Nebraska Press, 1998), 1–39.

19. The modern Muscogee (Creek) term for a cougar or mountain lion.

20. The Aztecs and other Nahuatl peoples of central Mexico referred to jaguars as *ocelotl*, which is the sources for the modern term applied to ocelots, the much smaller and now endangered spotted wild cats of Mexico and the brush country of southern Texas. The tern *jaguar*, which is the accepted modern term for these much larger cats, comes from the Tupi language, spoken in Brazil.

21. Colin Calloway, "Indian History from the End of the Alphabet; and What Now?," a presidential address delivered at the Annual Meeting of the American Society for Ethnohistory, Eugene, Oregon, November 15, 2008, 1.

22. Samuel Elliott Morrison, *The Oxford History of the American People* (New York: Oxford University Press, 1965), 3.

23. Richard C. Morgan, "Outline of Culture in the Ohio Region," in *Archaeology of the Eastern United States*, ed. James B. Griffin (Chicago: University of Chicago Press, 1952), 83–88; David Brose, James Brown, and David Penny, *Ancient Art of the American Woodland Indians* (New York: Abrams, 1985), 50–57; William Morgan, *Prehistoric Architecture in the Eastern United States* (Cambridge, MA: MIT Press, 1980), xxi, 10, 23.

24. John A. Walthall, Stephen H. Stowe, and Marvin Karson, "Ohio Hopewell Trade: Galena Procurement and Exchange," in *Hopewell Archaeology: The Chillicothe Conference*, ed. David Brose and N'Omi Greber (Kent, OH: Kent University Press, 1979), 247–50; Brose, Brown, and Penny, *Ancient Art*, 58–67; Thorne Duel, "Hopewellian Dress in Illinois," *Archaeology of the Eastern United States*, ed. James B. Griffin (Chicago: University of Chicago Press, 1952), 165–175; Morgan, "Outline of Culture," 88–93. Also see Mark F. Seeman, "Hopewell Art in Hopewell Places," in *Hero, Hawk, and Open Hand: American Indian Art of the Ancient Midwest and Southeast*, ed. Richard F. Townsend (New Haven, CT: Yale University Press, 2004), 57–71; and Bradley T. Lepper, "The Newark Earthworks: Monumental Geometry and Astronomy at a Hopewellian Pilgrimage Site," in ibid., 73–81.

25. David Wilcox and Lynette O. Shenk, *The Architecture of the Casa Grande and Its Interpretation* (Tucson: University of Arizona Press, 1977), 177–99; Coe, Snow, and Benson, *Atlas of Ancient America*, 69–70.

26. Stephen H. Larson, *Great Pueblo Architecture at Chaco Canyon*, Chaco Canyon Publications in Archaeology, 18B (Albuquerque, NM: National Park Service, 1984), 109–44; Coe, Snow, and Benson, *Atlas of Ancient America*, 71–79; Jennings, *Prehistory of North America*, 303–14. Also see Stuart, *America's Ancient Cities*, 81–111.

27. Timothy R. Pauketat, *Cahokia, Ancient America's Great City on the Mississippi* (New York: Penguin, 2000), 2–3, 26–27. Written by a recognized authority on Cahokia, this volume is designed for an educated, general audience and is an excellent introduction on this subject. The volume also discusses the archaeologists who have investigated the site and how their research has contributed to scholars' understanding of Cahokia's importance. General readers will find chapter 3, "Walking Into Cahokia," especially interesting.

28. William H. Morgan, *Prehistoric Architecture in the Eastern United States*, 48–56; Stuart, *America's Ancient Cities*, 31–33.

29. Roy Hathcock, *Ancient Indian Pottery of the Mississippi River Valley* (Camden: Hurley, 1976), 118, 204; Brose, Brown, and Penny, *Ancient Art*, 155–60; Stuart, *America's Ancient Cities*, 31–35. Also see Robert L. Hall, "The Cahokia Site and Its People," in Townsend, *Hero, Hawk, and Open Hand*, 93–103; and James A. Brown, "The Cahokian Expression: Creating Court and Cult," in ibid., 104–22.

30. "Cahokia-Prehistoric Legacy"; this multimedia presentation can be seen at the Cahokia Mounds State Historic Site in Illinois. It was produced by the Illinois Department of Conservation. Also see Brose, Brown, and Penny, *Ancient Art*, 96–97.

31. "Cahokia-Prehistoric Legacy." Also see Stuart, *America's Ancient Cities*, 35–36; and Pauketat, *Cahokia*, 62–64.

32. Pauketat, *Cahokia*, 2–3, 26–27. Also see Timothy R. Pauketat and Neal H. Lopinot, "Cahokian Population Dynamics," in *Cahokia: Domination and Ideology in the Mississippian World*, ed. Timothy R. Pauketat and Thomas E. Emerson (Lincoln: University of Nebraska Press, 1997), 103–23.

33. Tragically, this perspective continues. For example, on April 24, 2021, in an address to the politically conservative Young America's Foundation, Rick Santorum, a former congressman (R-PA) and current senior commentator for CNN, argued that European immigrants came to North America and "birthed a nation from nothing. I mean there was nothing here. . . . I mean, yes, we have Native Americans, but candidly, there isn't much Native American culture in American culture." See Philip Bump, "In Rick Santorum's Simplified Version of American History, Native Americans Are a footnote," *Washington Post*, April 26, 2021, www.washingtonpost.com/politics/2021/04/26/rick-santorums-simplified-version-american-history-native-americans-are-footnote.

34. For a detailed account and analysis of De Soto's foray into the Southeast and the cultures and communities that he encountered, see Charles Hudson, *Knights of Spain, Warriors of the Sun: Hernando De Soto and the South's Ancient Chiefdoms* (Athens: University of Georgia Press, 1997).

35. For an excellent overview of Moundville and its place within the Mississippian world, see Christopher S. Peebles, "The Rise and Fall of the Mississippian in Western Alabama: The Moundville and Summerville Phases, CE. 1000–1600," in *Mississippi Archaeology* 22, no. 1: 1–31; and Christopher S. Peebles, "Moundville from 1000 to 1500 CE, as Seen From 1840 to 1985, A.D.," in *Chiefdoms in the Americas*, ed. Robert Drennan and Carlos Uribe (Lanham, MD: University Press of the Americas, 1987), 21–41.

At the height of its influence, Moundville was enclosed by a log palisade on three sides; the fourth was defended by a river bluff. The area within the wall encompassed about three hundred acres, including numerous mounds, and sheltered a population of approximately three thousand.

36. Whiting Young and Melvin L. Fowler, *Cahokia: The Great Native American Metropolis* (Urbana: University of Illinois Press, 2000), 310–15. Young and Fowler's volume also includes brief synopses of several other scholars' analyses of the causes of Cahokia's depopulation and abandonment.

37. Ibid. Also see Neil H. Lopinot, "Cahokian Food Production Reconsidered," in Pauketat and Emerson, *Cahokia: Domination*, 52–68; Lucretia S. Kelly, "Patterns of Faunal Exploitation at Cahokia," in ibid., 69–88; and William Woods and George R. Holley, "Upland Mississippian Settlement in the American Bottom Region," in *Cahokia and the Hinterlands: Middle Mississippian Settlement of the Midwest*, ed. Thomas E. Emerson and R, Barry Lewis (Urbana: University of Illinois Press, 1991), 59–60.

38. Robert L. Hall, "Cahokia Identity and Interaction Models of Cahokia Mississippian," in Emerson and Lewis, *Cahokia and the Hinterlands*, 23–25.

39. James M Collins, "Cahokia Settlement and Social Structure as Viewed from the ICT-II," in Pauketat and Emerson, *Cahokia,*124–40.

40. Glenn Hodges, "Why Was the Ancient City of Cahokia Abandoned? New Clues Rule Out One Theory," *National Geographic*, April 12, 2021, www.nationalgeographic .com/environment/article/why-was-ancient-city-of-cahokia-abandoned-new-clues -rule-out-one-theory.

41. Pauketat, *Cahokia, Ancient America's Great City*, 161–70.

42. Young and Fowler, *Cahokia*, 287–327.

43. Melvin L. Fowler and Robert L Hall, "Late Prehistory of the Illinois Area," in *Northeast*, ed. Bruce E. Trigger, vol. 15 of *Handbook of North American Indians*, ed. William C. Sturtevant (Washington, DC: Smithsonian University, 1978), 566–68. Also see Alan G. Shackelford, "The Illinois Indians in the Confluence Region: Adaption to a Changing World," in *Enduring Nations: Native Americans in the Midwest*, ed. R. David Edmunds (Urbana: University of Illinois Press, 2008), 15–35.

44. See Christopher S. Peebles, "Paradise Lost, Strayed, and Stolen: Prehistoric Social Devolution in the Southeast," in *The Burden of Being Civilized: An Anthropological Perspective on the Discontents of Civilization*, ed. Miles Richardson and Malcolm C. Webb (Athens: University of Georgia Press, 1986), 24–40.

45. Alice Kehoe, *America before the European Invasions* (London: Pearson Education, 2002), 182–84; Newkumet and Meredith, *Hasinai*, 39–40. Also see Richard S. Townsend and Chester P. Walker, "The Ancient Art of Caddo Ceramics," in Townsend, *Hero, Hawk, and Open Hand*, 236–40; La Vere, *The Caddo Chiefdoms*, 29–30; and David LaVere, *Looting Spiro Mounds: An American King Tut's Tomb* (Norman: University of Oklahoma Press, 207), 187–93.

46. R. David Edmunds, Frederick E. Hoxie, and Neal Salisbury, *The People: A History of Native America* (Boston: Houghton Mifflin, 2007), 26.

47. An excellent discussion of the impact of disease on the Mississippian societies in the Southeast can be found in Hudson, *Knights of Spain*, 417–26. Using demographic statistics that can be found in Henry Dobyns, *Their Numbers Become Thinned: Native American Population Dynamics in Eastern North America* (Knoxville: University of Tennessee Press, 1983); and in Peter Wood, "The Changing Population of the Colonial South: An Overview by Race and Region, 1685–1790," in *Powhatan's Mantle: Indians in the Colonial Southeast*, ed. Peter Wood, Gregory Waselkov, and M. Thomas Hatley (Lincoln: University of Nebraska Pres, 1989). Hudson indicates that the population of the Mississippian chiefdoms in the Southeast shrank from approximately 1,294,000 in 1500 CE to about 200,000 by the last decade of the seventeenth century. See Hudson, *Knights of Spain*, 424–25.

48. Robert S. Grumet, *Historic Contact: Indian People and Colonists in Today's Northeastern United States in the Sixteenth Through Eighteenth Centuries* (Norman: University of Oklahoma Press, 1995), 61–62. Also see Collin Calloway, *New Worlds for All: Indians, Europeans, and the Remaking of Early America* (Baltimore, MD: Johns Hopkins University Press, 1997), 34–36

49. Calloway, *New Worlds*, 36.

50. Ibid., 38; Douglas H. Ubelaker, "The Sources and Methodology for Mooney's Estimates of North American Indian Population," in *The Native Population of the Americas in 1492*, ed. William M. Denevan (Madison: University of Wisconsin Press, 1992), 266. Also see Charles Callender, "Illinois," in Sturtevant, *Handbook of North American Indians*, 15:679.

51. Ubelaker, "Sources and Methodology," 243–88. Although scholars differ considerably in their estimates of the pre-Columbian population of the United States, they generally agree that introduction of Old World diseases into the Americas was catastrophic. See Dobyns, *Their Numbers Become Thinned*; Russell Thornton, *American Indian Holocaust and Survival: A Population History since 1492* (Norman: University of Oklahoma Press, 1987); David Stannard, *American Holocaust: The Conquest of the New World* (New York: Oxford University Press, 1992), 57–146, and Alfred W. Crosby, *The Columbian Exchange: Biological and Cultural Consequences of 1492* (Westport, CT: Greenwood, 1972).

52. Francis Jennings, *The Invasion of America: Indians, Colonialism, and the Cant of Conquest* (New York: W. W. Norton, 1975), 15–31. Also see Calloway, *New Worlds*, 42–67.

Chapter 2. Whispering Women and Shadowed Faces

1. The Potawatomi name for Green Bay was the Bay of Stinking Water or perhaps the Bay of Salted Water. See the letter by Father Claude Allouez, 1670, in Reuben G. Thwaites, ed., *The Jesuit Relations and Allied Documents*, 73 vols. (Cleveland: Burrows Bros., 1896–1901), 54:197–214; and "The Mississippi Journal of Jolliet and Marquette," in *Early Narratives of the Northwest*, ed. Louise P. Kellogg (New York: Charles

Scribner, 1917), 259. Also see R. David Edmunds, *The Potawatomis: Keepers of the Fire* (Norman: University of Oklahoma Press, 1978), 10.

2. Historians and anthropologists disagree over the exact mooring place of the *Griffon*. See Edmunds, *The Potawatomis*, 10, 20; James Clifton, *The Prairie People* (Lawrence: University Press of Kansas, 1977), 38. Also see Ruth Landes, *The Prairie Potawatomi: Tradition and Ritual in the Twentieth Century* (Madison: University of Wisconsin Press, 1970), 59; and Alanson Skinner, *The Mascoutens or Prairie Potawatomi Indians,* Bulletin of the Public Museum of the City of Milwaukee 6, no. 1 (Milwaukee: The Museum, 1924), 45–47.

3. James E. Fitting and Charles Cleland, "Late Prehistoric Settlement Patterns in the Upper Great Lakes, *Ethnohistory*, 16 (Fall, 1969): 297; George I. Quimby, *Indian Culture and European Trade Goods: The Archaeology of the Historic Period in the Western Great Lakes Region* (Madison: University of Wisconsin Press, 1966), 22–33.

4. For a discussion of the early trade between the Hurons and the Michigan tribes, see Conrad F. Heidenreich, "Huron" in Bruce Trigger, ed., *Handbook of North American Indians*, vol. 15 (Washington, DC: Smithsonian Institution Press, 1978), 383–87; and Quimby, *Indian Culture*, 68–72.

5. Edmunds, *The Potawatomis*, 4–5; George T. Hunt, *The Wars of the Iroquois: A Study in Intertribal Trade Relations* (Madison: University of Wisconsin Press, 1967), 109–19. Also see Louise S. Spindler, "Menominee," in Trigger, *Handbook*, 723–24; and Nancy O. Lurie, "Winnebago," in ibid., 706.

6. Hunt, *Wars of the Iroquois*, 103–15; Charles Garrad and Conrad F. Heidenreich, "Khionontateronon (Petun)," in Trigger, *Handbook*, 394–97; Ives Goddard, "Mascouten," in ibid., 668–72; Charles Callender, Richard K. Pope, and Susan K. Pope, "Kickapoo," in ibid., 662. Also see Burt Anson, *The Miami Indians* (Norman: University of Oklahoma Press, 1970), 3–4; and R. David Edmunds and Joseph Peyser, *The Fox Wars: The Mesquakie Challenge to New France* (Norman: University of Oklahoma Press, 1993), 9–11.

7. Quimby, *Indian Culture*, 68–76, 83–85, 115–16.

8. For a good discussion of acculturation patterns and the intermarriage between the French and Indians in the Great Lakes and Ohio valley regions, see Richard White, *The Middle Ground: Indians, Empires, and Republics in the Great Lakes, 1615–1815* (Cambridge, MA: Harvard University Press, 1991), 61–85.

9. Ibid., 25–27.

10. Ibid., 75.

11. Skinner, *The Mascoutens*, 299; Huron H. Smith, *Ethnobotany of the Forest Potawatomi Indians*, Bulletin of the Public Museum of the City of Milwaukee 7, no. 1 (Milwaukee, WI: The Museum, 1933), 32–124; Philip Alexis and Barbara Paxson, *Potawatomi Indian Black Ash Basketry* (Dowagiac, MI: Potawatomi Indian Tribe, 1984), 5–6; Robert Ritzenthaler, *The Potawatomi Indians of Wisconsin*, Bulletin of the Public Museum of the City of Milwaukee 19, no. 3 (Milwaukee, WI: The Museum, 1953), 168. Historians disagree over the extent of the dependency of the Wisconsin tribes' on European

trade goods. See Edmunds, *The Potawatomis*, 14–15; Edmunds and Peyser, *The Fox Wars*, 44–48; and White, *The Middle Ground*, 99–141.

12. Edmunds and Peyser, *The Fox Wars*, 3–30. Also see Raymond J. DeMallie, "Sioux until 1850," *Handbook of North American Indians*, vol. 13, part 2 (Washington, DC: Smithsonian Institution Press, 2001), 749–51.

13. Abel C. Pepper, a resident of Rising Sun, Indiana, was active in Democratic politics during the Jacksonian era and served as an Indian agent in the War Department, where he negotiated a series of treaties and land cessions with the Potawatomis and Miamis. He also served as a removal agent in the removal of tribal people from Indiana, Illinois, Michigan, and Wisconsin. The Potawatomis jokingly referred to him as Wasek Botagen (pepper grinder), because his raspy voice sounded like the pepper mills in use in frontier trading posts. His papers are located in the Indiana Historical Society. Also see Edmunds, *The Potawatomis*, 240–72.

14. Menominee was a village chief whose village was located on the Yellow River near Plymouth, Indiana. He was exposed to Catholicism before 1820 but was formally baptized into the Catholic faith by Father Louis Deseille in August 1834. See Helen Tanner, ed., *Atlas of Great Lakes Indian History* (Norman: University of Oklahoma Press, 1987), 134; and Irving McKee, ed., *The Trail of Death: The Letters of Benjamin Marie Petit* (Indianapolis: Indiana Historical Society, 1941), 12–15.

15. Keewawnay Lake, now known as Bruce Lake, is located in Fulton County, Indiana.

16. Willam Burnett, a trader of American origin, moved to the St. Joseph in the years following the American Revolution and married Kakima, the daughter of Nanaquiba, an aging village chief in the region. He established a trading post and warehouses on the St. Joseph and Kankakee rivers, and at Chicago. See Edmunds, *The Potawatomis*, 156, 188, 222–23, 228.

17. Jean Baptist Richardville, or Peshawa (the Wildcat) was a trader of mixed French-Creole and Miami descent whose business dominated the portage between the Maumee and Wabash river systems in northeastern Indiana. He was influential in Miami politics, and reputed to be the richest man in Indiana, when the territory became a state in 1816. See Bradley J, Birzer, "Jean Baptist Richardville, Miami Metis," in *Enduring Nations: Native Americans in the Midwest*, ed. R. David Edmunds (Urbana: University of Illinois Press, 2008), 94–108, Francis Godfroy was a trader of mixed Miami and French descent who maintained a very profitable trading establishment and a luxurious (by frontier standards) home on the Mississinewa River near modern Peru, Indiana. See Sarah E. Cooke and Rachel B. Ramadhyani, comps., *Indians and a Changing Frontier: The Art of George Winter* (Indianapolis: Indiana Historical Society, 1993), 25–30, 120–27, and plates 42 and 47. Winter's portraits of Potawatomi and Miami tribespeople in Indiana during this period provide a treasure trove of information regarding the material culture of many of these tribespeople during this period. As Winter's paintings and watercolors illustrate, many of the Potawatomis in northern Indiana prospered in the trade, attiring themselves and their families in expensive clothing and owning fine horses. Moreover, landscapes featuring their cabins and

houses indicate that many of their homes were similar or even superior to those inhabited by their white neighbors.

18. Nadewesiouz, Panis, and Wasaasa (Dakotas or Sioux, Pawnees and Osages).

19. George M. Jerolaman (the "healer" in the text) was a "physician" hired by federal officials to accompany several removal parties to the West. A notorious alcoholic, he was described as "abrasive, and bellicose." He was despised by the Potawatomis. See Joseph Holoman to John Tipton, October 16, 1838, in Nellie Armstrong Robertson and Dorothy Riker, eds., *The John Tipton Papers*, 3 vols. (Indianapolis: Indiana Historical Bureau, 1942), 3:751; Chauncy Carter to John Tipton, October 18, 1838, ibid., 752–53; and Jesse Douglas to John Tipton, October 21, ibid., 755–56.

20. Excerpts from Menominee's speech can be found in McKee, *Trail of Death*, 81–82n14.

21. For information on Massaw or D'Mouchekeekeeawh, see Cook and Ramadhyani, *Indians on a Changing Frontier*, 28–30, 59–62, 78–85, and plates 27 and 28. Also see Stewart Rafert, *The Miami Indians of Indiana: A Persistent People* (Indianapolis: Indiana Historical Society, 1996), 136–39. Unquestionably, the best discussion of the important role played by Potawatomi and other tribal women in the development of Native American commerce in Michigan and Indiana can be found in Susan Sleeper-Smith, *Indian Women and French Men: Rethinking Cultural Encounters in the Western Great Lakes* (Amherst: University of Massachusetts Press, 2002). For similar insights into the contributions of Sac, Meskwaki (Fox), and Ho-Chunk (Winnebago) women to the marketing of lead and the development of commerce in the upper Mississippi valley, see Lucy E. Murphy, *A Gathering of Rivers: Indians, Metis, and Mining in the Western Great Lakes, 1737–1832* (Lincoln: University of Nebraska Press, 2002); and Lucy Murphy, *Great Lakes Creoles: A French-Indian Community on the Northern Borderlands, Prairie Du Chien, 1750–1860* (Cambridge, UK: Cambridge University Press, 2014).

22. See White, *The Middle Ground*, chapters 1–5. Also useful is Michael A. McDonnell, *Master's of Empire: Great Lakes Indians and the Making of America* (New York: Hill and Wang, 2015). For the Potawatomi resettlement of southwestern Michigan and northern Indiana, see Edmunds, *The Potawatomis*, 24–38; and Tanner, *Atlas of Great Lakes Indian History*, 36–41, 58–59. Also see Michael S. Nassany, William M. Cremin, and Lisamarie Malischke, "Native American-French Interactions in Eighteenth-Century Southwest Michigan: The View from Fort St. Joseph," in *Contested Territories: Native American and Non-Natives In The Lower Great Lakes, 1700–1850*, ed. Charles Beatty-Medina and Melissa Rinehart (East Lansing: Michigan State University Press, 2012), 55–79.

23. See Edmunds, *The Potawatomis*, chapters 3–8.

24. Ibid.

25. Sleeper-Smith, *Catholic Women*, 11–53. Also see William McNamara, *The Catholic Church on the Northern Indiana Frontier, 1789–1844* (Washington, DC: Catholic University of America, 1931), 18–19.

26. Isaac McCoy, *History of the Baptist Indian Mission* (New York: Johnson Reprint, 1970), 133, 237–56; George A. Schulz, *An Indian Canaan: Isaac Mccoy and the Vision of an Indian State* (Norman: University of Oklahoma Press, 1972), 59–77.

27. See J. Herman Schauninger, *Stephen T Badin: Priest in the Wilderness* (Milwaukee: Bruce Publishing, 1956), 223–24. Also see Thomas T. McAvoy, *The Catholic Church in Indiana* (New York: Columbia University Press, 1940), 175–76.

28. R. David Edmunds, "'Unacquainted with the Laws of the Civilized World': American Attitudes toward the Me'tis Communities in the Old Northwest," in *The New Peoples: Being and Becoming Me'tis in North America*, ed. Jacqueline Peterson and Jennifer S. H. Brown (Winnipeg: University of Manitoba Press, 1985), 185–94. For a broad discussion of American attitudes toward the Creole French, see Edward Watts, *In This Remote Country: French Colonial Culture in the Anglo-American Imagination, 1780–1860* (Chapel Hill: University of North Carolina Press, 2006).

29. See Schauninger, *Stephen T. Badin*, 225–43. Also see "Remarks on Statement C, 1832," in Potawatomi File, Great Lakes-Ohio Valley Indian Archives, Glenn A. Black Laboratory of Archaeology, Indiana University, Bloomington, Indiana.

30. McKee, *The Trail of Death*, 15–16.

31. See Edmunds, *The Potawatomis*, 219–35.

32. Ibid., 240–72.

33. Ibid. Also see R. David Edmunds, "'Designing Men Seeking a Fortune': Indian Traders and the 1836 Potawatomi Claims Payment," *Indiana Magazine of History*, 78 (June, 1981): 109–12; and Robert Trennert, *Indian Traders on the Middle Border: The House of Ewing, 1827–1854* (Lincoln: University of Nebraska Press, 1981).

34. Anthony Davis to John Tipton, March 2, 1836, in *John Tipton Papers*, ed. Robertson and Riker, 3:233–35; Pepper to Deseille, May 16, 1837, in "Documents: Correspondence on Indian Removal, Indiana, 1835–1838," in *Mid-America: An Historical Review* 15 (January 1933): 185–86.

35. Deseille to Pepper, March 21, 1836, in "Documents," 182. Also see Edmunds, *The Potawatomis*, 265.

36. Pepper to Tipton, April 16, 1836, in *John Tipton Papers*, ed. Robertson and Riker, 3:259–60; "Articles of a Treaty made at a camp on Yellow River, August 5, 1836," in *Indian Treaties, 1778–1883*, ed. Charles Kappler (New York: Interland Publishing, 1972 [reprint]), 3:668–69. The other treaties negotiated by Pepper during this period can be found in Kappler, ibid., 457–72. Also see Sands to Pepper, May 20, 1837, in "Documents," 186–87; and Edmunds, *The Potawatomis*, 265–66.

37. Sands to Pepper, May 11, 1837, in "Documents," 183–84; Pepper to Deseille, May 16, 1837, ibid., 185–86; Sands to Campeau, May 28, 1837, quoted in McKee, *The Trail of Death*, 25.

38. Petit to Brute, November 27, 1837, in McKee, *Trail of Death*, 35–40; Petit to Brute, December 26, 1837, ibid., 47–51; Petit to De La Hailandiere, February 11, 1838, ibid., 53–58; Petit to Brute, May 26, 1838, ibid., 67–72

39. Edmunds, *The Potawatomis*, 267.

40. Ibid. Correspondence focusing on Pepper's, Wallace's, and Tipton's collusion in these events can be found in Robertson and Riker, *John Tipton Papers*, 3:660–96.
41. Edmunds, *The Potawatomis*, 267–68. See also Petit's correspondence and journal in McKee, *The Trail of Death*, 90–116, 126–32.
42. McKee, *The Trail of Death*, 90–116, 126–32.
43. For a brief overview of Potawatomi commercial activity in Kansas in the 1830s and 1840s, see R. David Edmunds, "Indians as Pioneers: Potawatomis on the Frontier," *Chronicles of Oklahoma* 65 (Winter, 1987–88): 340–53. Also see entries for March 1849 in *The Beginnings of the West: Annals of the Kansas Gateway to the American West, 1540–1854*, ed. Louise Barry (Topeka: Kansas State Historical Society, 1972), 801–2.

Chapter 3. Crooked Legs Walk No More

1. The orthography and translation of Arapaho words and idioms present certain problems to nonspeakers of the Arapaho language. Modern Arapaho usage differs somewhat from terms and definitions used in the late eighteenth and nineteenth centuries. When possible, the author has attempted to use spelling and terminology employed by ethnohistorian Loretta Fowler, or the lexicon compiled by Zdendek Salzman in *Dictionary of Contemporary Arapaho Usage*, no. 4, in the Arapaho Language and Culture, Instruction Material Series, ed. William J. C'Hair (Wind River Reservation, Wyoming: Arapaho Language and Culture Commission, 1983).
2. A general description of the pre-horse pedestrian hunting culture on the northern plains can be found in Brian Fagan, *Ancient North America: The Archaeology of a Continent*, 2nd ed. (London: Thames and Hudson, 1991), 136–43. Also see Virginia Cole Trenholm, *The Arapahoes: Our People* (Norman: University of Oklahoma Press, 1970), 12.
3. For a good discussion of the Plains tribes' use of dogs as pack animals or to draw travois, see Frank Gilbert Roe, *The Indian and the Horse* (Norman: University of Oklahoma Press, 1955), 11–32. The nineteenth-century artist George Catlin painted a scene that reflects the chaos that ensued when dogs hitched to travois engaged in a dogfight. See "Comanche Moving Camp; Dog Fight Enroute," in *Letters and Notes on the Manners, Customs, and Conditions of the North American Indians*, 2 vols. (New York: Dover, 1973), 2:65, plate 167.
4. Dressed in wolf skins, hunters on the plains continued to occasionally stalk bison well into the historic period. See "Buffalo Chase under Wolf-Skin Masks," in Catlin, *Letters and Notes*, 1:254, plate 110. Also see Brian Fagan, *Ancient North America: The Archaeology of a Continent*, 2nd ed. (London: Thames and Hudson, 1995), 144.
5. A good description of Arapaho methods of food preservation can be found in M. Inez Hilger, *Arapaho Child Life and Its Cultural Background*, Bureau of American Ethnology Bulletin No. 148 (Washington, DC: Smithsonian Institution, 1952), 175–79. Also see Loretta Fowler, *The Arapaho* (New York: Chelsea House, 2005), 20–21; and Trenholm, *The Arapahoes*, 66–67.

6. Arapaho methods of hide preservation are described in Alfred Kroeber, *The Arapaho* (Lincoln: University of Nebraska Press, 1983), 25–26; and in Hilger, *Arapaho Child Life*, 183–85.

7. Mountain sheep horn bows were very powerful and were highly valued by hunters on the plains. The Shoshones also constructed bows from elk antlers. See Colin F. Taylor, *Native American Weapons* (Norman: University of Oklahoma Press, 2001), 70–74. Also see "Archery in America," *Wind River Rendezvous* 21 (April–June, 1991): 3–16. This publication, produced by St. Stephens Indian Mission near Riverton, Wyoming, illustrates that artisans among the Wind River Shoshone people still manufacture the antler bows.

8. Loretta Fowler estimates that the Arapahos obtained horses "shortly after 1730." See Fowler, *The Arapaho*, 14–15. An excellent survey and analysis of the arrival of horses among tribal peoples on the plains can be found in Colin G. Calloway, *One Vast Wintercount: The Native American West before Lewis and Clark* (Lincoln: University of Nebraska Press, 2003), 267–312.

9. Arapaho tepees are described in Hilger, *Arapaho Child Life*, 180–81; and in Trenholm, *The Arapahoes*, 66–67. On the plains, difficulties in transporting aged or infirm family members too weak or ill to travel, particularly during the pre-horse era, is mentioned in Frank Linderman, *Pretty Shield: Medicine Woman of the Crow* (Lincoln: University of Nebraska Press, 1972), 92.

10. Trade between nomadic tribes such as the Arapahos and Cheyennes and village peoples such as the Arikaras, Mandans, and Hidatsas is discussed in Preston Holder, *The Hoe and the Horse on the Plains* (Lincoln: University of Nebraska Press, 1970), 89–137. Also see Roy W. Meyer, *The Village Indians of the Upper Missouri: The Mandans, Hidatsas, and Arikaras* (Lincoln: University of Nebraska Press, 1977), 16; Elizabeth A. Fein, *Encounters at the Heart of the World: A History of the Mandan People* (New York: Hill and Wang, 2014), 236. William Clark reported Arapahos trading in the Arikara and Mandan villages in 1804. See James Ronda, *Lewis and Clark among the Indians* (Lincoln: University of Nebraska Press, 1984), 48, 67.

11. William Clark mentions that the Arikaras bartered trade muskets and ammunition to the Arapahos and Cheyennes for horses and elaborately decorated skin clothing. See Ronda, *Lewis and Clark, among the Indians*, 50.

12. An excellent description of methods employed in hunting bison with a "buffalo runner" can be found in John Ewers, *The Blackfeet, Raiders on the Northwestern Plains* (Norman: University of Oklahoma Press, 1958), 76–80.

13. Good discussions of hunting buffalo in surrounds and other hunting techniques employed by Plains tribes can be found in Roe, *The Indian and the Horse*, 332–73; and in John Ewers, *The Horse in Blackfoot Indian Culture, with Comparative Materials from Other Western Tribes*, Bureau of American Ethnology Bulletin No. 159 (Washington, DC: Smithsonian Institution Press, 1955), 148–71.

14. The impact of horses upon warfare on the plains is discussed in Ewers, *The Horse in Blackfoot Indian Culture*, 175–215; and in Roe, *The Indian and the Horse*, 219–46. Also see Fowler, *The Arapaho*, 16–17.

15. Arapaho mourning practices are described in Kroeber, *The Arapaho*, 16–17. Also see Trenholm, *The Arapahoes*, 62–64.
16. Arapaho marriages are described in Fowler, *The Arapaho*, 28–30; and in Hilger, *Arapaho Child Life*, 193–216. Also see Kroeber, *The Arapaho*, 12–13.
17. The role of age-graded societies and ceremonies in Arapaho life is discussed in Fowler, *The Arapaho*, 27–39; and in Fowler, *Arapaho Politics*, 8–9, 54–55.
18. Scholars disagree over the size of the pedestrian pre-horse hunting population resident on the Great Plains. In the 1990s, Karl Schlesier suggested that previous assumptions that the pre-Columbian plains sustained only a small pedestrian hunting population were incorrect. In contrast, he asserted that the plains supported a relatively large number of pedestrian hunters until the region was swept by European introduced pandemics in the sixteenth century. Yet regardless of the population prior to 1500 CE, the plains were sparsely populated when Europeans first entered the region, and the population remained relatively sparse and diffuse until the advent of horses encouraged the settlement (or repopulation) of the region. See Karl H. Schlesier, ed., *Plains Indians, A.D. 500–1500: The Archaeological Past of Historic Groups* (Norman: University of Oklahoma Press, 1994), xx–xxiv, 316–23. Also see Fagan, *Ancient North America*, 126–36; and George Frison, *Prehistoric Hunters on the High Plains* (New York: Academic Press, 1978). An excellent, well-written, and beautifully illustrated account of the use of a cliff as a kill site can be found in Jack W. Brink, *Imagining Head Smashed In: Aboriginal Buffalo Hunting on the Northern Plains* (Edmonton: Athabasca University Press, 2008).
19. The most comprehensive discussion of the spread of horses can be found in Roe, *The Indian and the Horse*, 56–134.
20. David La Vere, *The Caddo Chiefdoms: Caddo Economics and Politics, 700–1835* (Lincoln: University of Nebraska Press, 1998), 60–63.
21. Roe, *The Indian and the Horse*, 53–134. Also see Ewers, *The Horse in Blackfoot Indian Culture*, 1–19.
22. Scholars disagree in their estimates of the relative size of horse herds among the different tribes. See Roe, *The Indian and the Horse*, 73–92, 282–315; Ewers, *The Horse in Blackfoot Indian Culture*, 20–32. Also see Pekka Hamalainen, *The Comanche Empire* (New Haven, CT: Yale University Press, 2008), 243–48; Thomas W. Kavanagh, *The Comanches: A History, 1706–1875* (Lincoln: University of Nebraska Press, 1996), 380–81; Donald J. Berthrong, *The Southern Cheyennes* (Norman: University of Oklahoma Press, 1963), 82–83; Gary C, Anderson, *The Indian Southwest, 1580–1830: Ethnogenesis and Reinvention* (Norman: University of Oklahoma Press, 1999), 226–28.
23. Roe, *The Indian and the Horse*, 123–34, 282–315; Ewers, *The Horse in Blackfoot Indian Culture*, 20–32. Also see Edwin Thompson Denig, *Five Indian Tribes of the Upper Missouri* (Norman: University of Oklahoma Press, 1961), 145–46.
24. Roe, *The Indian and the Horse*, 93–122, 282–315; Ewers, *The Horse in Blackfoot Indian Culture*, 20–32.

25. For a brief discussion of the spread of firearms onto the plains, see Colin G. Calloway, *Our Hearts Fell to the Ground: Plains Indians' Views of How the West Was Lost* (Boston: St. Martin's, 1996), 38–42.

26. Most historians agree that bows and arrows remained the weapons of choice for hunting buffalo. See Preston Holder, *The Hoe and the Horse on the Plains*, 114–16; Ewers, *The Horse in Blackfoot Indian Culture*,156–57; and Robert H. Lowie, *Indians of the Plains* (Garden City, NY: American Museum of Natural History, 1954), 75–76.

27. Ewers, *The Horse in Blackfoot Indian Culture*, 102–19, 129–48, 306–9.

28. Ibid., 309–13; Fowler, *The Arapaho*, 18–20; Hilger, *Arapaho Child Life*, 190–86;

29. Fowler, *Arapahoe Politics*, 8–9, 25–27, 38–39; Ewers, *The Horse in Blackfoot Indian Culture*, 309–11; Calloway, *Our Hearts Fell to the Ground*, 7.

30. Since the 1990s, several scholars have pointed out that the tribal hunting of bison, in addition to other factors, took a heavy toll of the bison population on the plains. See Dan Flores, "Bison Ecology and Bison Diplomacy: The Southern Plains from 1800 to 1850," *Journal of American History* 78 (September, 1991): 465–85; and Elliott West, *Contested Plains: Indians, Goldseekers, and the Rush To Colorado* (Lawrence: University Press of Kansas. 1998), 69–73, 84–88, 259–60, and passim. Also see Tom McHugh, *The Time of the Buffalo* (Lincoln: University of Nebraska Press, 1972), 247–99.

31. Holder's *The Hoe and the Horse on the Plains* contains an excellent discussion of the demise of the village peoples. Also see Elizabeth A. Fenn, *Encounters*; and Meyer, *The Village Indians of the Upper Missouri*.

32. Meyer, *The Village Indians*, 83–109; Fenn, *Encounters*, 322–25. Also see Russell Thornton, *American Indian Holocaust and Survival: A Population History Since 1492* (Norman: University of Oklahoma Press, 1987), 95–99; and "Fort Berthold," in *Tiller's Guide to Indian Country: Economic Profiles of American Indian Reservations*, ed. Veronica E. Velarde Tiller (Albuquerque: Bow Arrow, 2005), 794–96.

33. Meyer, *The Village Indians*, 105–33; Fenn, *Encounters*, 327–36.

34. La Vere, *The Caddo Chiefdoms*, 40–127; David J. Wishart, *An Unspeakable Sadness: The Dispossession of the Nebraska Indians* (Lincoln: University of Nebraska Press, 1994), 1–70.

35. For an insightful discussion of tribal migration onto the plains see Richard White, "The Winning of the West: The Expansion of the Western Sioux in the Eighteenth and Nineteenth Centuries," *Journal of American History* 63 (September, 1978), 319–43. Also see Virginia Cole Trenholm and Maurine Carley, *The Shoshones: Sentinels of the Rockies* (Norman: University of Oklahoma Press, 1964), 3–40; and Jerome A. Greene, *Nez Perce Summer, 1877: The U.S. Army and the Nee-Me-Poo Crisis* (Helena: Montana Historical Society Press, 2000), 1–5.

36. See David La Vere, *Contrary Neighbors: Southern Plains and Removed Indians in Indian Territory* (Norman: University of Oklahoma Press, 2000), 30–166; R. David Edmunds, "Indians as Pioneers: Potawatomis on the Frontier," *Chronicles of Oklahoma* 65 (Winter 1987–88), 340–53.

37. Robert Berkhofer, *The White Man's Indian* (New York: Knopf, 1978), provides an excellent analysis of the changing image of Native American people in American popular culture. Also see John M. Coward, *The Newspaper Indian: Native American Identity in the Press, 1820–1890* (Urbana: University of Illinois Press, 1999); Philip J. Deloria, *Playing Indian* (New Haven, CT: Yale University Press, 1998); and Philip J. Deloria, *Indians In Unexpected Places* (Lawrence: University Press of Kansas, 2004).

38. The best discussion of Native American participation in Wild West shows can be found in L. G. Moses, *Wild West Shows and the Images of American Indians* (Albuquerque: University of New Mexico Press, 1996). For information and commentary on tribal people in film, see Jacquelyn Kilpatrick, *Celluloid Indians: Native Americans and Film* (Lincoln: University of Nebraska Press, 1999); and the collection of essays edited by Peter C. Rollins and John E. O'Connor in *Hollywood's Indian: The Portrayal of the Native American in Film* (Lexington: University Press of Kentucky, 1995).

39. For an excellent photographic essay and insightful collection of vignettes illustrating the lives of modern Northern Arapaho people on the Wind River Reservation in Wyoming, see Sara Wiles, *Arapaho Journeys: Photographs and Stories from the Wind River Reservation* (Norman: University of Oklahoma Press, 2011).

Chapter 4. Herons Who Wait at the Spelawe-thepee

An abbreviated edition of this chapter was first published as "Herons Who Wait at the Spelawa-Thepee: The Ohio River and the Shawnee World," *Register of the Kentucky Historical Society* 91 (Summer 1993): 249–59.

1. The Shawnees called Anthony Wayne "Shemeneto," or "The Blacksnake," since like the reptile (and unlike previous American military commanders in the Old Northwest), they found him wary and difficult to surprise. See Wiley Sword, *President Washington's War: The Struggle for the Old Northwest* (Norman; University of Oklahoma Press, 1985), 296. Sword's detailed and well-documented volume is the best survey of the military encounters between the tribes and the United States in the "Ohio Country" during this period.

2. *Sauganash* was the term used by the Shawnees and other Algonquian speaking tribes to describe the English. *Onontio* was the term used by these same tribes to describe the governor general of New France. See Richard White, *The Middle Ground: Indians, Empires, and Republics in the Great Lakes Region, 1650–1835* (New York: Cambridge University Press, 1991), xi, xiv, 40; and R. David Edmunds, *The Potawatomis: Keepers of the Fire* (Norman: University of Oklahoma Press, 1978), 38, 172.

3. These early hunters from Virginia who crossed the mountains to hunt in Kentucky were called "long hunters" since their hunting trips into Kentucky kept them away from their homes for extended ("long") periods of time. See John Mack Faragher, *Daniel Boone: The Life and the Legend of an American Pioneer* (New York: Henry Holt, 1992), 49–50, 53–55. See also Otis Rice, *Frontier Kentucky* (Lexington: University Press of Kentucky, 1993).

4. Daniel Greathouse, a native of Maryland and Virginia, claimed over four hundred acres of land at "Mingo Bottom," near modern Follansbee, West Virginia.

5. For a much more detailed discussion of the pre-Columbian period, see chapter 1 of this volume. Also see David Hurst Thomas, *Exploring Native North America* (New York: Oxford University Press, 2000), 83–93, 106–13; and Philip Kopper, *The Smithsonian Book of North American Indians before the Coming of the Europeans* (Washington, DC: Smithsonian Institution, 1986), 125–134.

6. Although the volume does not focus on the tribes of the Ohio Valley, Richard White's *The Roots of Dependency: Subsistence, Environment and Social Change among the Choctaws, Pawnees, and Navajos* (Lincoln: University of Nebraska Press, 1983) offers excellent analyses of how the economic dependency of tribal peoples on introduced goods and economic systems had a profound impact upon tribal societies. Also see White, *The Middle Ground*; and Michael N. McConnell, *A Country Between: The Upper Ohio Valley and its People, 1724–1774* (Lincoln: University of Nebraska Press, 1992).

7. Excellent accounts of Shawnee migrations and occupation of the Ohio valley during the seventeenth and early eighteenth centuries can be found in Stephen Warren, *The Worlds the Shawnees Made: Migration and Violence in Early America* (Chapel Hill: University of North Carolina Press, 2014); and in Sami Lakomaki, *Gathering Together: The Shawnee People through Diaspora and Nationhood, 1600–1870* (New Haven, CT: Yale University Press, 2014). Faragher's *Daniel Boone* provides good descriptions of the movement of Virginians west into Kentucky, while excellent documentary accounts of the events surrounding Lord Dunmore's War can be found in Reuben G. Thwaites and Louise Phelps Kellogg, eds., *Documentary History of Lord Dunmore's War* (Madison: State Historical Society of Wisconsin, 1905; Philadelphia: Heritage Books, 1989).

8. There are several excellent accounts of the warfare along the Ohio frontier during the American Revolution. See Randolph C. Downes, *Council Fires on the Upper Ohio: A Narrative of Indian Affairs in the Upper Ohio Valley until 1795* (Pittsburgh: University of Pittsburgh Press, 1940), 179–279; Jack M. Sosin, *The Revolutionary Frontier, 1763–1783* (New York: Holt, Rinehart, and Winston,1967). Also see Faragher, *Daniel Boone*, 98–225; and William R. Nester, *George Rogers Clark* (Norman: University of Oklahoma Press, 2012).

9. See R. David Edmunds, Frederick E. Hoxie, and Neal Salisbury, *The People: A History of Native America* (Boston: Houghton Mifflin, 2007), 166; Colin G. Calloway, *Crown and Calumet: British Indian Relations, 1783–1815* (Norman: University of Oklahoma Press, 1987), 3–15; Larry L. Nelson, *A Man of Distinction among Them: Alexander Mckee and British-Indian Affairs along the Ohio Country Frontier, 1754–1799* (Kent, OH: Kent State University Press,1999), 131–34.

10. Francis Paul Prucha, *The Great Father: The United States Government and the American Indian*, 2 vols. (Lincoln: University of Nebraska Press, 1984), 1:58–60. Also see Vine Deloria Jr. and Clifford M. Lyttle, *The Nations Within: The Past and Futures of Native American Sovereignty* (New York: Pantheon, 1984); and John R. Wunder,

Retained by the People: A History of American Indians and the Bill of Rights (New York: Oxford University Press, 1994).

11. Excellent discussions of these treaties can be found in Downes, *Council Fires on the Upper Ohio*, 277–309; and in Francis Paul Prucha, *American Indian Treaties: The History of a Political Anomaly* (Berkeley: University of California Press, 1994), 42–58.

12. R. David Edmunds, *Tecumseh and the Quest for Indian Leadership* (Boston: Little, Brown, 1984), 26–30; John Sugden, *Blue Jacket of the Shawnees* (Lincoln: University of Nebraska Press, 2000), 65–98.

13. Downes, *Council Fires on the Upper Ohio*, 279–84.

14. Edmunds, *The Potawatomis*, 121–22.

15. An excellent, detailed account of these military actions can be found in Sword, *President Washington's Indian War*, 89–130.

16. A detailed account of St. Clair's ill-fated expedition and its defeat can be found in ibid., 145–203.

17. Ibid.

18. Ibid.

19. Ibid.

20. See R. David Edmunds, "'Nothing Has Been Effected': The Vincennes Treaty of 1792," *Indiana Magazine of History* 74 (March, 1978), 23–35.

21. Edmunds, *The Potawatomis*, 125–28.

22. An interesting, very readable narrative account of Wayne's activities during these two years can be found in Alan D. Gaff, *Bayonets in the Wilderness: Anthony Wayne's Legion in the Old Northwest* (Norman: University of Oklahoma Press, 2004), 37–204. For some interesting primary documents focusing on these events, see Richard C. Knopf, *Anthony Wayne, a Name in Arms: The Wayne-Knox-Pickering-Mchenry Correspondence* (Pittsburgh: University of Pittsburgh Press, 1960).

23. Reginald Horsman's *Matthew Elliott: British Indian Agent* (Detroit: Wayne State University Press, 1964), 92–95, provides a good discussion of the impact of Dorchester's speech and the construction of Fort Miamis on the tribes along the Maumee and Wabash.

24. For good accounts of the attack on Fort Recovery see Gaff, *Bayonets in the Wilderness*, 243–53; Sword, *President Washington's Indian War*, 272–78; Sugden, *Blue Jacket*, 164–68; and Edmunds, *Tecumseh*, 33–35.

25. Gaff, *Bayonets in the Wilderness*, 277–300; Sword, *President Washington's Indian War*, 279–88.

26. Gaff, *Bayonets in the Wilderness*, 301–13; Sword, *President Washington's Indian War*, 299–311; Sugden, *Blue Jacket*, 175–80; Edmunds, *Tecumseh*, 36–38.

27. Sword, *President Washington Indian War*, 306–11; Gaff, *Bayonets In The Wilderness*, 314–27.

28. Edmunds, *The Potawatomis*, 132–35; Horsman, *Matthew Elliott*, 105–12

29. See Edmunds, Hoxie, and Salisbury, *The People*, 164–66; and Wiley, *President Washington's Indian War*, 323–31.

30. List of US states and territories by historical population, US Census Bureau, https//en.wickipedia.org. The best discussion of Native American population numbers in this region can be found in Helen Hornbeck Tanner, ed., *Atlas of Great Lakes Indian History* (Norman: University of Oklahoma, Press, 1987), 65–55, 70, 95, 122,182, and passim. This volume, with its superb maps and text, is an invaluable reference work for any serious study of Native American people in the Great Lakes and Midwest.

31. Edmunds, *Tecumseh*, 147–96. Tecumseh's denunciation of Procter and the British betrayal of their Indian allies, delivered on September 18, 1813, ranks as one of the most inspiring speeches ever delivered by a Native American leader. See ibid., 188–90.

32. The treaties ceding these lands can be found in Charles J. Kappler, comp. and ed., *Indian Treaties, 1778–1883* (Mattituck, NY; Amereon House, 1972), 39–588. For the removal of the Midwestern tribes, see Grant Foreman, *The Last Trek of the Indians* (Chicago: University of Chicago Press, 1932); Mary Stockwell, *The Other Trail of Tears: The Removal of the Ohio Indians* (Yardley, PA: Westholme, 2014); and John P. Bowes, *Land Too Good for Indians: Northern Indian Removal* (Norman: University of Oklahoma Press, 2016).

33. Ironically, one century later, at the beginning of the twenty-first century, things had changed. In 2000, the six states (Ohio, Indiana, Illinois, Michigan, Wisconsin, and Minnesota) that bordered the Ohio River or the western Great Lakes contained almost 250,000 Native American people, and this enumeration included only those individuals who listed themselves as solely Native American, not the many others who identified themselves as multiracial, or "part-Indian." If people who identified themselves as of mixed descent are included, the numbers swell to over 460,000. Since Native American people in the Midwest have a long history of intermarriage with non-Indians, the latter figure probably is more accurate. Indeed, census reports indicated that in 2000, 17.4 percent of all Native Americans in the United States lived within this region. See R. David Edmunds, "A People of Persistence," in *Enduring Nations: Native Americans in the Midwest*, ed. David Edmunds (Urbana: University of Illinois Press, 2008), 1–2.

Chapter 5. Westbrooks Awash on a Trail of Tears

1. For information describing the size and physical properties of larger Cherokee farms and plantations during this period, see Theda Perdue, *Slavery and the Evolution of Cherokee Society, 1540–1866* (Knoxville: University of Tennessee Press, 1979), 55–60.

2. See William G. McLoughlin, *Cherokee Renascence in the New Republic* (Princeton, NJ: Princeton University Press, 1986), 396–401.

3. The Treaty of New Echota, December 29, 1835, can be found in Charles J. Kappler, comp. and ed., *Indian Treaties: 1778–1883* (Mattituck, NY: Amereon House, 1972; New York: Interland Publishing, 1972), 439–49. Citations refer to the Amereon edition.

4. Good discussions of these policies can be found in Francis Paul Prucha, *American Indian Policy in the Formative Years* (Cambridge, MA: Harvard University Press, 1962); and in Bernard Sheehan, *Seeds of Extinction: Jeffersonian Philanthropy and the American Indian* (New York: W. W. Norton, 1973).

5. For a brief, but accurate overview of the social, economic, and political culture within these tribes during the early nineteenth century see R. David Edmunds, Frederick E. Hoxie, and Neal Salisbury, *The People: A History of Native America* (Boston: Houghton Mifflin, 2007), 213–33.

6. William McLoughlin, *Cherokees and Missionaries, 1789–1839* (New Haven, CT: Yale University Press, 1984), 183–86, 233–36; Glen Fleischman, *The Cherokee Removal, 1838* (New York: Franklin Watts, 1971), 16–17. Also see Grant Foreman, *Sequoyah* (Norman: University of Oklahoma Press, 1938); and Ellen Cushman, *The Cherokee Syllabary: Writing the People's Perseverance* (Norman: University of Oklahoma Press, 2011).

7. For a good general description of traditional Cherokee society, see Theda Perdue and Michael D. Green, *The Cherokee Removal: A Brief History in Documents* (Boston: Bedford/St. Martin's, 2005), 1–14. A more detailed and lengthy discussion of these times can be found in McLoughlin, *Cherokee Renascence*, 3–205.

8. For an excellent discussion of the impact of these changes upon the role and influence of Cherokee women, see Theda Perdue, *Cherokee Women: Gender and Culture Change, 1700–1835* (Lincoln: University of Nebraska Press,1998).

9. McLoughlin, *Cherokee Renascence*, 316–19.

10. See Francis Paul Prucha, *The Great Father: The United States Government and the American Indian*, 2 vols. (Lincoln: University of Nebraska Press, 1984), 1:179–213; and Ronald N. Satz, *American Indian Policy in the Jacksonian Era* (Lincoln: University of Nebraska Press, 1975). For contrasting assessments of Andrew Jackson's Indian policies, see Francis Paul Prucha, "Andrew Jackson's Indian Policy: A Reassessment," *Journal of American History* 56, (December, 1969): 527–39; and Alfred A. Cave, "Abuse of Power: Andrew Jackson and the Indian Removal Act of 1830," *Historian* 65 (Winter, 2003): 133–53. Reprints of both of the preceding essays can be found in David S. Heidler and Jeanne T. Heidler, eds., *Indian Removal* (New York: W. W. Norton, 2007), 187–228.

11. Good general discussions of the Western Cherokees can be found in Gregory D. Smithers, *The Cherokee Diaspora: An Indigenous History of Migration, Resettlement, and Identity* (New Haven, CT: Yale University Press, 2015), 38–345. Also see Dianna Everett, *The Texas Cherokees: A People between Two Fires, 1819–1840* (Norman: University of Oklahoma Press, 1990)

12. See article 2 of the Treaty of New Echota, December 29, 1835, in Kappler, *Indian Treaties*, 440–41.

13. A good account of these assassinations/executions can be found in Thurman Wilkins, *Cherokee Tragedy: The Ridge Family and the Decimation of a People* (Norman: University of Oklahoma Press, 1970), 329–39. Also see William G. McLoughlin, *After the Trail*

of Tears: The Cherokees' Struggle for Sovereignty, 1839–1880 (Chapel Hill: University of North Carolina Press, 1993), 1–21.

14. See McLoughlin, *After the Trail of Tears*, 34–58, 75–76; and John W. Morris, Charles R. Goins, and Edwin C. McReynolds, *Historical Atlas of Oklahoma* (Norman: University of Oklahoma Press, 1976), plates 35 and 36.

15. McLoughlin, *After the Trail of Tears*, 59–76.

16. For an excellent discussion of slavery within the Cherokee Nation in Indian Territory, see Perdue, *Slavery and the Evolution of Cherokee Society*, 70–118.

17. McCloughlin, *After the Trail of Tears*, 77–80. Also see Edmunds, Hoxie, and Salisbury, *The People*, 246–47.

18. Edmunds, Hoxie, and Salisbury, *The People*, 247.

19. The best in-depth study of one of these seminaries is Devon Mihesuah, *Cultivating the Rosebuds: The Education of Women at the Cherokee Female Seminary, 1851–1909* (Urbana: University of Illinois Press, 1993). Also see Brad Agnew, "Cherokee Male and Female Seminaries," *The Encyclopedia of Oklahoma History and Culture*, www.okhistory.org/publications/enc/entry.php/entry=CH018.

20. Mihesuah, *Cultivating the Rosebuds*; Agnew, "Cherokee Male and Female Seminaries."

21. Perdue, *Cherokee Women*, 186–95; Carolyn Ross Johnston, *Cherokee Women in Crisis: The Trail of Tears, Civil War, and Allotment, 1838–1907* (Tuscaloosa: University of Alabama Press, 2003), 114–18.

22. See McLoughlin, *After the Trail of Tears*, 155–65.

23. Ibid., 168–221. Also see Laurence Hauptman, *Between Two Fires: American Indians in the Civil War* (New York: Free Press, 1995); and W. Craig Gaines, *The Confederate Cherokees: John Drew's Regiment of Mounted Rifles* (Baton Rouge: Louisiana State University Press, 1989).

24. Edmunds, Hoxie, and Salisbury, *The People*, 272.

25. "Treaty with the Cherokee," July 19, 1866, in Kappler, *Indian Treaties*, 942–50.

26. Morris, Goins, and McReynolds, *Historical Atlas of Oklahoma*, plate 33; Edmunds, Hoxie, and Salisbury, *The People*, 272–76.

27. Edmunds. Hoxie, and Salisbury, *The People*, 274.

28. See Devon I. Abbott (Mihesuah), "Ann Florence Wilson: Matriarch of the Cherokee Female Seminary," *Chronicles of Oklahoma* 67 (Winter 1989–90), 426–37.

29. For a perceptive analysis on the impact of Indian Removal on Cherokee women, see Theda Perdue, "Cherokee Women and the Trail of Tears," in *Native Women's History in Eastern North America before 1900*, ed. Rebecca Kugel and Lucy Elderveld Murphy (Lincoln: University of Nebraska Press, 2007), 277–302.

Chapter 6. Jumping Deer and New Badgers Still Walk in the Smoke

1. For Maidu and Nisenan terminology, the author has relied on William F. Shipley, *Maidu Texts and Dictionary* (Berkeley: University of California Press, 1963); and

A. L. Kroeber, *The Valley Nisenan (Southern Maidu of Central California Sierras)* (Berkeley: University of California Press, 1929).

2. For a good, brief discussion of both Maidu and Nisenan peoples, see Francis A. Riddell, "Maidu and Kokow," in *California*, ed. Robert F. Heizer, 370–86, vol. 8 of *Handbook of North American Indians*, ed. William C. Sturtevant (Washington: Smithsonian Institution, 1978); and Norman L. Wilson and Arlean H. Towne, "Nisenan," in ibid., 387–97.

3. An excellent account of John Sutter and his interaction with tribal people can be found in Albert L. Hurtado, *John Sutter: A Life on the North American Frontier* (Norman: University of Oklahoma Press, 2006).

4. An excellent analysis of the impact of American and other miners on the everyday lives of tribal people in California is contained in Albert L. Hurtado, *Indian Survival on the California Frontier* (New Haven, CT: Yale University Press, 1988). Also see Sherburne F. Cooke, *The Conflict between the California Indians and White Civilization* (Berkeley: University of California Press, 1976); and George H. Phillips, *The Enduring Struggle: Indians in California History* (Sparks, NV: Materials for Today's Learning, 1996).

5. Excellent accounts of the Spanish colonization and the mission system in California can be found in Steven W. Hackel, *Children of Coyote, Missionaries of St. Francis: Indian-Spanish Relations in Colonial California, 1769–1850* (Chapel Hill: University of North Carolina Press, 2005); and in James Sandos, *Converting California Indians in the Missions* (New Haven, CT: Yale University Press, 2004). David Weber's *The Mexican Frontier, 1821–1846: The American Southwest under Mexico* (Albuquerque: University of New Mexico Press, 1982) also provides a good discussion of Mexican Indian policy.

6. See Robert H. Jackson and Edward Castillo, *Indians, Franciscans, and Spanish Colonization: The Impact of the Mission System on California Indians* (Albuquerque: University of New Mexico Press, 1995); and Kent Lightfoot, *Indians, Missionaries, and Merchants: The Legacy of Colonial Encounters on the California Frontiers* (Berkeley: University of California Press, 2005). Lightfoot compares and contrasts how Native American people fared under both Spanish and Russian colonization.

7. Hackel's *Children of Coyote* provides a scholarly, detailed, and carefully documented discussion of Native American adaptation and resistance to the mission system. Also see Lightfoot, *Indians, Missionaries, and Merchants.*

8. An excellent survey of the California gold rush and its impact on both California and the United States can be found in Malcom J. Rohrbough's *Days of Gold: The California Gold Rush and the American Nation* (Berkeley: University of California Press, 1997). Kenneth Owens has edited a volume of informative essays focusing on the experiences of different ethnic groups (Chinese, Latin Americans, African Americans, etc.) in the California gold rush. Other essays focus on the role of women and young men and the nature of lawlessness in the mining camps. See Owens, *Riches for All: The California Gold Rush and the World* (Lincoln: University of Nebraska Press, 2002). Also see Susan Lee Johnson, *Roaring Camp: The Social World of the California Gold Rush* (New York: W. W. Norton, 2000).

9. James J. Rawls, *Indians of California: The Changing Image* (Norman: University of Oklahoma Press, 1984), provides excellent examples and analysis of how Anglo-Americans in California manipulated the image of Native American people to further their own economic goals.

10. Numerous contemporary documents, including letters, legal documents, and newspaper accounts vividly describing the violence perpetrated toward Native Americans in California during the third quarter of the nineteenth century, can be found in Clifford E. Trafzer and Joel H. Hyer, eds., *Exterminate Them: Written Accounts of the Murder, Rape, and Enslavement of Native Americans during the California Gold Rush* (East Lansing: Michigan State University Press, 1999); and in Robert F. Heizer, ed., *The Destruction of California Indians* (Lincoln: University of Nebraska Press, 1993). Also see Theodora Kroeber's *Ishi in Two Worlds: A Biography of the Last Wild Indian in North America* (Berkeley: University of California Press, 1961). This poignant biography of Ishi, a Yahi tribesman from the Mt. Lassen region of northern California, should be required reading for anyone interested in the history of tribal people in California.

11. In *An American Genocide: The United States and the California Indian Catastrophe, 1846–1873* (New Haven, CT: Yale University Press, 2016), Benjamin Madley presents a scathing survey of American Indian policy in California during the third quarter of the nineteenth century and argues very persuasively that however historians (past and present) prefer to describe genocide, "the direct and deliberate killing of Indians in California between 1846 and 1873 was more lethal and sustained than anywhere else in the United States or its Colonial antecedents" (358). Madley's volume also contains seven separate appendices detailing the numbers of tribal people killed in California during these years. Also see Trafzer and Hyer, *Exterminate Them*; and Heizer, *The Destruction of California Indians*. Both of these latter volumes were cited in the previous endnote.

12. Brendan C. Lindsay, *Murder State: California's Native American Genocide, 1846–1873* (Lincoln: University of Nebraska Press, 2012) provides an excellent detailed discussion of state and local efforts in California to eliminate the state's Native American population. Also see Rawls, *Indians of California*, 185.

13. Both Hurtado, *Indian Survival on the California Frontier*, and Rawls, *Indians of California*, contain extensive discussions of American miners' attitudes toward tribal women in California during the gold rush era.

14. Rawls, *Indians of California*, devotes much of chapter 4 to the apprenticeship program in California and its impact on Native American children. Also see Hurtado, *Indian Survival on the California Frontier*.

15. For an excellent discussion of the act of 1850, see Hurtado, *Indian Survival on the California Frontier*, chapter 7.

16. Both Hurtado and Rawls include brief discussions of the establishment of reservations in California. See Hurtado, *Indian Survival on the California Frontier*, chapters 7 and 8; and Rawls, *Indians of California*, chapter 6 and epilogue.

17. In his epilogue, Rawls briefly discusses demographic changes in the indigenous population in California in the first half of the twentieth century. See Rawls, *Indians of California*. For an interesting case study of one reservation community's perseverance during these years, see William J. Bauer Jr., *We Were All Like Migrant Workers Here: Work, Community, And Memory on California's Round Valley Reservation, 1850–1941* (Chapel Hill: University of North Carolina Press, 2009).

18. Additional information on Native American activism in California and other regions of the United States during the 1960s and 1970s can be found in Paul Chaat Smith and Robert A. Warrior, *Like a Hurricane: The Indian Movement from Alcatraz to Wounded Knee* (New York: New Press, 1996); and Kent Blantsett, *A Journey to Freedom: Richard Oakes, Alcatraz, and the Red Power Movement* (New Haven, CT: Yale University Press, 2018).

Chapter 7. Flower Girls, Fires, and Sausages

1. Otoe nomenclature in this paragraph is taken from Robert Rankin, Richard T. Carter, Wesley F. Jones, John E. Koontz, David S. Rood, and Irene Hartman, eds., *The Comparative Siouan Dictionary* (Leipzig: Max Planck Institute for Evolutionary Anthropology, 2015).

2. In 1915, the federal government opened the Sac and Fox Sanitarium near Toledo, Iowa. Although local residents assumed that it would primarily serve tribespeople in Iowa, Wisconsin, and Minnesota, it rapidly filled with additional patients from Kansas, Nebraska, and the Dakotas. See Brenda J. Child, *Boarding School Seasons: American Indian Families, 1900–1940* (Lincoln: University of Nebraska Press, 1995), 63.

3. See Margaret Connell Szasz, *Indian Education in the American Colonies, 1607–1783* (Albuquerque: University of New Mexico Press, 1999).

4. For a brief discussion of these missionaries and schools, see R. David Edmunds, Frederick E. Hoxie, and Neal Salisbury, *The People: A History of Native America* (Boston: Houghton Mifflin, 2007), 177–79.

5. Francis Paul Prucha, *The Great Father: The United States Government and the American Indian*, 2 vols. (Lincoln: University of Nebraska Press, 1984), 1:151–53, contains a good, brief account of the federal government's support of religious institutions' educational efforts among the tribes during this period.

6. An excellent discussion of these mission schools and their objectives can be found in William G. McLoughlin, *Cherokees and Missionaries, 1789–1839* (New Haven, CT: Yale University Press, 1984).

7. For information on the Choctaw Academy, see three articles published by Carolyn T. Foreman, all entitled "The Choctaw Academy," and all published in *Chronicles of Oklahoma*. These articles can be found in *Chronicles* 6 (December, 1928): 453–80; *Chronicles* 9 (December 1931): 382–411; and in *Chronicles* 10 (March, 1932): 77–114. Also see Christina Snyder, *Great Crossings: Indians, Settlers, and Slaves in the Age of Jackson* (New York: Oxford University Press, 2017).

8. Detailed information on McCoy's schools at Carey Mission and at other locations can be found in Isaac McCoy, *History of the Baptist Indian Missions* (New York: Johnson Reprint Corporations, 1970; New York: H and S Raynor, 1840); and in George A, Schultz, *An Indian Canaan: Isaac Mccoy and the Vision of an Indian State* (Norman: University of Oklahoma Press, 1972).

9. Good discussions of education within the Cherokee Nation can be found in William C. McLoughlin, *Cherokee Renascence in the New Republic* (New Haven, CT: Yale University Press, 1986); William C. McLoughlin, *After the Trail of Tears: The Cherokee Struggle for Sovereignty, 1839–1880* (Chapel Hill: University of North Caroline Press, 1993); and Devon Mihesuah, *Cultivating the Rosebuds: The Education of Women at the Cherokee Female Seminary, 1851–1909* (Urbana: University of Illinois Press, 1993).

10. Additional, more detailed Information on these Choctaw schools can be found in Angie Debo, *The Rise and Fall of the Choctaw Republic* (Norman: University of Oklahoma Press, 1934), 60–65, 96, 147; W. David Baird, "Spencer Academy, Choctaw Nation, 1842–1900," *Chronicles of Oklahoma* 45 (Spring, 1967): 25–43; and Justin D. Murphy, "Wheelock Female Seminary, 1842–1861," *Chronicles of Oklahoma* 69 (Spring, 1991): 48–61.

11. A. M. Gibson, *The Chickasaws* (Norman: University of Oklahoma Press, 1971), 248–49. Also see Amanda J. Cobb, *Listening to Our Grandmothers' Stories: The Bloomfield Academy for Chickasaw Females* (Lincoln: University of Nebraska Press, 2000).

12. See Edmunds, Hoxie, and Salisbury, *The People: A History of Native America,* 334–36.

13. Ibid. Also see David Wallace Adams, *Education for Extinction: American Indians and the Boarding School Experience, 1875–1928* (Lawrence: University Press of Kansas, 1995). Adams's scholarly monograph provides the best in-depth academic survey of boarding schools in this period.

14. Excellent examples of the loneliness and isolation experienced by students can be found in Francis La Flesche, *The Middle Five: Indian School Boys of the Omaha Tribe* (Lincoln: University of Nebraska Press, 1963); Luther Standing Bear, *My People, the Sioux* (Boston: Houghton Mifflin, 1928); and Zitkala-Sa, *American Indian Stories* (Lincoln: University of Nebraska Press, 1985). Also see Denise K. Lajimodiere, *Stringing Rosaries: The History, the Unforgiveable, and the Healing of Northern Plains American Indian Boarding School Survivors* (Fargo: North Dakota State University Press, 2019); and Michael Coleman, *American Indian Children at School, 1850–1930* (Jackson: University Press of Mississippi), 1993, chapter 5.

15. Child's *Boarding School Seasons* provides an excellent discussion of students who attended Haskell Institute in Lawrence Kansas because of deteriorating economic conditions on their reservations.

16. Myriam Vuckovic, *Voices from Haskell: Indian Students between Two Worlds, 1884–1928* (Lawrence: University Press of Kansas, 2008), 91–127. Also see Adams, *Education for Extinction*, 21–22, 142–45, 153–54.

17. Speech by Richard Pratt, 1892, in *Americanizing the American Indian: Writings by the "Friends of the American Indian," 1880–1900,* ed. Francis Paul Prucha (Cambridge, MA: Harvard University Press, 1873), 260–71.

18. See Vuckovic, *Voices from Haskell,* 74–76; Adams, *Education for Extinction,* 108–12; and Thomas J. Morgan, "Instruction to Indian Agents in Regard to Inculcation of Patriotism in Indian Schools," December 10, 1899, in *Documents in United States Indian Policy,* ed. Francis Paul Prucha, (Lincoln: University of Nebraska Press, 1975), 180–81.

19. For an excellent scholarly discussion of federal efforts to promote the use of English among Native American people, see Ruth Spack, *America's Second Tongue: American Indian Education and Ownership of English, 1860–1900* (Lincoln: University of Nebraska Press, 2002).

20. Excellent information on the attempts to eradicate tribal religions can be found in Vuckovic, *Voices from Haskell,* 128–38; and Adams, *Education for Extinction,* 164–73.

21. See Vuckovic, *Voices from Haskell,* chapter 5; Adams, Education for Extinction, chapter 6. Also see Kate Buford, *Native American Son: The Life and Sporting Legend of Jim Thorpe* (New York: Alfred A. Knopf, 2010); John Bloom, *To Show What an Indian Can Do: Sports at Native American Boarding Schools* (Minneapolis: University of Minnesota Press, 2000); and Margaret L Archuleta, Brenda J. Child, and Tsianina Lomawaima, eds. *Away from Home: American Indian Boarding School Experiences, 1879–2000* (Phoenix: Heard Museum, 2000). The Archuleta, Child, and Lomawaima volume contains many photos illustrating students participation in organizations and clubs sponsored by the boarding schools.

22. Adams, *Education for Extinction,* 156–63; Child, *Boarding School Seasons,* 81–86; Robert A. Trennert, *The Phoenix Indian School; Forced Assimilation in Arizona* (Norman: University of Oklahoma Press, 1988), 50–54, 72–73.

23. Adams, *Education for Extinction,*114–17; Child, *Boarding School Seasons,* 31–36. Also see Brookings Institution, *The Problem of Indian Administration* (Baltimore, MD: Johns Hopkins University Press, 1928), 314–45. Since one of the authors of this study was Lewis Meriam, a federal bureaucrat, this study by the Brookings Institution is often called the Meriam Report. Also see Estelle Aubrey Brown, *Stubborn Fool: A Narrative* (Caldwell, ID: Caxton, 1952), 60, 185.

24. Adams, *Education for Extinction,* 103–8; Child, *Boarding School Seasons,* 30–31. Both the above volumes contain photos of students in school uniforms. For illustrations of how uniforms changed through the years, see Archuleta, Child, and Lomawaima, *Away from Home.* For attitudes toward bloomers, see Tsianina Lomawaima, *They Called It Prairie Light: The Story of Chilocco Indian School* (Lincoln: University of Nebraska Press, 1994), 95–99.

25. Adams, *Education for Extinction,* 100–7. Also see Alice C. Fletcher and Francis la Flesche, *The Omaha Tribe,* 2 vols. (Lincoln: University of Nebraska Press, 1992), 2:495–96; John C. Ewers, *The Blackfeet: Raiders on the Northern Plains* (Norman:

University of Oklahoma Press, 1958), 106–8; Donald J. Berthrong, *The Southern Cheyennes* (Norman: University of Oklahoma Press, 1963), 39; and Vuckovic, *Voices from Haskell*, 68.

26. There is extensive information regarding health problems at the schools. See Trennert, *The Phoenix Indian School*, 75–77, 100–9; Child, *Boarding School Seasons*, 55–68; Vuckovic, *Voices from Haskell*, 179–210; and Donald J. Berthrong, *The Cheyenne and Arapaho Ordeal: Reservation and Indian Life in the Indian Territory, 1875–1907* (Norman: University of Nebraska Press, 1976), 141–47.

27. Lomawaima, *They Called It Prairie Light*, 96–98, 112–14, 124–25, 130–37, 154–58; Vuckovic, *Voices from Haskell*, 211–19, 224–26. Also see Coleman, *American Indians at School*, 154–57; and La Flesche, *The Middle Five*.

28. Excellent discussions and analyses of the end of the boarding school era can be found in Adams, *Education for Extinction*, 307–33; and in Prucha, *The Great Father*, 2:707–11, 791–840.

29. See R. David Edmunds, *The Otoe Missouria People* (Phoenix: Indian Tribal Series, 1976), 68.

30. In May 2022, the US Department of the Interior released a scathing report on boarding schools and their administration and the negative impact of these institutions on both Indian children and tribal communities. See Bryan Newland, *Federal Indian Boarding School Initiative Investigative Report* (Washington, DC: US Department of the Interior, 2022).

Chapter 8. Summer Hawks in Concrete Canyons

1. For a general discussion of tribal kinship systems in an urban setting and suggestions for further reading on this subject, see Russell Thornton, Gary D. Sandefur, and Harold G. Graswick, *The Urbanization of American Indians: A Critical Bibliography* (Bloomington: Indiana University Press, 1982), 32–38.

2. Ella Deloria, *Speaking of Indians* (Lincoln: University of Nebraska Press, 1998), 24–29, provides a good description of the avuncular system among the Lakotas.

3. For a brief survey of conditions among Native American veterans who moved to urban areas in the years immediately following World War II, see Alison R. Bernstein, *American Indians and World War II: Toward a New Era in Indian Affairs* (Norman: University of Oklahoma Press, 1991), 145–52.

4. Ella Deloria describes the role of familial respect and obligation within Lakota society in *Speaking of Indians*, 24–38.

5. Hand games or "stick games" are group guessing games played by many tribes across the western half of the United States. Usually accompanied by drums and singing, the games are played by two opposing teams who pass small sticks or pieces of bone from hand to hand while facing the opposing team, who then attempts to ascertain just which individual on the opposite team has the stick or bone. The opponents then point out the individual who has the bone, which causes them to surrender the

item. The object of the game is for one team to win as many of the bones as possible. These games are played by contestants of both sexes and all ages (adolescents through elders) and usually are social occasions accompanied by good-natured joking and conversation, similar to bingo, horseshoes, and bean-bag tossing games common among non-Indians. For more information, see Stewart Culin, *Games of the North American Indian* (New York: Dover, 1975; originally published in 1907 by the US Bureau of American Ethnology in *Twenty-Fourth Annual Report of the Bureau of American Ethnology, 1902–1903, 3–809)*, 227–327; and Frances Densmore, *Music of the Teton Sioux, Bureau of American Ethnology Bulletin No. 61* (Washington, DC: Smithsonian Institution, 1918), 485–92.

6. The best survey of federal policy during these years is Donald L. Fixico, *Termination and Relocation: Federal Indian Policy, 1945–1960* (Albuquerque: University of New Mexico Press, 1986). Also see Francis Paul Prucha, *The Great Father: The United States Government and the American Indian*, 2 vols. (Lincoln: University of Nebraska Press, 1984), 2:1013–84.

7. Fixico's *Termination and Relocation*, 134–58, offers an excellent survey of the federal government's goals in the relocation program .

8. In *Indian Metropolis: Native Americans in Chicago, 1945–1975* (Urbana: University of Illinois Press, 2002), 98–117, James LaGrand describes the economic conditions of tribal people in Chicago (including relocatees) during the 1950s and compares these conditions with those of tribal people in several other urban areas. Also see Ada Deer, with Theda Perdue, *Making A Difference: My Fight for Native Rights and Social Justice* (Norman: University of Oklahoma Press, 2019), 66–70. In her recent autobiography, Ada Deer describes these problems among urban Indians in Minneapolis-St. Paul during the 1950s.

9. See Elaine M. Neils, *Reservation to City: Indian Migration and Federal Relocation* (Chicago: Department of Geography, University of Chicago, 1971).

10. See Prucha, *The Great Father*, 2:1081–84; and Thornton, Sandefur, and Grasmick, *Urbanization of American Indians*, 28–31.

11. Donald L. Fixico, *The Urban Indian Experience in America* (Albuquerque: University of New Mexico Press, 2000), 173–80.

12. Neils, *Reservation to City*; and Joan Ablon, "American Indian Relocation: Problems of Dependency and Management in the City," *Phylon* 26 (Winter 1965): 362–71. Also see Donald L. Parman, *Indians and the American West in the Twentieth Century* (Bloomington: Indiana University Press, 1994), 143–44; LaGrand, *Urban Metropolis*, 133–35.

13. Fixico, *Termination and Relocation*, 183–88; Donald L. Fixico, *Indian Resilience and Rebuilding: Indigenous Nations in the American West* (Tucson: University of Arizona Press, 2013), 205–6. For good discussions of Ada Deer's fight to repeal Menominee termination, see Deer and Perdue, *Making a Difference*, 86–124; and Clara Sue Kidwell, "Ada Deer," in R. David Edmunds, ed., *The New Warriors: Native American Leaders since 1900* (Lincoln: University of Nebraska Press, 2001), 239–57.

14. LaGrand, *Indian Metropolis*, 112–21. Also see Fixico, *Indian Resilience and Rebuilding*, 113–14; Fixico, *Urban Indian Experience*, 80–84. Also see Kent Blantsett, *A Journey to Freedom: Richard Oakes, Alcatraz, and the Red Power Movement* (New Haven, CT: Yale University Press, 2018), 31, 80, 84–96; James LaGrand, "Indian Work and Indian Neighborhoods: Adjusting to Life in Chicago during the 1950s," in *Enduring Nations: Native Americans in the Midwest*, ed. R. David Edmunds (Urbana: University of Illinois Press, 2008), 203–8.

15. Blansett, *A Journey to Freedom*, 8. Blansett's volume also provides an excellent case study in the problems faced by young Native Americans attempting to forge a life in an urban setting.

16. See Fixico, *Indian Resilience and Rebuilding*, 113–14; Blansett, *A Journey to Freedom*, 7–9; and LaGrand, *Indian Metropolis*, 161–68, 177–78.

17. One of the best (and most balanced) surveys of the rise of Red Power and the American Indian Movement can be found in Paul Chaat Smith and Robert Warrior, *Like a Hurricane: The Indian Movement from Alcatraz to Wounded Knee* (New York: New Press, 1996).

18. See Smith and Warrior, *Like a Hurricane*, 1–11. Also see the series of excellent essays focusing on the Alcatraz occupation contained in Troy Johnson, Joane Nagel, and Duane Champagne, eds., *American Indian Activism: Alcatraz to the Longest Walk* (Urbana: University of Illinois Press, 1997). Blansett's *A Journey to Freedom* provides a well-researched, definitive biography of Richard Oakes and his integral role in these events.

19. Smith and Warrior, *Like a Hurricane*, 171–279. Also see Akim D. Reinhardt, *Ruling Pine Ridge: Oglala Lakota Politics from the IRA to Wounded Knee* (Lubbock: Texas Tech University Press, 2009).

20. Smith and Warrior, *Like a Hurricane*, 171–279. There have been several "eyewitness accounts" written by Native Americans who were occupants of the village during the siege. See Mary Crow Dog and Richard Erdoes, *Lakota Woman* (New York: Harper Collins, 1990). For a contrasting perspective from an FBI agent's point of view, see Joseph Trimbach and John Trimbach, *American Indian Mafia: An FBI Agent's True Story about Wounded Knee* (Denver: Outskirts Press, 2008).

21. Raymond Wilson, "Russell Means," in Edmunds, *The New Warriors*, 146–69. Also see Russell Means and Marvin J. Wolf, *Where White Men Fear to Tread: The Autobiography of Russell Means* (New York: St. Martin's, 1995); and Dennis Banks and Richard Erdoes, *Ojibwa Warrior: Dennis Banks and the Rise of the American Indian Movement* (Norman: University of Oklahoma Press, 2005).

22. The term *goon* was a derogative name used on the Pine Ridge Reservation to describe Guardians of the Oglala Nation, an auxiliary police force hired by Richard Wilson's administration and initially funded by the BIA. AIM's negative appraisal of this organization, also held by many Pine Ridge residents, can be found in Ward Churchill, "The Bloody Wake of Alcatraz: Political Repression of the American Indian Movement During the 1970's," in Johnson, Nagel, and Champagne, *American Indian Activism*, 242–84.

23. Porcupine, South Dakota, located on the Pine Ridge Reservation, about five miles north of Wounded Knee, was the staging point for many of the blockade runners who carried supplies into Wounded Knee or who slipped through the federal lines to join the ranks of the participants in the occupation. During the spring of 1973, the author served as the advisor to Native American students at the University of Wyoming and spoke personally with several residents from the Wind River Reservation who crossed into Wounded Knee via an overland route that originated in Porcupine.

24. *Wasichu* is the Lakota term commonly applied to people of European descent, that is, a "white" person.

Chapter 9. Moving with the Seasons, Not Fixed in Stone

An abbreviated version of this chapter was first published as "'Moving with the Seasons, Not Fixed in Stone': The Evolution of Native American Identity," in *Reflections on American Indian History: Honoring the Past, Building a Future*, ed. Albert L. Hurtado (Norman: University of Oklahoma Press, 2008), 32–57.

1. Erminie Wheeler-Voegelin, "The 19th and 20th Century Ethnohistory of Various Groups of Cayuga Indians," 1959, 109–12 (a copy of this report to the Indian Claims Commission is in the author's possession). Also see expert witness testimony in support of Seneca-Cayuga land claims, in R. David Edmunds, "The Origins and History of the Western Band of the Cayuga Indian Nation," 23 (2004, unpublished report; copy in author's possession).

2. Native American surnames often were changed, sometimes inadvertently, sometimes purposefully, by both missionaries and federal officials. White Hair, for example, a Potawatomi man from the Fox River in northern Illinois, was first mentioned in government records in 1811, but subsequent federal correspondence listed him as "White Hare." He was later listed as "White Rabbit." Among the Northern Arapahos, the surname "Iron Eyes" was changed by missionaries to "Goggles." See R. David Edmunds, *The Potawatomis: Keepers of the Fire* (Norman: University of Oklahoma Press, 1978), 176–204. Information on the nomenclature of the Goggles family was supplied in a conversation between Eugene Goggles and the author, Laramie, Wyoming, November 9, 1971.

3. Late twentieth-century Seneca-Cayuga life in Oklahoma is discussed in James Howard, "Environment and Culture: The Case of the Oklahoma Seneca-Cayuga," *North Dakota Quarterly* 29, nos. 3 and 4 (1970): 66–71 and 113–122.

4. The evolution of Seneca-Cayuga ceremonialism, including the role of the pot-hangers, is discussed in James Howard, "Cultural Persistence and Cultural Change as Reflected in Oklahoma Seneca-Cayuga Ceremonialism," *Plains Anthropologist* 6, no. 11. (1961): 21–30. Also see William C. Sturtevant, "Oklahoma Seneca-Cayuga," in *Handbook of North American Indians*, ed. Bruce E. Trigger, vol. 15, *Northeast* (Washington, DC: Smithsonian Institution, 1978), 537–43. The peyote faith is discussed at length in Omer C. Stewart, *Peyote Religion: A History* (Norman: University of

Oklahoma Press, 1987. Also see Douglas R. Parks, "Pawnee," in *Handbook of North American Indians*, ed. Raymond J. DeMallie, vol. 13, *Plains*, part 1 (Washington, DC: Smithsonian Institution, 2001), 543.

5. A brief description of the modern Seneca-Cayuga tribal government and its economic development programs can be found in "Seneca-Cayuga Tribe of Oklahoma," in *Tiller's Guide to Indian Country: Economic Profiles of American Indian Reservations*, ed. Veronica E. Tiller (Albuquerque: Bow Arrow, 2006), 871–72. Information regarding Seneca-Cayuga claims to lands in New York and the tribe's subsequent legal actions can be found in Edmunds, "Origins and History of the Western Band." Also see Cayuga Indians of New York et al. v. Mario Cuomo et al., United States District Court, Northern District of New York, Civil. Nos. 80-CV-930 and 80–960.

6. See "Preliminary Inventory of the Records of the Miami (Quapaw) Indian Agency," National Archives, Record Group 75, Southwest Region, Fort Worth, Texas, December 19, 2003.

7. Interview with Amanda Bearskin Greenback, Miami, Oklahoma, January 8, 2004.

8. On September 13–14, 2021, the author compiled information regarding blood quantum requirements through telephone interviews with tribal enrollment agents or through examining materials posted on tribal websites from the following tribal governments: Absentee Tribe of Oklahoma, Caddo Nation of Oklahoma, Cherokee Nation, Chickasaw Nation, Choctaw Nation of Oklahoma, Citizen Potawatomi Nation, Creek (Muscogee) Nation, Comanche Tribe of Oklahoma, Eastern Shawnee Tribe of Oklahoma, Fort Sill Apache Tribe, Kickapoo Tribe of Oklahoma, Ho-Chunk Nation, Kiowa Indian Tribe of Oklahoma, Lac Courte Oreilles Ojibwe Tribe, Mescalero Apache Reservation, Miami Tribe of Oklahoma, Mississippi Band of Choctaw Indians, Navajo Nation, Northern Arapaho Tribe, Oglala Sioux (Pine Ridge), Omaha Tribe of Nebraska, Otoe-Missouria Tribe of Indians, Pawnee Tribe of Oklahoma, Ponca Tribe of Oklahoma, Sac and Fox Nation, Sac and Fox Tribe of the Mississippi in Iowa (Meskwaki), Seminole Tribe of Oklahoma, Seneca-Cayuga Tribe of Oklahoma, Shingle Springs Rancheria, Three Affiliated Tribes (Mandan, Hidatsa, Arikara), Wichita and Affiliated Tribes, Wyandotte Nation.

9. For examples of removal rolls containing blood-quantum assessments, see "A Roll of Ottawa, Chippeway, and Potawatomi Emigrated Indians . . . under the Direction of Isaac L. Berry," 1838, National Archives, Records of the Bureau of Indian Affairs, Letters Received by the Office of Indian Affairs (M234), roll 752, 189; Muster Role of a Band of Pottawatomie Indians Delivered at the Osage River Agency," October 6, 1840, ibid., roll 642, 234–36. Also see "A Census of the Cherokee Nation of Indians, 1896" (a copy of this census can be found in the National Archives Depository at the Federal Records Center in Fort Worth, Texas); and "Census of Indians at the Quapaw Agency on June 30, 1913, taken by Ira C. Deaver, Superintendent," Tribal Archives, Seneca-Cayuga Tribe, Miami, Oklahoma.

10. Russell Thornton, *American Indian Holocaust and Survival: A Population History since 1492* (Norman: University of Oklahoma Press, 1987), 236–37. Also see Russell

Thornton, "Health, Disease, and Demography," in *A Companion to American Indian History*, ed. Philip J. Deloria and Neal Salisbury (Malden, MA: Blackwell, 2002), 76–80.

11. Thornton, *American Indian Holocaust*, 236–37; Thornton, "Health, Disease, and Demography, 76–80.

12. The historical literature contains ample evidence of this phenomenon. For example, among the Potawatomis, Shabbona, a leading early nineteenth-century chief, was born an Ottawa, while Billy Caldwell, who led part of the tribe during the removal period, was of Irish-Mohawk descent. See Edmunds, *The Potawatomis*, 172; and James A. Clifton, "Personal and Ethnic Identity on the Great Lakes Frontier: The Case of Billy Caldwell," *Ethnohistory* 25 (Winter, 1978): 69–94. Also see Margaret Schmidt Hacker, *Cynthia Ann Parker: The Life and the Legend* (El Paso: Texas Western Press, 1990); Sarah E. Cooke and Rachel B Ramadhyani, comps., *Indians and a Changing Frontier: The Art of George Winter* (Indianapolis: Indiana Historical Society, 1993), 133; and Susan Sleeper-Smith, "Resistance to Removal: The 'White Indian,' Frances Slocum," in *Enduring Nations: Native Americans in the Midwest*, ed. R. David Edmunds (Urbana: University of Illinois Press, 2008), 109–23.

13. Alexandra Harmon, "Wanted: More Histories of Indian Identity," in Deloria and Salisbury, *A Companion*, 254–55.

14. Ned Blackhawk, "I Can Carry on from Here: The Relocation of American Indians to Los Angeles," *Wičaza Ša Review* 11 (Fall, 1995), 16–18; and Joane Nagel, *American Indian Ethnic Renewal: Red Power and the Resurgence of Identity and Culture* (New York: Oxford University Press, 1997), 137–40.

15. See Susan S. Harjo, "Why Native Identity Matters: A Cautionary Tale," *Indian Country Today*, February 10, 2005.

16. Telephone interviews with enrollment agents, September 13–14, 2021; see note 8, above. Also see Ronald I. Trosper, "Native American Boundary Maintenance: The Flathead Indian Reservation, Montana, 1860–1970," *Ethnicity* 3 (1976): 256–74.

17. Jeremy Finch, director of cultural resources, Citizen Potawatomi Nation, telephone interview, March 29, 2005. Also see www.potawatomi.org/blog/2020/07/14/citizen -potawatomi-nation-land-management-and-soverignty. For tribal opposition to termination and efforts by tribes to reestablish reservations or trust lands, see Donald Fixico, *Termination and Relocation: Federal Indian Policy, 1945–1960* (Albuquerque: University of New Mexico Press, 1986); and Nicholas C. Perrot, *Menominee Drums: Tribal Termination and Restoration, 1954–1974* (Norman: University of Oklahoma Press, 1982).

18. Telephone conversation between Kenneth McIntosh and the author, September 21, 2021. McIntosh, a professor of history at Clarendon College, Clarendon, Texas, is the grandson of W. W. ("Dode") McIntosh (Tuskenugge Micco), the last appointed chief of the Creek Nation and the son of the late Chinnubbie McIntosh (Haccoce), who also actively participated in Creek tribal government. Also see "Grace Thorpe," in *Always a People: A History of Contemporary Woodland Indians*, ed. Rita Kohn and Lynwood Montell (Bloomington: Indian University Press, 1997), 254.

19. For a discussion of the growth of tribal sovereignty and the "new federalism," see Stephen Cornell, *The Return of the Native: American Indian Political Resurgence* (New York: Oxford University Press, 1988), 202–13; and Donald Parman, *Indians and the American West in the Twentieth Century* (Bloomington: Indiana University Press, 1994), 175–81.

20. "Winstar Convention Center Media Kit." This information packet provided by the Chickasaw Nation is available from the marketing office at the Winstar Convention Resort or can be downloaded from www.winstarworldcasinao.com; "Choctaw Casino and Resort, Durant." This information packet provided by the Choctaw Nation can be downloaded from Choctaw Casinos, www.choctawcasinos.com/meetings/durant.

21. See Inn of the Mountain Gods, https://innofthemountaingods.com/activities/; and Oneida Casino, https://oneidacasino.net/radisson-hotel-conference-center. For a critical analysis of Native American gaming, see Gerald Vizenor, "Gambling," in *Encyclopedia of North American Indians*, ed. Fred E. Hoxie (Boston: Houghton-Mifflin, 1996), 212–14. Also see Steven Andrew Light and Kathryn R. L. Rand, *Indian Gaming and Tribal Sovereignty: The Casino Compromise* (Lawrence: University Press of Kansas, 2005), for a detailed study of the issues surrounding this subject.

22. Information regarding the Oneida Nation of Wisconsin comes from a telephone interview with James Bithorff, legal counsel, Oneida Law Office, August 13, 2021. Also see "Oneida Nation of Wisconsin," in Tiller, *Tillers Guide to Indian Country*, 1053–57; Wisconsin Department of Public Instruction, Error! Hyperlink reference not valid .https://dpi.wi.gov/amind/tribalnationswi/oneida; and "About Us-The Bay Bank," www.baybankgb.com/About-Us.

23. Information regarding Citizen Potawatomi economic enterprises comes from a telephone conversation between the author and Jeremy Finch, March 29, 2005, and from more recent information currently available on the Citizen Potawatom Nation's website at httpsc//www.potawatomi.org.

24. See paragraph in text denoted in note 18.

25. There are many legal cases that have both expanded and contracted tribal sovereignty and Native American retention over tribal lands during the past century. For example, California v. Cabazon Band of Mission Indians 480 U.S. 202 (1987) spurred the growth of Native American gaming by limiting the authority of states to regulate gaming on tribal lands. Solemn v. Bartlett, 465 U.S. 463 (1984) ruled that the opening of reservation lands to settlement by non-Indians did not diminish the boundaries of a reservation unless diminishment was specifically determined through an Act of Congress. Nebraska v Parker, 577 U.S. 483 (2016), strengthened tribal sovereignty over reservation lands which had been sold to non-Indians, by further limiting definitions of diminishment. McGirt v. Oklahoma 591 U.S. 2452 (2020) ruled that since the reservations were never officially disestablished by Congress through the Oklahoma Enabling Act of 1906, these reservations remain, and prosecution of crimes by Native Americans in the region are under the jurisdiction of tribal or federal courts, not state

courts. Obviously, this decision has the potential to markedly alter questions over sovereignty on lands in eastern Oklahoma.

26. Brief descriptions of all these natural resources can be found in Tiller, *Tiller's Guide to Indian Country*. The references to resources on specific reservations can be found on the following pages: Navajos, 536–42; Crows, 653–54; Northern Cheyennes, 667–69; Wind River (Eastern Shoshones and Northern Arapahos), 1085–87; Southern Utes, 509–12; Ute Mountain Utes, 512–16; Colville Reservation (Confederated Tribes), 961–964; Flathead Reservation (Salish and Kootenai), 655–58; Red Lake Reservation (Ojibwes), 628–29.

27. The history of federal supervision over Native American land and resources is replete with instances of Indian agents' acquiescence or complicity in this misadministration of tribal lands, resources, and ways of life. For a good overview of these events, see R. David Edmunds, Frederick E. Hoxie, and Neal Salisbury, *The People: A History of Native America* (New York: Houghton Mifflin, 2007), chapters 13 and 14 (322–72). For an excellent collection of documents reflecting the sometimes well-intentioned but often naïve policies that shaped American Indian policy during the late nineteenth century, see Francis Paul Prucha, ed., *Americanizing the American Indian: Writings by the "Friends of the Indian," 1880–1900* (Cambridge, MA: Harvard University Press, 1973).

28. Mike Baker, "Amid Historic Drought, a New Water War in the West," *New York Times*, June 1, 2021, www.nytimes.com/2021/06/01/us/klamath-oregon-drought-bundy .html.

29. Support for tribal languages is widespread. For example, see the interviews with tribal leaders and elders in Kohn and Montell, eds., *Always a People*; Benton White and Christine Schulz White, "Philip Martin," in *The New Warriors: Native American Leaders since 1900*, ed. R. David Edmunds (Lincoln: University of Nebraska Press, 2001), 195–209. Information regarding current tribal language programs can also be found on most tribal websites. Additional information on the Mississippi Choctaws' tribal language programs was provided to the author in a telephone interview with Roseanna Thompson, the Mississippi Choctaw director of cultural preservation and tribal cultural affairs, on August 12, 2021.

30. For information on several leading Native American professional organizations, see the American Indian Science and Engineering Society, aises.org; the Native American Right Fund, https://narf.org; the Association of American Indian Physicians, https:// https://aaip.org; the National Alaska Native American Indian Nurses, https://nanaina .org; and the Index of Native American Resources on the Internet, https//hanksville .org/NAresources//.

31. For a description of the Seneca-Cayuga Strawberry Dance, see Charlie Diebold, "Strawberry Dance—May 30, 2021, at Newsletter-May 2021," http://sctribe.com/wp -content/uploads/2021/05/Newsletter-May2021.png.

Index

References to illustrations appear in italic type.

Act of 1850 for the Government and Protection of Indians (Calif.), 187–88
Adams-Onís Treaty (1819), 147
Adena Cultural Complex, 23, 111
Alabama River, 29
Albuquerque Indian School (N.Mex.), 228
alcaldes, 182
Alcatraz Island, 190, 259–60
American Board of Commissioners for Foreign Missions (ABCFM), 221
American Indian Movement (AIM), 190, 259–60
American River (Kummayo River) (Calif.), 162–66, 169, 182–83
American Revolution, 60–61
American Society for Ethnohistory, 21
Amherstburg, Ontario, 120
Anadarko, Okla., 214
Ancestral Pueblos, 10–12, 24–25
Apaches (Apachus, Savus), 10, 86, 261–63; Mescaleros, 273
Arapahos, 73–85, 91, 230, 276; receive horses from Kiowas, 87; size of horse herds, 87. *See also* Wind River Indian Reservation (Wyo.)

Arikaras, 80, 85, 91, 277; attacked by other tribes, 90; population decline, 90
Arkansas River, 7, 16, 88, 154–55
Arkansas Valley Railroad, 155, 159
Assiniboines, 87; size of horse herds, 87
Auglaize River (Ohio), 97, 107–8, 116–17

Badin, Stephen T., 62, 63, 65
Banks, Dennis (Ojibwe), 260–61
Bannocks, 86, 259
Baptist Mission Society, 221
Barrett, John "Rocky" (Potawatomi), 274
Bearskin, Amanda (Seneca-Cayuga), 267
Beatrice, Nebr., 207–10
Big Black River. *See* Ohio River
Big Sandy River (Ky./W.Va.), 96
Bird, Henry, 102–3
bison hunting, 75–77, 81, 85, 88; depletes herds, 89; kill sites at cliffs, 75–77, 86; using surrounds, 82, 86; using wolfskins, 75
Blackfeet, 86, 87, 91, 276
Black Fish (Shawnee), 102
Black Hawk (Sac), 32
Black Hills, 86–87, 92

Printed in the USA
CPSIA information can be obtained
at www.ICGtesting.com
LVHW091416131023
760933LV00026B/143/J

9 780806 192765